OVER HERE

A Novel by James Hockenberry

Published by HN Books, LLC, James Hockenberry and Colleen Nugent
HN Books, LLC, P.O. Box 4214, New Windsor, New York 12553, USA

Endpapers, maps, interior and cover illustrations by HN Books, LLC

ISBN: 978-0-9915612-0-9 (paperback)
ISBN: 978-0-9915612-1-6 (electronic book)

Library of Congress Cataloging-in-Publication Data
Hockenberry, James L.
Over Here/James Hockenberry

viii, 484p. | c22.86 cm.

Library of Congress Control Number: 2014955873

1. Action & Adventure, 2. Suspense Thriller, 3. Thriller, 4. Fiction,
5. Literature & Fiction, 6. Spy Stories & Tales of Intrigue,
7. Contemporary Literature & Fiction, 8. Mystery, Thriller, Suspense,
9. Historical Thriller, 10. Teen & Young Adult,
11. World War One, 12. War, 13. Military History

Printed in the United States of America
Book Design by HN Books, LLC

For Catherine

Acknowledgments

So many have contributed so much to *Over Here*. Without their help, support, and inspiration, I could not have completed it.

I owe a great deal to my brilliant editor, Gayle Wurst, of Princeton International Agency for the Arts, who pushed me to new levels, taught me to question every word, and insisted on extra research. Her contacts and advice have been invaluable. Thanks, too, to my sister, Hope Yelich, former librarian at William & Mary College, who aided in the research.

My friend Colleen Nugent, who always believed in me, came forward to make this book happen. Whenever I hit a roadblock, Colleen managed to find a way around it. She made the book a published reality.

I am particularly indebted to four people who provided invaluable technical assistance and expertise: Detective Kevin Canavan, of the NYPD's current Bomb Squad; University of Rhode Island Professor Jimmie Oxley; Lafayette College Professor William Miles; and Bob Bearden, WWII 507 PIR, 82nd Airborne veteran.

I give special thanks to Philip Schwartzberg at Meridian Mapping, my mapmaker; Howard Brower, my artist; Diana Groden, my copy editor; Anne Waldron Neumann and her writing group; and Daniel-Gary Holderman, my friend and first writing instructor.

Many family and friends have encouraged me to keep going. Their insights and suggestions improved the novel at every stage. These people stand out: my brother John, his wife Nina; all my friends in the Financial Executives Network Group (FENG); and Angela, Charlie, Charlene, Chris, Glenn, Greg, Louis, Mary, Rich, Pascal & Kathy, and Tim. Thank you all.

New York Harbor, 1916
NEW JERSEY
Communipaw
Claremont
Caven Pt.
Black Tom Island
Ellis Island
Statue of Liberty
Hudson River
Manhattan
Battery Park
East River
Governor's Island
New York Harbor
Red Hook
Brooklyn
Upper Bay
Gowanus Bay
Robbins Reef Light
Staten Island
Bay Ridge
0
1 mile

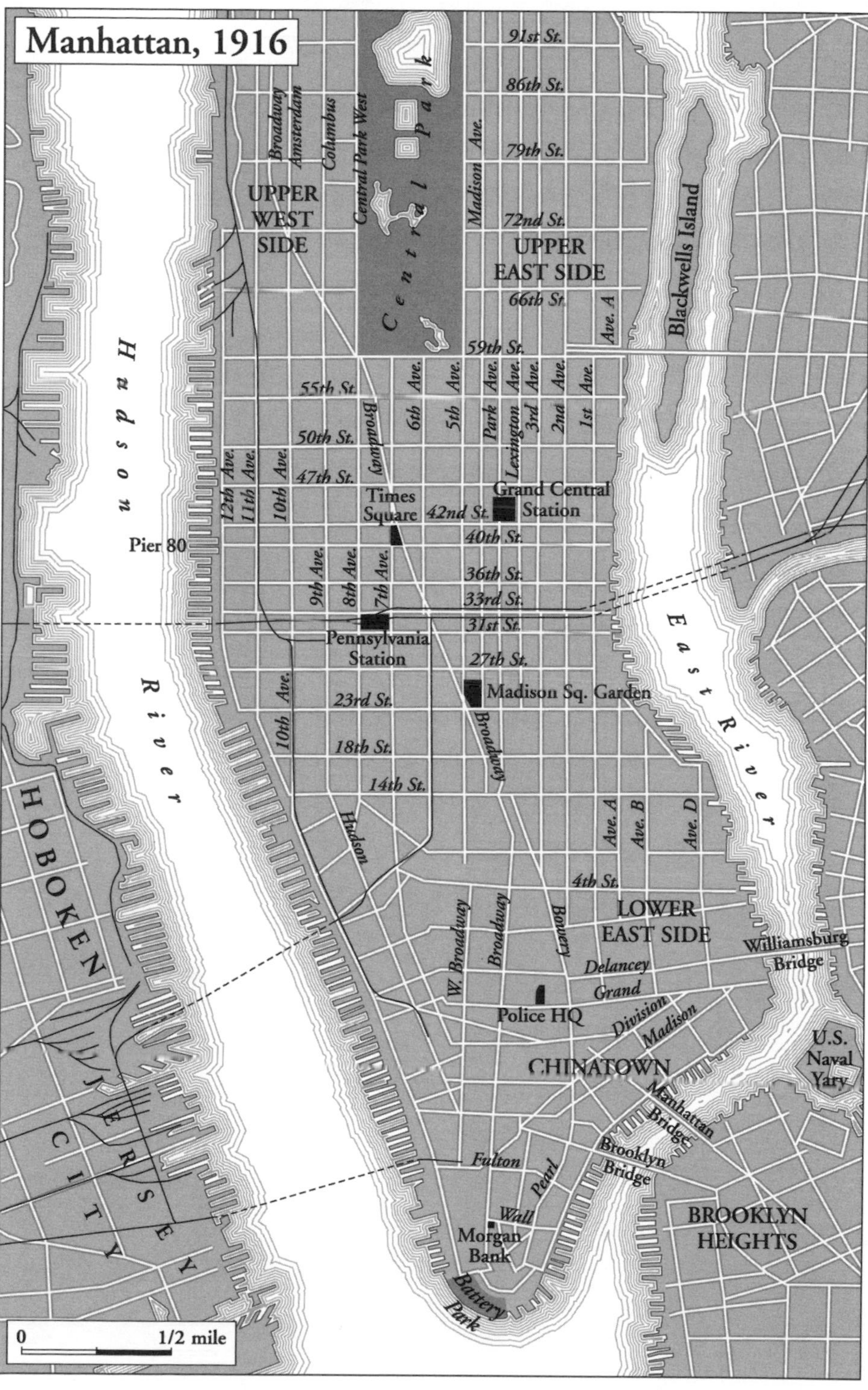
Manhattan, 1916
91st St.
86th St.
79th St.
72nd St.
66th St.
59th St.
55th St.
50th St.
47th St.
42nd St.
40th St.
36th St.
33rd St.
31st St.
27th St.
23rd St.
18th St.
14th St.
4th St.
Broadway
Amsterdam
Columbus
Central Park West
Central Park
Madison Ave.
UPPER WEST SIDE
UPPER EAST SIDE
Blackwells Island
Ave. A
12th Ave.
11th Ave.
10th Ave.
9th Ave.
8th Ave.
7th Ave.
6th Ave.
5th Ave.
Park Ave.
Lexington Ave.
3rd Ave.
2nd Ave.
1st Ave.
Hudson River
East River
Times Square
Grand Central Station
Pier 80
Pennsylvania Station
Madison Sq. Garden
Hudson
Ave. A
Ave. B
Ave. D
HOBOKEN
JERSEY CITY
W. Broadway
Bowery
LOWER EAST SIDE
Williamsburg Bridge
Delancey
Grand
Division
Madison
Police HQ
CHINATOWN
U.S. Naval Yary
Manhattan Bridge
Brooklyn Bridge
Fulton
Pearl
Wall
Morgan Bank
Battery Park
BROOKLYN HEIGHTS
0
1/2 mile

Germany desperately needed to stop the flow of American arms and pack animals to the Allies in order to win World War One. They had helped turn a German victory on the Western Front into a bloody stalemate. But, how could Germany stop the endless supply of these goods without provoking America's hostility?

On January 26, 1915, it initiated a plan when the German Foreign Office sent the following coded message to its attachés:

> *"In the United States, sabotage can reach all kinds of factories for war deliveries. Under no circumstances compromise embassy."*

German agents then commenced an extensive and well-financed program of sabotage in the United States.

THE WAR IN AMERICA HAD BEGUN

Prologue
Mules

Baltimore, Maryland: March 1915

The herd of mules going off to war seemed strange, calm. Mickey, the eighteen-year-old stable hand, saw how they quieted down when the lanky blond veterinarian entered the loading pen at the Baltimore dockyard. Something about him seemed different. He had all the ways of a veterinarian, but he showed an uncommon understanding of the animals. Mickey guessed he grew up a farmer. He sure enough had a farmer's tan. He wore a dusty fedora and never wasted a movement or retraced a step. Mickey liked how the vet treated each mule: a gentle whisper in its ear, a soothing caress across its neck, and then a determined jab of the long needle into its tough backside. Finally, a carrot reward.

The vet saw Mickey. "Last-minute shots," he said.

Mickey nodded. He couldn't make out the man's accent, but he was just a Midwestern farm kid – everyone's accent outside Missouri sounded funny.

The vet injected Judy, one of Mickey's favorite mules, then slipped on some muck. He irritated the animal when he grabbed her to right himself. Judy started to kick. The mule could have knocked the vet into kingdom come, but Mickey had never seen a man move so fast. Once Judy settled down, the vet looked at Mickey. "You've been watching me," he said.

Mickey poked at his teeth with a piece of straw.

"You care about the mules, don't you?" The vet wiped his brow.

"Sure enough, sir. I love them animals."

"I feel sorry for them." The vet patted a mule. "These animals deserve better. This isn't their war, but they're dying on the Western Front faster than the Tommies." The vet continued to inject the mules. "I'm almost finished, son. Then you can load them up."

A voice shouted from the ship. "What's holding things up, you chowder-head?"

"Don't worry, I'm done." The vet wrapped the needle and the empty vial in a small blanket and removed his thick, sturdy gloves. "They're all yours, son." He walked toward the gate.

Mickey turned away to calm one of the mules near the fence. When he looked back at the gate, the vet had disappeared. Mickey didn't think anything of it. Later, in his bunk, Mickey couldn't recall much of their conversation. It didn't matter. No one ever asked him about the incident. He was glad. He reckoned he liked the vet more than his crewmen.

~

The *Henry Morgan*, a six-thousand-ton cargo steamer, departed Baltimore with a crew of forty-five and a cargo of six hundred mules. A day into the voyage, Mickey asked the first mate, "Where's the vet at?"

"Who? There's no vet on this ship."

Two days later, the mules were dying. By the fifth day, the *Henry Morgan* had jettisoned the carcasses of forty-six mules. Judy was one of the first. Heavy sons-of-guns they were, Mickey thought. Dead weight.

Near Liverpool, less than five hundred mules were still alive. Half of those had a fever. "I ain't goin' through this no more." Mickey started to cry. "Muck is one thing. Blood and rotting carcasses is another. I can't stand to see another one of my mules shiver hisself to death."

When they reached Liverpool, a British doctor boarded the *Henry Morgan*. He ordered everyone to stay on board while he assessed the situation. The captain took the doctor to the mule pens, where Mickey showed them the latest dead mule. It lay on its side. Blood covered its mouth and nostrils. "It stumbled its last stumble." Mickey petted the mule.

"It died of convulsions," the captain said.

The doctor pulled at his mustache. "I need to open it up." He put on a cotton mask and leather gloves and handed a pair to the captain and Mickey. "Put these on." He pulled out the scariest knife Mickey had ever seen and started to hack at the mule's insides. "This is the second animal transport ship I've had to board this month." The doctor buried his hands elbow-deep inside the mule and pulled out something black. "Liver." It looked like an old deflated football. The doctor turned the organ over. He brought it up close to his nose and sniffed. "You Yanks have a problem. See these lesions?" The doctor pointed to several spots. "Feel them." He handed the diseased organ to the captain.

"They're hard. I've seen this before." The captain handled the dead liver as if it were a live bomb. "I grew up around livestock. Is this what I think it is?"

"Yes. Anthrax."

SECTION I

NEW YORK POLICE HEADQUARTERS

May 1915 - June 1915

Chapter 1
Bomb Squad

Police Headquarters: May 1915

"Men, we're at war." Captain Thomas Tunney's eyes narrowed. His jowls bulged over the collar of his high-buttoned uniform. In the corner of the fifty by forty-six foot basement assembly room in New York City's Police Headquarters at 240 Centre Street, the twelve men of his Bomb Squad, the top explosives experts in the country, listened and exchanged silent glances.

Detective Sergeant Gil Martin looked at his captain and knew exactly what the other men were thinking, because he was thinking it too: the United States was a neutral country. Martin was a cop's cop. He was honest, calm under pressure, and fearless, once having stood down three bank robbers with an empty gun. The men looked up to him; they valued his intelligence and opinion.

"Not officially, of course." Tunney's voice boomed off the thick basement walls. Martin noticed the captain's thick muscles press against his tight uniform. "But since we're selling munitions to the Allies, we've already picked sides – that's as good as a declaration of war. At least that's how Germany must see it." Tunney stopped and looked at each man. His large body seemed to magnify the gravity of his words. He paused a moment. "What I'm about to tell you is strictly confidential. I'm instructing you not to divulge this information to anyone outside the squad."

Several men nodded. A few murmured, "Yes."

In a loud, clear voice, Martin said, "Yes, sir." He was shaken. He considered any attack on New York City a personal affront and an unforgivable crime. The city was his home, the home of his family, and now the war was over here.

"There have been more than twenty incidents already, and I believe German agents are responsible," Tunney said.

Martin knew Tunney was a man who never said anything he couldn't defend and grew angry when the captain mentioned Germany's involvement. At an early age, Martin's French parents had taught him to hate Germany. Germany had killed his two uncles during the Franco-Prussian War in 1870, forced his parents to leave France the next year, and committed countless atrocities in the prosecution of the current war.

"The sabotage has picked up. Last month, the *Cressington Court* caught fire at sea. The same thing happened to the *Samland*. We found a bomb in the cargo hold of the *Devon City*, but some crewman threw it overboard – no evidence. Just last week, the *Anglo Saxon* nearly sank."

Martin tightened his fist around the arm of his chair and forced his compact body to be still.

"I won't stand for it." Tunney pounded the lectern. "We're going to find the bastards responsible and shut them down!"

The men cheered. Martin was proud to be a member of the Bomb Squad, the most elite unit in the New York City police force. Known for his perseverance, quick intellect, and uncommon good luck, he had risen quickly through the department. At thirty-one, he was one of the Bomb Squad's youngest sergeants ever. First named the Italian Squad, the Bomb Squad had been created to fight the Black Hand, thugs who victimized poor Italian immigrants on the lower East Side, applying extortion and terror. Dynamite was their favorite weapon. The Italian Squad fought back and cut crimes against the city's Italian community in half.

By 1914, New York City had become a refuge for European anarchists from Italy, Spain, Ireland, and Austria-Hungary. An Italian anarchist group called the Brescia Circle started a bombing campaign. Explosions erupted in front of Saint Patrick's Cathedral and on the steps of St. Alphonsus Catholic Church in Brooklyn. When Captain Tunney, the new squad leader, infiltrated the Brescia Circle, he solidified the Italian Squad's reputation, and Tunney's boys became known as the Bomb Squad.

Things in the squad had become too quiet. Martin sensed this was going to change. He looked at his new partner, Detective Paul Keller, who shifted in his chair. Martin knew Keller preferred action to talk and would want to start the investigation. Tall, with short, brown hair that spilled over his forehead, Keller looked like the athlete he was. Still a bit boyish in his mid-twenties, he loved baseball, chasing girls, and police work, and he was good at all three.

"Questions?" Tunney's energy and confidence were contagious. He looked ready for a fight. Only his salt-and-pepper mustache suggested he was older than forty.

"Any leads?" Martin asked.

"No, but I'll tell you this. We're dealing with someone good," Tunney said. "These are not the crude street toughs we're used to."

Seymour Griggs, one of the oldest Bomb Squad detectives, asked, "How big a gang are we dealing with?"

"I wish I knew. I'm sure it's larger, better financed, and more sophisticated than anything we've dealt with before. This bombing ring is complete with paymasters, technicians, informants, suppliers, and operators."

"Something this big must be easy to find," Keller asserted in his usual impulsive way. "Surely we know where to start."

"We don't know anything," Tunney said. "We think Irish dockworkers are planting the bombs, but we believe German saboteurs are behind it. That's the maddening certainty, but we need proof. You are the best policemen in this country. The city is relying on us to stop these bombings. I'm confident we'll do it. God help us if we don't. You men wanted action?"

Twelve men stood up and wildly agreed, Martin's voice loudest among them.

"Well, you're going to get it."

Chapter 2
The Bitter-Ender

North Bay, Ontario, Canada: May 1915

Spring had arrived in Ontario as temperatures inched above freezing. Danie Caarsens scratched the four-day stubble on his jaw and waited. The soles of his boots were comfortably worn, but the cold reached through the holes of his socks and stabbed him like icicles. Caarsens shivered, tucked his checkered wool shirt deeper inside his patched trousers, and pulled his wide-brimmed slouch hat low on his determined brow. Like him, it had seen too many campaigns. He hated the cold, but he hated the British more. One hate attacked his body from the outside. The other knotted his gut tight from within.

"*Blerrie* hell," Caarsens said as he swatted away the hordes of black flies gnawing his flesh. "*Fokking* things." He picked up his German military field glasses and observed the scene from an outcrop of rock overlooking the bend in the railroad tracks thirty yards below. It gave him proper concealment, an excellent view of the approaching train, and a hard-to-track escape route. Everything was ready. Having not eaten all day, he poured maple syrup on two-day-old campfire bread and savored it while the minutes ticked by.

Caarsens was on a mission to sever Canada's east-west railroad connections. The head of German sabotage operations along the East Coast wanted to choke off the flow of goods to Canada's eastern ports. "How you do it is your business. Here's money for your expenses." When Caarsens opened the envelope, he found ten thousand dollars, a small fortune.

Caarsens had studied Canada's railroad connections for a

month. He concluded the railroad tracks here, near North Bay, provided the optimal spot for sabotage. North Bay was Canada's critical railroad juncture, and the Royal Canadian Mounted Police were thinly dispersed in the area.

Caarsens had perfected railroad attacks in the Boer War, and was confident he had minimized all risks for this strike. He was certain this was a military train – no women and children. He didn't give a thought to eliminating combatants, but he didn't kill innocents – the British did that. The area around the railroad was a vast and deserted wilderness, ideal for a skilled guerrilla fighter like him. An accomplished rider on a good horse could escape easily.

Exhausted and desperate, the Boers had signed the peace treaty on May 31, 1902. The treaty provided amnesty to rebel commandos except the most violent ones. Caarsens had refused to surrender and encouraged others not to sign the pledge of allegiance to King Edward VII demanded by the British. The locals called men like him "bitter-enders." Falsely accusing Caarsens of an atrocity at the end of the war, the British had placed a reward of five thousand pounds sterling for his capture, forcing him to leave South Africa. Now, thirteen years later, the reward was still in effect, making Caarsens an itinerant exile, well appreciated in those international circles that understood the value of his extraordinary knowledge of demolitions and guerilla tactics, and his passionate hatred of the nation that had murdered his loving family, ruined his land, and stolen his country.

A shrill train whistle vibrated through the air. Caarsens looked up and saw a column of smoke heading toward him. The sun reflected off his veldt-hardened face. A familiar pre-battle tension filled his body, and the veins in his long, powerful arms seemed to bulge out of his skin. He fastened two bandoliers filled with bullets across his chest, grabbed his Winchester repeating rifle, and moved to the detonator hidden behind the outcrop.

The iron horse chugged forward. Forty train-cars loaded with goods followed. When the train slowed down and swayed around the curve, he pressed the detonator. Two mighty explosions, his trademark, shook the ground beneath him and lifted the locomotive off the ground. The middle car blew apart and the rest toppled over, car by car. Flames grabbed the sky as the kerosene he had poured along the tracks ignited. The fire became so bright Caarsens had to shade his eyes with his hand.

Fire spread to the tender. Its coal turned red. The heat intensified, and Caarsens began to sweat. Bullets exploded by the caseload. An ammunition train. The smell of gunpowder was everywhere, and caustic black smoke filled the air. Caarsens coughed. The train wreck became a volcano, erupting scores of human fireballs screaming inhuman sounds. Their burning flesh smelled like pigs roasting over a campfire. A man in uniform shouted orders and directed the survivors with his good arm. A flying piece of metal cut him in two. Another officer replaced him. Ten seconds later, a stray bullet struck his head. No one took their place. Those who could ran away. The wounded crawled. The dying wailed.

Caarsens was satisfied with his work. He mounted his horse and vanished into the forested rocky hills. After riding hard for several hours, he emerged from the thick wilderness and established a campsite a mile off the Champlain trail, near a small lake, where he secured his horse and rinsed his face. His dusty, sweat-stained clothes needed washing, but he was used to their coarseness and odor. After he set up camp, he baited his hook with hands toughened from years of physical work, cast his line, and within minutes reeled in a trout, then another. In five minutes, he had dinner and breakfast. He grabbed his gray crank-handle Demag bayonet and cleaned the trout with deliberate, efficient movements.

When he finished cleaning the fish, Caarsens tenderly wiped the Demag, admiring it from tip to hilt to tip. He loved how the light from the campfire reflected off its well-polished blade, how it felt like a perfect extension of his hand and an able tool for his will. He glided the edge of his blade lightly across his cheek, providing a familiar steel caress and a cold reminder he was still alive. He marveled at the bayonet's precise balance and utilitarian design as he ran his finger over the rounded grooves on either side of the blade, designed for easy extraction from its victim.

He held up the bayonet and watched it glint in the flickering firelight. His once handsome face had become scarred by battle, weariness, and forty hard years. He was no longer the young man girls whispered about at dances despite warnings from their silently jealous mothers, no longer the prosperous farmer with a loving family, no longer the most respected man in the county.

He was still a superb horseman, a knowledgeable adventurer, and fearless soldier. How many men had he killed with the Demag? Not enough. How many people had the British killed in the Boer War? Too many. Although the fighting had stopped in 1902, Caarsens's war was far from over. It was still very personal.

He reached for a stone to sharpen the bayonet. He enjoyed the scraping sound of its blade against the rough surface. With each stroke against the stone, Caarsens thought about the war against Britain. It was a war he and the other Boers did not want, but they fought to defend their independence against a resource-greedy and plundering imperial power. For almost three years, Boer commandos fought Britain to a standstill until the Anglo intruders changed tactics and destroyed everything the Boers had – their land, their animals, and their people, including almost an entire generation of children in British concentration camps.

Despite his foolhardy bravery and willingness to die, Caarsens had lived. He believed he was spared to seek retribution. Such was his attack today. He rolled up his sleeve and stared at the round cigar-sized burn marks that covered his arm. "You brought the fires of hell down upon Canada today, didn't you, Major Westerly?" He rubbed the scars and recalled the searing pain. *God curse the British Empire and its American paramour.*

A wolf howled in the distant blackness and seemed to share his emptiness. He sheathed the bayonet and read his daily passage from the *Old Testament* while his trout sizzled in the frying pan. He ate it with overcooked beans and boiled coffee. He leaned against a rock, opened his billfold, and removed a worn, stained photograph of a young woman. He looked at it for a long time.

A flying ember singed his cheek. He brushed it away, and his thoughts moved to the current war. Hoping for a German victory, he prayed his efforts would make a difference. He had further plans to cripple the Canadian railroad system, but time was short. He feared the Mounties had his scent. As in so many of his battles, Caarsens was outnumbered.

Chapter 3
The *Lusitania*

Washington, D.C.: May 1915

John Wittig, a vice president for J.P. Morgan Bank, listened with a negotiator's guile to the representative from E.I. du Pont de Nemours make his pitch for a considerable government-guaranteed loan to build a plant to fulfill a new government contract for explosives. The U.S. congressman in attendance, whose committee would approve the contract, was looking bored when an excited aide interrupted the meeting. "Excuse me, gentlemen. We just got the news – the *Lusitania* was sunk off the Irish coast today!"

"How?" All three men spoke in alarmed unison.

"German U-boats."

The men groaned. "Young man, do you know how many died?" Wittig asked.

"About twelve hundred, sir, as far as we know."

"How many Americans?" The congressman's face was white.

"Over one hundred. There may be more."

Tempers erupted as an argument ensued among them.

"Gentlemen, calm down." Wittig wanted to know all the facts. He couldn't believe Germany's U-boats were so reckless. "There are two sides to this. Maybe the *Lusitania* carried weapons. If she did, she was a legitimate target."

The du Pont man waved his hand mockingly with apparent dismissal.

"Don't forget, Germany published a warning last month," Wittig said. "They announced their U-boats would attack any British ship. Every passenger knew he was traveling at his own peril."

"Of course, you'd say that. You're one of those Huns." The du Pont man pointed a finger at Wittig. "Your name and your haircut give you away."

Proud to be a German-American, Wittig was angry at having to defend Germany yet again, and tired from long, stressful hours working on Morgan Bank's biggest deals. His normal reticence left him. "My parents were German. I was born in Brooklyn, and I'm as loyal to this country as you are. The difference between us is that I despise *all* wars."

"U-boat attacks are an outrage to humanity." The du Pont man stomped his foot.

The congressman stood up and straightened his waistcoat. "Torpedoing merchant ships and killing innocent Americans are unconscionable. Germany has proven it is our enemy. The next thing you know, they'll be sabotaging American ships and blowing up our factories. We must do something to stop them." He looked at the others as if he was expecting applause. It didn't come.

"You're wrong." Wittig felt a spasm in his gut. "Germany is just trying to defend itself."

"As it fights for world domination," the congressman snapped and reached for his hat. "Let us adjourn. My committee will not approve these contracts without modification."

~

On the train back to New York, Wittig worried about the sinking of the *Lusitania*. American outrage would grow, and war was a real possibility. War, Wittig was certain, would bring persecution of German-Americans like himself. Hundreds of German-Americans had already returned to Germany. Wittig closed his eyes. *Would the bank fire him? Would America deport him? Could Germany try to draft him if he returned?*

His German nephew, Ernst, had already been killed fighting the British at Ypres. An artillery shell obliterated his body. His two daughters loved their cousin and had cried for days. His wife, Nora, an Irish-American, had started to challenge his turn-the-other-cheek philosophy. "Can't you see?" she asked in exasperation. "England is our enemy, and America is helping them. The English starved the Irish for a century. Now they're starving Germany, *your* Germany."

~

The next day, Wittig visited Consul General Felix Beck at the German Consulate at 25 Broadway, just a short walk from his Morgan Bank office on Wall Street. Wittig, a major contributor to the German Red Cross, had talked with Beck at several Red Cross functions. As he waited outside Beck's closed office, he heard Beck arguing with a man with a high-pitched voice, but he could not understand their words. Suddenly, the consul's door flung open, and a bald man as big as a bear walked out. His shoulders almost touched either side of the frame. He put on a black hat and coat, looked at Wittig with threat in his eyes, and stalked away.

Beck came to the door, his face arranged in a smile.

"Herr Wittig, what a surprise. I hope you have not waited long. It is good to see you. Please come in." A little man with short, dark hair and a thin nose, Beck was dressed in a well-cut suit similar to those worn by Morgan Bank partners.

Beck's office was twice the size of Jack Morgan's, the son of the bank's founder and its current head. Blood-red Persian carpets as thick as the heel of Wittig's shoe covered the floor. A black, white and red German flag decorated the far wall. Beck gestured to a straight-backed chair.

Sitting, Wittig noticed two photographs on Beck's desk. The first showed a young Beck in a fencing uniform with his hands up in triumph. "I always wanted to be an athlete, but I was too busy at school," he said.

"You have done well, Herr Wittig. Your education and your business success demonstrate that." Beck pointed to the photograph. "I was a Dresden champion in foil. That was a long time before this God-forsaken war. No matter. My life has turned out well."

Wittig was impressed by the second photograph, which showed Beck in a German major's uniform with an Iron Cross First Class decoration. He looked at it a bit too long to be polite. "How did you earn it? The Iron Cross."

"What brings you to my office, Herr Wittig?" Beck folded his hands on his desk, pointedly ignoring the question.

"I want to discuss how Germany is going to handle the *Lusitania* disaster. One of my neighbors drowned when she sank. I don't want to lose any more friends."

"My condolences, Herr Wittig. The sinking was an unfortunate business. I regret the loss of life."

"But public opinion."

"We will manage that. Everything will be fine." Beck assured Wittig that Germany wanted peace with America and would try to solve any further issues with President Wilson. Thirty-five minutes later, his worries about the war greatly assuaged, two questions he had not asked continued to bother him. *Who was that rough-looking man? And what was he doing with the consul general?*

Chapter 4
The *Kirk Oswald*

Brooklyn Dockyards, New York City: May 1915

The big man in the black hat and coat stood alone and watched the *Kirk Oswald* sail out of New York Harbor. His mouth turned up in his corrupted version of a smile. He was confident the *Kirk Oswald*, loaded with food supplies, would never reach its destination in Archangel, Russia. He knew what no one on board the ship knew – his agents had buried powerful incendiary bombs inside four sugar bags. They were timed to explode when the *Kirk Oswald* neared Archangel.

His agents had already conducted a series of successful attacks on other U.S. munitions ships. His sabotage campaign was accelerating, but the police were unaware of his activities. All they knew was that he was a law-abiding German national who was head of security for the Hamburg-American Shipping Lines. The men along the docks knew the big man differently. They had witnessed his violent and coercive ways, and understood without a doubt that he controlled New York Harbor.

~

Halfway across the Atlantic Ocean, the captain of the *Kirk Oswald* received orders to change course and sail to Marseilles, France, a change of itinerary that reduced the length of the voyage by several days. The rest of the journey proceeded without incident.

Upon arrival, North African laborers scrambled to unload the sugar and grain. They had removed one-third of the goods from cargo hold #2 when one of the sugar bags burst open in a man's arms. Something heavy dropped to the ground. One of the mates recognized a bomb and quickly alerted the captain.

Captain Philippe Boudreaux, a bomb expert from French military intelligence, arrived to lead the investigation. Dressed in a neatly pressed uniform, Boudreaux was a compact man with a military bearing and a pencil-thin mustache. An artillery man by training, he had risen through the officer ranks because of his thoroughness, hard work, and engineering skills. He found three more bombs. Their quality and workmanship were excellent, and their design was unlike anything he had ever seen before.

Unexplained bombings and fires on board U.S. munitions ships were a serious concern for France. She, like Britain and Russia, depended on supplies from America to sustain her desperate war effort. Without America's goods, the Allies could not continue the war. The *Kirk Oswald* bombs were the first clue to the mystery. Boudreaux cabled Captain Thomas Tunney and suggested he come to New York to consult with Tunney's bomb experts. The message concluded: "Most urgent. Delays will cost lives."

~

The poorly controlled detonation knocked Martin off his bench. Working in the basement laboratory of the New York City police department's headquarters for fifteen straight hours, he had been testing timing devices. Once again, the luck that made all of Martin's police colleagues envious held. Clad in the same protection the British used in their munitions design laboratories, Martin escaped unharmed. He dusted himself off, reviewed his notes, and concluded he had used too little pressure on the primer.

His body ached for a cigarette, but for safety reasons he had pledged to give them up when he joined the Bomb Squad. His ears still ringing from the misfire, Martin couldn't understand the garbled words coming from the doorway. "You have to shout."

The messenger cupped his hands around his mouth. "Sergeant, your visitor from France has arrived."

Captain Philippe Boudreaux greeted Martin with a crisp salute.

"Thank you for coming, *Capitaine*," Martin said in French and offered his hand. "You arrived sooner than we expected." He escorted the Frenchman to an empty office.

Boudreaux maintained military and Gallic formality. "Here are the bombs from the *Kirk Oswald*." He presented a leather satchel to Martin. "We have neutralized them. We call them cigar bombs."

"How do they work?" Martin asked.

"They are ingenious." Boudreaux explained that the bombs were made from ten-inch-long metal pipes the diameter of a large cigar. A copper disk separated the pipes into two compartments. One compartment contained sulfuric acid; the other, potassium chloride or another flammable chemical. Wax sealed each end of the tube. At a fixed rate, the sulfuric acid ate away the copper. When the two chemicals combined, flames spewed from either end of the bomb like a juggler's torch. "The thickness of the copper determines the timing."

"The thicker the copper disk, the longer it takes the bomb to explode. Is that right?" Martin examined the bomb.

"*Oui*. Everything about them says German design and engineering."

"Why didn't they detonate during the journey?"

"By chance." Boudreaux pulled some papers full of formulas

and calculations from the satchel. “The *Kirk Oswald* was redirected en route. The ship docked before the bombs could explode. Whoever set the fuse overestimated the time of the journey,” Captain Boudreaux said.

“Possible,” Martin said. “Or the copper case was too thick. It prevented the acid from burning through at the planned rate.”

“Unlikely with a German-made bomb.” Boudreaux paused for a moment and lowered his head. “This war is so terrible,” he said. “May I speak frankly to you, a French-American?”

“*Bien sûr*.” Martin nodded his head in assent.

“My brother died last week,” Boudreaux continued. “He was shot down in his aeroplane. France needs your help.”

Martin had conflicting views about the war. He loved France and knew that, had his parents not emigrated when the Germans annexed Alsace, he would be fighting in the trenches by now. However, he was born in America, and his allegiance was to her. Where did his loyalties start and end?

Regaining his composure, Boudreaux resumed his official persona. “I brought the materials to make a crude cigar bomb. Do you want to test it?”

~

Tunney and Detective Keller joined them for the test in an open field in the upper Bronx. The bomb produced a white-hot blast of fire that shot out about four inches from each end. Its force and intensity startled Martin. “Is that what we’re up against?”

“My test was only one-third strength,” Boudreaux said in excellent English.

“Impressive.” Tunney didn’t flinch. “If there’s anything flammable nearby, it would ignite an inferno.”

"Even better." Boudreaux picked through the remains of the bomb. He gathered a handful of tiny fragments and showed them to Tunney. "The metal has melted – no evidence."

"No wonder the fires are mysterious," Martin said.

"Captain Boudreaux, can you think of any reason why the bombs were hidden inside sugar bags?" Keller asked.

"Two reasons. One, the bombs are easy to smuggle on board if they're concealed in bags. Two, sugar is highly flammable. A sugar fire is hard to control. Much water is needed to fight it, and the water ruins the munitions still in the hold. It doesn't matter if the ship sinks or not."

"Very clever." Keller sifted through the debris.

"Yes, it is." Boudreaux looked at Keller. "Your name, Keller, is German, is it not?"

Keller stared back. "Yes, and I'm proud of it. But I'm as American as anyone."

"Just asking."

Wanting to deflect the tension, Martin said, "Whoever is planting the bombs, he'll make a mistake. We'll find him."

Tunney acted as if he hadn't heard. "These cigar bombs are easy to conceal, powerful, and efficient. They are perfect for a saboteur." Tunney asked, "Captain Boudreaux, do you have any other thoughts?"

"These bombs are a threat. The people who made them are resourceful, motivated, and will not hesitate to sink every munitions ship sailing out of New York Harbor. If these saboteurs are not stopped, they will soon start to blow up your city. The war has come to America."

Chapter 5
On to New York

Canadian / United States Border: May 1915
Caarsens sensed danger. He was vulnerable in open enemy country he did not know. He had blown up two more trains and demolished a bridge on the Cross Canadian Railway in Ontario. The Mounties on his trail had multiplied and were searching for him with flying machines. Now, the Mounties' Indian trackers were getting close. They were as good as the Zulus. He used all his guile and experience, but he couldn't lose them.

Closing the gap hour by hour, the Mounties chased him to the United States border. A fresh mustang he stole saved him. When the horse collapsed in front of the Niagara River, Caarsens grabbed his weapons and money and ran to the water. He commandeered a leaky boat and was halfway across the river when he saw Mounties. They stopped at the river's edge and fired their Lee Enfield rifles; their bullets struck Caarsens's boat. It started to sink and capsized sixty yards from the New York shore. Despite the powerful currents and icy water, Caarsens made it across.

~

A week later in a Delaware hotel, a warm breeze blew across Caarsens and distracted him from his nightly torments. It took him a moment to remember where he was, a second more to understand he was safe, and a third to control the dull pains in his body, legacies of a past never far from his mind. He turned over in bed. The soft mattress felt uncomfortable. His body was used to hay, dirt, or hard wooden slabs. The stiff bed sheets scratched his rough skin, and the borax smell irritated his nose. He preferred a saddle for a pillow and a blanket that smelled like a horse.

He rolled over again but couldn't sleep. What was sleep? Merely fitful periods of rest. He felt as if he'd been running a lifetime. Yet, he had only become a fugitive at the end of the Boer War when a British military court convicted him in absentia of burning six British soldiers alive in a blockhouse and assassinating two British magistrates the same day. The main witnesses against him were two known Boer collaborators, three drunken British soldiers whom Caarsens's lawyers proved were not at the scene of the alleged crimes, and Major Westerly, his old adversary, who had earned a special place in Hell. Caarsens swore he'd deliver the major there some day.

Caarsens fled Africa and first found refuge in Quebec, where his knowledge of French and his hatred of the British proved useful. He earned a good living with his farming and explosives expertise, but he had to leave when Canadian police started to inquire about his background. For the next year he traveled around South America, occasionally working for mining companies.

In 1906, he returned to South Africa to join an unsuccessful Boer rebellion. Almost captured, he escaped to Turkey, outside the reach of the British Empire, where he offered his services to the Ottoman sultan. His military experience and excellent German made him a frequent guest at the German Embassy in Istanbul, where he met German military advisors.

When Archduke Francis Ferdinand, the heir apparent to the Austria-Hungary Empire, was shot in Sarajevo, triggering the outbreak of World War One, Caarsens volunteered to work for Germany against Britain. They accepted and sent him to America, where he impressed the German spymaster in New York on his first assignment. The spymaster later boasted to Count von Bernstorff, Germany's most senior ambassador to the United States, how Caarsens had infected the entire herd of mules on the *Henry Morgan*. He had proven himself again by destroying Canada's railroads.

Today, he had a munitions plant to destroy.

A rooster announced sunup. He forced himself out of bed and remembered it was Sunday. As he did every morning, he started the day with a prayer. He prayed to be courageous in battle and asked for mercy for the meek. He added a special request: to know that his work would not be in vain.

This was his last job before he moved to New York. He wanted the police to waste their time chasing someone who didn't exist, so he let the innkeeper live. He couldn't tell the police much: a middle-aged, blond-haired, French-Canadian man named Jacques Levert of Quebec City stayed one night. He was polite and quiet. No, he didn't seem dangerous. I didn't see any weapons. He said he had some business in Dover, I think. Took care of his own horse – brown mare, it might have been black; no special markings. You're welcome, Officer. If I see anyone suspicious, I'll call you.

Caarsens had a morning's ride to reach his objective: two buildings that manufactured black powder at du Pont's Wilmington, Delaware plant. The week before, he had entered the plant disguised as a government inspector, memorized the plant layout, learned its vulnerabilities, and mentioned he would return. A guard had told him there was only token security on Sundays.

Once again pretending to be the government inspector,

Caarsens rode up to the plant and hitched his horse to the post by the front gate. He threw his saddlebags full of explosives over his shoulder, waved to the drowsy gatekeeper, and walked into the plant unchallenged. He went to the shipping area of Plant #1, where he knew hundreds of pounds of powerful grade powder waited to be shipped the next day. The plant was empty, and he set his explosives with no problems. He repeated the process in Plant #2 and walked to the main gate. He tipped his hat to the guard, mounted his horse, and rode away. He had been in the plant less than an hour.

The first bomb detonated when he was four hundred yards down the road. His next bomb ignited seconds later and triggered a series of secondary explosions that sounded like an artillery duel between two heavily armed adversaries. He felt the earth rumble as debris crashed behind him. He steadied his whinnying horse amidst the yelling and cries for help. The explosions intensified.

After another half a mile, Caarsens guided his horse off the main road into a thick forest and crossed Brandyglass Creek. He tied up his horse and climbed the tallest tree. He adjusted the wheel on his Carl Zeiss 6x24 DF German field glasses and assessed his work. The scene came into sharp focus. The utter devastation surprised even him. Nearby trees were either uprooted or twisted into kindling. The plants had turned into exploding infernos. Five minutes later, the roofs collapsed, and the walls of the buildings toppled with a thundering bang. A few men stumbled around dazed. He was thankful casualties seemed light. He didn't like to kill on the Sabbath.

Chapter 6
A Family Sunday

Bronxville, New York: June 1915

As Caarsens was riding away from the Delaware plant, John Wittig sat down in a pew at Bronxville's Dutch Reformed Church. He ignored the other parishioners as they entered and stared at the empty spots on either side of him. A draft of cool air flowed through the wood frame building. Wittig bowed his head and thanked the Lord for his family, their good health, and his professional success. Then he cursed Him.

Although he apologized and prayed for forgiveness, Wittig hated the religious separation he and his family endured each Sunday morning. He didn't understand why social conventions forced him to go to church alone every Sunday. Accepting the split was the agreement he and Nora Fitzpatrick, a Catholic, had made when they married. Neither would convert, and neither would abandon the other. Those days seemed so distant now.

During communion his mind drifted. The U-boat that sank the *Lusitania* had torpedoed his life as well. Over the last month, personal attacks against him and his German heritage had increased. He had become German, and not German-American. Last week, he had lost another loan deal to a New York banker, an elder at an Episcopalian church. Some of the children in his daughters' school refused to play with them because of their German background. Wittig grew his hair longer and told strangers and new clients he was Dutch.

After church, he walked down Kraft Avenue and met Nora

and their two girls walking up from the Catholic Church on Park Place. Hannah and Mary saw their father, ran toward him, and nearly knocked him over. The girls skipped in front of them as he and Nora walked home together hand-in-hand.

When they got there, Nora prepared lunch. Wittig went to the living room and slumped in his reading chair. Nora joined him a few minutes later. "What's wrong?"

"I fear this war in Europe will change our lives."

"Mary Mother of God, it's about time you realized that."

"Girls, why don't you play outside?" Wittig said.

"When are we going to the beach?" Mary asked.

"That's my favorite part of the week," Hannah chimed in, clutching her Raggedy Ann doll.

"Soon." After the girls ran outside, Nora said, "You think too highly of people, John. The difference between us is that I'm a practical person. You see the good in people. I see the bad. Growing up in Ireland does that to you. Most Americans will side with the Allies, and we'll feel their hate."

"But we're good people," Wittig said. "Surely our friends will know –"

"No, they won't. We'll become outcasts." Nora wiped her hand on her apron. "But let's not argue. Hannah is right. It's Sunday afternoon. We have given God our morning. Now it's our time to be together." Nora leaned out the back kitchen window. "Pack the motorcar. We're going to Milton Point for a picnic," she announced to cheers from the girls.

~

Wittig drove the Hudson Super-Six Touring Sedan up the Boston Post Road and reached secluded Milton Point in nearby Rye by mid-afternoon. Wittig loved its spectacular view of Long Island Sound. They passed a rich landscape that changed from tall meadow grass to woods of oak and maple full of robins, jays, and sparrows. The smell of the sea mixed with the smell of the land to produce an odor sweeter than honey, saltier than pickle brine, and more intoxicating than Wittig's best whiskey.

He stopped the motorcar on the side of the deserted dirt road, and the family walked to the shore behind the woods. Nora spread out a blanket. They ate her ham sandwiches spiced with the last of their imported German mustard, the incomparable Wittig potato salad, and Oreo cookies for desert. The girls took off their shoes and stockings and chased each other to the water. Splashes back and forth left them drenched and laughing.

The girls built a sandcastle with thick walls and an eight-inch wide moat. Hannah finished a tower four drinking cups tall. Mary carved decorations with a stick.

The tide moved in. Amidst the girls' delighted giggles, waves began to crash into the sandcastle. Its walls began to slide into the charging water. For another ten minutes, the girls saved their creation with frantic repairs. "Come on, Mary," Hannah pleaded. "Work faster."

Amused, Wittig lay down on a blanket and Nora joined him. She rested her head on his stomach.

"Papa, come, hurry," Hannah called. Wittig ran to the water.

"It's scary." Mary backed away from the water and pointed to a horseshoe crab floating upside down. Wittig grabbed it by its tail and carried it away. He returned just as the foamy seawater washed away the sandcastle.

Chapter 7
The Sugar Trail

Police Headquarters: June 1915

Follow the sugar trail, Martin told himself. At what point in the process from sugar processing to loading the munitions ships did German agents smuggle the bombs into the sugar bags?

Completing their three-week investigation into the local sugar processing industry, Martin and Keller visited their last sugar plant in Yonkers on the Hudson River, just north of New York City. Dressed in their usual detective attire, dark suits, Prince Albert coats, and high black derbies, they walked through the entire production process, watched every delivery, and asked every worker questions. They observed every step in the refining process from goods receipt to bagging. They concluded that the only opportunity for a saboteur to plant a bomb occurred after the sugar bags were initially closed in the plant.

The bags were sewn closed either by hand or machine and held in storage until they could be transported. But which bags? Martin had a theory, but he needed to test it. The detectives took a number of filled sugar bags back to Bomb Squad headquarters. Keller and Griggs planted fake bombs in some of the bags and resealed them. Could Martin determine which ones held the bombs?

Martin inspected and smelled each bag. He studied every closing, took out a knife, and opened them. "I can tell which of the machine-sewn bags have been tampered with. I see no difference with the hand-sewn ones. Since we're sure that the bombs are placed in the sugar bags after they've been closed, we've cut our search in half. Our bombers are using the hand-sewn bags, since they obviously can't re-close the machine-sewn ones without someone noticing. Now we can concentrate on the shipments of hand-sewn sugar bags only."

"I bet Griggs that's what you'd find." Keller held out his hand, and Griggs dropped two fifty-cent pieces into it with a frown.

The detectives examined the shipping process next. Only two people knew the destination of the sugar before it was actually placed in a ship's hold: the shipping clerk at the refinery, and the captain of the large flat-bottomed barges, called lighterboats, used to transfer the bags from the plants onto the ships. The shipping clerk handed the bill of goods with the destination to the lighterboat captain.

When the next shipment of hand-sewn sugar bags was ready for delivery, the detectives revisited the refining plant and waited for the lighterboat captain. Martin was surprised when a Teutonic-looking man came into the shipping department and introduced himself. "Reinhardt Lerchmacher. Are the goods ready?"

Martin stepped forward and explained that he wanted to follow the sugar to the munitions ship.

"You're not welcome on board. We don't accept strangers on our lighterboats, sir."

"You have no choice." Martin flashed his badge.

"It wouldn't be wise to interfere with us."

Keller moved up to Lerchmacher belly-to-belly and looked down at the much shorter man. "You're losing your hair."

Lerchmacher stood his ground. "You need a bath."

Martin separated the men. "We're going to inspect your ship, Captain. Let's be gentlemen about this."

"Or not," Keller threatened.

Lerchmacher conceded. “Go ahead, but don’t get in our way. I have a schedule to keep. Excuse me.” He left shouting orders to his men.

“Most of these lighterboat captains are of German descent,” the shipping clerk said.

Martin looked at Keller – they were thinking the same thing. They followed Lerchmacher to his lighterboat. When they were satisfied it contained nothing incriminating, Martin let Lerchmacher proceed.

“About time. You’ve just cost me money,” Lerchmacher said.

“Be glad that’s all it cost you,” Martin replied. The lighterboat sailed into New York Harbor and headed to the big munitions depot at Black Tom Island, just behind the Statue of Liberty. It pulled up to the pier alongside the merchant ship to be loaded. As soon as the lighterboat tied up to the ship’s side, stevedores rushed the cargo into the hold. When they were done, the crew sealed the hatches, and a cargo-checker gave the consignment receipt to Lerchmacher.

During the loading process, the detectives saw no sign of mischief. Still, Martin was certain bombs were sometimes – but not always – placed in the sugar bags during transit on the lighterboats and smuggled onto the ships by the lighterboat crews. Proving who did it and when would be a challenge. The miles of shoreline to cover were daunting, and lightering was often done at night, which made the lighterboats hard to watch. After almost three weeks of work, the sugar trail had gone cold, and Martin was no closer to finding the saboteurs. His frustration and fear of failure mounted. Captain Tunney was quick to replace men who disappointed him.

The mysterious bombings continued.

Chapter 8
New Approaches

Manhattan: June 1915

Freshly shaved and cleanly barbered, Caarsens arrived in New York City by train from Baltimore. He disembarked at Penn Station, took a horse-drawn taxi to the Plaza Hotel on 59th Street and 5th Avenue, and registered for a week as Maurice DuBois. The clothes he had bought in Baltimore made him look like the successful French-Canadian businessman he pretended to be.

He hated New York City crowds, noise, and smells, but he could easily disappear here; he was just another immigrant in a city of almost five million. Getting around was easy after he figured out all the transportation routes, and the rivers and harbor offered attack and escape possibilities. Best yet, the city contained numerous vulnerable targets.

On his third day, Caarsens walked down Fourth Avenue to the newly opened Brooks Brothers store on 44th Street. He walked out in a new blue suit and boater. He later visited an army surplus store and purchased an old campaign hat and uniform from the Spanish-American War, a strong rucksack, and some working man's clothes. Before he returned to the Plaza Hotel, he bought several things in a store that supplied to Broadway shows and Vaudeville actors.

The following week, he found a safe place to stay – convenient, crowded, and away from the police. Once settled, he spent many hours in the New York Public Library preparing his next operation. He laughed at the irony. *Imagine a place that provides someone the information to attack it and doesn't even charge a fee.*

~

A week later, Caarsens sat against a tree at the edge of the woods and studied the approaches to the German Consulate's summer house in Milton Point, near the Wittig family's favorite picnic spot. The big house sat on a large wooded property along the shore of Long Island Sound. Good reconnaissance and careful observation were mandatory in his line of work, and he excelled in both. He had already scouted the grounds for fresh footprints and the pier for activity, but sat vigilant and patient for another half-hour.

Inside, Consul General Felix Beck, head of German sabotage operations along the East Coast, reviewed the financial accounts of his activities. His superior, Colonel Walter Nicolai, head of Section III-B – German Military Intelligence – had provided him with five million dollars to establish his spy network and insisted on proper accounting and documentation for expenditures.

Before the war, Beck had been chief accountant for Krupp Industries, where he had had a reputation for outsmarting bankers and always securing the best rates. This talent and Beck's purchasing prowess had increased Krupp's profits by three percent in 1912. When the war started, the powerful General Erich Ludendorff snatched him from Krupp and employed him as a quartermaster. Major Beck soon displayed his loyalty and ruthless competence in a variety of dangerous and unpleasant assignments.

Chief among the major's services was his success in smashing a Russian counterfeiting ring that no one else had been able to crack. Fake Reichsmarks had been flooding into East Prussia. Beck traced the source, tracked down the printing presses, and captured two Russian conspirators in an old warehouse along the border. When the Ivans were slow to provide desired details, Beck had his men stake one of them to the ground. When the man still refused to talk, Beck stabbed him with a pitchfork at six-inch intervals all along his body, starting at his ankles. The man's screams stopped when he punctured his groin. His breathing stopped after two more thrusts. His partner revealed all and was rewarded with a bullet to the head. The counterfeiting stopped, and Beck, without protest from the diplomatic corps, became a consul general.

Caarsens rose from his post at the foot of the tree, circled the house one more time, and approached the front door.

Beck came outside. "You are very thorough. Your reputation is deserved." He was a small man with restless eyes, delicate hands, and a large wart on his left cheek, who nevertheless commanded respect. "I am glad to see you again, Herr Caarsens. You have done well in Canada."

A rabbit hopped across the front pathway. Beck picked up a rock and threw it at the animal, missing by inches. "Shame. It is a mistake to antagonize me."

Caarsens followed the little man inside. The house was as well furnished as a sultan's summer residence, with elaborate ivory decorations, beautiful tapestries, and large, comfortable couches. Burning candles released an Oriental fragrance. They sat down and talked in a mixture of German, French, and English. Caarsens thought Beck sounded like a pompous aristocrat. He outlined what Caarsens needed to know about his operation in New York. "We must arrange a place to exchange messages."

"I agree." Caarsens nodded, but wondered how much he could trust him.

"You are a religious man, are you not?" asked Beck.

"*Ag man*. My religion is my own business."

"Of course, but you go to church?"

Caarsens didn't answer.

"I suggest we exchange messages and other things at Saint Luke's Lutheran Church on 42nd Street between 7th and 8th Avenues. The minister is discreet and sympathetic. But he is not very bright. He will not ask questions or bother us as long as we keep his collection plate full."

"I am anxious to get started, Herr Beck. How can I help?"

Beck hesitated a moment. "I have an immediate problem, a request from Germany." He held up some papers that appeared to be in code. "I understand you have a broad knowledge of your, ah, profession."

A test? "What do you want me to do?"

"One of my tasks is to procure key raw materials and supplies for Germany. I must do it legally."

"But the blockade?"

"Yes, the damn blockade. It is more effective than Germany has acknowledged, but U.S. laws still allow us to ship some goods across. With some ingenuity, you can maintain the letter of the law without abiding by its spirit, but not in the quantities Germany needs."

"What are you looking to provide specifically?"

"Lubricating oil. Germany needs it badly." Beck swallowed.

Caarsens thought a moment. "How are you planning to get it there?"

"I have men who do this work."

"Yes, smuggling is a possibility, but I have a better idea. You can still ship fertilizer to Germany, can't you?"

"So far, yes. It is a non-military good."

"Here's what you do. Mix the oil with magnesium carbonate. Then add fertilizer into the mixture. It will absorb the oil – impossible to detect. Falsify the manifest and claim it is fertilizer. Once it reaches Germany, have your chemists put it in benzene, salt, and water. The oil will float to the top."

Beck made a few notes, then slid a thin silver case out from his inside lapel pocket. "A gift from General Ludendorff."

The General Ludendorff? Caarsens raised an eyebrow ever so slightly.

"No other," Beck responded.

Caarsens made a mental note that Beck seemed so attuned to reading facial responses, he must have a gift for reading minds.

"The general arranged to have me assigned here. He calls me the Black Ferret. I like the name. Cigarette?" The consul proffered an all-but-invisible smile.

"No, thank you."

Beck eased one out of the case, attached a holder, and lit it. "These Americans are fools. They make good cigarettes, though. They want to shut down our beer halls. An outrage. It is just another attack on German culture."

"I'm more concerned about America's shipment of goods to the Allies," Caarsens said.

"Worst of all, they want to give women the right to vote. Women. That's insane. Women are stupid and useless."

Caarsens disagreed, but let Beck talk.

"President Wilson is no better than a woman – he does not have the stomach for war. That is why Germany will win. We are bold, we make our own luck. Let me show you." Beck produced a Morgan silver dollar from his pocket. "Beautiful, is it not?"

Caarsens watched and waited.

"One coin. Two sides – heads and tails, yes?" Beck showed Caarsens each side of the coin. "It is made by one creator, but it looks different depending which side you see. It buys the same goods regardless which side is shown to the merchant. Like life, it produces a game of chance. Flip it: heads – one thing happens; tails – another thing happens. Care to guess who wins this war?" Beck flipped the coin in the air, caught it, and hid it in his fist.

No comment.

"You are a careful man, Herr Caarsens. I like that. Let us try again. Heads – the Central Powers win. I guarantee it." Beck snatched the coin in mid-drop. He opened his palm – heads.

"I pray you're right," said Caarsens.

Beck turned the coin over – also heads. "Luck will not determine the outcome." He handed Caarsens the coin. "Control the game, make your own luck. That is how the Central Powers will win this war – we play by *our* rules. Here is what I want you to do."

When he finished, Beck laughed sarcastically. "We will make a marvelous partnership. What I cannot buy, you will blow up."

"I have many other ideas." Caarsens gave back the coin.

Beck smiled, showing small, uneven teeth and flipped the two-headed coin again. "I'm listening."

~

When Wittig arrived in early evening at his suburban home at 2 Dellwood Road in Bronxville, fifteen miles north of Manhattan, the house seemed oddly quiet. The girls were not playing in the front yard, the front door was closed, and the new trumpet-horned Victrola scratched no music. Entering the house, he realized the warm smells that usually emanated from the kitchen were missing.

He found Nora in the master bedroom with a letter on her lap. “I’m worried about my brother.”

“What’s he up to now?” Wittig didn’t like his brother-in-law, Rory Fitzpatrick.

Nora and Rory had written each other frequently ever since she had left Ireland as a teenager. “He’s become a leader in the Irish Republican Brotherhood. Sure as the Lord made us, he will either lie in an English prison or in an unmarked grave,” Nora said.

“With all his hate, I expect he’ll soon be the Lord’s problem. I really don’t want to know about his revolutionary plots. They’ll either result in bloodshed for him or questions for us from the police about our loyalties.”

“This war will affect this family whether you like it or not, John.”

“You’ve asked me to decide. I have. The only cause I’ll support is the one I truly believe in – the peace movement. I’m going to the peace rally tomorrow.”

~

Martin sat at his desk on the main floor on the north end of police headquarters wondering what to do about the German lighterboat men when Keller suggested something. “I speak their language, and I know enough about lightering to infiltrate them,” Keller suggested. His idea fit his confident and aggressive nature, and Martin admired Keller’s courage and physical skill. Keller had been captain of his high school baseball team, and his keen batter's eye made him an excellent marksman. The same quick hands that made him a great shortstop made him deadly with the dagger he kept strapped to his leg. Keller was not a man easily defeated.

"It's worth a try, but the lighterboat men are a closed and suspicious lot, even to someone who speaks German, like you. Besides, there are so many lighterboats, it'll be impossible to infiltrate all of them." He leaned forward, rested his elbows on his legs, and cradled his drooping head.

"What's wrong?" Keller asked. Martin rarely showed fatigue or lack of confidence.

"Corinne has morning sickness, and I want a smoke."

"You know you can't do that. Tunney will have your head. You could blow us all up."

Tunney marched in and everyone in the squad jumped to his feet up. "Any progress?"

"Nothing conclusive, Captain, but I have a thought. Take a look." Martin gave the captain a poster. "I want to attend the Friends of Peace rally tomorrow. Our saboteur will be there. I'm sure of it. A successful peace movement would be more effective than a thousand cigar bombs."

Chapter 9
The Peace Rally

New York City: June 24, 1915

Early Thursday morning, June 24, hours before the peace rally was scheduled to start, Martin attended his first Mass since he had joined the Bomb Squad. He found peace and guidance at Saint Cecilia, where he had met Corinne and where they had married not so long ago. He knelt, thanking the Lord for his blessings, and prayed for the success of the new Pope, Benedict XV, the health of his wife and their soon-to-be-born baby, and asked for a long life together. He asked to be the judge and executioner of the German saboteurs. He knew it was wrong to kill, but he also knew the meek shall not inherit the Earth in times of war. And with more bombing attacks on ships, war it was.

~

That same morning, sitting in the last car of the 8:02 a.m. train from Bronxville, Wittig put down his newspaper as the train ground to a halt outside the tunnel leading into Grand Central Station. Workmen outside were yelling, eliciting harsh responses from the train crew, and the morning heat had already begun to seep into the stalled train, making the passengers all the more irritable and vocal in their protests.

The conductor ambled down the corridor, attempting to calm riders' nerves. Recognizing Wittig as one of his morning regulars, he stopped a moment to apologize for the delay. "Thank you for not complaining, Mr. Wittig. I only wish everyone was a gentleman like you."

"Do unto others, Hank," Wittig said and returned to *The New York Times*, engrossed in an article predicting that a German victory would destroy the American economy. Britain, France and Russia owed so much to the United States that if the Allies lost the war and defaulted on their debts, the write-offs would cripple America and its banks, including his own. The stock market reflected the same sentiment, closing lower after a Central Powers victory and propelling upward with an Allied win. Wittig had invested well both ways.

Getting off the train at Grand Central Station, Wittig fervently hoped today's peace rally would start to redirect the country toward pacifism. He was convinced that without American support the Allies would seek peace, and he could return to his prosperous and happy pre-war life. He picked up his pace, anxious to arrive early at the rally.

~

A few blocks away, the 3rd Avenue El train clanged into 23rd Street. Caarsens descended and headed to Madison Square Garden. Unshaven, sporting a false mustache and dark hairpiece, he was dressed in an old cap and a trench coat that concealed his Demag. He had been in New York City just over three weeks.

Caarsens believed his mission today was curious. "Peace rallies are not about peace. I want you to observe two Bomb Squad detectives who are sure to be at the rally," Beck had told him yesterday, describing Martin and Keller in detail. Martin, the sergeant, was older, maybe thirty, of average height, thin, with dark-brown hair combed back, a plain dresser. Determined and smart, he thought before he acted. The younger man, Keller, was impulsive but capable. He was tall, over six feet, and had dirty-blond hair, combed down onto his forehead. An athletic man, he also had a tic – he often made baseball-type gestures. Caarsens, unfamiliar with the game, watched as Beck illustrated several of Keller's typical movements. "Follow them. Test their reactions, I want a full report," Beck admonished, leaving unexplained his interest in the pair or how he knew they would be at the rally. Caarsens decided to look for the detectives near the entrance to the Garden at 26th Street.

~

Around the corner, Martin met Keller near the thirty-two story Moorish-style tower, one of the tallest structures in New York, which rose above Madison Square Garden. Martin wore a gray felt hat and business suit complete with tie and waistcoat. Keller was dressed like a common laborer. Thousands of people thronged the streets around Madison Square Garden. Lines trying to enter the rally were backed up around the block as hundreds of cops, including horse-mounted policemen, controlled the crowd. Other than the occasional madwoman or doomsday ranter, everyone was well-behaved and orderly – no one shouted or pushed. The detectives circled the Garden and talked for a few minutes in front of the 26th Street entrance. "Let's split up. I'm positive someone here is involved in these bombings," Martin said.

~

Caarsens had been observing the two men at the entrance for several minutes. It was unusual for a businessman to stand speaking to a worker for so long, and although he could not see the hair of the older man, who was dressed in a hat and formal business attire, both men otherwise fit Beck's description perfectly. When the blond man turned away and pounded his left hand with his fist as if it were a baseball mitt, Caarsens knew he had identified his quarry. Wanting to focus on the senior man, he let Keller walk away.

~

Martin remained near the entrance, listening to the swirl of comments all around him: "America will have to fight!" "No, peace is the only answer." "Leave Europe to the Europeans – let them kill each other, not us." "The Apocalypse is upon us!" Martin checked his pocket watch and decided to go inside. Just as he was walking toward the queue to enter the Garden, a dark-haired man in old clothes bumped into him. Martin tensed, assessing his man, but relaxed when the man raised his arms.

~

"Pardon me." Caarsens lowered his arms and stepped aside. The detective's reaction had been swift and controlled. *This man knows his business.*

~

Inside the Garden, Wittig had taken his seat some thirty minutes earlier. Waiting in anticipation, he watched the crowd enter and was pleased to see attendance grow beyond the arena's stated 8,000-seat capacity by what looked like several thousand. Chairs filled the main arena. They faced a large platform at one end. His seat in the middle, about twenty rows up a section that angled straight back to the wall, offered an excellent view of the proceedings. The attendees seemed polite and restrained, unlike the fans at boxing matches he had also attended here.

As the key speakers and special guests mingled around the dignitaries' chairs on the platform next to the podium, Wittig recognized his friend Henry Weismann, chief sponsor of the rally; William Jennings Bryan, former secretary of state; Gerhart Zabel, head of the German Red Cross in New York; and Felix Beck.

Weismann approached the podium and waved to the packed crowd, eliciting a roar of applause. "Welcome! Thank you for coming. I'm overwhelmed by your attendance. I'm afraid that thousands of our supporters couldn't make it in. We are organizing another rally outside." Waiting for the wave of further applause and cheers to die down, he then began: "The Friends of Peace join hands today to guard our beloved country against those whose words and acts make for war. We are opposed to being drawn into this bloody conflict!"

Yes we are, God willing, Wittig said under his breath.

Once he began, Weismann dived right in, and Wittig was all attention, feeling the excitement of the crowd. Weismann continued speaking with the same authority and passion throughout. He demanded that the U.S. government place an embargo on munitions and arms exports.

Excellent, that will stop America's slide into this conflict. This is what I've wanted since the war began, Wittig thought.

A few minutes later, Weismann mentioned that "miserable little Roosevelt." The crowd booed and hissed, none louder than Wittig, who knew that if Teddy Roosevelt were president today, America would already be at war. Weismann called for charity toward fellow men and finished to overwhelming applause.

Felix Beck spoke next. In accented English, he stated flatly that Germany wanted to be friends with America and that Ambassador von Bernstorff was working with President Wilson to resolve Germany's differences with America.

Is that all? Wittig was disappointed. He had hoped Beck would pledge to seek peace with all belligerents, or at least announce cessation of U-boat activity. As an afterthought, he looked around the podium to see if the big man with the black coat was there, but to Wittig's relief, he was not.

Weismann next introduced William Jennings Bryan, "the new leader of the American people who stand for peace."

At last, someone to lead the peace effort, and who better? Having heard Bryan speak during his presidential campaigns, Wittig thought Bryan was undoubtedly the best orator he'd ever heard. Wittig had voted for him in each of his runs for president, and wondered why Bryan had resigned his position as secretary of state two weeks ago. His friends in government suggested that Bryan believed President Wilson favored the Allies too much, and had left his job because of his anti-war beliefs. The German-American community was convinced the president would lead America into war against Germany.

"I believe it is my duty to crystallize the peace sentiment until the demand for peace drowns the demand for war," Bryan proclaimed, midway into his speech.

Wittig stood up and applauded so hard his hands hurt.

Bryan next criticized the press for supporting President Wilson. "I am not as surprised as you are by the position taken by the New York press, because I am used to it. I have been in politics for a quarter of a century, and I have never yet known the New York press to take the side of the American people in any question."

Yes! At last someone with authority had the gumption to attack the press.

Toward the end of the speech, one man in the back stood up and called for war. He was shouted down and threatened. Bryan continued for another twenty minutes as Wittig listened, captivated.

~

In a seat far to the back of the arena, Martin listened to the speech, having slipped into the Garden just before Bryan began. He had heard more than enough platitudes about national honor and the need for peaceful solutions by the time Bryan had finished. The cause seemed noble but naïve. Martin didn't want war, but he believed that force was sometimes necessary, and he was prepared to fight. It was like being a cop on the beat: if you surrendered ground, the gangs would take over. After all, Germany was nothing more than a big gang, wasn't it?

Martin left his seat before the next speaker reached the lectern, and headed outside to find Keller as applause reverberated behind him. The street was alive with thousands of people chatting, cheering, and waving various flags and banners for causes that had nothing to do with peace. He walked by the 24th Street speaking stand, one of six that had been established outside to handle the throngs, estimated to be seventy thousand in the area, to his appointed meeting place with Keller. They bought five-cent hot dogs from a street vendor as Keller summarized his frustrating day, which was on a par with Martin's. Eying Keller as he smeared mustard on his hot dog, already piled high with sauerkraut, Martin could not resist commenting: "I'll tell you, Paul, you always seem American, but you eat like a German."

"Why not? It's good." Keller took a big bite. "My father was born in Milwaukee and my father's family has been in the States longer than I know, but my mother makes all the traditional dishes. We often speak German at home to keep the old ways going. What about you? Except for Corinne, you never talk about your family."

"I grew up poor. It was a struggle. My parents came over from France. Both of them died last year. I had some breaks along the way and was lucky to get into the police." Martin tossed his half-eaten hot dog in the street.

"You're lucky to have Corinne. Everyone likes her."

"I don't know what I'd do without her." Martin wanted to change the conversation. "What do you make of the peace movement, Paul?"

"I'm glad I'm an American and living in America, but I don't want America to fight Germany. The thought stays with me like an old injury. But I'll tell you what bothers me most – it's all this anti-German sentiment."

"I support France."

"German-Americans are proud people and good citizens. All kinds of us, including pacifists like these." Keller pointed to the crowd. "Most of us still care about Germany, but we know right from wrong. These bombers, I hate them because they are criminals. They make all of us look bad."

"I just hate them," Martin said.

~

Inside the Garden, Wittig felt agitated and uncomfortable. The air had become thick and the temperature rose to match the outside heat. He mopped his brow and loosened his collar and felt his hopes sink after the high point of Bryan's appearance. Many others in the crowd also appeared restless, sitting back and fanning themselves.

As the speeches wore on, they were often too long and academic, drawing applause from the crowd out of courtesy, not conviction. Much to Wittig's disgust, one speaker twisted Bryan's arguments and turned them into class struggle nonsense, and the rest were merely forgettable. He concluded in spite of himself that the Friends of Peace leadership was ineffective. He felt trapped in the stifling heat of the crowded auditorium.

When the rally finally ended, Wittig walked with relief into the afternoon air, drawing deep gulps into his lungs, hoping the crowd in the streets would be more enthusiastic, but everyone was using the peace rally to forward his own cause. A man wearing an International Workers of the World badge started to lecture him. Wittig silenced him with a cold stare. *I'm a businessman being accosted by a union man. I'm a pacifist in a world at war. I'm of German heritage in an English-speaking country married to an Irish-Catholic who wants to topple the world's greatest imperial power since Rome. Is anyone on my side?*

~

Throughout the rally, Caarsens had remained on the streets around the Garden, feeling nothing but disdain. The atmosphere was no better than a carnival. Tubas belched, drums thundered and the whole Flatiron District smelled of freshly baked pretzels, apple strudel and sweaty people. *Let the idiots enjoy themselves. War will put an end to their mindless fun,* he thought, as he searched anew for the Bomb Squad detectives.

~

About the time Caarsens was making his assessment, Martin and Keller decided the day had been a complete waste of time. "Support the Industrial Workers of the World!" someone shouted at the ebbing crowd.

"I hate those Wobblies," Keller said. "Abolishing wages, can you imagine? You might as well stop war." Keller spit on the sidewalk as they continued their walk. "I'll never support anything they stand for."

"Me either," said Martin as a suffragette shoved a flyer into his hands. He handed it to Keller without glancing at it.

Keller read it and crumpled it up. "The world has enough problems already."

Martin and Keller crossed 23rd Street and scanned the crowd. Three men caught Martin's eye. "I don't like the looks of them. Why would they be here?" He pointed to a big, stout man with a black coat who appeared to be giving orders to two men who looked like longshoremen. The unshaven older man had leathered skin, bulging forearms, and a low brow. The younger man was broad-shouldered, with narrow hips and a big skull.

"Don't recognize them, but they'd sure be useful in a bar fight," Keller said.

"Me either, but they're up to something."

~

When the detectives looked at him, the man in the black coat turned away and told his men to act natural. "Those men are a threat to my business. We'll get our chance to teach one of them a lesson later. Walk away."

~

"Come on, Gil, let's find your saboteur," Keller said. "Nothing we can do about those three until they break the law."

"They will." In the next half-hour, Martin and Keller searched the area for more men who looked suspicious, but all they found was a nervous man waiting for his wife, a cripple who sat on a park bench too long, and a reporter taking notes.

"Not much of a day's work," Martin commented as the crowd thinned out. He and Keller were walking south on Broadway when he leaned over and said with new interest, "Don't say anything. Do you see that man?" Martin nodded toward a tall, lanky, dark-haired man with a cap shoved into his back pocket standing alone at the corner of 21st Street.

"The one eating peanuts?" Keller asked. "What's he want?"

"Don't know, but he's looking at us. He bumped into me earlier, in front of the arena. He's not interested in the rally, is he?"

"Don't you think it's too hot for that coat?"

"He looks like a coiled snake." Martin caught the man's eye.

~

Caarsens tensed, then looked away. The sergeant had recognized him. *If I leave now, I'll lose my advantage.* He took another handful of peanuts and started to shell them, acting nonchalant, waiting to see what the detectives would do next.

~

"He doesn't frighten off, does he?" Martin commented.

"No," said Keller. "He ain't the non-violent type. Think he's hiding something under his coat?"

"Let's see," said Martin, heading toward the lone man on the corner. "I want to talk to him. He's a threat for sure." Just as the detectives started toward him, a motorcar swerved into a horse-drawn carriage nearby. The sound of the impact reverberated across the street. The frightened horse broke away, charged, and headed straight for a woman pushing a pram across 21st Street. She looked up and screamed as the horse bore down on her.

Martin ran toward her but was too far away to help. The man in the trench coat deftly intercepted the horse, grabbing its reins and stopping it just a few feet in front of the woman. *He is fast,* thought Martin. The man rubbed his hand across the horse's nose, calming it within seconds as throngs of people converged on the scene. By the time Martin reached them, the man in the trench coat was gone.

Keller arrived a few seconds later. "He disappeared!"

"Go that way." Martin pointed north. "I'm headed east."

The detectives had no sooner split up than Martin caught sight of his man. He chased him into Gramercy Park, drawing his revolver and yelling a warning. Ignoring him, his man escaped from the east exit of the park, gaining ground with every step. Stopping at 23rd Street to catch his breath, Martin glimpsed his man board the 3rd Avenue El platform just as a train was arriving. The man jumped on, leaving Martin, too far away to reach it, cursing and still gasping for breath.

~

As the El pulled away, Caarsens made his way through the passengers to the rear of the busy train. *I couldn't let that woman and baby die. They were innocent.* From the back window, he saw the sergeant, framed in mid-shout, his face contorted in anger, and watched him walk away as the El picked up speed. *Lucky man. I would have killed you if you'd gotten closer.*

~

Heading north, Keller saw a familiar-looking man – the same broad-shouldered goon he had observed earlier – cross 27th Street, heading right at him. The man in the black coat must be nearby. He turned around quickly, but the stout longshoreman had already moved to block him. A punch to his kidney doubled him over. The next blow landed on Keller's jaw, loosening two teeth and rocking his head sideways. He steadied himself and punched his assailant in the chest. No effect. Another punch knocked Keller to the ground, as he glimpsed the man in the black coat watching from a distance.

Passersby ignored his cries for help and walked away quickly. Others froze. "Get out of here unless you want the same!" the stout man hissed at them. They ran while the broad-shouldered man continued to pummel Keller. Spitting up blood, he forced himself onto his hands and knees, all the while trying to regain his balance. His last chance was the blade strapped to his leg, but his reactions were too slow. The stout man knocked his arm aside, and the broad-shouldered man pushed him down with the heel of his boot. Keller landed prostrate. "What do you want?" he gasped.

SECTION II

TIMES SQUARE

June 1915 - August 1915

Chapter 10
Berlin

Berlin, Germany: June 1915

Kaiser Wilhelm II rested his shrunken left arm on his desk and cursed. With his right hand, he crumpled and tossed away President Wilson's response to Germany following the sinking of the *Lusitania*. The paper landed on his desk like a bomb. "That impudent dog, Wilson. Who does he think he is? He accuses Germany of being 'deliberately unfriendly.' Deliberately unfriendly? What diplomat wrote that line? He demands we stop our U-boat attacks on non-military ships immediately."

Grand Admiral Alfred von Tirpitz, Commander of the German navy, glared. "By that, he means all American vessels."

Gottlieb von Jagow, Germany's foreign minister, squirmed in his chair. "President Wilson is trying to keep his options open, Your Excellency."

"Why doesn't he just say our naval policy constitutes an act of war?"

"He wants Germany to appear belligerent, Your Excellency. As he always does, President Wilson sees himself as a great moral champion," von Jagow said.

"A great trouble-maker is more accurate. After he dies, Wilson will go to heaven and run for God." Tirpitz tugged at his long white beard. It parted at the chin to form two points and looked like the roots of a molar. "He has no guts for war, Your Excellency."

Von Jagow looked over at the Kaiser. No reaction. He looked Tirpitz right in the eye. "Our indiscriminate use of U-boats will bring

America into the war, Herr Tirpitz." Von Jagow started to fill a pipe. "We must comply with Wilson's request."

"I disagree." Tirpitz's face turned red. "Our U-boats are strangling them. We are sinking 600,000 tons of merchant shipping each month. Britain can't sustain those losses. We must continue our U-boat policy, Your Excellency."

Von Jagow frowned. His high forehead was as impressive as Tirpitz's beard was long. "The British blockade is working."

"True," the Kaiser said. "We are having a more difficult time obtaining critical war materials than we had expected. We've had to close some clothing factories because we can't get enough cotton. I've ordered some factory workers to the mines in Silesia. Soon, Germany will have to impose systematic price restrictions on all goods related to the war effort."

"How are the food supplies, Your Excellency?" Von Jagow lit his pipe. "I've heard rumors that –"

"Damn the rumors." The Kaiser pounded his desk. "This is a delicate issue."

"What can you tell us?" Tirpitz asked.

"Germany is deliberately shifting nitrates away from our fertilizers to munitions plants. Lack of fertilizer is hurting our farm production. We're having trouble importing all the nitrate we need from neutral companies."

"So long as the military receives the munitions it requires, I am sure the German people can endure." Tirpitz's face turned stone-cold.

"Only for so long, Herr Tirpitz." Von Jagow looked back at the Kaiser. "The cost of this war must be exorbitant. How are our finances managing?"

"Up to now, the Reichstag has granted twenty billion Reichmarks for war purposes. I have just read Herr Heifferich's Treasury report." The Kaiser summarized the figures. The amount was equal to five billion U.S. dollars, the equivalent value of the entire German railroad. Each month, the war cost Germany two billion Reichmarks. This was one-third higher than the cost of the entire 1870-1871 war.

"We will go bankrupt." Tirpitz's voice boomed again. "We must win soon. You cannot restrict the U-boats, Your Excellency."

"With all due respect, Your Excellency, I disagree. We must find alternatives." Von Jagow re-lighted his pipe. "If we do not, America will declare war on us."

"I understand and share your concerns, Herr Tirpitz." The Kaiser shifted his left arm. "I will give President Wilson what he asks for – for now."

"Stopping the U-boats is risky, Your Excellency," Tirpitz said.

"I am aware of the implications, gentlemen." The Kaiser stood up to leave. "One final issue, Herr von Jagow. We must compensate for the reduced impact of our U-boats. Tell your man in New York, Beck, that he has to do more than blow up some munitions."

Chapter 11
The Birth of a Nation

Bellevue Hospital, New York City: June 1915

Martin reached the emergency room of Bellevue Hospital just as the doctor finished taping Keller's ribs. A bandage covered the side of his head and the area around his left eye was turning purple. Wads of cotton wool jutted from his nose. "How are you, Paul?"

"'Stay away from our lighterboats.' That's all they said. 'Stay away from our lighterboats.'" The wadding blocking his nose made him hard to understand.

Martin moved closer to the bed. "Paul, what the hell happened?"

"Some broken ribs and a concussion. They sure got me good."

"Who did?"

Keller described the events. "Did you get that man you wanted?"

"No, but we will." Martin tried to sound positive. He was furious at himself for losing him and angry that Keller's face was beaten in.

"Good." Keller looked nauseated.

The doctor injected something into Keller's arm.

"That big man with the black coat. You were right about him. He watched as they beat me up, but we can't arrest him for ..." Keller turned his head into the pillow and passed out.

The doctor chased Martin away. "Your friend will be fine in a few weeks. He was lucky. Nothing more for you to do tonight. Go home."

Martin left the hospital deep in thought. *How did they know we'd be at the rally? Was it a coincidence that the man I chased and the man in the black coat were both watching us there? No. They're hiding something on those lighterboats.*

~

A moment of panic struck Martin when he arrived home to his Brooklyn apartment. His wife, Corinne, did not welcome him at the door. *Had the Germans gotten to her, too*? The vase of fresh flowers that normally greeted him on the front table beside their wedding picture was missing. *So they know where I live*? He fought back his anxiety. A few seconds later, he heard someone scamper up the stairs two floors below him. "Corinne?" He tried to look down the stairwell.

"Gil? It's me." Out of breath, she reached the open door of their apartment. She dropped the bouquet of white lilies, stood on her toes, and kissed him. She studied his face. "You don't look good."

"Keller was beaten up."

"My God. How is he?" Corinne's eyes bore right into his. "Are you all right?"

"Am now." He hugged her tight. Her patient eyes and welcoming face calmed him. The kerchief tied around her head made her look attractive in a way Martin could not explain.

"Why? I was just around the corner. You know how I love my lilies." Corinne looked at the flowers on the floor. "Oh my ...." She picked them up and arranged them in a neat stack in her arms. "I'm sorry, I haven't finished cleaning yet." Corinne took off her kerchief, unpinned her long brown hair, and shook it loose. "I haven't started supper."

"I'm not hungry." He flopped on the secondhand couch they

had bought with money from their wedding. He closed his eyes and fell asleep.

When he awoke, Corinne was sitting next to him. She held a bottle of his favorite red wine. "What's wrong?" She pulled the cork and poured the wine into two glasses.

Martin emptied his glass. He rested his head on her firm belly, her pregnancy still not apparent. "This case. It's consuming me. I'm sure the Boches are involved, but I can't prove it." He fell back on the couch.

"You will." Corinne bent over and kissed his eyes.

Good. But he couldn't relax. "Now, they're attacking my men. I can't allow Germany to do that." Martin turned away. He didn't want Corinne to see the failure he felt.

"One policeman in New York won't determine who wins the war." She cradled his head.

Martin wanted to say something, but remained silent. He had no energy left to argue.

"These saboteurs are fanatics." Corinne looked into his eyes. "That's their weakness."

"You're right." Martin kissed her passionately. "You're always right."

"Now I have a suggestion – you need a break, and I'd like to be with you for an evening. We won't have too many more chances." She patted her belly.

Martin smiled.

"We've been talking about going out for a night; tonight's our chance. Let's go see *The Birth of a Nation*. I've wanted to see it since it first came out. All my friends are talking about it."

"Are you sure we can afford it? The tickets are expensive – $2 each." Martin checked his billfold to make sure he had the money.

"Let's splurge. It's playing at the Strand Theatre on Broadway. It's a short subway ride. Let me get ready. It'll be fun."

~

After the movie, Gil left the Strand at 47th Street with Corinne on his arm. Night had overtaken day, but Times Square's lights made it hard to tell. Martin looked toward The New York Times' building at 42nd Street. A full moon seemed to dance over it. A minstrel walked through the streets strumming his guitar.

He stopped to kiss her. "*Je t'aime.*"

"I love you too, but I'm concerned, Gil."

"Why?"

"Your job. It's dangerous. Your partner just got beaten up. These saboteurs seem like a dangerous lot. All these bombs – your work is too risky."

"The Bomb Squad is the best unit in city. We haven't lost a man yet."

"I'd rather you work in a safer unit." She clasped his hand. Suddenly, Martin heard something like a gunshot behind him. He pushed Corinne to the ground and covered her with his body. He looked around. A police motorcar sped south on Broadway, its siren screamed and its engine misfired again.

When he was sure there was no danger, Martin stood and pulled Corinne up.

"See, you're jumpy too," she said.

"It's been a long day."

She clasped his hand. "I wish this war in Europe were over. I want to raise our baby in a better world – with you." They said nothing for another block. "What did you think of the movie, Gil?"

"Too long."

"You never have any patience except when you do your detective work. What did you like about the movie?"

"The battle scenes. I think they got them right."

"You men and your wars." She squeezed his hand tight. "I was upset when they treated the Ku Klux Klan like heroes."

The night turned chilly. He mumbled something.

"I think your saboteur reminds me of a Klan member," Corinne said.

"How could you say that? You're being too dramatic."

"No, I'm not. In his mind, he's a patriot." Corinne stopped and looked right at him. "The Ku Klux Klan was fighting for its country just like your saboteur is fighting for his. They are both wrong, but your saboteur would disagree."

"He's worse than an anarchist. Lynch him, I say – like the Klan lynched those poor colored boys in the movie."

"It's more complicated than that, Gil. They believe in their cause and will do anything to defend it. The Ku Klux Klan tried to scare people, same as your saboteurs. You might do the same thing if you were in their shoes."

"Never." The people walking next to Martin looked at him in surprise. Martin gestured an apology. "Those Klan men are godless criminals and killers – same as my saboteurs."

"The British thought that way about our Minutemen," Corinne said. "The South fought for their cause just like the North did. Our dear France is doing the same."

"No. Justice must prevail."

"Remember the final line in the movie?" Corinne asked. "'Dare we dream of a golden day when the bestial war shall rule no more?'"

"Now you sound like those people at the peace rally. God gave me a gun, and I will use it against our enemies." Martin spoke through clenched teeth.

"Isn't that a bit dramatic?" Corinne pulled her coat tighter. "I assume you believe God is on your side?"

"Of course."

"Everyone believes God is on his side. Whose God is right if there is only one?"

Martin struggled to answer. Just then, a stout man grabbed Corinne's purse from behind and ran. Martin recognized him. He was the same longshoreman who had talked to the man in the black coat earlier today. Martin started to chase him into the Times Square subway entrance, but stopped. *What am I doing? I've left Corinne unguarded.* He rushed back just in time to see a broad-shouldered man approach her. "Get away from him. Run, Corinne."

When the broad-shouldered man saw Martin, he ran west on 43rd Street. Martin wanted to chase him, but Corinne was still alone. He called for the police, but got no response. Before he disappeared from sight, the broad-shouldered man turned back and said, "Stay away from our lighterboats."

Chapter 12
New Opportunities

Police Headquarters: June 1915

Martin was still angry the next day when he went to work. The Germans had attacked his partner and threatened his wife. Did they really think they could intimidate him? For them to be so bold, he knew he was close to uncovering their secrets. Tunney agreed, but preached caution and assigned someone to guard Corinne. These men were dangerous.

At Police Headquarters, a report came through that two naked bodies were found floating by the Brooklyn Bridge. They matched Martin and Keller's descriptions of their attackers. Each man had a bullet hole in the back of his head. Parts of their faces were missing. Martin went to the morgue and confirmed they were the goons who had threatened his wife. Had they intended to harm Corinne or to scare her? Martin wasn't sure if they were killed to stop further investigation or to punish incompetence. Who was that man in the black coat?

Until Keller could return to duty, Tunney partnered Martin with Detective Griggs. Aside from Keller, Griggs spoke the best German of anyone else in the Bomb Squad. Martin urged the captain to adopt a new strategy. Taking Keller's idea, Martin proposed they go to the places where the lighterboat crews meet after work.

"But they'll recognize you," Griggs said.

"Maybe, but I'll take that chance. Keller's told me where they drink."

"I like a man with guts," Tunney said. "Be careful."

~

For three nights in a row, Martin and Griggs frequented the lighterboat men's favorite German bars. Nothing happened. The places were crowded, but the lighterboat men, a closed and suspicious lot, avoided them. Martin and Griggs could only stay in the back corner of the bar and observe. Martin refused to give up. He was confident that this approach would work and was willing to take risks. Corinne was feeling the strain and starting to have difficulties with her pregnancy.

It was after 11 p.m. when he and Griggs entered the Hapsburg Inn in Hoboken, New Jersey. It smelled like bilge water and piss. The beer was cheap. Dressed like poor stevedores who had just finished a day at the wharves, the detectives were unshaven and looked like the other workers. Unlike previous nights, Martin suggested they bring attention to themselves. Griggs protested, but Martin talked him into it by reminding him that he was aware of Griggs's love of gambling, a weakness the captain abhorred.

Speaking a mix of German and broken English, Griggs walked up to the bar and started buying drinks for everybody. He told them he'd just won some money on the horses. Martin mingled. Everybody talked and drank for an hour when Martin saw the big man enter. He recognized him immediately. He wore the same black coat and hat he had worn at the peace rally. Martin moved closer to get a better look. The man was circus-strongman big; he was six feet tall and well over two hundred pounds. He had an immense bald head and spoke German in a funny, high-pitched voice. Everyone seemed to know him, but they left him alone. Out of respect or fear, Martin guessed. He signaled Griggs to meet him in the latrine.

"That's my man." Martin wanted to arrest him but he had no cause. *Start a fight*? Despite the brass knuckles in his pocket, he knew that he and Griggs couldn't win, and he might end up in a hospital like Keller.

Griggs wanted to leave. "Call in reinforcements, at least. Please, Sergeant."

"No, let's play this out." Martin flushed the urinal and returned to the bar. He acted drunk and moved to the end of the bar near the big man but away from his field of vision. As he neared, one of the lighterboat men grabbed his arm and said in accented English, "Don't get too close to that one. He don't like nobody who ain't German."

"Why?" Martin pulled his coat collar around his ears to hide his face.

"He's crazy. On the wharf, I once saw him pick up a Polack and drop him across an anchor for no good reason."

"What's his name?" Martin looked over and saw the big man breaking walnuts in a nutcracker.

"Goes by the name of Eugene Traub. He works for the Hamburg-American Shipping Company. That's all I know. I'm leaving. I don't want no trouble with him." The lighterboat man chugged his beer and left quickly.

So that's who you are? Martin ordered a beer and moved closer. He was prepared to fight if Traub recognized him, but the big man seemed relaxed and chatted with the men around him. He displayed none of the vigilance Martin had seen at the peace rally. *Thank you, God.* He noticed that part of the big man's left ear was missing. The rest was scarred and red. Traub rolled walnut shells across the bar. His behavior changed when another lighterboat captain entered – Otto Meyerhoff. Because Meyerhoff's lighterboat had loaded sugar onto three of the munitions ships that had blown up, Martin had been investigating him for weeks.

Meyerhoff seemed bothered about something and walked up to Traub, who gave Meyerhoff a few winks and pushed him away. They left the Hapsburg Inn together. Martin shadowed them to an alley while Griggs stayed in the bar to make sure no one followed.

Martin knelt behind some garbage cans and listened to their argument. He knew enough German to understand.

"Not now. They'll get the money tomorrow." Traub seemed angry.

"Where?" Meyerhoff sounded jumpy.

"Pier 80, just off 40th Street."

"What time?"

"Midnight."

~

Caarsens sat on a blanket in New York's Central Park. It had been six weeks since he blew up the du Pont plant. He ignored Beck, who sat next to him. The scene reminded him of good times long past. In the Sheep Meadow, men rode horses, kids chased each other, and fathers watched mothers with babies. He shook his head a few times, bent down, and scooped up some earth. He rubbed it between his fingers, then smelled it. "Good dirt." *Across the ocean, men wait to die in trenches cut into ground similar to this.* The thought made him restless. He tossed the dirt on the ground and looked at Beck. "What's happened to the Bomb Squad detectives I shadowed at the peace rally?"

"Don't worry. I'm sure they've learned a lesson. If they are smart, they will not bother us again." Beck picked up a stick and began to clean his nails. "Are you ready?"

"Of course." Caarsens scanned the area to make sure no one could overhear them.

"Good. Berlin is pleased with your plan. It is ingenious." Caarsens had never seen Beck so enthusiastic. "Stop the plant, stop the shipments. What's your target?"

Caarsens described the Chesapeake Iron and Steel Works factory in Maryland. It manufactured 20,000 artillery shells daily, mostly filled with shrapnel and high explosives. The owner was an inventor and an engineer. Before the war, he had developed a patented process. Using high-quality lathes, Chesapeake Iron manufactured shells with high tensile strength. The shells contained two acids; their proportions and concentrations were secret. When combined, the acids helped create a terrific explosion, more powerful than conventional shells.

Upon detonation, the shells fractured into unusually small pieces. The acids contaminated the shell fragments and caused agonizing wounds that killed the victim within four hours unless he received medical attention. Getting a wounded man from the trenches to a field hospital in that time was almost impossible. The wounded man's suffering often incapacitated his comrades with fear and helplessness. The company's advertisements bragged that no effective antidote existed for the poisoned fragments.

Caarsens was sure his plan would work. Before the war, its white workers went on strike for more money. The company brought in Negro workers from the South as scabs. They even paid their expenses to move. Once they started work, Chesapeake Iron paid them half what they paid the white men. When war production accelerated, Chesapeake brought in more Negroes. Currently, most of the factory workers were southern Negroes. The plant's supervisors and managers remained white.

"Do you think you can convince those darkies to strike?" Beck asked.

"Yes, the men want a fair deal." Caarsens reached for a peach in his haversack and took a big bite. It was sweet and satisfying.

Beck lay back on the blanket and stared at the sky. "Let me think a minute."

After a few minutes, Beck propped himself up. "We'll get the newspapers involved. Liberal New York papers will love the story. Once you are down south, I will start alerting a few of them."

"Do you really care about these men?" Caarsens finished the peach and flung the pit away.

Beck seemed baffled by the question. "Of course not." He paused. "Oh, I almost forgot." He reached into his waistcoat and pulled out a set of papers and a thick wad of paper money. He handed them to Caarsens. "You are now a union organizer for the Labor National Peace Council."

"Who am I this time?" Caarsens thumbed through the money.

"Jens Rasmussen."

Caarsens secured the cash and papers in his inside coat pocket next to his Demag. "I'm leaving tomorrow."

"Good luck." Beck ignored Caarsens's outstretched hand. "If you get into trouble, I cannot help you."

Chapter 13
An Arrest

Pier 80, Manhattan: June 1915

Midnight approached. To make sure they covered all escape routes, Martin brought Griggs and two extra men from the Bomb Squad to Pier 80. Keller joined them at the last minute. "Nothin' going to stop me tonight. My ribs are taped up nice and tight. Don't ask me to run the bases, but I can handle a shotgun."

Hiding behind stacks of crates ready for loading the next day, Martin prayed for a break. Keller said he felt tense, like he was playing in front of a full crowd at the Polo Grounds during the World Series. Griggs fidgeted with his revolver. The other two men shuffled their feet.

A few minutes later, Meyerhoff walked onto the pier alone. He did not appear to be carrying a weapon. He stopped, put his hands in his pocket, and waited. By midnight, nothing had happened. Meyerhoff whistled. *Was he nervous*? Griggs started to grumble when Martin heard a motorboat approach at full speed. As it neared the pier, Martin saw the pilot's big body and black coat. "That's Traub."

Meyerhoff lowered a rope. Traub slowed down, tied a canvas bag to the rope, and sped away. They exchanged no words. Meyerhoff lifted the bag, looked around, and ran when he saw Martin. During the chase, the bag fell to the ground. Within seconds, Martin had caught and cuffed him. Breathing heavily, Keller caught up and punched Meyerhoff in the ribs. They both grimaced. Martin picked up the bag and looked inside. "There's over three thousand in here." He looked at Meyerhoff. "We're going to have a long talk."

~

Martin and Keller dragged Meyerhoff into the basement of Police Headquarters, past the gauze curtain in the line-up area that separated perpetrators from their accusers. The basement was hot or cold, depending on the location of the steam pipes. Instead of placing him in one of the sixteen jail cells, they put him into a room so small it could have been a storage closet, next to the 130-foot pistol range. "For effect." Martin winked to Keller, who shot him an approving look. Here was their first chance to confront the cursed Germans, and Martin wanted to make sure they got all the information they could from him. The bombings had to stop.

The darkness of the room made it feel smaller, and its confines reeked of mold. The whooshing of a toilet in the bathroom sounded above them. Drops of condensation landed on Martin from the leaking ceiling. He hoped it was water. Despite the hour, one man practiced on the range. The noise from his gun vibrated like a drum beat into their room. Martin could almost feel the bullets hit their target. From his movement, Martin could tell that Meyerhoff could, too.

For an hour, the detectives sat on wooden boxes and forced Meyerhoff to stand while they fired off questions. Acting confused, Meyerhoff babbled and kept repeating, "Why am I here? Where is my bag?"

A machine gun burst from the pistol range seemed to jar Meyerhoff.

"You going to talk?" Martin asked.

Meyerhoff just looked at the wall separating them from the shooting range. The gunfire next door stopped, and the sound of heavy shoes moved away from them.

Martin turned to Keller, “We’re alone now. He’s yours.”

Not constrained by his aching ribs or maybe motivated by them, Keller pressed Meyerhoff against the wall with an animal fierceness and punched him in the kidney. Then he twisted his arm. “Tell us what’s going on.”

“Nothing. Why don’t you believe me?”

“Liar.” Keller said in German. He wrenched Meyerhoff’s arm up high behind his back – a soft crack.

Meyerhoff yelled and almost fainted.

“We know you load more than sugar on those ships.”

Meyerhoff gritted his teeth and shook his head.

Martin looked away. “Paul, why don’t you help him remember?”

More yells.

“I talk.” Meyerhoff reached for his shoulder. “Fix it.”

Keller popped it back. Meyerhoff almost passed out.

“Speak. *Beeilen sie sich.* Hurry up,” Keller said.

Once he decided to confess, Meyerhoff’s English improved. The arrangement he described was simple. Several of the lighterboat crews stole sugar bags as they loaded the ships. They left about one in every twenty sacks on board the lighterboats during the transfer. The cargo checkers responsible for verifying the count were part of the scheme. They were paid off later. Meyerhoff didn’t know their cut.

“What was in it for you?”

"I sell the bags to river pirates – Italians – one-sixth street price, a fixed rate." Meyerhoff massaged his shoulder. "That's the deal across the harbor. Don't ask me what or how, but I learnt Italians sell them sugar bags for five-sixths street price."

"So they made a lot of money on the deal."

"I need smokes." Meyerhoff coughed. "Water, too."

"Get him water," Martin said. "You'll learn to live without cigarettes where you're going."

Before Keller could leave, Meyerhoff's eyes narrowed into dark slits. "I talk enough. Go to hell."

Keller stopped, turned the big ring on his finger inward, and slapped Meyerhoff with his open hand. The ring had the same effect as brass knuckles. Meyerhoff grabbed his head and almost fell over. The stone on the ring left a cut. Blood spilled down his neck.

"That's enough, Paul. I think he gets the idea. Go on, Mr. Meyerhoff."

Meyerhoff covered his wound with his hand and described the smuggling operation. It involved other German lighterboat captains, go-betweens, payoffs, secret meetings, and transfers along the harbor.

"Was it Traub who gave you the sack of money?" Martin asked.

"Yes, payment to the Italians. We usually used middle men to make them, but they needed their money quick. I was their contact, and Traub had to get it to me fast."

"It wasn't a payoff for planting bombs?"

"*Mein Gott*, no. I swear." Meyerhoff removed his bloody hand from his head. "Can you get me a cloth?"

Martin handed him a dirty rag. He looked at Meyerhoff's

wound. "Not bad." Martin motioned to Keller, who circled behind Meyerhoff. "I'm going to ask you something important. Your answer will determine how much time you'll do in prison. Understand?"

Meyerhoff twitched and coughed a few times. "I fought Serbs and Arabs. I ain't scared of you Yankees. Germans scare me more." He spit at their shoes, but his hand began to quiver.

Martin looked at Keller and said, "It's late. No one's around. I think we should take our friend next door."

Meyerhoff panicked. "What? Are you going to shoot me?" He tried to fight them off, but Keller subdued him with a knee to the gut and dropped a foul-smelling sack over his head. Each detective grabbed Meyerhoff by an arm and dragged him backward, his heels scraping the ground, to the bathroom on the southwest corner of the building. They removed the sack, dumped him into one of the tubs and turned on the water. Keller clutched Meyerhoff's neck and braced his head against the bottom of the tub as the water rose to his ears.

His legs kicking helplessly, terror growing in his eyes, Meyerhoff croaked something the detectives didn't understand. When Keller released his grip, Meyerhoff spat out some water and shouted, "Enough!"

"Good boy." Keller patted him on his head and pulled him out of the tub. The detectives walked him back to the interview closet and offered Meyerhoff a cigarette. He grabbed it with shaking hands. Keller lit it, and Meyerhoff burned down a third of the cigarette in one long drag.

Martin pulled the cigarette away from Meyerhoff, dropped it on the ground, and stamped it out. He raised Meyerhoff's chin and forced him to look right at him. "What do you know about the bombings on the cargo ships?"

Meyerhoff's head fell, his mouth wide open. "*Wass*?" Beads of sweat dripped from his face.

Keller moved closer and said in German, "Tell us about those ships that blew up in the Atlantic, you bastard." He turned the ring on his finger, raised his hand.

"I swear. It wasn't me."

"Liar." Keller's voice echoed through the basement room. He swung again. His ring grazed Meyerhoff's cut, and Meyerhoff covered his head.

"Let's go back to the bathtub." The detectives moved to pick him up.

"No. I knew about 'em. We all knew." Whatever fight was left in Meyerhoff vanished.

"Who was responsible?" Martin asked.

"Not sure."

"You must," Martin said. "How did the bombs get on board those ships? You lighterboat men planted them, didn't you? Three boats you loaded blew up."

"*Nein*. I just steal sugar; earn extra money for my family. Sometimes I look away, *ja*?"

"If you lighterboat men didn't plant the bombs, who did?" Keller asked.

Meyerhoff shrugged his shoulders.

"Who is the leader of this operation?" Martin tightened his fist. He wanted to slug Meyerhoff but restrained himself knowing he had to turn Meyerhoff against the Germans. His knuckles turned white.

"Not me. Don't know."

Keller moved closer.

Meyerhoff shivered. "On the grave of my mother, I don't know. The bombings helped us."

Keller looked at him perplexed. "That's crazy. Make sense."

Meyerhoff talked fast. "With boats sinking, no one notices a few missing sugar bags each load. No way to check the count if bags in Atlantic, *ja*?"

Martin opened his notebook. "Mr. Meyerhoff, I've got enough to send you to prison for a long time ... unless ..."

"Unless what?" Meyerhoff looked scared.

"You help us."

"*Wie*? How?" Meyerhoff asked.

"Tell us who is behind the bombings. You can find out things we can't. If you do that, maybe ..." Martin paused.

"What if I can't?"

"You will."

Chapter 14
A Fateful Lunch

The German Club, Manhattan: July 1915

At his lunch with Felix Beck at the German Club on 59th Street, John Wittig hardly ate. Beck finished his chateaubriand. "Dessert?"

Wittig shook his head no. "Coffee."

"How are your daughters?"

"How did you ..." Wittig tried to hide his nervousness.

"Relax, Herr Wittig. Do not be surprised. I make it my business to know something about everyone I meet regularly." Beck dabbed his lips with his napkin.

What more does he know about me? Wittig felt an impulse to look over his shoulder.

"My friend, you are quiet today. What is bothering you?" Beck waved for a waiter.

"I saw you speak at the peace rally," Wittig said.

"I know you are a pacifist, but I am sorry to say that the peace movement will amount to nothing." The waiter brought a coffee for Wittig and a torte and tea for Beck. "Let me assure you, Herr Wittig. Germany does not want war with America. The lies against us are hard to fight."

"I know."

Beck added sugar to his tea. "I assume you still want to help the Fatherland?"

"Of course. I have many ideas. I would like to discuss them."

"Give me one."

"I assume that Germany would like men and materiel from America. Thousands of men are willing to return to Germany to fight. I can help."

"How? I already have people who forge passports for me. I have sent hundreds of men back to the Fatherland already."

"I was thinking of something of a political nature." Wittig gulped his coffee. "I know many people in Washington. Congressman Joseph Alpert is an acquaintance of mine."

"New York Congressional District 5?"

"Yes, I can speak to him about ..."

"I, too, have many friends in Washington, Herr Wittig. They can be greedy." Beck floated his hand through the air. "No matter, I can afford them."

"You misunderstand. I must have expressed myself badly, Herr Beck. I will not be party to bribes or anything illegal." The meeting's sudden turn frazzled Wittig. He put his cup aside – the coffee had turned cold.

"Who said anything about that?" Beck asked. "Germany obeys all U.S. laws. I am not clear what you are saying, Herr Wittig. I was hoping that you would offer your financial expertise to our cause."

Wittig hesitated, not sure what Beck had implied. "How?"

"You tell me." Beck smiled wolf-like.

"I did have one idea about setting up ..." Wittig stopped himself. He knew mentioning it would start him down a dangerous path.

"Setting up what? Tell me your idea."

Reluctantly, Wittig mentioned the main points. When he

finished, Beck said, “Excellent. We need to pursue this.”

Wittig left the club and thought to himself, *it’s too late to turn back now.*

Chapter 15
The Harbor Master

Macy's Department Store, Manhattan: July 1915

Martin tried to calm Meyerhoff down. They sat alone in the private security area in Macy's basement. Half an hour ago, Keller and he had met him in the store for their next meeting. Keller now stood guard while Martin interrogated him.

"If that gorilla finds me talking to you, I'm going to die." Meyerhoff wrung his hands.

"What gorilla?"

"Eugene Traub. That man has a temper. No one crosses him. I heard he once shackled a man and tossed him overboard just because he owed him six dollars. I saw him beat up three men in a bar fight – two had knives and one had a club. Traub walked away without a scratch."

"He's bald? Wears a black hat and coat?" Martin asked.

"That's him."

"The same one who gave you the money four nights ago?"

"He runs the smuggling operation." Meyerhoff tapped his feet. His nervousness had reappeared.

Martin's excitement grew. At last, he was getting closer to his adversary. "Who does he work for?"

"He's the head of security at the Hamburg-America Shipping Line, but that's not all."

"What do you mean?"

"That gorilla is already watching me." Meyerhoff tapped his feet faster.

"How do you know?"

"That man has two looks – scary and real scary. I know what that second one means. That's the one he's using on me. I've said too much. I'm sorry, I have to ..."

"I can still arrest you." Martin held him back. "Why are you so afraid?"

"Traub's the most powerful man in New York Harbor. He patrols it like a Sing Sing guard patrols the prison. They both know how to maintain order and how to make money on the side. Traub can always find men to do what he wants. He boasted to me there wasn't a man on the dockyard he couldn't buy – at his price. Just talking about it makes me nervous." Meyerhoff took out a cigarette. "You got a light?"

"Here." Martin lit the cigarette and welcomed the smoke. "And what does he want?"

Meyerhoff took a puff and calmed down. "Information." He revealed that Traub's connections cover everyone along the harbor: captains, paymasters, tugboat skippers, lighterboat men, wharf-rats, dive-keepers, and every criminal gang and member. He knows where men hide, and where they don't want to be found. He knows the name of every ship coming and leaving. He can predict which cargo businesses will make money and which will fail. He can quote the rates for every rope, barrel, piece of coal, or boat sold along the wharf. Meyerhoff believed Traub set the rates for every loading job in the harbor. "Ya gotta protect me."

"We will. Go on."

Meyerhoff said Traub had recruited a private guerrilla army from interned German merchant marines, employees of his shipping line, German-American sympathizers, and German reservists like him living in America. To complement his army, Traub has spies everywhere. He employs hotel workers of every type – bellhops, maids, waiters, clerks, bartenders, receptionists. He uses common laborers – street vendors, telephone operators, window washers, taxi drivers, stable boys, clerks – anyone who has access to information he needs. He brags that he knows more about what is happening along New York's waterfront than the mayor and the chief of police combined.

Martin interrupted. "Must be highly profitable. What does he do with all that money?"

Meyerhoff shook his head.

"After we arrested you and let you go, what did you tell Traub?"

"Nothing. I paid the Italians like you said." Meyerhoff reached for another cigarette. The ashes were piling up at his feet.

"Last match." He made Meyerhoff reach for it. "And to your knowledge, Traub suspects nothing?"

"He suspects everything, but about this? *Nein.*"

Martin stood up and glowered at Meyerhoff. "You haven't given me anything. I need to know who plants the bombs. How? When?"

Meyerhoff gulped. "Listen. I'm paid to look away, so I do. I don't know what the other lighterboat captains do. I don't ask questions."

"If you don't tell me something useful, you're going to die in jail and your family will be sent back to Germany without a penny." Martin grabbed Meyerhoff's shirt and shook it. "Who runs the bombing operation?"

Meyerhoff began to tremble. "I'll tell you this – I'm sure Traub knows about anything illegal happening in the harbor."

"I'm going to break up this ring. And when I do, I'm going to tell every German I arrest that you helped me. Then, I'm going to make sure the judge sends them to Sing Sing, just like you." Martin ripped the cigarette out of Meyerhoff's mouth and threw it down. "I wouldn't give a penny for your chances after that."

"I'll ... help." Meyerhoff could hardly say the words.

"Good. When we meet next time, you're going to tell me how we can trap Traub."

Chapter 16

Join My Union

Chesapeake Iron and Steel Works, Maryland: July 1915

Caarsens studied the fifteen Negro factory workers in front of him and wondered how they were going to react. The men gathered outside the factory grounds of the Chesapeake Iron and Steel Works located in Twin Corners, Maryland, just west of Baltimore. They were tough, well-muscled men, used to physical labor. Their overalls were patched and faded but clean. Some men stood while others sat on the ground and opened their lunch sacks. A breeze blew steam from the plant toward them, raising the temperature to over 100 degrees. Sweat dripped from all the men and darkened their clothing. No one looked at him except Lucius "Choo-Choo" Madison, the informal leader of the group.

Some men shuffled their feet; others placed their hands on their hips. One man lifted his shirt to scratch his belly, revealing the handle of a large knife. A few men carried shovels. Caarsens suspected that most of the other men concealed switchblades, shanks, or guns.

Caarsens looked over at Choo-Choo for the signal to speak. It had taken him two weeks to convince Choo-Choo that his plan would help the men. In that time, he had gotten to know Choo-Choo. He had shoveled coal on the railroads when he was thirteen and moved to Baltimore with his wife and baby when he was nineteen. Caarsens had won his trust when he convinced Choo-Choo that unionizing would not get them all killed. He told Caarsens he could speak to his men, but had warned him the men would be skeptical and defensive. He would have one chance to make his pitch. This was it.

Caarsens asked the men to move closer. "I suspect that most of you don't trust me."

A few nods.

"You have every right."

Several men looked at him.

"I know that America's high-minded values don't reach your world."

"Amen."

"Things need to change here." Caarsens pointed at the factory.

One man in the back shouted, "About time!"

Sensing the men were listening, Caarsens added more emotion to his speech. "Germany is not your enemy, but your shells kill Germans."

"Who cares? We need work."

Caarsens ignored the heckler. "America denies your basic freedoms. Germans don't lynch people; Americans do." Caarsens waited as a few workers moved closer. "I guess there've been about fifty lynchings across the South in these last few years. At least five of them were women."

"Lord help us and save us."

"Shoot them crackers."

"But I'm not here to talk about the war in Europe. It's not your war, but this factory profits from it. Do you?" Caarsens asked.

"No."

"America supports England and France, but what does it do for you?"

"Nothing."

"That's an outrage. Fight for what's right – equal pay for equal work. I'll help you. Join my union."

Half the men clapped mildly when he was done. Many kept looking at the front gate. Caarsens stepped back, and Choo-Choo stepped forward. From the corner of his eye, Caarsens saw a truck pull out of the factory. It was riding low on its wheels. Caarsens knew the truck contained high-explosive shells bound for Europe. How many German soldiers will those shells kill? Bile rose up from his stomach.

After he stopped speaking, a few men stayed and approached Choo-Choo. When they finished talking, Choo-Choo went over to Caarsens and said, "The men need to get back to work. Let me talk to them after their shift ends. I'll meet you later, as we arranged."

"Do you suspect trouble?" Caarsens asked.

"Yes," whispered Choo-Choo.

Chapter 17
Losses and Gains

Battery Park, Manhattan: July 1915

Martin ignored the view of the harbor as Keller and he waited for Meyerhoff at the Battery Park Aquarium. They were its first visitors of the day. He flipped open his grandfather's silver Swiss pocket watch and checked the time. Worried, Martin looked at Keller and shook his head. Meyerhoff was late.

Two hungry seals fighting for breakfast thrashed in the water tank in front of them. Their throaty high-pitched barks reminded Martin of his squabbling neighbors. The animal feeder in his rubber boots walked past them. He carried a pail of smelly fish. "Mornin'." He waved. "You're early."

New York Harbor was already alive. From inside the aquarium, Martin heard engines and whistles coming from boats entering Battery Park's Ferry Port. The constant deep-pitched shouts from men docking their boats and the chatter of people disembarking on their way to work disturbed Martin. For a moment, he envied their carefree routine and easy burdens, so different from his.

"It's not like Meyerhoff to be late." Keller's loud voice rose above the clamor. "Whatever else he is, he's a German."

"Did we push him too far?" The chilly morning air made Martin shiver.

"I hate fish." Keller rubbed his nose. "I'm wondering if he betrayed us or just ran away."

"Doubt it. He'll be here. He has no other choice," Martin said.

"He can take care of himself," Keller said. "We got the meeting place right, didn't we?"

"Sure. He told me over the phone eleven o'clock – twice. Mentioned the code word 'remember.' That moves the meeting time to –"

"Nine o'clock." Martin looked at his watch again. "Half an hour ago. He told you to meet him at the bathhouse, didn't he?"

"Yes. Crazy code."

"Meyerhoff said it's similar to the one Traub uses. It will work for us. This is a good meeting point – away from the harbor but close enough." Martin checked his watch again. The minutes ticked by. Two seals chased each other in an underwater game of tag. A third seal stared at him, clapped his flippers and barked. "I love seals."

"Not me." Keller started to pace. "Where is Meyerhoff? 'Be careful,' I told him over and over. Traub's got people everywhere. 'You're in danger, Otto,' I told him."

"We squeezed him hard, but he understands the risks. He'll be here soon," Martin hoped. "I'll bet on it."

"You and your luck. A gambling man might take those odds, Gil." Keller stepped in a shallow pool of water. "But I don't bet. Let's go outside before this water ruins my shoes."

Once outside, Martin saw a cargo ship steam away from Brooklyn. *What are the chances there's a bomb on board?*

"The lighterboat men are busy today." Keller pointed to the small boats scurrying around the harbor.

"My parents came through there." Martin looked at the Statue of Liberty on Bledsoe's Island just beyond Ellis Island's four turrets.

"She's beautiful." He remembered first seeing it as a boy when his parents from Alsace brought him there. They tried to explain how they felt when they arrived in New York and what it was like to be processed through Ellis Island. They rarely talked about the Prussian invasion at the start of the Franco-Prussian War and their journey to America. He knew they were happy to leave France. His two uncles died at the Battle of Sedan. His family vowed never to return to Alsace after it became part of Bismarck's new Germany.

They fled to America instead. Gil's earliest childhood memories were of his parents cursing the Boches. His father was thrilled when France prepared for war in the summer of 1914. "We'll be in Berlin by snowfall," he said cheerfully. He died of a bad heart at the end of August, as waves of German armies crushed the French. Much to Martin's regret, his father never lived to hear about the miracle on the Marne, the turning point in 1914 when French troops rallied to halt the German advance.

His mother's health deteriorated after her husband died. Connections to her relatives in German-occupied France had been severed. She did not have the strength to fight the cancer. She died that Christmas. With her last labored breath, she cried, "Kill the Boches." Martin always blamed Germany for his parents' deaths. "Let's give Meyerhoff another fifteen minutes."

Twenty nervous minutes later, however, they left Battery Park. Martin headed to the closest police signal box located next to the Whitehall Building off of West Street, the largest building overlooking Battery Park. He opened the signal box drawer and pulled down the lever that transmitted the box number to his headquarters. The newly installed Gamewell Company system automatically recorded the number and time of receipt. New York

City had the largest telephone switchboard in the world outside of the telephone companies themselves. Martin removed the telephone receiver from the signal box. It sent a signal for headquarters to pick up.

Martin said little while the desk sergeant told him the news. Martin nodded his head a few times, then replaced the receiver down hard. For a moment, Martin's lungs tightened, as if he had been handcuffed and dumped in the seal's tank. Drowning and suffocation were his biggest fears.

"Meyerhoff's dead."

~

Before dinner, Caarsens tried to nap in Twin Corners' only hotel. He could not get comfortable and shifted positions every few seconds. He was upset. He had just learned that Germany had surrendered its Southwest Africa colony to Britain. Caarsens regretted that he hadn't been able to go there to fight the British, but he knew he was still a wanted man in South Africa. The British would kill him on sight. As hard as it was to accept, he understood he could do more for his cause in America.

Caarsens left his hotel at 5:30 p.m. and hiked a road covered with horse manure toward the outskirts of town. He reached Sherman's Grill, a "coloreds only" restaurant, in twelve minutes. He surveyed the surroundings. The restaurant was set back thirty yards from the dirt road. Its paint was peeling and part of the front-porch railing was missing. Behind Sherman's Grill, he could see thick woods. Two dogs fought in the back.

He and Choo-Choo sat down by the window with the best view of the road. Although he was the only white man in the place, everyone was cordial to him. The waiter said, "We appreciate what you doing for us, sir."

Caarsens ate chicken, corn, and mashed potatoes with thick, lumpy gravy. The food reminded him of meals he had as a boy. Just as he dropped the last gnawed chicken bone on his plate, Caarsens heard someone call his name.

"Mr. Rasmussen? We want you out here. Now."

Choo-Choo dropped his fork and looked out the window. "The Klan. I know they'd be here sometime."

The few patrons picked up their things, dropped some money on their tables, and fled through the back door. The employees followed.

Caarsens looked out the window. Two men out in front and four behind them headed toward the front door. They were dressed in white sheets and pointed white hoods that covered their faces. The one who was speaking twirled a thick rope. The man next to him carried a torch and a Bowie knife in his belt. Of the four men behind him, two carried torches. Another carried a club that could have been a baseball bat, and the last man held a double-barreled shotgun.

"We don't like northerners interfering none with our business down here." The leader was a heavy man and had a throaty southern accent.

"I wondered when they'd show up." Caarsens finished his potatoes and corn.

Choo-Choo stared out the window. "Those boys mean trouble. If I were ..."

Caarsens wiped his mouth and left. He didn't stay to hear Choo-Choo's last words.

"You comin' out, or do we come in for you?" the leader called.

Once out back, Caarsens circled around the building. Just the six men – no ambush, no reinforcements. Good. He picked up a stout branch about three feet long and tapped it across his hand, feeling its heft. This will do. He checked his Demag. The Klansmen moved toward the front door. Caarsens crept up behind them.

"We're waiting!" the leader called. "Any of you boys still around, why don't you just git. Our bus'ness is with Rasmussen."

Before any of the Klan men knew what was happening, Caarsens had snuck up behind them. He swung his wooden club across the leg of the man with the shotgun. Crack! The man tilted sideways and sunk like a merchant ship hit by a torpedo. Reversing direction but with the same fluid motion, Caarsens smashed the arm of the man with the baseball bat. The bat hit the ground an instant before the Klansman. Caarsens jabbed a third man in the face. He felt teeth shatter and saw a dark puddle form in the white hood around the nose. The fourth man started to react and waved his torch like a sword. Caarsens dodged out of the way, spun around, and with both hands swung his club. It struck the man's back. The man fell forward, gasping for breath. Caarsens hit the man again, knocking him unconscious.

Slow to react, the two leaders turned around. Caarsens dropped his club, picked up the shotgun, and fired into the air. The two men froze. "Why don't you gentlemen go? I've got lawful business here."

The two men started to move apart. Caarsens moved with them so he could keep both in his field of vision. *These boys won't back off*. The second man flashed his Bowie knife and charged.

Caarsens could have killed him with the shotgun, but he didn't want to risk arrest. The attacking man slashed wildly in reckless windmill-like motions. Caarsens side-stepped the Klansman, blocked the Bowie knife with the shotgun and jammed the stock into the man's ribs. The man bent double and spat blood. Caarsens grabbed his arm, twisted it, and moved behind him. With a vicious kick upward, he shattered the Klansman's arm. Howling in pain, he dropped the Bowie knife. When he tried to clutch his dangling arm, Caarsens kneed him in the groin. The man collapsed.

The leader with the rope stood frozen. He looked at his five wounded companions writhing on the ground. Caarsens walked up to him and pulled off his hood. Caarsens drew his Demag out of its sheath and shoved its point under the leader's chin. He pushed it up slowly. The man's head tilted up to counter the blade. When the man's chin was at forty-five degrees, Caarsens said, "I guess it's just you and me. What do you think you're going to do with *this*?" Caarsens took the rope.

"What happens down here ain't none of your bus'ness. Leave," the leader croaked.

"You boys don't know when you're whipped." Caarsens pushed the bayonet up harder and felt blood drip on his hand. "Why don't you get your men out of here? They look like they need some help. Bar fight among friends, wouldn't you agree? That's what you'll tell the cops, right?" Caarsens searched the man's pocket and found a Colt 45 Caliber M1911 semi-automatic pistol. Caarsens slid it into his pocket.

The leader tried to spit at Caarsens. Before anything left his mouth, Caarsens punched him in his big soft belly. He dropped.

Caarsens spotted Choo-Choo in the shadows. “Do you know this man?”

“Yeh, that’s Cole Tiegs down at the bank.”

Caarsens grabbed Tiegs by the hair and pulled him up. “Well, Mr. Tiegs, nice to meet you. Let me tell you – I’ll find out where you live. If you and the rest of your Klan friends make any trouble for the Chesapeake workers, or if any harm comes to any colored man or woman in this county, I’ll hear about it, and I’ll come back. After I do that, I’m going to find you, and we’re going to have another talk. Then, I’m going to blow your house into kindling or kill your entire family. Your choice.” As he started to leave, Caarsens turned back and slashed his Demag across Tiegs’s cheek, cutting a four-inch gash half an inch deep.

Choo-Choo walked out of the shadows. “I never seen nothing like that, Mr. Rasmussen. Where did you learn to fight like that?”

“I think the Klan will leave you alone for a time. What will your men do?”

Chapter 18
Friends, Old and New

Brooklyn Dockyards: July 1915

Martin told Keller the police found Meyerhoff's body on the Brooklyn dock by his empty lighterboat. When they arrived there, Martin jumped over the barrier the police had erected. Low tide's rotting smell rolled in. Overhead, a flock of gulls circled. Their droppings and the wet boards made the dock slick. Keller slipped, but Martin grabbed his hand before he fell into the water. The roundsman who had found the body rushed to help.

"Thanks." Keller pulled himself up.

Martin recognized the roundsman. "Sean Clancy. How are you? It's been a long time." Martin patted his back. When he was a rookie in Brooklyn, Clancy had saved Martin's career. "It's quiet around here, old friend."

"Death does that," Clancy said. "In the dockyards, the police are the enemy. Silence is the first commandment. We got an understandin', me and the dockyard men. I ignore petty crime and personal fights, so long as nobody gets hurt too bad. I got the safest rounds along this here harbor." Clancy reached down and rubbed his badge. "Nothin' ever real bad happened on my watch. Until today." Studying Martin for a few seconds, Clancy hesitated a moment, then said, "You don't look so good, Gil. You all right?"

"What happened here, Sean?" Martin was angry at Clancy for seeing how the stress and fatigue had affected him.

Clancy explained that he found the body by accident. "I knew something was wrong when I saw all the lighterboats gone but

Meyerhoff's. I never saw the pier so quiet and empty like this." Clancy waved his arm in a long arc. "Not early morning anyways. I'm used to seeing men fixing nets, repairing boats, loading up supplies."

"More like a graveyard than a shipyard," Martin said.

"I hear you're in the Bomb Squad now. Me and the other roundsmen are proud of you, son." Clancy wrapped his arm around Martin's shoulder. "A sergeant, too. We knew you'd go far. You always had more luck than a leprechaun with two pots of gold."

"I'm good, too."

"I hear Eloise Bauer is helping you over at the Bomb Squad."

"Yes."

"She's my wife's aunt by marriage."

"Nice lady."

"I guess I'm not supposed to ask, but what was Meyerhoff up to?"

"Can you tell us about the body?"

Clancy thought the body had been dead for several hours. Becoming rigid, it lay face-down and was covered with a blanket. His clothes were ripped. "Meyerhoff was no angel; none of these men are, but nobody deserves this." Clancy started to roll the body over but couldn't. "I'm getting old. Give me some help." With Martin's help, Clancy flipped the body over.

"Holy mother of God," Keller said. A shotgun blast had obliterated his groin. What was left of Meyerhoff's insides spilled out. A railroad spike had been driven into his forehead. Flies buzzed around the corpse.

Martin whistled. "Even the del Gaudio Brothers weren't this brutal." He brushed away the flies, but more returned.

"It's the Lord's truth when I say I never seen nothing like that." Clancy crossed himself.

"He didn't die easy, that's for sure." Martin could still read the pain in Meyerhoff's marbleized eyes.

"What kind of animal does that?" Keller floated the blanket back over the body.

When he calmed down, Martin asked Clancy some questions. What did he know about Meyerhoff? Good captain; his crew liked him. Had he talked with Meyerhoff recently? No, but Clancy had talked to him often. Enemies? Around here, nobody really has friends. Honest? Better than most.

"Sorry I can't help you more." Clancy wished Martin well as the detectives departed.

"*Scheisse*," Keller said when they got off the pier. "As soon as Meyerhoff starts to help us, he gets killed. He was our best chance to crack that ring of Kaiser-lovers. I got to figure that ape Traub did this."

"I agree," Martin said. "We must be getting close to their operation."

"What now?"

"I want to shadow Traub to the devil's door."

~

Two days after his fight with the Klan, Caarsens met Choo-Choo outside the Twin Corners hotel. "The men agree to join your union," Choo-Choo said. "They'll demand fair wages. If they don't get 'em, they gonna strike. Thank you, Mr. Rasmussen." Choo-Choo extended his hand. Their eyes locked for a few seconds.

Choo-Choo's sincerity startled Caarsens. He was not

accustomed to helping other men, especially Negroes. "Thank you, Mr. Madison, but the real work begins now. You've got the papers, and the union will send some people down to get you started."

Choo-Choo turned to leave but stopped. He called back to Caarsens. "One last thing, Mr. Rasmussen. If you ever in New York, my cousin lives in Harlem. Name's Jelly Brown. He's mighty well connected around that harbor up there. People say he runs a dock gang. One thing I do know is he's resourceful like me, so he's a good person to know. I'll tell him about you. Don't be afraid to look him up."

Caarsens made a mental note of the name; "Jelly Brown" should be easy to remember. He started to go back to the hotel when someone in a straw boater approached and pointed a camera at him. Caarsens was able to get his hand up in time to cover part of his face before it flashed. He wanted to take the camera, but he knew he couldn't ask the reporter for the picture without raising suspicion.

"Hello. I'm from the *Baltimore Daily News*. I just heard about the union. Can I ask you for an interview?"

"Later. I'm in a hurry. I'm sure Mr. Madison over there will be able to answer all your questions."

~

Back in New York, Caarsens briefed Beck on the events. "Well done, except for one thing," Beck said.

"What?"

Beck slid over a two-day old copy of the *Baltimore Daily News*. "Page five. Look."

The paper contained an article about Chesapeake Iron's new union and Mr. Rasmussen's picture.

"Too much publicity, wouldn't you agree?" Beck's voice was stone cold.

"The picture is a bit grainy. I don't like it, but you can see only some of my face."

"But anyone who has seen you before might be able to recognize you."

"Let's pray that doesn't happen."

Chapter 19
Bronxville

Bronxville: July 1915

On this hot summer day, John Wittig shivered as he looked out his front window at the two men walking toward his house. Who was the man with Beck? At least it wasn't the man in the black coat. He felt he was losing control of his offer to help Germany and wondered how things would change after their visit.

He hated doing business in his suburban home on a Saturday. Normally a good negotiator, he wasn't sure how Beck had talked him into this meeting. Originally, he had intended to help Beck indirectly. However, after several lunches, Beck had coaxed him into providing more assistance. After Wittig mentioned his idea about forming a German-backed U.S. munitions company, Beck demanded more details. Wittig would provide them at today's meeting, but why had the matter become so urgent?

Wittig greeted his guests at the front door. Felix Beck waltzed in like an aristocrat at a banquet. He introduced his tall colleague as Pieter Knopp. Nora hurried from the kitchen to meet the visitors. She patted her hands against her apron, causing flour to puff outward. The men moved to the living room, and Nora returned to her chores. The smell of baking bread filled the house.

Wittig's two daughters were playing hop-scotch in the back yard. He could hear their laughter through the open windows.

His two guests occupied chairs at either end of an antique couch. Wittig sat between them on the couch. They made Wittig nervous. He noticed that Knopp seemed to be keeping one eye on Beck. The quiet blond man had the arms of a steelworker and a leathery, weather-worn face. He reacted to every sound and sudden movement like a watchdog.

Beck gestured with his hands and his courtly manners seemed an affectation. Wittig guessed he was not the aristocrat he claimed to be. Beck spoke first. "Herr Knopp is Dutch and one of my most trusted associates. He's a former agriculture engineer, and sympathetic to Germany. I have mentioned your ideas, and he is anxious to hear more."

Nora entered the living room with a large silver tea service and hot bread. After she served the men tea, she returned to the kitchen.

"Herr Beck, how should we start?" Wittig asked.

"Herr Wittig, I assume you have thought further about your idea of a German-funded business. Please share your ideas with Mr. Knopp."

"I believe a plant in America sympathetic to Germany's interests could have a large impact." Wittig relaxed as he moved to the topic of the plant. "I'm convinced such a plant could reduce or slow the flow of arms across the Atlantic."

"Makes sense." Knopp broke off a piece of bread.

"How much money will the plant have, Herr Beck?" Wittig was an expert on economic problems of new businesses.

"We will start with two million dollars. Additional funding is available if the plan succeeds." Beck took two pieces of bread and left crumbs for Wittig. He slathered both pieces with butter and put them together. "As a banker, do you think this is sufficient capital,

Herr Wittig? We plan to call the company New Haven Projectile."

"Two million dollars is a start, but my ideas will require more money." Wittig was startled that Beck had already selected a name and location for the company.

"Herr Wittig, summarize for Herr Knopp what you want this plant to accomplish."

Intuition told him he needed to please Beck. Wittig stood up and faced them. "One, New Haven Projectile can place contracts for delivery to U.S. and Allied companies that it has no intention of honoring. It should set contract terms so that it would not suffer significant losses when it fails to deliver. Two, it can make long-term agreements for delivery of important machinery and manufacturing tools. This will allow us to prevent their productive use for as long as possible. When New Haven Projectile delays receipt or rejects the goods outright, penalties should be minimal. You have good lawyers, don't you, Herr Beck?" He sat down.

"Of course," Beck chuckled.

"Don't forget the common worker," Knopp said. "We can upset labor markets by paying higher wages than our competitors. Better wages will attract key employees away from actual U.S. manufacturers and cause unrest in the whole industry."

"Delicious." Beck finished his bread.

"What will you do with all the munitions the plant purchases, Herr Beck?" Knopp asked.

"That's the best part of this whole plan. I've already made inquiries." Beck licked his fingers. "We'll sell them to Spain. They will be most grateful, especially with the prices we will offer."

"We could also learn about the U.S. munitions industry."

Knopp placed his right hand on his brow as if he was thinking. "What companies are in trouble? Who buys what? Where would the deliveries go? Maybe we'll learn our competitors' payment terms so we can offer them cheaper and never deliver."

They all laughed.

"I was hoping the plant could try to secure a monopoly on key raw materials too," Beck said.

Outside in the back yard, children's laughter turned to screams. "Help!" Hanna yelled. "It's Mary."

~

Caarsens, who was used to using false names like Knopp, jumped to his feet when he heard the calls. Nora rushed to the living room window. "Oh, no. John, come quickly." She ran outside. He followed her. Wittig joined them. Beck remained behind.

Mary grabbed her left leg and writhed on the ground. "It hurts bad." She gulped through her tears.

Nora clutched Mary. "What happened?"

Hannah pointed to the tall oak behind them. "She fell."

"I told you not to ..."

Caarsens rushed over. "Let me. I know what to do." He saw her foot bent at an angle.

Nora stepped back and placed her hands over her mouth, tears streaming down her face. "Is it bad?"

Caarsens cradled Mary's head and whispered soothing words. When her cries turned to whimpers, he rested her flat on her back. With a surgeon's skill, he felt her leg. "It's a fracture, but she'll be all right, Mrs. Wittig. Get me some bandages and something to clean the wound and wash my hands. Also, wood to make a splint."

Nora returned with the two pieces of a broken broom handle and clean towels. She handed him a bottle of whiskey, soap, and a wet cloth. "Will this do?"

"Fine." Caarsens washed his hands and poured the whiskey onto the wound. Mary winced but didn't cry. "Good girl. You're very brave." When he was ready to set the leg and fix the splint, he took Hannah's hand and guided it gently across Mary's leg. "Can you feel the break, Hannah? Careful. Be gentle."

Nora comforted Mary while Wittig started the car.

"Let me carry her to the motorcar. Is the hospital far?" Caarsens asked Nora.

"Its a few minutes up the road. I've got her." Nora brushed away tears from her gray-blue eyes and picked Mary up. "I don't know what to say. Thank you so much."

Caarsens backed away. "I hate to see innocent people suffer, especially children." After they left, he found Beck still seated in the living room writing notes.

"Most successful day." Beck put away his pen and checked his watch. "We can still catch the 4:38 train back to New York."

As they walked to the train station, Caarsens asked, "Since my union work is completed, I assume you don't want me to run this plant. There's too much publicity concerning what I did in Maryland, isn't there?"

"I have the perfect man to run the plant." Beck walked faster. "Karl Bier is second-in-command of the Hamburg-American Shipping Line. He's been most helpful to me, but he will need help. You will work for him as well as do various things for me."

"When do you want me to start there?"

"Soon. The plant is half completed."

Chapter 20
The Freedom March

Brooklyn Dockyards: August 1915

Caarsens did nothing for ten days as he waited for orders from Beck. Used to action, he became more frustrated each day as he sat by the harbor and watched ships stuffed with munitions sail to Europe. Beck had lectured him to be patient and stay hidden. That was like asking a soldier to sleep during an artillery barrage. His only pleasure was eating the fresh peaches and peanuts he bought from street vendors.

To hell with Beck. Caarsens grabbed the initiative. Since much of America's munitions shipped out of New York, Caarsens decided to find Jelly Brown, Choo-Choo Madison's cousin who worked the docks in Brooklyn. It wasn't hard to find Negro work crews, but getting them to talk? Now that proved difficult. They either ignored or threatened him. Violence would have gained him nothing, so Caarsens resorted to money.

It cost Caarsens three silver dollars to find Brown's work gang. A young boy took Caarsens to a shaky old pier with rotted pilings. Caarsens opened his palm to show another coin. "Which one is Jelly Brown?" The boy grabbed the coin, pointed to a huge bare-chested Negro man booming instructions in a deep baritone voice, and ran away. Just then, Brown shouldered a barrel all by himself. Sunlight reflected off his gold front tooth. No question who the leader was.

Caarsens decided to wait for Brown's crew to break for the day. He smelled oily water and tidal waste. Swarms of flies covered the piles of garbage washed up at the shoreline. He approached Brown as the crew walked off the docks. "Just a minute of your time. Is your name Jelly Brown?"

Brown's men surrounded Caarsens and tightened their ring around him. Brown, a head taller and thirty pounds heavier than the other men, stepped forward. "You crazy? This is my dock. You got a death wish or somethin'?"

Caarsens noticed the outline of something that could have been a knife in Brown's waistband. "I'm a friend of your cousin, Choo-Choo Madison. I think he talked to you about me. Jens Rasmussen?"

"Mister, you got a crazy way of introducing yourself. Good thing my cousin sent me a note. Stand down, boys." He wiped grimy sweat from his brow with a red bandanna he took from his back pocket.

Caarsens smiled broadly and turned on the charm. Because of his time with Choo-Choo he knew he could gain this man's confidence. "Choo-Choo told me your Grandma Dolly is a rotten cook. He wouldn't feed her chitlins back to the hogs."

Brown stomped his feet and hooted with laughter. "She surely is that. If he told you that, you know him good. Good to meet you, Mr. Rasmussen."

Brown's men moved back.

"We may be able to help each other," Caarsens said.

Brown waved his men away and walked to a bench near the water. He sat down, pulled out a knife and a stick, and started to whittle. With each swipe of his knife, another curled shaving dropped by his worn boots. "What you got to say?"

Caarsens started to talk about Choo-Choo, but he had to

check to see if Brown was listening. His grunts indicated he was. When he finished, Brown put down his knife and looked up. The whittled stick was now a sharpened spear. "That's a good story. Good thing for you Choo-Choo wrote me the same thing. You really take down eight Klansmen?"

Caarsens didn't take his eye off of Brown. "It was six. They weren't so tough."

"Damn. I wished I'da seen that. You something, that's for sure. But I got a question."

"Ask."

"Why you do it? Go down south and help some Negro boys?" Brown fought off flies with his stick.

"It was the right thing to do."

"Yeh and Abe Lincoln freed the slaves. So what?" Brown spit into the river. "Now you lying to me. If you want me to trust you, I want the truth."

Caarsens and Brown stared at each other like boxers in the ring.

"I hate America," Caarsens finally said.

"I know why I hate America, but why you?"

"It supports Britain. I despise Britain. I want Germany to win the war."

"What else?" Jelly asked.

"Whatever else is my own business." Caarsens revealed his personal affairs to no one.

"So there's somethin' in it for you – helpin' us. If there ain't no war, would you still be here?"

"No."

"So you want my help. How?"

"Information from time to time. What's going on at the docks – rumors, scuttlebutt, things that don't add up."

"And what do I get in return?" Brown snatched a fly and squished it.

"I can help organize your people like I did for your cousin." Caarsens swatted a fly away from his face. "I expect your pay is lower than the white men."

"Yeh. Nothin' new 'bout that." Brown wiped his hand on his bandanna. "Man needs to live. For me, I can never get enough dough."

"Maybe I can help."

"How?" Brown lashed out at more flies with his stick.

"My friends have some influence around the docks."

"Who they?" Brown lowered his stick.

"That's my business. Let's say I might be able to get your men a better deal."

"Prove it, and I'll believe you."

Caarsens adjusted his collar. "One more thing. I don't want anyone to know about me. I don't use the name Rasmussen any more. I go by Carpenter these days. "

"I don't tell nobody nothing, Mr. Carpenter. We all got things to hide. Around here we never turns our back on no one. If you help us, we'll protect you. If you Judas us, we skin you alive. One thing 'bout me. Like my cousin Choo-Choo, when I sets my mind to doin' somethin', you can't stop me with a freight train."

"I like an honest man." Caarsens stood up. "I think we understand each other."

"We talk again. I got to check on some things. We meet two nights from now. Come here." Brown jotted something on a small scrap of paper and handed it to Caarsens.

"Jack Johnson's pool hall in Harlem?" Caarsens looked at Brown. "I can find it."

"If you ain't there, we never talk again."

~

Brown was already playing pool when Caarsens entered Jack Johnson's dusty pool hall and bar. Beck had approved the meeting, saying, "These darkies can be useful. Cultivate the friendship and give them what they want – I am happy to pay for some trouble along the docks." As Caarsens walked in, the customers moved away from him. He walked by them with his head and shoulders erect. He noticed the bartender reach down – most likely for a club. Wary but not intimidated, he watched him from the corner of his eye knowing his Demag was within easy reach.

The men relaxed when Jelly Brown went up and greeted him. "We good to talk. Glad you came."

The bartender poured two beers. Brown and Caarsens each took one and sat at the quietest table in the joint. They touched their glasses.

"Let me say right off, I'm mad," Brown said.

"What's bothering you?"

"Our minister preaches restraint, but violence begets violence. Hate begets hate." Brown pulled at the cross around his neck.

"I know about that. Once hate eats into you, it rots your insides and freezes your soul." Caarsens felt a draft coming through the boarded windows.

"Somethin' like that." Brown's eyes were blank. "I'd like to invite someone over to talk to you. He got an idea."

Caarsens read Brown's eyes and decided this was not a trick. "Why don't you bring your friend over," Caarsens said.

Brown approached a white-haired Negro man standing at the bar and bowed. After a few words, they sat down next to Caarsens. Brown's friend had skinny but tough hands hardened by his share of physical labor. Brown introduced him as William Bouchet, a preacher and supporter of Negroes' rights.

Brown shifted his seat and let Bouchet face Caarsens. "Mr. Brown says you are a friend. I will settle for a compatriot." For an old man, Bouchet projected authority.

"I support equality and justice, Mr. Bouchet. Mr. Brown's cousin will vouch for me, if that helps you in any way." Caarsens leaned closer to Bouchet. "How can I help you?"

Bouchet summarized his frustration. Two weeks ago, a riot had occurred in St. Louis, Missouri. Trustworthy firsthand accounts were spreading through Harlem like an epidemic. Anger was rising faster than the temperature. The riot had started when several Negro men were hired by a factory that supplied goods under government contract. A number of white men got angry because they thought the Negroes had stolen their jobs. A rampage ensued. It caused more than forty thousand dollars in damage. Two policemen were killed. At least forty Negro men, women, and children were beaten, stabbed, or lynched. Almost six thousand Negro families became homeless when their homes in East St. Louis were burned down. The police and local militia did nothing to help.

When he finished, Bouchet's face was lined with worry and determination. "We are tired of being oppressed."

"I understand."

"We can no longer tolerate this treatment. We are God-fearing folks and good Christians." Bouchet pounded the table so hard the glasses vibrated.

Bouchet's passion impressed Caarsens, who understood their plight. "I wish that mattered, Mr. Bouchet."

"Tell him your idea." Brown's words burst with excitement.

"I want to do something that everyone will notice." Bouchet's arm muscle coiled.

"Many ways to do that," Caarsens said. "I know something about fighting. Maybe I can advise you on –"

"No. I am sorry. You misunderstood me," Bouchet said. "I want to prove that Negroes can handle their problems better than white folks."

"What are you thinking about?"

"This is gonna be good." Brown's face widened into a broad smile.

"I want to organize a march of colored folks down Fifth Avenue. A peaceful march. Solemn like a funeral."

"How can I help you with that?"

"I work for Mr. W.E.B. DuBois. He's one of the founders of the NAACP. Have you heard of it?"

"No."

"The National Association for the Advancement of Colored People. Mr. Brown will be happy to discuss the details with you later. I'm guessing you've been wronged in the past, Mr. Carpenter – I can see it in your face – and you are looking for retribution."

"Why do you say that?" Caarsens didn't like Bouchet picking at his scabs.

"I know men. Your hate will consume you," Bouchet said.

Damn you.

Bouchet stood up. "Good luck. I'm leaving. I hope to see you again, Mr. Carpenter. Remember, God forgives us our sins. Reach out to him."

After Bouchet left, Brown said, "That man is somethin'. Did you know he a writer too? He clings too much to the Good Book, but the NAACP does good. Can we help each other, Mr. Carpenter?"

"I'm sure we can," Caarsens said. "When we last talked, I told you I was interested in some information."

"I might be willin' to trade you for it, provided it don't hurt us."

"If I ask for something that you feel might hurt your people, I'll understand if you don't share it."

"That's fair." Brown took a long drink from his beer. He put down the glass and looked at it for several seconds. Then he looked up at Caarsens. "Mr. Carpenter, I need something right away."

"What?"

"I need to help organize Mr. Bouchet's march. He wouldn't accept your offer, but I can. Anything you give me will help us. Let's say that's a start to our friendship."

"How much of an advance do you want?"

"Two thousand."

"I'll give you three. When do you need it?"

~

Caarsens waited for the parade from the steps of the New York Public Library on 41st Street. He heard the muffled drums first. Three hundred children led the march. They carried numerous signs. One caught his attention: "Give us a chance to Live."

Thousands of women dressed in white dresses and their Sunday hats followed. They marched in orderly rows, twenty across in some places. No one spoke. Signs carried their message: "Thou shalt not kill." A particularly tall woman carried the largest one: "Mr. President – Why not make America safe for democracy?" She held it up with the same pride and determination as a regimental flag carrier.

W.E.B. DuBois and William Bouchet led the men. Jelly Brown walked behind them. Caarsens thought he saw Brown wipe a tear away as he walked past the library. Men, more numerous than the women, followed. They were dressed in black suits, ties and shirts whiter than the white on the American flag. Every man wore a hat – boaters and top hats, mostly.

Caarsens guessed the parade numbered between eight and ten thousand people. No funeral procession was more orderly, respectful, and somber. Only the steady beat of drums interrupted the sound of thousands of shoes hitting the pavement. A few men handed out leaflets and NAACP pamphlets. The sidewalks were crowded with people of all walks of life. They lined both sides of Fifth Avenue as far as Caarsens could see.

A few policemen guarded the street. They seemed tense but quiet. The policeman nearest him shuffled back and forth and kept his hand on his nightstick. He turned away as the Negro men walked by.

When he could no longer hear the drums, Caarsens thought, *I've helped you, Mr. Brown; let's see if you do your part.*

~

John Wittig, who had taken an uptown subway, stood on 43rd Street and watched the march. It inspired him and gave him hope for a better world.

SECTION III

GRAND CENTRAL STATION

August 1915 - December 1915

Chapter 21
The Economic Conference

Denver, Colorado: August 1915

As the train chugged across seemingly endless farmland, Secretary of the Treasury William McAdoo felt like he was crossing the same ground again and again. He drifted in and out of what others would call a nap. To McAdoo, it was the closest thing to sleep that he had had in months. McAdoo considered the Denver conference vital. There, he would ask the top financial men in the country to agree to provide direct private lending to the Allies.

McAdoo had calculated that, by year's end, America's exports would exceed its imports by two and a half billion dollars. At that rate, the Allies would be unable to pay America without additional financing. If the financing was unavailable, the Allies would stop ordering goods.

He roused himself, washed his face, and headed to the dining car to meet his traveling companion, Dr. G.G. Carlsen, chief of the Federal Bureau of Foreign and Domestic Commerce. Dr. Carlsen organized the conference and served as its chairman. After ordering wine, McAdoo turned to Carlsen. "Let's get down to business. I gather you still have reservations about the president's lending policy."

Carlsen shifted in his padded velvet seat. "I am not criticizing or objecting to the European loans. I'm merely raising the question: Is it sound economic policy for the United States to loan our money to our best customers so they can destroy each another?"

The waiter returned and poured a finger-height of wine into McAdoo's glass. The secretary rolled the wine around in the glass, held it up to the light, and then to his nose. He closed his eyes and tasted it. “Quite satisfactory.”

The waiter wiped a cloth around the top of the bottle and filled their glasses.

“Excuse the interruption. Please continue, Mr. Carlsen.”

Carlsen reached for his glass and took a gentle sip. “Couldn’t our money be better used to develop those countries, such as those in South America, Africa, Australia and the Far East, that are ardently seeking capital? With such funds, they can grow and keep the very wheels of commerce moving.”

“I wonder if the Europeans realize they are going to destroy themselves either militarily or economically.” McAdoo savored the wine.

The waiter returned. “Would you gentlemen care to order?”

Without looking at the menu, McAdoo said, “My usual. Steak. Rare.”

Carlsen closed the menu. “I’ll have what he has.” His face sagged. “What concern is Europe to us? This is not our war.”

“Not our war? I don’t agree. Our trade with the Allies will increase from about eight hundred million dollars before the war to three billion next year.”

Carlsen’s eyes widened. “But certainly we have lost trade with Germany. Aren’t your figures misleading, Mr. Secretary?”

“No. Before the war, we exported about one hundred-fifty million dollars to Germany. It will drop to less than a million this year. The difference is millions lost and billions gained.”

The waiter brought their steaks. McAdoo grabbed his knife, sliced off a big chunk, and stuffed it in his mouth. Carlsen poked at his potato.

"The problem gets worse." McAdoo rained salt and pepper over his food. "By next January, the Europeans will no longer be able to fund their purchases. I don't have to tell you what that means to our economy."

"But, we've just invested in these industries and shifted resources to meet the demand." Carlsen started to cough. "If the Allies stop buying ..."

"They will lose the war, and we will have a crisis – people out of work, companies going bust, bank loans worthless."

"So we are on a fast train with no brakes."

"I'd rather be in our position than any European nation." McAdoo finished his meal and patted his belly. "The only means to avoid a crisis in the U.S. is to float the loans."

"Yes, I understand," Carlsen said. "We must loan money to the Allies in order to keep our foreign trade moving, but won't our loans only create a bigger problem later?"

The waiter returned. McAdoo ordered a large cognac. "We can always take their gold as collateral. Do I have your support?" McAdoo reached his hand across the table.

"With the possibility of gold-backed loans if necessary, yes, but Germany will be angry." Carlsen extended his hand.

McAdoo took it. "Let them. What can they do? Blow up a few more of our ships?"

They both laughed.

~

During a break at the end of the conference, John Wittig, who had helped organize it, felt dizzy and returned to his hotel room. He looked at himself in the mirror and realized he was aging fast. He skipped lunch and took a nap. The conference reconvened at 2 p.m. when Dr. Carlsen stood at the lectern and pounded his gavel twice. "I ask our secretary, Mr. John Wittig of Morgan Bank, to come forward and read the final proposal."

The motion to extend the loans to the Allies was seconded. The vote carried unanimously. After the conference, Wittig met Secretary McAdoo, who congratulated him on his diligence and thoroughness. "I will personally call Mr. Morgan to thank him for lending us your services. You have done outstanding work at the conference, Mr. Wittig. I'll tell Mr. Morgan you deserve a promotion. What position do you aspire to?"

"I would like to be part of Mr. Swanson's munitions purchasing group. Thank you, sir." Wittig started to walk away when he overheard McAdoo say to Carlsen. "I wish all German-Americans were as dedicated as that man. I'm sure he'll contribute to the war's outcome."

Chapter 22
Shadows

Police Headquarters: August 1915

Days after he saw Meyerhoff's dead body, Martin learned that the devil's door opened at 45 Broadway. The building contained the offices of the Hamburg-American Shipping Lines, Eugene Traub's employer. But before he could concentrate on Traub, Martin had to face Tunney.

At headquarters, the desk sergeant ordered Martin and Keller to report to the captain at 10 a.m. Tunney kept them waiting for thirty-eight tense minutes. To pass the time, Martin reviewed every aspect of the case in his head, scrutinizing all his mistakes. At first, Keller mimicked tossing a baseball into a gloved left hand over and over again, then stood, stretched, and started to pace.

When Tunney opened his door, his voice was harsh, his face Irish-red, and the rut over his nose more pronounced than ever. "Sit down," he growled, slamming the door. Before they could sit, he opened a thunderous barrage. "You promised that Meyerhoff would lead to arrests. Now he's dead! The mayor is furious. The chief of detectives wants answers. Do you want to go back to doing rounds?"

Martin tried to sound confident. "I believe Eugene Traub is at the center of everything. I'm sure he killed Meyerhoff."

"What about the sabotage, damn it? All you've given me so far is a dead body, a second-rate pirate operation, and some theories. It's been over four months, and the ship bombs are still going off. Last week, the *S.S. Fayette* went down. The reputation of the Bomb

Squad is sinking faster than those ships!" Tunney pounded his desk. "I want results! And soon!"

A numbed silence ensued. For once, even Keller sat stock-still. Martin felt all the color drain from his face. Only when he was absolutely sure Tunney had finished did Martin trust himself to speak. "I want to shadow Traub," he said, carefully, controlling his composure. "Find out how he conducts business; whom he sees; where he goes. We'll get our proof."

"So, you want to shadow Traub? Good idea," Tunney replied, much to Martin's relief. Keller audibly let out a breath. "But before we go further, I want someone to hear this." The captain rose, opened the door, and called, "Shannon?"

An attractive red-haired woman in her mid-twenties, about five-foot seven, entered. The men stood up. "My niece, gentlemen, Miss Shannon Connolly. I've asked her to join our department as my secretary. She's also the best shadow I know. She's a natural – instinctive and intelligent. I taught her myself."

With widening eyes, Keller straitened his hair, jumped up, and offered the young woman his chair. "She'll sit over here, Detective." Tunney gestured to the chair beside his desk.

Keller and Shannon exchanged glances. *She's trouble*, thought Martin.

Tunney turned to Shannon. "Aside from her secretarial duties, she will do research, and anything else I think she can handle. I want her to listen to our conversation."

"Hello," said Martin, keeping his voice as neutral as possible. *Wonderful. I've got a target on my back for sure.*

"Great to have you on our team." Keller beamed with boyish charm.

"Let me tell you about Traub." Tunney's face darkened. "I've known him for a long time. Before the war, I learned Traub was involved in some dockyard crimes involving his company, but couldn't prove it. He's a tough character – smart and thorough. We must build a strong case against him; it won't be easy. Things are sensitive enough with the German community already. We don't want to make them madder than necessary, so let me tell you what it takes to shadow someone."

Martin glanced over at Shannon to evaluate her reaction, but she remained composed and impossible to read. *Was she more than Tunney was saying*?

"A good shadow needs to think fast and know how to hide in the open," Tunney said. "Every detail and gesture is important. He must know how to pretend to read a newspaper while noticing everything around him; how to pretend to sleep with his eyes open; how to call for a taxi and make sure he doesn't get one." He looked at Shannon. "I'm sure you have something to add."

"Thank you, Uncle." Her voice was strong, confident beyond her years, yet feminine. "From what my uncle has told me, Traub is very good," Shannon began quietly.

Oh no, Martin moaned inwardly. *Can things get any worse? Keller is smitten, and she knows more about Traub than I do. Worse, she's not afraid to say it.*

"There are three things a man can't change: his height, the proportion of his shoulder width to the size of his head, and his feet. Given Traub's large physique, this puts him at a disadvantage."

So she knows what she's talking about, Martin admitted grudgingly.

"I always notice how a man walks and how he angles his feet. I look at his shoes. The man being followed can change coats, put on a hat, and even use spectacles to change his appearance, but it's difficult to change shoes very quickly."

Tunney looked pleased for the first time that afternoon. "Let me add that if a man takes a circuitous route and doesn't buy anything along the way, he knows he's being followed."

"I find you can learn a lot if you can get up close to him," Shannon added.

"How do you do that?" Keller piped up.

Martin shot him a sidelong glance. Had he already ceded his status to a know-it-all secretary?

"Surprise him," Shannon answered. "Catch him off guard. Be something he doesn't suspect."

Tunney agreed. His niece seemed to have a calming effect on his nerves. "The moment the target realizes, or even suspects, he's being followed, he acts differently. He changes what he's doing. Either he stops what he was about to do, or he starts to behave in ways he wouldn't otherwise. When that happens, the shadow may have to abandon the hunt."

"The most important thing is to react to what's going on. To do that, I think of myself as an actor," Shannon added.

"I never looked at it like that," Keller said, much to Martin's dismay. *Why is she really here?* he asked himself. *Does the captain really mean to let his pretty red-headed niece run this investigation?*

"That's part of it," Tunney said. "But shadowing is more than reacting. A good shadow is like a good fisherman – someone who knows how much line to run out and when to reel it in. And, our friend Mr. Traub is a very slippery fish. Shannon will help us a lot. I value her brains and her moxie. She's so good, she could be the next Isabella Goodwin," Tunney bragged, referring to the highest-ranking woman police officer in the United States, the NYPD's Detective Lieutenant Goodwin.

We'll see about that, Martin glowered. *The day I report to a woman a good deal younger than me is the day I give up my badge.*

~

For the next several weeks, Martin and Keller shadowed Traub through the streets, dockyards, and various shit-holes of New York. Traub made sure he had a good view of the surroundings whenever he stopped. His pockets always jingled with change. He used public phones often and never the same phone twice. He held his frequent meetings in public places, where it was difficult to eavesdrop, and covered his mouth making it impossible to hear his conversations. In the subway, for example, he would wait for a speeding train before he'd say anything. Trailing him was nothing but an exercise in frustration.

Traub knew how to disappear, despite Shannon's comment about his size. He left buildings through back exits, walked off subway cars at the last minute, and was expert at dodging the detectives in elevator buildings. No matter how many times they shadowed him to Macy's, he vanished without a trace in the store. "He's a better magician than Harry Houdini," Keller declared, disgusted.

Martin's frustration reached its limit when Traub started to use the ferry to go to the Communipaw Station in Jersey City. It was the perfect place to lose a tail. To avoid the purchasing queues, he always had a ferry ticket ready. Three days in a row, Traub walked onto the ferry but jumped off just as it was leaving Manhattan. On the fourth, he boarded the ferry, leaving Martin and Keller behind. By the time they arrived in Communipaw, Traub was already crossing back. He waved to them mockingly from the deck of the departing ferry.

Martin wondered aloud, “Who is the shadow and who is being shadowed?”

On their way back, Keller asked, “What’s so important over there?”

“We’ll never find out this way,” Martin said. “We’ll have to tap his phone.”

Chapter 23
We Germans

Bronxville: September 1915

Wittig vowed he would enjoy this Saturday away from work. He had been back from Denver for six weeks and had not spoken to Felix Beck since his visit to Bronxville. Beck had sent a note to apologize for missing their regular meetings.

Wittig sat at the circular mahogany dining room table and waited for the surprise he knew was coming. The swinging door to the kitchen opened. "Happy birthday to you; happy birthday to you; happy birthday, dear Papa, ..." Wittig turned and saw Hannah emerge. She juggled a cake that was almost too big for her to carry. Mary hopped behind on crutches. Nora followed. Hannah placed the cake in front of her father. "We baked it ourselves. It's –"

"Chocolate." Mary raced to say it first.

"Chocolate on chocolate." Hannah stressed the last word. "Your favorite."

"I made the frosting." A speck of frosting decorated Mary's nose.

"They did a wonderful job. Didn't you, girls?" Nora wrapped an arm around each girl. They beamed.

"My gracious. Where did you find all those candles?" Wittig tried to act amazed. "Let's count them." The girls stood on either side of him and giggled.

"You know how many there are, silly." Hannah nudged her father.

"One, two, three ..." Wittig pointed as he counted.

"You're taking too long. I want to eat." Mary pulled her father's sleeve.

"I want to make sure. Seventeen, eighteen, ..."

"Oh, Papa."

"Oh, no. You made me lose count. I have to start over. One, two, ..."

"No!" Both girls laughed.

"Let's see. Where was I?" Wittig put his index finger on his chin. "Oh, yes. Forty-one, forty-two, forty-three. They're all there."

"You have to make a wish." Nora smiled.

He closed his eyes and thanked God for his family. He loved the girls. They were a joy – smart and fun. Both were slender and strong. Hannah was going to be a beauty – turquoise-blue eyes and brown hair with reddish tints from her mother and the compact body and high cheekbones from her father. Mary was short for her age and had a rounder face. She was temperamental like her mother and strong-willed like her father. She added excitement wherever she was. She reminded Wittig of his mother – stubborn, resilient, and loving. She was on the mend from her fall. Her crutches hadn't slowed her down.

"Come on, Papa. How long does it take to make a wish?" Hannah's voice brought Wittig back to the present. He opened his eyes, took a deep breath, and blew out all the candles. Both girls cheered.

"What are we going to do tomorrow?" Mary asked.

"What we do every Sunday. We'll go to church, then we'll drive to the beach. It's still warm enough." Wittig said. "But, while we're there, Papa's got to meet someone nearby."

"John?" Nora seemed surprised.

"It's important. It's Mr. Beck's friend at the German-American League. I told you about him."

"Oh. That's all right, then."

~

After church the next day, Wittig and his family drove to Milton Point. After lunch, Wittig kissed everyone, apologized, and left for his meeting a few miles away. Wittig was excited to have a rendezvous with Matthias Weil, the head of the Federal German-American League in New York. The League was the most active political group speaking for German interests and culture in the United States. It tried to advance German-American organizations and businesses; arranged fundraising events for German-American causes; and supported the German-language press in America, such as Bernard Ridder's German publication, *New-Yorker Staats-Zeitung*.

The League had two and a half million members across the country and chapters in forty-four states. The League was particularly strong in large German pockets in New York, Pennsylvania, and the Midwest, and Wittig contributed to it generously. German-Americans like him supported the League's opposition to the prohibition movement. Since German culture in America was so intertwined with beer halls, he could not understand the feeling against alcohol. Prohibition was an attack on his way of life.

Wittig was convinced that German-Americans could gain more influence over America's policies. After all, German-Americans were the largest immigrant group in the country. Out of a pre-war

U.S. population of ninety-two million, two and a half million people were direct immigrants from Germany. Another four million people were born in America to German-born parents, just as he was. By including people of earlier German extraction, at least ten percent of the U.S. population considered themselves German-American. Irish-Americans were the next largest immigrant group. They numbered less than half the German-Americans. No other hyphenated-American group matched these two in size.

The German-Americans' biggest enemy was the bellicose former president, Theodore Roosevelt, who never ceased to argue for the build-up of America's army in anticipation of war. In his latest affront, Roosevelt had started a campaign to oppose the use of hyphen designations for immigrant groups.

Wittig saw the marker to turn off the main road. He drove onto a dirt path slightly wider than his Hudson. After a few hundred yards, his wheels started to sink into the sandy ground. He could go no further. He'd have to drive back in reverse.

He walked the rest of the way. A big house separated the yard from the water. He walked around the house and reached the shore. He saw a lone boat, the *Lorelei,* tucked beside a small dock just where Beck had told him it would be, and a man wearing a German navy captain's cap. Wittig climbed aboard the *Lorelei*, introduced himself in German, and said the greeting common to German-Americans, "God curse the English." Weil clicked his heels together, removed his hat, and bowed.

Weil, neither tall nor short, looked menacing. He had a widow's peak on his wire-stiff almost white-blond hair, and his complexion was so smooth, Wittig couldn't guess his age. He wore a leather apron and resumed cleaning fish. "Beautiful, aren't they?" Weil took a cleaver and whacked off the head of a striped bass. "Took all morning to catch them, but it's worth it when you fry them up."

Wittig saw four more bass on the cleaning table. "I've never fished."

"Too bad." Weil tossed the fish head into a bucket and wiped his hands on the apron. Weil's palms were smeared with blood when he extended his hand to Wittig. He shook it anyway. Weil studied Wittig. "Life is treating you well, Herr Wittig." Weil pulled Wittig's suspenders out and let them snap back into place leaving a smear of blood.

Wittig ran his hand through his thinning hair. This was going to be a long afternoon.

"I understand you want to discuss something with me." One bass continued to flop on the table. "That one still has some life in it." Weil took a mallet, held the fish down, and bashed its head. He hit it again a second time and then chopped its head off. "What is so important?"

Wittig started by explaining why he thought Germans were culturally arrogant. He then talked about life in America. After a few minutes, Weil interrupted. "Excuse me, Herr Wittig, but you seem like one of those 'Germany is my mother, America is my bride' type of German-Americans."

"I'm not sure what you mean."

"Heaven help us and save us. What don't you understand?" Weil took the headless bass and used a boning knife to cut around the fin. "The husband has bonds to both his wife and mother, *ja*?"

Wittig tried to grasp his meaning.

"Yes, but who is more important?" Weil pulled out the fin and the bones attached to it. He threw them into the bucket.

"It depends." Wittig grew defensive.

"Ultimately, you have to choose – your wife or your mother. You can have only one allegiance, Herr Wittig." Weil slit open the fish and yanked out its innards.

"My wife would agree with you."

"Then she's smart. Why are you so against America sending arms to the Allies? I know why I am, but you? I don't understand. The war is making you rich, isn't it?"

"Why do you say that?" Wittig was shocked by the question.

"Herr Beck told me, of course. Don't you think he knows everything about you?"

Wittig wasn't sure what to think.

"For instance, I know about your gains in the stock market," Weil said.

"Beck couldn't know that." Wittig tried to sound indignant. "I give my money to good causes." Wittig did not feel guilty about his investment success, but he understood it was connected to the munitions trade. Giving to German charities made him feel better.

"The only good cause is Germany's. I don't care how you make your money. Let's continue."

Wittig struggled to return to his thoughts. After a long discussion, he finished by saying he was concerned that American society was not ready to accept a political movement based on non-Anglo-Saxon traditions. Although it was legal, the growing German-American political force made Americans uneasy. It was new and misunderstood. "If we can change our approach, Herr Weil, I'm sure the American people might be more sympathetic to our arguments."

"I fear you are being too optimistic, Herr Wittig." Weil finished cleaning and filleting the bass. He reached for the next one. "I suppose you think the Kaiser is arrogant and pompous, too," Weil said.

"I don't want to say anything against the Kaiser."

"Your-mother-or-your-wife dilemma again. You can't say anything about him because he's Germany's leader." Weil reached for his boning knife and wiped it up and down on his leather apron like a barber sharpening his razor.

"That's not the issue. We need to change America's thoughts about us."

"I wish it were that easy. We Germans are hard people to like."

Chapter 24
The Telephone Tap

Lower Manhattan: September 1915

From his look-out spot, a rented office three stories up and across the street from 45 Broadway, Martin spotted Traub walking down the street. If Traub worked Sundays, so did his team. Seven-day weeks had become normal for them. "There he is, right on schedule. His church service ended half an hour ago. I don't understand it. Traub's always so punctual on Sundays, but not during the week."

"Maybe we'll get something this time." Keller crunched into an apple.

After the captain had obtained the warrant legalizing the tap and the police and telephone company connected the wires linking Traub's circuit to their tap, Martin, Keller and Mrs. Bauer, Tunney's sixty-something-year-old assistant who helped them with the phone tap, waited for a breakthrough. But after three weeks, Traub had proved as elusive on the phone as he was on the street. "Is it hot in here?" Martin loosened his collar. If they didn't get results soon, the captain was going to shut down the tap.

"Don't worry, Gil. If this doesn't work, we've got plenty of other options to get that fat pig. I think we should consider using one now." Keller swung an imaginary bat against a lampshade.

"Calm down, Paul. He's the criminal." Martin turned to Mrs. Bauer. "Get ready, dear. I think Mr. Traub should be in his office by now." Martin had to repeat himself to make sure Mrs. Bauer heard him.

With surprising efficiency, Mrs. Bauer connected switches,

cranked something Martin didn't understand, and dialed some numbers. We're ready." She adjusted her thick glasses. A few minutes later, Traub's phone rang, and Mrs. Bauer adjusted the equipment. "There's a call, Detective."

Keller slid his chair over to the telephone receiver so he could listen and translate if necessary. "That's Traub. I can recognize his squeaky voice anywhere." He grabbed his notepad and a pencil and transcribed the call. When he finished, Keller broke the pencil in two. "Shit. I hate that voice. I can't make any sense of it. He's using the same gibberish code he's been using for weeks – just like Meyerhoff said he would. We'll never figure this out."

"All it takes is one call." Martin walked to the window and stared at the street. "But we need it soon."

"This is like catching smoke with a bear-trap," Keller threw the broken pencil to the floor.

"Excuse me, Detective," Mrs. Bauer said, "Another call is coming through."

Martin jumped up when Mrs. Bauer announced the call. Keller went to the receiver to listen. He began to write. When the call ended, Keller scratched his head. "That was strange."

"What was?" Martin asked.

Keller described the call. "All in German, but it wasn't in code – somebody demanded money from Traub. He was angry. That's for sure, but there was something else." Keller closed his eyes. "That's it." He jumped up and fought to keep his balance. "Loss of control. The way he hung up. He just ended it. That's not like him. He's always a good talker – confident and in command. But he wasn't during this call."

"Maybe our friend has a weakness after all."

Chapter 25
We've Got a Problem

Milton Point, New York: September 1915

Weil had just started to clean another bass when Wittig heard a lone voice come from the woods. "Herr Weil?"

Weil answered in English. "Here. On the *Lorelei.* Who is it?" Weil stopped cleaning the bass but kept the boning knife in his hand.

"Nicholas Dallmann. From the German-American League." A raspy voice. "You remember me, don't you?"

Weil responded in German. "*Ja.*" He reached for a Mauser rifle near the steering wheel and studied the area. Convinced Dallmann was alone, he put down the rifle, cupped his hands around his mouth, and shouted, "Come aboard." Weil turned to Wittig and said, "Don't say anything. This shouldn't be long."

Still focusing on the Mauser, Wittig nodded and sat down on the far corner of the *Lorelei.*

Dallmann was panting and sweating hard when he came aboard. His hair hung in wet strings across his face, and his clothes were wrinkled and smelled of body odor. He carried a knapsack that looked full. "Water." He placed his hands on his knees and panted.

Weil reached under the cleaning table and tossed Dallmann a canteen. "What's wrong?"

Dallmann drank greedily. He put down the canteen and took several hard breaths. He lifted the canteen and took two more gulps. He looked dizzy. "Any food?"

Weil turned over a wooden crate and stood over him. "Sit there. Tell me what happened."

"I failed."

Wittig wanted to leave. "Maybe it would be better if I –"

"Don't go anywhere." Weil pushed Wittig back onto the gunwale. "You're part of this now." Weil flashed his long boning knife. He turned around and gestured for Dallmann to continue.

Dallmann's stomach made a noise. "Don't you have anything to eat?"

Weil tossed him a half-eaten roll that was on the fish-cleaning table. "What happened?"

Dallmann ate the roll in three bites. "I did as you told me. I went down to see Congressman Alpert."

My God, thought Wittig. *I gave Beck that name.* Wittig swallowed hard.

"Well, I was going to give him that envelope you gave me. I went to the Hotel Monroe just like you told me."

While he listened, Weil grabbed another bass and started to scale it. With the boning knife he started to scrape from the tail to its head in short powerful strokes. "And ..."

"I was about to knock on the door, room 209, like my instructions said, but I heard voices."

"Voices?" With a powerful chop, Weil whacked off the tail and threw it into a bucket with the rest of the fish slop.

"Yes." Dallmann looked squeamish. "That stinks something terrible."

"Stop looking at the fish and tell me what happened."

"I, I got nervous. You told me Congressman Alpert would be alone."

"Should have been." Weil took his flailing knife and slit the fish end to end.

Dallmann looked away. "I didn't know what to do. I thought a moment. I didn't want to make a mistake."

"So what happened?" He hacked out the fish's innards and dumped them in the bucket.

Wittig concentrated on the bucket and hoped to stay inconspicuous.

"I ..." Dallmann stopped in mid-sentence. "Ran."

Weil looked at Wittig. "Are you thinking the same thing I am?"

"A trap?" Wittig asked.

"Had to be."

"They knew I was coming." Dallmann gulped down more water.

"The congressman talked. Must have," Weil said. "Now, we've got a problem. Did anyone see you?"

"Two cops."

Weil placed the fish on its side and made a cut behind the gill cover that ran from top to bottom. A splash of blood landed on Wittig's trousers. He looked for something to clean it off and found an oily rag on the deck. He wiped off the blood, but a stain remained.

"Too bad. How did you get here?" Weil asked.

"I took a train back to New York. That was the plan."

What plan? Wittig began to worry.

"You think those cops could identify you again?"

"Yes." Dallmann had a blank expression.

"Then they can find you?" Weil plunged the knife into the

bass he was cleaning. "Jesus Christ."

"I suppose, but –"

"If they can find you, they can find me." Weil kicked the side of his boat.

"I guess."

"I guess? I guess! Is that all you can say?" Weil circled around the table and moved toward him. Dallmann backed away until he bumped against the back of the boat. He looked like he wanted to jump.

Dallmann looked at Wittig.

Weil slapped Dallmann, then pushed him. Dallmann almost fell in the water. He righted himself and put his hands up to his chest, palms forward. He talked fast. "The cops never saw me last night. I swear. I slept in the woods. I knew you had a boat out here. It's all secluded. I remember the party you had here last year for the German-American League. I hoped you'd be here."

"What did you do with the envelope?" Weil looked Dallmann up and down.

"Got it in my sack."

Weil snatched the sack from the deck and dug into it. He discarded what he didn't want: clothes, a pair of shoes, some papers. When Weil found the envelope, he dropped the sack, ripped open the envelope and counted the cash. Wittig saw a thick wad of bills. "It's all here." Weil folded the money and put it in his pocket.

"You'll help me, won't you, Herr Weil?"

"Of course." Weil turned to go to the cabin.

Wittig started to breathe normally again. He stood and buttoned his coat. Weil saw him and pointed to the gunwale. "Stay."

Wittig noticed Weil pick up something flat and heavy from the cleaning table. Weil moved closer to Dallmann. He pulled his arm back and swung. The cleaver landed in Dallmann's cheek and continued down into his neck. The blow separated his jaw. A chunk of Dallmann's cheek flopped away from the rest of his face. Muscles, tendons, and skin prevented it from falling off. He wailed in panic. Blood splattered onto Wittig's face, temporarily blinding him. Dallmann dropped to his knees. After some effort, Weil pulled out the cleaver and swung again at his head, splitting it. Blood spurted everywhere, and the body flopped to the deck.

Wittig wiped the blood off his face. He pointed to the body. "What the hell? What about his family? Won't someone look for him?"

"No! Now move. It's a good thing for you Beck said you were important."

He was important? Wittig was more startled by what Beck said than the sight of Dallmann's exposed brains.

"Be smart and we'll be fine," Weil bent down and fought hard to retrieve his cleaver buried deep into Dallmann's skull. "Get something heavy so we can sink him."

It took Wittig several minutes to collect enough rocks and get back on board. He fought the urge to flee. *Just run away back to the woods where Dallmann had stood alive and hungry not more than ten minutes ago.* But he couldn't risk getting shot. Besides, his legs were so wobbly he wasn't sure he could run at all. Wittig just sat still and silent as the boat headed into Long Island Sound.

Together, they worked to tether the stones to hold the body down. After fifteen minutes out to sea, Weil said, "This is far enough.

Grab the body." Wittig hurried to Dallmann's feet and needed all his strength to lift the legs. They rested the faceless body on the edge of the boat and pushed it overboard. Wittig stared as it landed in the water and sank. Dallmann's knapsack and contents followed.

"Good riddance. That's the price you pay for being stupid." Weil spit into the water. "Help me clean up this mess. Then wash yourself. Soap's by the wheel."

Wittig obeyed. He could hardly swallow.

When they got back to shore, Weil said, "I'll talk to Beck tomorrow. No way the cops can trace him to you. He handed Wittig the fish he had previously filleted. "Tell your wife we went fishing. She'll be worried. That's why you're later than expected. If she sees any blood, tell her it's fish blood. You helped me clean them. If anyone asks, you never heard of our friend out there." Weil pointed toward the water. Weil handed him the bucket of bloody fish parts. "Get rid of this."

Wittig recoiled in horror. He'd had enough blood and guts for one day. "What do I do with it?" Wittig asked.

"Toss it by those rocks. The crabs will love it."

Wittig walked away. *My God. I'm an accomplice to murder.*

Chapter 26
The New Haven Projectile Company

New Haven, Connecticut: September 1915

In the middle of September, Caarsens took the position as the number two man in Beck's newly formed New Haven Projectile Company. The plans that Beck, Wittig, and he had discussed last summer were becoming a reality. Caarsens now used the name Pieter Knopp. To prevent someone from recognizing him from the widely circulated newspaper picture taken of him during his union organizing work, he had dyed his hair brown and let it sweep across his brow. He also wore glasses and had grown a mustache. To look thinner, he wore clothes that were too large.

In the weeks since Caarsens had started, New Haven Projectile's facilities had grown. Next to the original two-story brick building, one section of the plant was already completed and a second was under construction. The grounds met Caarsens's security concerns. A new six-foot brick wall topped with barbed wire surrounded the complex located outside of town. The only accesses into the plant and offices were the railroad tracks running into the back of the plant and a gravel pathway in front. A guardhouse and gate controlled the entrance.

Caarsens and the head of the company, Karl Bier, worked well together. One of the earliest participants in Germany's sabotage activities in the United States, Bier, a tall red-headed man, was an excellent manager. He was smart enough to give Caarsens leeway, savvy enough to negotiate excellent business deals, and strong enough to run a tight operation. He followed Beck's instructions and took the initiative when opportunities developed.

Bier and he had already produced results. In order to provide technology for Germany, they acquired aeroplane patents from the Wright Company and sent them to Berlin. New Haven Projectile had begun to disrupt industry labor markets. They had hired ten of the best machine designers in the area at higher wages. Caarsens-Knopp was recruiting another five. They drove up local pay scales many legitimate companies in the Northeast could not afford. Every New Haven Projectile worker earned wages at least five percent more than the competitive rate. Bier had received complaints from the other manufacturers. His answer was always the same: "It's a competitive market. I can afford to pay these wages. I'm sorry if you can't, but I need these men."

Higher wages had sparked a three-week strike at Camden Iron Works of New Jersey. Camden settled, but Bier predicted that it would go bankrupt. If it did, Caarsens told Beck they should buy Camden Iron for pennies on the dollar and start a second New Haven Projectile-type plant. He was monitoring the situation.

At a cost of $417,550, Bier was about to sign an order for 534 hydraulic presses for making shells. Bier had done such a good job disguising the deal that he was certain the company thought it was selling to an English-based U.S. company.

Their biggest disappointment was their failure to buy the Union Metallic Cartridge plant. Bier had been outbid. On the train back to Connecticut after negotiations ended, he told Caarsens, "I can only pay so much. If someone wants to pay the crown jewels, I'll let him. He'll go under soon. We win either way."

Caarsens-Knopp was close to completing a deal with the Aetna Powder Company, one of the largest producers of explosives in America. He offered to buy its next four-month output, almost one million pounds, and planned to resell it to Spain.

At the end of October, Bier and Caarsens had their first argument when Felix Beck started to interfere with New Haven Projectile's operations. He ordered them to corner the wool market.

"What does wool have to do with projectiles?" Caarsens reasoned.

"Think beyond munitions," Beck said. "If we can create a wool monopoly, imagine the possibilities."

Bier supported Beck.

"But it will cost too much," Caarsens said.

"If we can corner the market, we should. I have got the financing to support the effort and have valuable sources that will give us a negotiating edge," Beck said.

"Don't forget, it will hinder our other operations," Caarsens stressed.

"You're wrong." Bier looked sharply at Caarsens.

"Worst of all, it will expose us to scrutiny and unnecessary risk. We are doing well. We don't want government people sniffing around. Our success depends on staying inconspicuous."

Caarsens lost the argument. For six weeks, Bier traveled across North America and contacted every supplier possible. Because Beck somehow knew the timing, delivery points, and buyers of all wool shipped into New York, New Haven Projectile was able to move faster and outbid other buyers. Twice, when shippers did not agree to sell to Bier, their cargo disappeared after it reached New York's docks. Wool suppliers soon learned that New Haven Projectile provided the safest deals and best prices. By the beginning of December, Bier controlled nearly all of the U.S. wool market and prices rose fifteen percent.

It was early December, and New Haven Projectile had started to construct a new warehouse to store the wool. Bier wanted to insure the inventory. Once they did, Beck suggested that an accidental fire might be a profitable way to dispose of it. The first indication of a problem occurred when no company would insure them. New Haven Projectile's stockpile of wool continued to grow.

As Caarsens worried what to do with the wool he could no longer store, he looked out his second-floor office window and saw a small, vaguely familiar figure enter the front gate. The apathetic guard hardly noticed the man. Caarsens would sack the guard tomorrow. As the man walked past the front gate, Caarsens couldn't believe it was his old enemy. He looked closer and was sure he was right. His problems were about to get worse.

~

Caarsens remembered every detail about the man, Major Percy Westerly of the Royal Westminster Fusiliers, who was now walking toward the office building. Westerly had weak shoulders, a bullet-shaped head, and turned-up thick, black eyebrows. Scars across his face gave him a permanent sneer. Dressed as a civilian, he was rounder and grayer than when Caarsens last confronted him. *Blerrie hell. What was he doing at the New Haven Projectile Company?*

Caarsens recalled their confrontation fifteen years ago as if it was yesterday. He had been riding with Christiaan De Wet's commando, the most successful Boer guerrilla unit in the Orange

Free State. They captured trains at will and forced thousands of British soldiers to chase them. De Wet further infuriated the British when he thanked them politely for re-supplying his men as they unloaded their spoils.

De Wet's successes had forced the British to change tactics. The war became harder for the Boers and successes fewer. Casualties mounted, and food became scarce. Their numbers dwindled while British forces multiplied. Their horses tired; the British replaced theirs with fresh ones. The men worried about their families. Atrocities mounted, and the war became a malignant brawl.

The Boers' biggest advantages were the veldt's open space and their knowledge of the land. To counter this, the British carved the land into smaller and smaller sectors using barbed wire and fortified blockhouses. Each new blockhouse reduced the open space. Once a sector was small enough, roving British cavalry attacked the commandos and drove them into merciless crossfires. De Wet's options shrunk daily.

Finally, De Wet's commando unit was cut off and trapped. Surrender was out of the question. Boer prisoners were routinely tortured, sometimes maimed, and often shot. Danie knew that if they could break through the barbed wire and avoid the blockhouses, they could outride the British encirclement. He devised a bold but risky escape plan and volunteered to lead it. De Wet accepted, with misgivings.

De Wet's men rounded up the cattle in the area. Danie rode ahead, dismounted, and cut through a section of the barbed wire. Then, the Boers shot their Mausers in the air and drove the panicked cattle toward Danie's opening. The cattle stampeded toward him followed by De Wet's men. The British were in close pursuit.

As the cattle charged, Danie's horse bolted before he could remount. The Boers rode past him and tried to scoop him up but couldn't. Danie dodged and shifted to avoid being trampled. A bullet nicked him in the leg, and he fell as the last Boer commando streaked by him. De Wet's men drove the cattle straight at a British unit that had been set up to block their escape and scattered them. Danie cheered as his friends galloped to safety.

A British major rode up and signaled most of his men to pursue the Boers. Injured and choking from dust, Danie looked up. The major dismounted and ground his boot into Danie's wound. Two British soldiers threw Danie over a horse and took him to their camp, where they tied him to a wooden chair in a large tent. The British major entered, put his foot on Danie's chest, and pushed him over. "My name is Major Westerly, and you are going to tell me everything you know." A Boer collaborator translated, but Danie did not reveal he understood English.

A British sergeant sat him up, and Westerly punched him in the gut. He kept asking, "Where is De Wet?" Danie cursed him in his native tongue. Another punch. Silence. The major lit a cigar and ground it into Danie's arm again and again. He tried to ignore the pain. More beatings, but Danie said nothing. The major gestured to the sergeant, who struck Danie in the head with the butt of a rifle. He passed out.

When he awoke, Danie discovered one eye was swollen shut. Rope bound his legs together so tightly they had begun to swell. His untreated wound ached. The sergeant pulled back each of his little fingers until they broke. Then they dragged him to a tent pole, positioned him four feet in front of it, and forced him to stand on his tiptoes and lean toward the pole so he had to support the weight of his body on his undamaged fingers. His broken fingers dangled. The major repeated, “Where is De Wet’s camp?” Danie shook his head. The sergeant said, “He can’t take this for long.”

Danie maintained the position for several minutes until his breathing began to labor. Sweat dripped off his brow. Seeking temporary relief, he tried to shift his position, but the sergeant forced him back. Fatigue began to overpower his defiance. He gritted his teeth. Cramps tore through his insides. He became disoriented and felt strong spasms contort his leg and arm muscles. Refusing to surrender to the pain, Danie faltered but maintained the position. His body begged for relief until he slipped into delirium. Then something poked him in the groin, jerking him awake. He refused to yield. Nearing the limits of endurance, he saw the sergeant reach for a rattan cane and say, “Don’t pass out yet.”

The sergeant rapped the cane across the back of Danie’s thighs. He collapsed, unconscious. Someone slapped him awake. Two soldiers picked him up and forced him back into the position. Danie cursed them as they laughed. He fell after nineteen seconds.

Danie regained consciousness when they threw a bucket of horse piss in his face. They tied his legs and arms to the front legs of two chairs lashed together back to back. Stripped naked, he felt like an inverted “V”. The backs of the chairs pressed into his stomach, and he struggled to breathe. Major Westerly pounded a baton against his hand and leered. The translator interpreted. “Things will only get worse. He says he can continue this longer than you can take it.” With the baton, the major struck Danie across his buttocks. Numbing pain spread through his body. After several swings, something rammed into his rectum. He passed out again.

Danie woke when someone rushed into the tent and said, "Major, come quick. I think we have a lead on De Wet." The next thing Danie remembered was riding in a wagon. He had no way of knowing how long it had been since his capture. The wagon bounced across the rutted trail. Each bump intensified his pain. He had to lie on his side to tolerate it. His stomach ached both from Westerly's beatings and lack of food. He was desperately thirsty and tried to lick moisture from his vomit and sweat-soaked shirt. Through one eye, Danie saw blistered burn marks up and down his arms. The bullet wound in his leg throbbed, and blood leaked from his anus.

Two drivers were talking. "I've never seen anyone take that kind of punishment."

"Should have shot him."

"Wait 'til we get to Bloemfontein. He'll talk then."

"Or die. I hate those –" A rifle shot silenced the driver. Danie heard him tumble out of the wagon, which rolled to a stop. Another shot; the second man went down. Danie heard many horses approach fast. Gunfire. Shouting. Rifles dropped to the ground. Boer orders. Pleading English voices. Three pistol shots. Silence. Someone shouted in his local Dutch tongue. "Caarsens, you all right?" Smits, his friend. "Can you ride?"

~

Fighting back his anger, Caarsens calmed himself and went downstairs where Westerly was standing in the waiting area. Westerly addressed their head secretary, Mrs. Riley, whom Bier had hired despite protests that she was a woman. "My good lady, I humbly request a meeting with your company's president, Karl Bier." Despite words to the contrary, Westerly's words sounded like a demand.

"Do you have an appointment?" Mean as a hippo and about as wide, Mrs. Riley stood and placed her hands on her hips. She had been a woman's prison guard before starting at New Haven Projectile.

"No. Would you be most kind to inform me when he is available?" Another demand.

"He's busy. When he's free, I'll tell him that you're here. Please sit, Mister ...?"

"Oh, I apologize. Most rude of me. Colonel Westerly, Percy Westerly. I work in His Majesty's Quartermaster Corps." He oozed condescension and lit a cigarette from an expensive silver lighter.

When Caarsens heard that Westerly was responsible for supplies, he was sure his visit related to wool. The cigarette sparked memories. Caarsens rubbed his arm. He gambled that Westerly would not recognize him as he walked toward Mrs. Riley and told her to detain Westerly.

Westerly paced and ignored Caarsens. "I beg your pardon, but is Mr. Bier free now?" He asked a third time.

Caarsens coughed and said in a wheezy voice, "Just a few moments, sir." He headed to Bier's office.

Westerly started to follow, but Mrs. Riley blocked his way and pointed to the chair. "Sit down."

The British colonel complied.

Caarsens looked back. *I knew you wouldn't stand up to someone stronger*. In Bier's private office, he told him that Westerly could be a problem. They talked for several minutes, then Bier sent word to Mrs. Riley to allow Westerly to pass.

Westerly marched into Bier's office. "Mr. Bier?"

"Yes." Bier stood up.

"My name is Colonel Percy Westerly. I am in charge of securing wool supplies needed by the British army."

Caarsens stayed in the background and, careful not to show his face, looked down and pretended to take notes.

"I have been looking for you." Westerly leaned forward onto Bier's desk.

"I do not tolerate rudeness." Bier put his two fists on his desk and leaned so close to Westerly that their foreheads almost collided. "Why don't you sit down and state your business."

Westerly pulled up a chair. "I understand, sir, that your company controls a large supply of wool."

"What does that have to do with New Haven Projectile?"

"Our Canadian supplier is having difficulty obtaining it. If it cannot purchase sufficient quantities, it will be unable to fulfill its contract to supply us winter uniforms. I will not let that happen."

"I make projectiles. Your problem has nothing to do with me."

"Do you deny that you are purchasing every bale of wool between New Orleans and Montreal?"

"I don't know what you're talking about." Bier stared at Westerly. "What proof do you have, sir?"

The muscle over Westerly's eye twitched.

"Mr. Westerly, why don't you leave?" Bier said.

"You have not heard the last from me. My solicitors are

Cronin, Withgate, and –"

Bier stood up and raised his voice. "We have done nothing illegal. If you don't leave peacefully, I'll evict you myself." Bier moved away from his desk.

Westerly scurried off.

After he was gone, Caarsens said, "I told you something like that would happen. Cornering the wool market brings too much attention to us. This problem will not go away."

"I agree. This Westerly fellow is not the first person to complain about our wool business. I think it is time we leave it. I'll let Beck's lawyer sort it out and make sure Westerly's Canadian company gets its wool. Unless we do, more trouble will follow. I'll talk to Beck tomorrow." Bier reached into his desk, pulled out a bottle, and poured two whiskeys. "How should we handle Westerly?"

"He's a separate issue." Caarsens downed the whiskey in one shot. "Let me handle him."

"Don't leave a mess." Bier drained his glass.

"I never do."

Chapter 27
A Capitalist Caesar

Morgan Bank, Manhattan: October 1915

Wittig headed up the wooden stairs from his office to his interview with Robert Swanson, the second most powerful man in Morgan Bank. He was pleased. Despite his personal problems surrounding the war in Europe, his career had flourished, and he was relieved nothing had happened following the Milton Point incident. His fear that police would arrive at his home or office had lessened, but the thought of wearing handcuffs and living in a prison cell without seeing his family haunted him daily.

He pushed his fears away and prepared mentally for the interview. If America's munitions industry had a beating heart, it rested in the body of Robert Swanson. In just a few months, he had become the subject of more gossip and speculation than anyone else in Morgan Bank. The former head of the Midwest Match Company and a commodity speculator in the Chicago trading pits, Swanson had been selected to coordinate all Allied purchases of U.S. materiel. Rumor had it that President Wilson approved Swanson himself. People who worked with him said Swanson combined the bravado of Bluebeard, the cunning of Cochise, and the coolness under pressure of General Grant. He possessed an accountant's compulsive obsession for detail and could count coins faster than Midas. If provoked, he had a more extensive vocabulary than a British seaman.

In his position at Morgan Bank, Swanson had become a capitalist Caesar. U.S. industry had become his empire. His staff had grown to more than one hundred people since he had started at Morgan last January. So important were his duties that Morgan Bank had to post guards around the building. If Swanson wanted something or someone to work for him, all he had to do was ask.

Wittig straightened his tie and brushed his suit. He approached Swanson's secretary, who glanced at the clock on the wall. Each tick reminded Wittig of a cash register ringing up another sale. The secretary noted something in his log and, without looking at Wittig, pointed to a bare wooden bench. "Right on time, Mr. Wittig. Please sit. Mr. Swanson will be with you shortly."

Wittig looked around. The walls were barren except for the clock and twelve monthly calendars – October 1915 through September 1916. Each was as big as a Red Cross poster and filled with an intricate pattern of neat marks, letters, and numbers, all written by a precise and firm hand. The secretary put down his pen and asked Wittig, "Do you know what Mr. Swanson's employees are called?"

"Of course, slaves of Swanson. I'm not afraid of hard work."

The secretary laughed and checked the clock. "Mr. Swanson expects everyone to fit seventy minutes of work into each hour. He will see you now. There." He pointed to the closed door in the corner.

Wittig knocked and entered when he heard a voice from inside. Like a general studying battle plans, Robert Swanson was leaning over, his fists resting on his desk. Not sure what to do, Wittig remained standing. Swanson sat down and began to process paper with Ford production-line efficiency: pick up paper, read it, make notes, render a decision, stamp paper, sort it into its proper pile, straighten and organize piles. Repeat process. No wasted movement.

Swanson's head never looked up. His large hands seemed too big for his slender arms.

"Well, sit," he said.

Swanson continued to review papers until he crumpled one and threw it on the floor. "Can't he do anything right?" He pulled out a memo book and started to write. "Note to self – fire Livingston." He slid his chair back. "Yes?"

"Hello, Mr. Swanson. I'm John Wittig. I have –"

"I know who you are, Mr. Wittig. I have a schedule to keep. Time's a-wasting. Let's get started."

"Fine."

"Mr. Morgan recommended you himself, but I have a question, Mr. Wittig – I'm sure you know what we do here. Doesn't that bother a pacifist like you?"

"Yes, but I'm a businessman first. I can separate my feelings about my work and the war."

"Good." Swanson rubbed his ear.

"You, Mr. Swanson, are doing the most important business deals in the country. I want to be part of it." Wittig paused to swallow. He did not reveal that Felix Beck insisted he apply for the position. "And I'm sure my career will –"

"I like ambitious men. I understand you have a degree from Columbia University."

"That's correct."

"Excellent school. You're mine starting tomorrow."

"Very good, sir."

"Let me tell you about our operation." He fired facts and figures at the rate of a machine gun. Seventy minutes squeezed into one hour was not an exaggeration. "You can start dealing with loans we make for new factories. Your first assignment will be a new plant Bethlehem Steel wants to build in Easton, Pennsylvania. Here is the file." The file was thick and orderly. The words "Strictly Confidential" were printed in large letters on the cover.

Wittig thought, *Here's an irony. I'll be helping do the very thing Beck and Nora want to stop.*

~

Over the next few weeks, Wittig learned much about Swanson's operation. He was impressed by its size and complexity. The purchasing operation handled everything from artillery pieces to livestock to wheel chairs. The contracts amounted to almost $10 million a day. Wittig calculated that Swanson's group handled contracts that had the same value as the world's total economic output at the turn of the century.

Swanson's group was immensely profitable. It earned a one percent commission on its purchases, which increased Morgan Bank's coffers by about half a million dollars a week. Wittig understood the importance of the information he possessed. Each night on the train home, he thought, *I hope Beck never learns the exact details and scope of Swanson's operation, because I won't tell him everything.* He woke up that night with the unnerving idea that Beck might already know.

Chapter 28
Edith Cavell

Morgan Bank: October 1915

Wittig's heart jumped when he saw the headline: "Edith Cavell Executed." He had lived with an infantryman's sense of foreboding and acceptance for months. Now, the fragile balance he had achieved between work and his personal life was shattered. The newspaper article stated that the British nurse was shot as a spy. Germany had arrested her in her Belgium hospital, extracted a confession, and tried her. They claimed that, while she trained Belgian nurses, she had helped Allied soldiers escape to neutral Holland. Yesterday, she was killed. Wittig imagined the firing squad's bullets ripping into her.

When he arrived at work, news of her death had already spread around Morgan Bank like an infectious disease. Everyone had sought leniency for her, but Germany ignored the entreaties of the American and Spanish ministers to Belgium.

Wittig's colleagues delivered the most vicious verbal attacks on Germany and him since the sinking of the *Lusitania*. This time, the attacks were more personal and hateful because there was no ambiguity about Germany's actions. Everyone could sympathize with a nurse. The comments struck Wittig like verbal bullets and hurt more because he himself believed the shooting was barbaric. Wittig could not forgive Germany for an act that shattered his world. A firing squad? Germany might as well have shot the Virgin Mary for all the uproar it created. He began to question his support to

Germany, which at the moment he considered immoral. Maybe they *had* committed all those atrocities in Belgium the Allies had claimed at the start of the war.

It was almost midnight when Wittig opened the door to his house. He fought a headache that felt like a cannon ball rolling around inside his skull. He had a bit more than seven hours before he had to leave to catch the morning train. Everyone was asleep. With his last reserve of energy, he changed into his nightclothes, went to the living room, reached under the couch for his blanket, and fell asleep.

Chapter 29
So Who's the Woman?

Lower Manhattan: November 1915

After the "I need money" call, Martin convinced Tunney to continue the telephone taps. Still, more weeks went by with no results. Keller checked the morgue daily to see if any unclaimed stiff had a connection to Traub, but the dead remained silent. The days became shorter and colder.

It was another routine, boring Friday. Martin paced, wondering what he'd do after Tunney lost all patience and fired him. Keller read old sports sections and relived the World Series play by play. Mrs. Bauer was busy knitting an ugly sweater with colors that clashed.

Traub's fourth call that afternoon produced the same useless results as the first three. But on the fifth call, Martin watched Keller turn energetic. He transcribed the message with determined speed and handed his notes to Martin with a grin from ear to ear. "We're back in the game. Some woman just called, and called him *Eugene*."

"Only someone who knows him well would do that," commented Mrs. Bauer, as she disconnected the tap.

"They arranged to meet tomorrow – for *Spanferkel* and asparagus."

Martin wrinkled up his face. Suckling pig did not agree with him. "That's all we know? We'll have to follow him to that meeting. Any idea what restaurant that might be?"

Mrs. Bauer cut in. "Luchow's has it. It's the best in the city."

"He wouldn't go there," Martin said. "Too many people. There'd be a chance someone would see him. No, this is a meeting where he doesn't want to be seen. Any other ideas, Paul?"

"I'll ask around, but just in case, I'll stake it out myself."

~

The next morning, Traub arrived at his office at 7:55 a.m. From his stake-out across the street, Martin watched the entrance of Traub's building while Keller briefed his two shadow teams. At 9:10, Traub left 45 Broadway. Martin saw the first team encounter problems immediately. Ten paces from the door, Traub tripped over a newspaper boy. He shouted something and pushed the boy to the ground. The urchin got to his knees and wiped his face with his sleeve. One of the shadows went over to him and didn't see where Traub had gone. The boy pointed in Traub's direction, picked up his papers, and went the same way. Martin shook his head, and Keller left for Luchow's.

Six hours later, Keller returned, and the shadow teams reported back to Martin that Traub had evaded them. Martin slumped down in his chair and scowled; Keller kicked the wall and hurt his toe; Mrs. Bauer's knitting needles picked up speed. After several silent minutes, she got up to prepare tea.

"We did our best. I have to speak to the captain," Martin said. "He'll demand changes." Martin walked to Battery Park, where he bought a pack of cigarettes and smoked four of them one after the other. The tobacco calmed him. No longer able to postpone his fate, he finally returned to headquarters. It was the longest walk of his life.

~

When Martin walked into Tunney's office, the captain did not acknowledge his presence. He just tapped his fingers on his desk. After several seconds that seemed much longer, Tunney spoke. "I understand you lost him." His voice rumbled like a French 75 mm artillery piece.

"Yes, sir."

"You have no idea who Traub met, do you?"

"No, sir."

"Your shadow teams failed – mine didn't." Tunney went to the door and called down the hallway. "Shannon, would you come here?" She walked in carrying a small bag.

"You had red hair last week," Martin blurted, taken off-guard.

"Yes I did, Sergeant." Shannon pulled off a short brown wig, removed her hairpins, and shook out her glorious Titian-red hair.

"But I didn't see you near Traub," Martin said, trying to recover his composure.

"Remember that raggedy-looking newspaper boy with a cap outside 45 Broadway this morning? That was me."

Angry at himself again, this time for missing the significance of the event, Martin said tensely, "But I never expected you to be the shadow."

"That's the point," Tunney said. "No one expects a woman. That's one reason she's so good. Vassar with honors is another. Plus, she's tougher than a cheap steak. Shannon, tell Sergeant Martin what happened today."

"I pretended to be the newspaper boy to get in Traub's way. I wanted to judge his mood," she continued, all business. "He was jittery. Unusual. He wouldn't have pushed me if he'd been more in control. I knew right away that you were right about how important this meeting was. I had to get a good look at him from the start, to see how he was dressed and smelled. He wasn't dressed for a romantic meeting. This helped me eliminate a hotel room for his rendezvous. He also uses some expensive fragrance, French soap or maybe cologne. Men do little things a woman notices, Sergeant."

"She learned more about our friend in five seconds than you and your men learned all day," Tunney interjected, rubbing salt into the wound.

Martin kept his tongue, thoroughly irritated but also intrigued. What was really going on here? Did the captain use her to upstage him for a purpose? If so, did he really need to use a secretary to do it? What was his game?

"Uncle Thomas's man, Detective Griggs, helped," Shannon continued. "He drove the taxi I used to get around, and I changed disguises in the back seat."

"One of my teams lost him at the ferry to Communipaw. Why didn't you have any trouble shadowing him?" Martin asked.

"Traub had to stay in Manhattan. If he took the ferry, he couldn't get back in time for his lunch so I stayed in the taxi."

"Wasn't that a risk?" Martin questioned, partly as a challenge, partly from genuine interest.

"I had to go with my gut, and my gut said he'd stay in Manhattan. Besides, I'd asked around and knew there weren't any good German restaurants near Communipaw, so Griggs and I waited for him to leave the ferry station, then followed him to Macy's."

"My other team lost him there," Martin admitted, his admiration growing in spite of himself. "Why didn't you?"

“We waited outside, guessing he would leave through the delivery entrance, and then followed him to Herald Square. He waited on a bench and checked his watch a few times.”

“Was he nervous or just passing time?” Martin jumped in, realizing too late he had abandoned all appearance of indifference.

“Both. He waited a bit, then took the northbound El. Mr. Griggs and I followed in our taxi. Traub got off near 42nd Street, and I left the taxi and shadowed him on foot. He tried the usual methods – crossing and re-crossing streets. Doubling back. Ducking into stores. He has one quality we can rely on: he’s never late. It was getting close to midday. I figured he had to be at the restaurant soon. He lost me when he walked into Grand Central, but I was sure he was headed to Yorkville. Other than Luchow’s, which Detective Keller covered, it has the best German restaurants.”

“But, how did you cover Yorkville by yourself? You’d lost him.”

“Yes, but only three restaurants in Yorkville serve the dish that Traub mentioned. I visited them all last night.”

At this, Tunney shot Shannon a smile, eliciting a blush Martin would not have expected. “Well,” she covered, picking up the thread again, “as I said, Traub lost us at Grand Central. However, it was 12:35, so he didn’t have much time. I changed wigs, put on some jewelry and a suitable coat while Detective Griggs drove me to the first restaurant, the Bavarian House at 86th Street. Traub wasn’t there, but he was at the second restaurant. He was talking to an attractive woman, maybe forty years old.”

Shannon paused to take a deep breath. “This was the most dangerous part for me. Traub had situated himself so he could observe the entire restaurant. Luckily, it was getting late and it wasn't too crowded, so I used my charm with the maitre d' to get a small table next to them in a quiet corner. I was sure Traub wouldn't recognize me in disguise. I sat with the woman behind me and Traub looking at the back of my head. They spoke pretty low, but I could understand them."

Martin gave her a quizzical look. "So, they didn't speak –"

"German?" Shannon interjected. "Yes, they did. I majored in languages and classical studies in college."

"So," Martin asked, eager to get to the punch, "who's the woman?"

"The mother of Traub's nephew. His brother has an illegitimate son."

Chapter 30
Even the Score

Police Headquarters: November 1915

Shannon Connolly's words hung in the air of Captain Tunney's office like poison gas over no-man's land. "Did I understand you right?" Martin rubbed his eyes. "Illegitimate son?"

"Yes."

"How in God's name?"

She repeated what she had overheard. "The woman – Traub called her Renate – kept asking what was more important than blood. That was when she mentioned her son, Rupert. Traub called him a lazy bastard and said he never approved of his brother's relationship with her. Renate asked why he didn't pay Rupert what he owed him. Traub said Rupert had not finished his work. He owed him nothing and refused to help him anymore.

"She asked why he had beat Rupert up. Traub said Rupert was lucky that's all he did. When Renate said the boy was in trouble, Traub offered to send him back to Germany, where he could be more useful fighting in the trenches. Traub didn't care if Rupert died, even if he was the last in the Traub bloodline."

"Excuse me for interrupting, Miss Connolly, but do you think Traub had any suspicions you were there?" Martin admitted to himself he was amazed by what she had learned.

"No. Not at all. I'm sure he believed he'd lost all the shadows. He felt safe in the restaurant – as safe as he ever does. Besides, he never would have expected me; I'm a woman. I had gotten what I needed and left. I waited for Renate to leave and shadowed her to a Brownstone apartment on 83rd Street. I slipped inside the doors to the foyer and took a look at the post box – R. Kleinmann. I'm going to visit her tomorrow to find out more." Miss Connolly's determination was unmistakable.

Captain Tunney applauded. "Excellent." He turned to Martin. "Sergeant, I think we've got our hands around Mr. Traub's testicles. And we're going to squeeze."

The next day, Martin and an uncharacteristically nervous Keller followed Shannon, who rode in Griggs's taxi, to the brownstone at 244 East 83th Street. They parked around the corner and met the postman, who confirmed that Renate Kleinmann was a tenant, and that her son Rupert also lived there. He described the young man – scrawny, dirty, and a drunk.

Keller explained that Shannon had her meeting with Renate all worked out. She'd pretend to be a woman whose fiancé was cheating on her. Shannon would enter the building with feigned righteous anger and demand justice.

"Don't worry about her," Griggs said as they walked to a nearby café. "She's good. She can take care of herself."

Thirty-five minutes later, Keller started to tap his spoon against his coffee cup. "She's taking too long. We should go in."

"The building looks peaceful," Martin said, trying not to worry. He didn't like putting women, even one as independent as Shannon, in harm's way. "We'll stay."

A few minutes later, Shannon met them at the café. "I know where Rupert likes to drink."

~

Following Shannon's information, Martin and Keller found Kleinmann at the Bridge Café on Water Street, just under the Brooklyn Bridge. Rumored to be haunted by ghosts of pirates who used to drink there, its wooden floors soaked up spilled beer, and the dirty windows filtered the sunlight into gray streaks. The few men at the bar looked like they'd been there longer than the stick-wood furniture. Martin pulled his shirt half-way out and mussed his hair.

"There." Martin pointed to the skinny young man sitting alone at the corner of the bar. "Exactly where Shannon said he'd be." A quick glance convinced Martin that none of Traub's men were nearby. Sensing victory, Keller sat next to Kleinmann while Martin lingered close behind. Pretending to recognize a fellow German, Keller bought him a beer.

"Why don't you leave me alone? I got enough troubles." Kleinmann sounded funny, because his nose was bashed in.

Martin joined their conversation a few minutes later.

Kleinmann's lazy-eye drifted to him. "Who are you? His valet? I'll drink your whiskey, but I don't got to talk to you."

"Just being friendly," Martin said.

"I don't trust nobody. Just this." Kleinmann raised his glass. "I ain't too sociable these days. See this?" Kleinmann pointed to his crushed nose. "I got a pug's nose now. Can't hardly breathe."

"Who did that to you?" Martin guessed the answer.

"Some ape. Bald like a cue ball. Ruined my life. Hit me when all I was trying to do was collect what's mine. Do you know how much that was?"

Martin and Keller shook their heads.

"Five dollars and fourteen cents. Can you believe it?" Kleinmann stretched out both hands, palms up. "He squashes my nose for five dollars and fourteen cents. But I got him back."

"How?" Martin liked the thought that a weakling like Kleinmann could do anything to Traub.

"I damn near shot his ear off, that's what I done."

"When?"

"I don't remember too good. Early June, I think."

Just about the time he saw Traub with Meyerhoff after the rally, Martin recalled.

"That ape. Thinks I was scared after he beat me up. When I get out of the hospital, tape all over my nose, I go into his office and shoot him. I wanted to kill him, but I guess my aim weren't too good."

They continued drinking for another twenty minutes. Kleinmann excused himself to piss. When he returned, Kleinmann asked, "Why you so interested in Traub?"

Martin had been waiting for the question. "He killed a friend of ours. We want to even the score."

"That's one mean bastard." Through bloodshot eyes, Kleinmann looked first at Keller, then at Martin. "I'd do anything to see that ape roasted in a pit."

"What about putting him in jail?" Martin asked.

"Dead would be better. Who are you guys?"

Martin flashed his shield. "Police officers."

"Great. You guys going to put the squeeze on me now?"

"What can you tell us about his business?" Keller asked.

"Get me another beer and settle my bill with the bartender." Kleinmann licked his lips. "I got an interesting story for you."

Chapter 31
Henry Ford

Manhattan: November 1915

"Ford to Captain Peace Crusade in Chartered Liner"

John Wittig read the November 24th story with the same concentration as a colonel studying progress reports from the front. The newspaper described how Henry Ford, America's most successful businessman, intended to promote peace negotiations with the help of neutral countries: "I've chartered a ship, and some of us are going to Europe," he had said. "I've assembled the biggest and most influential peace advocates in the country. Men sitting around a table, not men dying in a trench, will finally settle the differences. We're going to try to get the boys out of the trenches before Christmas."

Wittig had followed Ford's newspaper writings for a long time. Ford's anti-military stance particularly appealed to Wittig even if his anti-Semitic view did not. As early as 1901, Ford had warned America about the danger of its growing militarism. "It is the duty of Congress to keep the country out of a war for which there is no reason," he had editorialized.

Since the war broke out, Ford had written essays and placed ads in newspapers supporting the anti-war movement. He had challenged traditional patriotic arguments. "Patriotism does not consist of merely dying for one's country. I believe it consists more in living for the benefits of the whole world, of giving others a chance to live for themselves, their country, and the world" – sentiments Wittig shared.

The prospect of Ford's peace campaign excited Wittig. For the first time since the spring, he felt relief. Could this be the solution he had prayed for? Stop the war and end all his troubles. The stakes were high. Like a gambler going all in with a questionable hand, Wittig committed his hopes on the chance Ford's peace mission would succeed.

Wittig wanted to be part of it. But his superior, Robert Swanson, said, "Why are you even asking?" He was willing to quit his job at Morgan to go to Europe with Ford, but his wife, Nora, said he was foolish. The family could not live without his salary. Felix Beck said he was wasting his time and was as crazy as Ford. He agreed to let Wittig go only if he talked to Eugene Traub about the matter. That ended that.

Because he couldn't go, Wittig wanted to know everything he could about the peace mission. It occupied his every free moment. He read all he could. To Wittig's dismay, the American press was skeptical and critical of Ford's mission. Some newspapers accused Ford of hubris. Others questioned the vagueness of his plans. More than one compared him to P.T. Barnum. *The New York World*, a paper that generally supported Ford, wrote that the mission was "an impossible effort to establish an inopportune peace." *The Baltimore Sun* said, "All amateur efforts of altruistic and notoriety-seeking millionaires only make matters worse." A *New York Herald* editorial claimed the trip was "one of the cruelest jokes of the century."

The New York Times raised more serious concerns. The peace settlement that Ford was expected to propose would have allowed Germany to occupy Belgium and northern France, maybe even annex them. To *The Times*, the only acceptable outcome to the war was a full German retreat from the territories it gained both from the 1870-1871 war and this one.

Prominent politicians raised other objections. Teddy Roosevelt was quoted as saying, "Mr. Ford's visit abroad will not be mischievous only because it is ridiculous." Former presidential candidate Alton B. Parker called Ford "a clown strutting on the stage." Former New York Senator Chauncey M. Depew wrote, "In uselessness and absurdity, it will stand without an equal."

Wittig couldn't understand why such a noble and worthy effort was being subjected to such scorn. As the criticism mounted on the newsstands, Wittig's despair grew. He felt every insult to Ford was an attack on him. Every article pierced him like poisoned spears; each one cut into his confidence and infected his morale.

Chapter 32
Vengeance

Grand Central Station, Manhattan: December 1915

After Westerly left New Haven Projectile's office, Caarsens moved fast. He snatched his emergency bag from his office and took a taxi to the train station. The bag contained weapons and changes of clothing. Now, disguised as a white-haired Spanish American War veteran with a moth-eaten campaign hat and a limp, Caarsens sat five rows behind Westerly on the train back to New York. He was sure Westerly would take no notice of him.

After watching Westerly for some time, Caarsens concluded that the ravages of time and the doldrums of paperwork had decayed his senses and made him weak. He was no longer a hardened soldier and showed no sense of danger. During the train ride, Westerly drank something out of a silver flask and ate two sandwiches, a large apple, and some cake. When he wasn't eating, Westerly shuffled through some papers and trimmed his fingernails. He snored for half an hour.

Caarsens decided to make his move at Grand Central Station. For much of the trip, the train rocked and bumped up and down; the rail beds needed repair. Twice, the lights flickered and almost blacked out. Time seemed to crawl, and Caarsens had time to remember his wounds, as his cramped seat gave him pain. Finally, they reached Grand Central in the early evening. Caarsens had his quarry in his sights. Before the train stopped, the old war vet limped past Westerly and moved forward to the door so he could exit first. Caarsens checked back and saw Westerly put on a thick cashmere coat and expensive leather gloves.

Caarsens positioned himself along the platform so he could catch Westerly's attention as he walked by. He pulled the campaign hat low on his brow and fingered some old medals pinned to his coat he had bought in a Brooklyn pawn shop. As Westerly neared, Caarsens approached him. "Pardon me, sir. Can I trouble you?"

Westerly tried to avoid the old vet. He used his brief case to push him away.

"I saw you on the train; I thought I'd ..."

"Get away from me, you vagabond. You reek." Westerly tried to walk past him.

Caarsens grabbed Westerly's coat and pulled him near. He reached into his own coat pocket for the Colt semi-automatic pistol he had taken from the Klansman in Maryland. Through the fabric, he pushed the barrel into Westerly's side.

Westerly jumped when he felt the gun. "What do you want?" The panic in his voice was unmistakable.

"Let's take a walk."

"Who are you?"

"An old friend." Caarsens jabbed the pistol deeper into Westerly's ribs. It felt like he was pushing the gun into butter. "Go."

Other passengers walked by and paid no attention to the old vet and the dapper businessman walking arm in arm.

When they reached the end of the platform, Westerly made a feeble attempt to escape, but Caarsens was fueled by anger and easily restrained him. "Follow me to the restroom. If you make a sound, I'll kill you where you stand," Caarsens said in a hushed voice.

"Why are you doing this?" Westerly's knees buckled.

"Quiet." Caarsens seized him by the arm and almost carried

him to the lower level men's room.

"What have I done to you?" Westerly asked as they walked through the main concourse.

"Satan will answer that."

Westerly tried to break away, but Caarsens tripped him. A police officer noticed the scene and walked over. Caarsens gritted his teeth and said, "If you make a sound, that cop will watch your brains scatter."

"Can I help you, old timer?" The policeman asked.

"My nephew. He's drunk again. Just like his mother. I'm taking him home. I can handle this, officer. Thank you and have a good night."

"Get home safe." The policeman walked away.

Caarsens moved his mouth against Westerly's ear. "Good soldier."

He lifted Westerly to his feet, as it appeared he would have sat there all night. Westerly's legs wobbled. Caarsens hauled him to the men's room. It was dark and smelled like an enlisted men's latrine. As they entered, Westerly lost control of his bladder. "I don't want to die. I –"

Caarsens dragged him into a stall.

"I'm going to be sick."

Caarsens forced his head over the bowl. Dry heaves. Westerly collapsed. Caarsens closed the stall and removed his glasses. He moved his face inches in front of Westerly's. "Do you recognize me? Take a good look, you *rooinek piel,*" he said calling Westerly a redneck dick in his native tongue.

Westerly shook his head. "I don't know you." He blinked his

eyes several times. "Should I?"

Caarsens rolled up his sleeve. "I'm sure you did this to many Boers, but I bet I'm the only one to escape and become wanted for murder." Caarsens stomped on Westerly's leg.

A cry of pain followed. "I don't know who you think I am, but –"

"Liar. *Jou bliksem*!" Caarsens grabbed Westerly's hair and slammed his head into the edge of the porcelain toilet bowl. A deep gash opened and blood dripped onto the urine-stained tiles.

Someone entered the men's room. "You got a problem?"

"No. My friend drank too much." Caarsens covered Westerly's mouth until the man left. "Remember me now?"

Westerly shook his head, but his eyes narrowed.

"I'm going to make this hurt." Caarsens bent Westerly's index finger back. Snap. He broke the middle finger next. When he reached for a third, Westerly spat into his face.

Caarsens laughed in contempt. "You just made this very easy for me."

Westerly's eyes bulged. With a burst of energy that surprised Caarsens, Westerly made a last-ditch effort to get away. Caarsens had to hold him down with all his might, but he was fueled with vengeance brewed from years of hatred. He covered Westerly's mouth with one hand and punched him twice in the gut with the other. Westerly's bowels emptied. Seconds later, the contents of his stomach erupted upward. With no exit, the vomit was trapped. Westerly shook and tried to cough, but Caarsens's grip remained firm. When whiskey-smelling puke escaped through Westerly's nose, Caarsens pinched it tight. Another wave of vomit ran down into

Westerly's lungs. He weakened, convulsed, and started to turn blue. His eyes turned to sightless marbles.

Caarsens patted down his pockets and took Westerly's money and identification. He left him in the stall in his expensive cashmere coat and gloves, covered in his own blood and excrement. The cops would find another dead drunk. They would conclude he had either been in a bar fight or had fallen, drunk, and cracked his head on the crapper. Maybe both. He choked on his own vomit. Somebody had robbed him either before or after he died. Case closed. Too much else to do.

~

The next morning, Caarsens went to the Lutheran Church, where he and Beck exchanged messages. Beck knew that Caarsens was scheduled to be in New York that day. Caarsens opened the Bible in front of his usual seat and took out the folded message. It was a matrix of meaningless numbers and letters. He decoded it.

"Something has developed. Drop everything. Meet me in Washington Square Park at 4 p.m. Most urgent."

Chapter 33
The Good Ship Nutty

Hoboken, New Jersey: December 1915

Wittig woke up early to make sure he'd get to Hoboken in time to see Henry Ford's chartered liner, the *Oscar II,* sail away on its peace mission. Since Ford had arrived in New York City only nine days before, he'd had little time to organize the mission.

Ford's lack of preparation showed. The *Oscar II* sailed with 115 delegates. The list of people disappointed Wittig. No prominent names like William Jennings Bryan or Thomas Edison were on board. According to the papers, about half the delegates were writers, including socialists, suffragettes, and pacifists; the next largest segment consisted of lecturers and workers for causes; the last group included government officials, ministers and teachers. One member intrigued Wittig: William Bullitt, a Philadelphia correspondent whose columns had impressed him. Wittig was upset that Ford was the only businessman on board.

From his early-bird vantage point, Wittig was able to stand close to the *Oscar II.* Behind him, he guessed the crowd numbered well over ten thousand. It was a raw, cold day, more like Norway, where the *Oscar II* was headed, than New Jersey. An argument started near him. Shouts and taunts bounced among pacifists, pro-Allied groups, and German sympathizers. Allied supporters sang "*La Marseillaise*" and "God Save the King." The pro-Germans countered with "*Deutschland Über Alles.*" The pacifists did not sing. Wittig prayed.

The confrontation stopped when the band struck up, *I Didn't Raise My Boy to Be a Soldier*. The crowd applauded when Ford appeared. He seemed excited and bowed many times. To Wittig, Ford's broad smile seemed cherubic.

Before he boarded the ship, Ford talked to reporters. Wittig was close enough to hear.

"Mr. Ford, do you have a last word for the public?"

"Tell the people to cry peace."

"What if the expedition fails?"

"I'll start another." As Ford turned toward the gangplank, a prankster broke through the phalanx of reporters and handed Ford a cage containing two squirrels. Attached to the cage was a large sign that read, "To the Good Ship Nutty." One of Ford's assistants wrestled the man to the ground. Several people laughed and applauded the jokester as the police dragged him away.

Suddenly, from somewhere behind him, Wittig recognized the growling laugh of Matthias Weil. Wittig couldn't believe his ears, but there he was. "What are you doing here?" The tone of his voice drew the attention of the people standing nearby.

Weil pushed them aside. "My friend. Such a surprise. How are you?" Weil extended his hand.

Wittig felt his heart beat faster. Pain shot through his chest.

Weil smirked. "You've lost weight, Herr Wittig."

"Pleasure to see you too, Herr Weil." Weil's taunting made it obvious to Wittig that Weil's presence here was a message. Beck had instructed Weil to be there and wanted Wittig to realize he was following his every move.

Wittig looked up as the crowd cheered. He was just in time

to see Henry Ford, gold-handled cane in hand, boarding the *Oscar II*. Someone opened a crate of white doves. They flew overhead and quickly disappeared. Ford stood on the *Oscar II* and tossed red roses to his wife, who remained on the dock. She was crying.

While the *Oscar II* pulled away from the pier, the crowd waved. When the ship turned south on the Hudson River, a fully dressed man broke from the crowd and shouted. “I’m Mr. Zero.” He jumped in after the ship. A tugboat plucked him out of the water after a few minutes.

Wittig couldn’t understand why anyone would be so crazy. He headed home confused and depressed. Events were becoming chaotic. His last thought before he went to sleep was *I fear what’s next*.

Chapter 34
A Confession

Police Headquarters: December 1915

Martin and Keller stopped their auto in front of 240 Centre Street. Kleinmann, Traub's nephew, got out of the car and gawked at the huge dome that towered above him. "I always knew I'd be inside a police station. I'm finally here." Keller pushed forward up a couple of steps and through the main doorway of Police Headquarters. They turned left past the two-story marble entrance hall with its circular staircases and coffered ceiling into the Bomb Squad offices on the Broome Street side of the building across from the homicide bureau.

"Take him to the consultation room, Paul," Martin instructed. "I have to see the captain." When Martin returned, Kleinmann spoke first. "I'll do anything to get Traub."

"With your help, we will." Martin removed his coat and put it on the back of his chair. "Tell me about him."

Kleinmann told his story through a string of questions and personal observations. "What happened to me? I was smart. That bald ape ruined my life."

Keller interrupted and tried to clarify things, but Martin told him, "Let him tell it his own way."

Kleinmann continued: "Why did my father have to die? I was too young to lose a father. Hiking accident. I don't want to talk about it. I guess my mother loved him. That's what she said. She never told me why they didn't marry. Class difference? Religion? I think the Traubs were big-shots in Dresden. Uncle Eugene looked after me when my father died. Can't say why. My mother went along. She was poor and followed him to New York. I really need a drink. Please?"

Keller gave him a glass of water. "This is going to be as hard as trying to decipher Traub's codes."

"Rupert, why don't you tell us what Traub paid you for?"

"If you call them wages." Kleinmann stopped for a moment and checked his pockets. He relaxed when he heard some coins knock together. He told them he did small jobs around the waterfront for Traub, such as recording ships entering and leaving New York Harbor, and guard duty around Hamburg-America's offices. Occasionally, he delivered messages.

Kleinmann believed Traub employed him to make sure he made enough money – $2.57 each day – for him and his mother. He said Traub paid for their apartment on 83rd Street, "a costly family obligation," Traub called it. "I never understood that. He never accepted me or Mother into his family. I guess he loved his brother and felt a strange blood loyalty to me," Kleinmann said.

"Get to the point. Did you ever take orders directly from Traub?" Keller raised his voice.

"I did what he told me. He demanded that I follow his directions to the letter. 'I'm not paying you to think,' Traub told me." Kleinmann shrugged his shoulders.

"So you weren't sure what Traub was doing?" Martin said.

"I really didn't care. I just wanted the money."

"What did you and Traub fight about?" Martin knew Kleinmann had something useful to say. He just had to find the right question to get to it.

"One day, I got sick and couldn't go to work on the riverfront," Kleinmann said. "Traub blamed the liquor, but it weren't that. I had piles."

Keller chuckled.

"You ever have piles?" Kleinmann reached down and rubbed his backside. "I was out for two days. Traub laughed at me when I told him. 'No excuse, the booze caused the piles,' he said. I got real mad. A week later, one of his men just gave me a paper. Told me to get off their property. I got the paper at home – Traub insists on keeping good records – everything very efficient. He fired me for 'constant quarrelling with another operative, drinking, and disorderly habits.' I'll quote that line at his funeral after I piss in his grave. Then, Traub refused to pay me my last two days wages. Come to $5.14."

"Does Traub keep a record of his private business deals? Give me something I can use." Keller banged his fist on the table.

"Don't know." Kleinmann's eyelids shrunk into defensive slits. "You're starting to sound like him. You another German brute? All I can tell you is Traub has a memory like an elephant. He don't forget nothing."

"When did he punch you?" Martin tried to deflect Keller's aggression.

Kleinmann slumped in his chair. "When he didn't pay me, I called him asking for the money. $5.14. Can you believe it? Cheap bastard. It was due me, and I was going to get it. I know he likes to go to the German House on 59th Street after work, so one night I waited for him. We started to argue. That's when he punched me. He crushed my nose. I guess I started drinking more after that. I swear I'll get him. You're going to help me, right?"

"At the bar, you mentioned you had an interesting story to tell us. What was it?" Martin said.

"Let me think." Kleinmann rested his head on his arms, smacked his lips, and fell asleep.

Martin cringed. "Let him rest. Why don't we get some coffee? He isn't going anywhere. This is going to be a long night."

~

When Martin and Keller returned a half-hour later to continue the interview, Kleinmann was thrashing around like he was having a bad dream. Martin nudged him awake. He seemed more sober. He sat up and drank coffee they had brought. "Except for Mother, no one cared much about me. I wasn't always a drunk." Little by little, Kleinmann told them what he knew about Traub's organization. They were unconnected bits and pieces, a start. But nothing to use to arrest Traub.

"Do you remember the story you were going to tell us?" Martin asked. "To get Traub."

"Oh, the story. I almost forgot." Kleinmann yawned. "What do you know about the Welland Canal?"

Martin and Keller looked at each other. Because of their explosives expertise, the Canadian government had asked the Bomb Squad to advise them on guarding such a strategic target as the Welland Canal against a dynamite attack. Captain Tunney used the report to train his men.

"Welland Canal? Don't know it." Martin lied. "Where is it?"

"You must know it," Kleinmann said. "It's real important. U.S. – Canadian shipping operations depend on it." Kleinmann didn't seem to care that he was cutting the key to his own prison cell lock.

"Isn't that the one that connects Lakes Erie and Ontario?" Keller asked. "What about it?"

"You got a pencil? Let me draw you a picture. Can I get some more coffee? I draw good. Mother said I should have been an artist."

Kleinmann sketched a map of the U.S.-Canadian border with Lake Ontario in the north and Lake Erie on the south. "This here stretch of land, it's about twenty-seven miles, separates the lakes. On the western side of the land is Ontario; the east is New York. Buffalo is here." He circled a spot at the northeast tip of Lake Erie. "Niagara Falls is maybe halfway between the two lakes. The Welland Canal is about twenty miles west of the border. It has eight locks. Take away the canal and shipping would be ruined. Cargo ships couldn't get around Niagara Falls." It was clear from the map that Kleinmann was right. Without the canal, no shipping from Ohio and Michigan could reach Lake Ontario, and from there sail past Montreal, through the Saint Lawrence Seaway and into the Atlantic.

This man knows what he's talking about, thought Martin.

"What does the Welland Canal have to do with Traub?" Martin asked.

"That fat ape had plans to destroy it. I helped." Kleinmann smiled proudly.

"What happened?" Keller asked.

"Well, Traub knew I needed work, and I wanted to help Germany. I had good grades in school, and Traub knew I could draw pretty good. He didn't want any of his New York goons to do the job – couldn't trust them, he said. Besides, he wanted a fresh face to do it. Someone the police couldn't connect to his organization. I was happy to have a chance to show him I could do good work. He paid me to go to Niagara and gather information. The canal was closely guarded."

Martin remembered from Tunney's report that Canada used one thousand men to guard the canal. Traub wasn't the only man who realized its importance.

"Pretend you're fishing, but make diagrams and drawings of the area. If you're undetected, take photographs, Traub told me. I made the drawings – I still have 'em at home. I took notes of shipping schedules, the canal's construction, guard positions, the vulnerable spots."

"When was this?" Martin became more excited.

"This spring. I took a train up to Buffalo and then connected to Welland, Canada. I registered at the Welland House – can't forget that name – close by the waterway. Next day, I rented a boat and traveled south to Port Colborne, at the mouth of Lake Erie. Stayed the night. Headed north the next day."

We can check these facts, Martin thought.

"I thought I done good. I wanted to be part of the team to blow it up. Do something really important. Traub said no. 'Need to keep things separate.' He told me he'd hire men to row a boatload of dynamite across the upper Niagara River and smuggle it into Canada. Don't know what happened."

I do, thought Martin. Traub's men panicked and botched the job. *Now I can connect Traub to that attack.*

"Thought he'd give me some bonus or something, but I never heard nothing from Traub again on the canal. I was real disappointed. He ignored me until my mother went to see him. She came home that night with a black eye, but he gave me work on small jobs, like I said."

"Do you still have your notes and drawings on the Welland Canal?" Martin asked.

"Got everything in a box in my closet. What you want them for?"

"They're going to help us destroy your uncle." Martin imagined how he'd feel when he put the cuffs on Traub. He turned to Keller and said, "What do you think, Paul?"

"If Kleinmann's evidence is good, we can trace Traub to Niagara Falls and the attack on the Welland Canal."

"Then we can arrest Traub on a violation of the Neutrality Act – conspiracy to use American soil as a base of unlawful operations against Canada," Martin added.

"I agree." Keller already had his coat on.

The morning sun had been up for an hour when they borrowed a police car, shoved Kleinmann in the back seat, and headed north. All three men were walking up the stoop to Kleinmann's home when a shot rang out from behind them.

Chapter 35
It Will Destroy Him

Upper East Side, Manhattan: December 1915

One shot was enough. One shot was always enough when Caarsens pulled the trigger. Since daybreak, he'd been waiting on the roof across from 244 East 83rd Street. He was cold and hungry and patient. When the police arrived and escorted Kleinmann to his building, he was ready. "Kill only the boy – he is betraying my entire organization to the police." Beck's instructions had been absolute. "Just him. We don't want every cop in the city chasing us on a revenge mission."

The bullet traveled 2,900 feet per second and struck the young man in the head. His brain exploded in a red spray mixed with gray pulp. The body spun and fell onto the detective behind him.

From his sniper's position, Caarsens watched the detective, who had been in front of the young man, turn and gape. The detective recovered his composure, tore off his coat, and wrapped it around what was left of the young man's head. He knelt down and frantically tried to revive him. "A doctor! A doctor! Where's there a doctor?"

Caarsens recognized the detective as the one who had chased him at the peace rally last summer. He reworked the bolt and assessed potential threats. Satisfied he was safe, he lowered the M1903 Springfield rifle and wiped it clean. The gun barrel felt warm in the freezing air; the trigger cold. He pocketed the spent 30.06 cartridge.

Before he left, Caarsens glanced over the roof and saw the

younger, more athletic detective look up. When he started to concentrate on Caarsens's location, Caarsens backed away from the ledge. He'd be gone before the New York police swarmed the building.

Except for the Springfield and an old rug Caarsens had used to smuggle it up to the roof, the police would find nothing. They would determine the rifle was part of a cache that had been stolen from a local armory. From his knapsack, Caarsens took out tinted glasses and his Colt pistol. He changed into a dirty old trench coat, and put on a wool cap. He then secured his gray crank-handled Demag bayonet in the leather scabbard hidden inside his coat. He stuffed some dry sausage into his mouth. Its skin was wet and the meat was salty.

He jumped over to the adjacent roof and walked down the stairs to the street. Bent over like a cripple and leaning on his cane, Caarsens walked past the chaotic scene. The younger detective dashed by him into the building. *Reckless fool.* He heard a woman wailing. "My son. Somebody get a priest."

He said a silent prayer for the boy, turned the corner, and walked away. Two blocks later, he found a garbage can in an alley. He broke the cane into pieces, and buried it, the wig, and the glasses in the bottom of the can. He folded his coat into the knapsack, and put on a workingman's cap.

On his way toward Central Park, Caarsens walked past a woman walking with a young boy. "Hey mister, didn't I see you a few minutes ago?" the boy said.

Caarsens pretended he didn't hear.

The boy persisted. "You were blind."

Caarsens didn't want to hurt the boy. Killing enemies was acceptable; he refused to kill women and children. He ignored them and walked away. Time was short.

~

Two hours after Kleinmann's shooting, Martin sat on the stoop of Mrs. Kleinmann's building and watched the cops and detectives crawl over 83rd Street like crabs on a beach at low tide. He knew they'd leave hungry. The shot proved Kleinmann's killer was no Black Hand amateur. Most likely, he had fled the scene minutes after the shooting and left nothing incriminating behind.

One after another, frustrated policemen told Martin the problems they were having with the investigation. Witnesses argued. Stories conflicted. People exaggerated. Many had seen nothing. Some claimed they saw everything. No one was sure where the sniper was located until a policeman came out of the building across the street carrying a Springfield rifle. "Nothing else up there but a dirty rug."

"Keep trying. Something may turn up." Martin tried to be encouraging but knew his words lacked conviction. He ordered Keller to coordinate the investigation while he steadied Mrs. Kleinmann. Martin looked down at Kleinmann's body, wrapped in a flimsy moth-eaten blanket, and prayed. *Tell me, God. Tell me I didn't escort this man to his execution.*

An hour later, he saw a horse-drawn hearse, covered in freezing snow, pull in front of the building. The driver, an old ruddy-cheeked man, wore a black coat, top hat, and white gloves. Embroidered white netting covered the back of a gray horse. Black ostrich feathers were attached to its head. Two oversized lanterns, like wide unseeing eyes, flanked the driver and seemed to give Martin an accusing look.

Martin was exhausted from lack of sleep and tension. While Mrs. Kleinmann prayed over her son's body, he walked toward Keller, who sat silent on the building's steps, wet with snow and brown from coagulated blood. Keller admitted he needed a break. "Just want some quiet, Gil."

Keller's brooding worried Martin. "Nothing we could have done, Paul."

Keller covered his head with his hands. "You sure we didn't make a mistake? How come everyone we get close to in this case dies?"

"This is the hardest case we've ever had." Martin scratched his day-old whiskers. He forced himself to stop. "Damn it. Kleinmann didn't die for nothing. We owe him. Get up." Martin yanked Keller to his feet.

"Thanks, Gil." Keller wiped a wet hand through his hair.

At that moment, the undertaker walked past them and headed toward Kleinmann. Mrs. Kleinmann, guarding his body, looked up when he neared. The undertaker removed his top hat and bowed his head. "I'm so sorry, Renate. I came when I heard."

"Thank you, George." Her head rested on his chest. Tears flowed down her cheeks. "He hasn't received last ..." She began to cry, a deep desperate cry.

"We'll take care of him. Father Brandt knows what to do." He patted her back. It's time to say goodbye. I'll fetch you when he's ready."

Martin helped the undertaker carry Kleinmann to the back of the hearse. The undertaker climbed onto the driver's seat, released the brake, and signaled the horse to go.

Martin found Keller. "Come on. Time to see Mrs. Kleinmann."

As the hearse rounded the block, Mrs. Kleinmann turned and wandered to the building. Martin caught her at the front door. "I'm sorry, Mrs. Kleinmann, Rupert had a good heart. I know you are in shock, but could you help us?"

"What?"

"Could you answer some questions? Do you think you can manage that?"

"My son is dead, and it's your fault." Her eyes seemed to shoot arrows of hate at him.

"Rupert was helping us," Keller said in German.

"Speak English. I'm American now. Haven't you done enough? You brought him here to get killed."

"Whoever killed him was waiting for him. We're trying to help," Martin said.

"Why now? Where was you police when I needed help?"

"We're here now. Don't you want to help us find Rupert's killer?" Martin asked.

"I know who killed my boy – his own blood." She tensed and closed her eyes tight; her clenched hands shook.

"Who?"

"You must know." Mrs. Kleinmann looked surprised. "You were with him when he died. Rupert kept saying he'd go to the cops. I never believed him."

"We don't know."

She looked up and down the street and then whispered, "Eugene Traub."

"We need to talk to you about him," Martin said in his softest tone.

"Upstairs." Mrs. Kleinmann's face was pale. "I'll do whatever I can."

"Good." Martin knew she was right about the murder. No one would kill Kleinmann without Traub's say-so. However, shooting him in front of his apartment on a Sunday morning was bold and risky. How did he know we'd be here? Something didn't add up.

~

Mrs. Kleinmann's flat was small, plainly furnished, and German-neat. She closed the door, and asked, "What do you want to know?"

Martin summarized what Kleinmann had told them. "We need to know more."

She confirmed what Rupert had told them the previous night. They asked her if she knew about his trip to Buffalo in June. "Eugene arranged the trip. Rupert was real secretive about it. I was amazed, but after that, Eugene seemed to care a bit more about him. He put Rupert on his payroll and gave him steady work. Do you want to see some pictures of him? I don't have many."

"Of course." Martin fought fatigue.

When she was finished, Martin asked what had happened after Rupert started to work for Traub. Mrs. Kleinmann closed the thin album and put it on the side table. Her hand rested on it. She cleared her breath and continued. "I saw Eugene about once a week over the summer. He paid the rent. I don't want to discuss it."

"Of course not," Martin said. "We just want to know about Rupert's work for Traub."

"Something happened between them. I can't say. Eugene just

fired him."

Martin made a note in his book.

"They had a big fight. That was when Rupert's nose got all smashed in. He was never the same after that. He started to drink all the time. Then Eugene said Rupert tried to kill him."

"Do you know anything about Traub's work?"

"Besides working for Hamburg-America? No. He loves Germany though. That's all he loves; except himself, and I'm not sure of that."

"Can you tell us anything more?" Martin asked.

She hesitated for a few painful seconds. "No."

"I know this is hard for you," Martin said, "but Rupert swore he wanted to get Traub. He wanted to show us something. That's why we were here this morning. Can we see his room?"

Mrs. Kleinmann took them to a small chamber. She held the doorknob for several seconds before she entered. When she saw his empty bed, she nearly fainted.

"Why do you think Eugene killed Rupert?" Martin asked.

The words seemed to trigger something in her. "*Eins,* he could do it. He has men all over the city. How many killers are out there? *Zwei*, Eugene has the devil's soul – not like his brother. Violence excites him. *Drei*, he never forgave Rupert for shooting him. His personal code demanded revenge." Mrs. Kleinmann clasped her hands together. "I have nothing left. Give me your gun."

"Please don't think like that. Why don't you see your priest? We'll help by catching Traub."

"You promise?" She looked at him. Martin saw faint signs of hope in her face.

"Yes, but we need to find something. If he had something important to hide, where would Rupert put it?" Martin asked.

"He keeps his valuables in here." She showed them a cigar box on the floor of his closet."

Martin held his breath as he bent down to pick up Rupert's box. He felt elation and sadness. He regretted Kleinmann's death but hoped he was getting closer to arresting Traub. Over seven months of investigation and the murder of two key informants, a breakthrough in the case might be hidden in the contents of a cheap cigar box. Martin picked it up with religious reverence and clutched it so hard the box began to bend inward. His mouth was parched.

The box weighed a couple of ounces, but to Martin it felt as heavy as a pirate's chest. He hoped it contained Kleinmann's promised treasure. His anticipation mounted while he lifted the lid. He found precious nuggets of information: Kleinmann's notes, drawings, and photos he took of the Welland Canal. Other evidence included hotel receipts under his assumed name, Earle Foxx and details, all thoroughly documented, of all his expenses – train tickets, boat rentals, meals, cab fares, and clothing, such as gloves and boots. The big surprise was the most incriminating detail. They were all initialed as paid by "ET" – Eugene Traub.

Martin blessed the heavens. "Thank you, Mrs. Kleinmann." He smiled reassuringly. A sense of victory welled up inside him. "This is what we needed. Rupert would've been glad you gave it to us."

"What will that do to Eugene?"

"Destroy him."

"Good. Make him suffer." Silent tears rolled down Mrs. Kleinmann's face.

When they were once more outside the building, most of the policemen had left 83rd Street. Keller filled him in. The temperature had warmed and the ice on the steps had started to melt. They climbed into their motorcar and headed to Police Headquarters. Keller sighed. "Don't we still need Kleinmann as a witness?"

"Not any more." Martin tapped the box. "This will be enough to make an arrest."

Chapter 36
Worthy Adversaries

Upper West Side, Manhattan: December 1915

Rushing to his next assignment, Caarsens remembered Beck's words from their meeting the day before in Washington Square Park. "Traub has become a liability. We cannot let the police talk to him. Make sure there is nothing they can use. Remember, our entire operation is at risk."

"Understood."

"Meet me at the Yale Club after your business is done. I assume there will be no complications."

"Why would there be?" Caarsens knew killing Traub would be a challenge. Good. Traub was a brawler – mean, unpredictable, and ruthless. Physical power and bulk were his assets. Agility, cunning, and skill were Caarsens's strengths. Worthy adversaries. Survival of the fittest – as it should be.

It was mid-Sunday afternoon when Caarsens knocked at Traub's door. "What do you want?" a high-pitched voice asked.

Caarsens used the code words Beck had given him. "I have the strudel you ordered."

The door opened a crack. Traub peeked at him. "What's so important?"

"Got a message for you."

Traub appeared to study his visitor cautiously. He unlocked the chain, and gestured for Caarsens to enter. As he walked in, Traub closed the door, keeping himself between Caarsens and the entranceway so he now blocked the door. An expert move – Caarsens had no exit. He cursed himself for losing the advantage and moved back to widen the distance between them. "I just finished a project for Herr Beck in Maryland. He wants me to join your operation, Herr Traub." Partial truths make the best lies. He took off his brown fedora and handed it to Traub, hoping to distract him.

Never taking his eyes off Caarsens, Traub took the hat and tossed it on a nearby table. "I pick my own people. Don't want your help." To gain another advantage, Traub walked one step closer to Caarsens so they almost touched. "What do you really want?"

"Came to warn you." Caarsens moved away – he wanted space that Traub wouldn't concede.

"About what?" Traub followed to keep close.

Ending the dance, Caarsens changed tactics and stood his ground. To gain Traub's trust, he used the story Beck had conveyed. "Your nephew."

"That all? He's a weakling and no threat to me." Traub relaxed and smiled dismissively.

"He's talking to the police. You must –"

Traub's interest reappeared. "What's he saying?"

"He's implicating all of us."

"Why isn't Beck telling me this?" Traub snarled and flexed his massive chest. "Who are you?"

Caarsens tried to calm him down while he studied the apartment for the fight he knew was coming. He had to get out of the hallway.

"I only talk to Beck. He knows that. Why are you here?" Traub looked at Caarsens's hands. "Why the gloves?"

He knows I'm here to kill him.

Traub closed in. Talk moved to action. Caarsens stepped backward, all the time watching Traub's eyes. Caarsens reached inside his coat, but the big man reacted with unexpected speed and seized Caarsens's arm before he could withdraw his Demag. With his free arm, Caarsens grabbed Traub's ring finger and pulled it back until it broke. Traub released his grip and shook off what little pain he must have felt, giving Caarsens just enough time to jump away and backpedal into the living room.

Traub closed the distance between them and snarled. He shifted into a boxer's stance: balanced, arms up, ready to strike or deflect a blow. He punched twice, but Caarsens dodged each one. Traub followed with a powerful left-right combination that Caarsens blocked with his arms. The punches felt like bricks, but Caarsens fought off the hurt. Countering with a fast jab, Caarsens bloodied Traub's nose.

With wild eyes, Traub wiped the blood away with his sleeve and rushed Caarsens, trying to wrestle him to the ground. Caarsens stepped quickly to the side and pushed him forward. Traub stumbled over the couch.

Caarsens pulled out the Demag.

Enraged, Traub sprang to his feet, looked at the bayonet, and leered. "I love a knife fight." His nostrils flared. Traub grabbed the neck of a bottle on the table, broke it, and slashed upward. Caarsens felt the glass cut his forehead. Blood trickled into one eye. Traub reversed the direction of his arm and whacked Caarsens in the mouth with his elbow. Caarsens reeled and spit out tooth fragments. *Had he met his match? He never expected to die like this.* Caarsens wiped his stinging eye, but his vision was blurred.

Savoring his impending victory, Traub hesitated, giving Caarsens the chance to recover. Turning his head to see with his good eye, Caarsens kicked Traub's shin with enough force to break it, but Traub only buckled. He regained his balance and bent over to pick something up off the floor. Traub stood upright and waved an eight-inch long truncheon studded with steel spikes.

Where had that come from? Under the couch?

Traub moved toward him and grinned like a crazy man. He swung the truncheon from side to side. With his depth perception impaired, Caarsens dodged awkwardly, but one swing ripped into his arm. He was hurt, but he had to fight on or die.

Traub tried to finish the struggle with one vicious swing. He overplayed his advantage. Instead of moving away from the blow as Traub had expected, Caarsens moved into it and ducked. The truncheon passed over his head. Caarsens drove the six-inch blade of his Demag into Traub's gut. The bayonet struck deep. He forced it up several times. Before he fell, the gorilla punched Caarsens in the ribs. Caarsens couldn't believe a dying man had such power.

Caarsens went to the bathroom and washed out his eye. He opened the cabinet and, true to form, Traub kept a military first aid kit there. With it, he bandaged the wound. Unfortunately, the painkiller assigned to the kit was gone. He searched the apartment and found one of the two secret books Beck had described and burned it in the fireplace. He threw other papers into the fire and continued to look around. As sirens neared, he took his hat and fled, having failed to find the second book.

~

Several hours after Kleinmann's murder, Martin and Keller returned to Police Headquarters with the evidence. The captain approved Traub's arrest immediately, and the detectives, well-armed and prepared for a fight, rushed to his apartment building on 93rd Street off of Amsterdam. Martin checked the mailbox – E. Traub, #1B – and entered the front door. The hallway leading to Traub's apartment was narrow, empty, and too quiet. As they moved to #1B, Martin pulled out his revolver. "Careful, Paul. Who knows how Traub will react?"

"Shouldn't we wait for the rest of the posse?" Keller loaded a double-barreled shotgun and snapped it ready.

"No, this is our arrest. We can handle him. Keep your distance. If he gets violent, shoot. Both barrels. If that doesn't stop him, crack his head open with your nightstick. Just don't kill him." Martin took three deep breaths and pointed his revolver. "Go."

Keller knocked on the door. "Police!" No answer. He rapped twice more. Nothing. Keller leaned forward and put his ear to the door. "Can't hear anything, Gil."

"Knock it in." Martin's heart beat faster.

With all the force he could muster, Keller pounded the door with a sledge hammer he had brought with him. The door jamb broke and Martin rushed in. The apartment was dark, cold, and barren. Keller ducked into a crouch, pointed the shotgun, and followed Martin. Smoke hung in the air and a few glowing embers struggled to spit out their last bit of heat in the fireplace. All the curtains were drawn. "Is this a trap?" Martin whispered, sensing danger.

"Something's wrong. Careful, Gil."

Martin turned on a light in the hallway. "Look, a trail of blood."

"I've got you covered." Keller raised his shotgun to his shoulder while Martin, ready for anything, crept into the living room and around the couch, where Traub's inert body lay curled on its side. A pool of syrupy black ooze spread in front. Guts that looked like uncooked sausages spilled from his insides. His right hand still formed a fist. Traub's scrunched-up face showed the pain of his last few seconds. To Martin, it seemed to sneer. Even in death, the gorilla taunted him.

Keller joined Martin and poked Traub's dead body with the barrel of his shotgun. "Can't believe it. You dodge us for months, you fat ape. We can finally arrest you, and you get killed." They rolled Traub over. A five-inch wound stretched from his groin to his liver. "Look at that bruise from the knife hilt." The cut was saw-toothed, as if the killer had forced his knife up in zigzags. "Takes a strong man to do that."

Keller looked the body up and down, amazed that someone had been able to kill Traub like this. "That's some butcher's cut. Bastard got what he deserved."

Martin thought of the Kleinmanns. *Yes, Mrs. Kleinmann, Traub suffered in his last minutes. You got your wish, Rupert; he died like a stuck pig*. "What's that?" Next to the body, Martin picked up the broken bottle. Red smears covered its jagged edges.

"Gil, see this?" Keller found a truncheon lying near the body with clumps of flesh and shreds of fabric attached to its steel studs. "Must have been some fight."

"He knew the killers," Martin declared.

"Why do you say that?"

"Traub doesn't make mistakes." With his experienced

detective's eye, Martin scanned the room. We're missing something. This place has been ransacked. The killers wanted something, and they wanted it bad. What was it?" Martin stared at the fireplace. "There." Remnants of what looked like papers were burning. Martin ran over and grabbed a handful of gray ash. "Too late." Martin crumbled the ashes and let them fall. "We can't end it here. Let's hope the killers missed something."

Over the next two hours, they hunted for false walls, loose floorboards, and hidden compartments in the furniture and closets. They looked through his books and behind the bookcases. They opened every item, drawer, and cabinet in the kitchen but found nothing. Dismayed and tired, Martin buried his head in his hands. "I'm going to call the captain. We need the whole team over here. I want to interview everyone in this building. Somebody's got to know something. Check the hospitals, too. There's at least one killer out there who's hurt, and bad, if I'm right. Bring in the fingerprint team. On the reading table next to him, Martin noticed a copy of the German-American newspaper *The Fatherland*. "Paul, have you ever read that?"

"Trash. It's full of distortions and mistakes. It's a disgrace to German-Americans."

Fighting defeat, Martin sat in Traub's red leather reading chair near the window and tried to imagine the scene. It was a winter Sunday afternoon. The days were short. Traub had been to church and had eaten at a good German restaurant. He sat in this very chair and relaxed, probably for the only time all week. He was reading *The Fatherland* when the killers knocked. Most likely, it was a surprise. Martin doubted Traub had many visitors. He got up from the chair and, for some reason, let the men in. There had been no signs of damage to the front door before Keller knocked it in. Either Traub knew the men or they said something, most likely a code word, to identify themselves. Even so, Traub would have been careful. They talked for a bit until Traub became suspicious. When the fight erupted, it turned deadly, fast. It hadn't lasted long.

On the floor near the reading table, hidden by darkness, Keller sifted through a stack of fallen books. "What's this?" He picked up something from the bottom of the pile. Keller read the front cover. "*Die Bibel*?"

"Traub with a Bible? Let me see that." Martin opened it. "What the ...?" Traub had hollowed it out. Something was hidden inside. Martin picked up a six-by-four inch black book with loose-leaf rings at the top. It was thick with typewritten pages in English. Martin flipped through the book and grinned. "Mr. Traub might still be helpful."

"How?"

"He left us his book. Codes and all."

Chapter 37
Victory Is the Only Thing

Midtown Manhattan: December 1915

Caarsens was a block away when he saw the cops arrive at Traub's apartment. He took off his gloves and tossed them in a bin. As he crossed Central Park, the tension from the fight had begun to subside. Feeling mortal, he realized he'd nearly lost the fight with Traub, something he never thought possible in a one-on-one fight. His long trench coat covered the bandage he'd placed around his damaged left arm. The brown fedora pulled low on his forehead partially concealed his head wound, and his ribs felt like a poker was sticking him from the inside.

Caarsens considered the freezing rain and growing darkness his friends. Few people walked outside in such unpleasant weather. Those who did were more interested in their own comfort than a shivering laborer with a head wound. Anyone who noticed he was taking in short breaths would think he had consumption.

Caarsens entered Grand Central Station and fetched the canvas bag he had stored in a locker. He walked to the men's room and checked the mirror. He realized he was lucky he hadn't lost an eye. Moving to a stall, he rested for a minute, then removed a cloth from his bag, disinfected it with liquor from his flask, and cleaned the cuts on his face. Praying infection wouldn't set in, he removed the bandage from his arm and examined the wound. Traub's truncheon had gouged out a chunk of flesh. The wound was deep, but to his relief the bone was intact and the major vessels and tendons undamaged. Caarsens removed his sewing kit, sterilized the needle with a match, and disinfected the area with alcohol from his flask. He took a healthy swig and closed the wound with four stitches.

Before he left the men's room, Caarsens washed his face, changed into a business suit, and applied makeup. To fortify himself, he opened his billfold and removed the oft-folded paper and picture. Even though he knew the words by heart, he read it several times. Then he looked dreamily at the picture, and for a second, he was happy. He returned them to his billfold; he had things to do. Checking the mirror one last time, he was satisfied with the change and returned the bag to the locker. He headed across the street to the newly built Yale Club on 44th Street and Vanderbilt.

"Ask for me at the front door – they know me." Beck had boasted. "I'm an honorary member – diplomatic connections and a bit of money go far. I love this country. Privilege is purchased, not inherited."

Caarsens entered the club and was directed where to find Beck. The main lounge's wood-paneled walls and portraits of Yale nobility, including former American President William Howard Taft, gave Caarsens the impression he was visiting a Marquis's chateau. Light from the fireplace reflected off polished silver trophies. The oriental rugs were deep and luxurious; the whiskey glasses were full. Caarsens understood the Yale Club, like similar clubs in London and Vienna, housed a world where rich men perpetuated their superiority; powerful men decided common men's fates; and undeserving political men accepted glory they did not earn and rejected all the problems they had caused. It was a world he hated.

Caarsens found Beck in the library by himself staring at a

chess board. Beck looked up. "My friend. Glad you could make it. Sit." Beck moved a black piece and studied the new position. "Do you play?"

"Everything is done," Caarsens said studying the board. "I found Traub's book on the bomb-makers you were concerned about."

"Good."

"I burned it and whatever else I could find."

"What about the second book?"

Caarsens shook his head.

"No matter." Beck moved a white knight. "Check."

Wrong move.

Beck moved his chair away from the chess board. "I think it is ironic that I am sitting near the spot where Nathan Hale was hanged. Or that's what they tell me. 'I regret that I have but one life to give' and all that patriotic nonsense. Dying is for fools. Victory is the only thing I care about." Beck reached for a whiskey – "To Herr Traub. He served the Fatherland and died for the cause," and emptied his glass. He ordered another drink. "With your help, Herr Caarsens, I am going to change our strategy. We will lie low and create some diversions. When we strike, we will strike hard."

Chapter 38
The Code Book

Police Headquarters: December 1915

The morning after Traub's death, Martin, Keller, and Tunney studied his black book in the captain's office. Anticipation, a feeling of victory, and pots of coffee fueled their excitement. After examining the first few pages, Martin realized they'd found gold. Captain Tunney called the book "the most valuable source of information about German activities in the United States I've ever seen." The official name of Traub's organization was "*Geheimdienst*" or Secret Service Division. Traub referred to his sabotage operations as "D files" – "D" for destruction. The book documented the division's activities, agents, and codes.

None of them had ever seen anything close to the book's detail, completeness, and precision. It covered the period from April 1915 to the day before Traub's death. It included a complete record of each assignment – its purpose, the agent, aliases used, time frames, and all costs down to the penny: compensation, dinner, tips, and transportation. The book was no fake. Its worn cover and weak binding indicated that Traub used it every day. The detectives cross-referenced their investigation record with the book – every date agreed.

Martin was interested in events surrounding June 24, the day of the peace rally. He found nothing about the man Martin had chased through Gramercy Park or the attack on Keller, but the book referred to a meeting Traub had with Agent 27 at the Hapsburg Inn that night and a payment he made to Agent 27 for his Italian middlemen. Traub's written description matched Martin's recollection of the events that led to the arrest of Otto Meyerhoff, who had to be Agent 27. No mention of his assassination.

"Anything about Rupert Kleinmann's killer?" Keller asked.

"Sorry. The references stopped Saturday night."

"Let me look at that, Detective." Tunney scrutinized it. "An efficiency fanatic might have developed something so complete, but only a German would maintain it like this." Martin detected a tone of admiration in Tunney's voice.

Every German agent had a number and alias. Traub's was 101 and QQQ. He used different names for each case: Wegenkamp, Kelly, Boem, and many others. In a section titled "Notes to Agent QQQ," Traub indicated that he maintained a private file with newspaper clippings dealing with D-cases. "Go after those tomorrow," Tunney said. "I'm sure we'll find some useful material in Traub's office."

A few minutes later, Keller started to laugh. "Listen to this. Traub gave himself rules: 'It has been decided that I refrain from drinking beer or liquor with my supper prior to receiving Agent B.I., for the reason that I wish to be perfectly fresh and well-prepared to receive his reports.'"

Tunney snickered. "When a German voluntarily forswears his beer, something serious is afoot."

Martin added up thirty payments the German government made to Traub. He put down his pencil and said, "Comes to $159,073.38."

Keller looked up. "That kind of money can buy a lot of influence."

“And weapons. Anything else?” Tunney asked.

“Yes, Captain.” Martin continued to search Traub’s book. “Lots of references to Operative 51; the case reference is D-343. It seems like Traub meets him a couple of times a week. His name is Klaus Schiller.”

Keller’s head shot up. “I remember Meyerhoff mentioned his name a few times, but we never tracked him down. He started to work for Traub in April.”

Tunney pulled out his file drawer and looked at some papers. “That’s when we started to record an increase in ship bombings.”

Martin turned the page and said excitedly, “Look at this! Traub has a meeting scheduled with him tonight.”

~

Martin and Keller drove to the Algonquin Hotel on 44th Street near Times Square to meet Schiller at 6:30 p.m., his scheduled meeting with Traub. From Traub’s book, Martin had learned that Klaus Schiller was a clerk at Morgan Bank. He handled telegrams, cables, and letters concerning Allied purchases of war materials. Because of his work, Schiller learned details on money transfers, specific descriptions and prices of the goods, the suppliers, means of transportation, and their carriers. Schiller also had access to information about when and which ship would carry the goods out of New York Harbor. According to the book, at each meeting Schiller gave Traub the bank’s traffic in cables and letters. Schiller would replace the papers each morning before the bank opened for business. Meanwhile, Traub directed his dockyard saboteurs to targets based on Schiller’s information.

Martin and Keller waited for Schiller at the meeting point

in the hotel lobby. Schiller was on time, but "Dieter Woehler," Traub's alias when he dealt with Schiller, was not. From the front desk, the detectives observed how Schiller became increasingly nervous with each passing minute. Pencil-thin with twitching eyes, Schiller glanced at his watch and paced. He looked out the window several times. Obviously not a trained agent, Schiller turned to leave, but Martin walked toward him while Keller moved to block the door. "I'm afraid Mr. Woehler won't be coming tonight." Martin showed his badge.

"I ... I don't know who you're talking about." Schiller's voice cracked when he spoke.

Keller walked over and hooked his arm roughly around Schiller's. "Why don't you come with us? We have some questions." They drove him to 240 Centre Street and took him to the smallest interrogation room near the prison in the basement of the building. Keller shoved Schiller into a straight-backed wooden chair. "We haven't slept in two days. Don't make this harder than it has to be."

"Wh ... what d-do you want?"

"Information about Mr. Woehler." Martin stared over him. "You know who we're talking about. Big man. Bald. Works for the Hamburg-America Shipping Line."

"No. I ... I don't ..."

Keller slapped Schiller so hard his hand stung. "That was a love tap compared to the next one." Keller rolled his ring around so its bulging stone-edged top pointed down and rubbed it across Schiller's cheek.

Schiller gulped.

"Let me see what's in your pockets." Keller reached into Schiller's coat.

"No. No. What are you doing?" Schiller tried to grab Keller's hand, but instead of reaching down farther, Keller pulled back his hand and jerked his elbow into Schiller's lower jaw. When Schiller reached up to check his face, Keller removed papers from Schiller's pocket. Two documents, dated Friday, December 10, 1915, were addressed to Morgan Bank. One was from the Banque de Lyon Pour Etrangers and concerned a shipment of two hundred thousand artillery shells. The other document was a cablegram from the Italian government authorizing the bank to extend four million dollars of credit to its naval attaché and Italian purchasing agent, Colonel Paulo Cianci. The documents were enough to convict Schiller of stealing information. Keller handed the papers to Martin and backed away.

Martin approached Schiller. "I assume you were about to return these papers before the bank opened tomorrow. Am I correct?"

"I, I can ..."

Martin seized Schiller's lapels. "You're under arrest for document theft."

Schiller started to plead.

"You're going to tell us everything you know."

"Yes. Just keep him away from me." Schiller nodded toward Keller. "He scares me."

"Who hired you at Morgan Bank?" Martin asked.

The name Schiller blurted out meant nothing to Martin.

~

Martin and Keller locked up Schiller, and went to see the captain, who was talking to the chief of detectives, the police commissioner, and the mayor's top assistant. Tunney waved them in and introduced everyone. “We are about finished, gentlemen; I’ll brief you on further developments. By the way, tell the mayor my wife wants to know all about President Wilson’s wedding next week. I heard he was lucky enough to get an invitation.”

After the men left, Martin asked, “Has Griggs picked up the other operatives?”

“He made the arrests,” Tunney said. “They all went peacefully. Nobody was hurt. We arrested the German lighterboat captains and the other Hamburg-America captains who were implicated in Traub’s book.”

Bursting with anticipation, Martin asked, “What about the people who planted the bombs?”

Tunney told them what Griggs had learned. After they had arrested the sugar pirates based on Meyerhoff’s information, the German lighterboat men refused to partake in the bomb-planting operation. After that, Traub paid Negro and Irish dockworkers to plant the bombs. Both groups were sympathetic to Germany. Griggs arrested the leader of each group.

The Negro leader, Ty Jefferson, was uncooperative at first, but finally admitted that he had helped Traub after Jelly Brown, another black gang leader, refused to cooperate. Jefferson said that Traub was a mean son-of-a-bitch, but he paid good and treated Negroes like men. His men planted fewer bombs because Negroes were always the last men chosen to load ships.

“What about Donovan, the head of Irish dock workers?” Keller asked. “I saw his name several times in Traub’s book.”

“His men planted some bombs. He didn’t know the Negroes planted bombs, too. Donovan was angry about that. Professional jealousy between criminals, I guess," Tunney said.

"Competition among thieves – what a concept. Did Donovan or Jefferson say where they got the bombs?" Martin asked.

"No. That's the bad part," Tunney said. "They never knew the bombers. They picked up the bombs at various drop-off points, but Traub never used the same one twice. Another dead end. We'll have to catch the bomb-makers some other way." Tunney leaned back in his chair. "What are your next steps, Sergeant?"

"We need to interrogate Mr. Schiller some more. Then, we have to go to Traub's office. I also want to go to Morgan Bank and interview people who knew him. I'll start with the man who hired him."

"Who's that?"

"Somebody called John Wittig."

Chapter 39
Case D-343

Police Headquarters: December 1915

The morning after Schiller was arrested, Martin entered Police Headquarters at the back of the building. For the third night in a row, he hadn't slept. He was worried about Corinne; she was having difficulties in her last two months of pregnancy. He wanted to believe her doctor, who ordered her to stay in bed and said everything would be fine if she just rested. Martin wasn't sure. He never left things to chance, but he was helpless in these matters, which only magnified his concern. Heartburn rose from his stomach.

He stopped halfway up the basement stairs leading to the main entrance hall when he heard Keller enter behind him and leap up the stairs to greet him. "We've got some bad guys to catch. Get moving, Gil. You look like an old lady today." Keller wore the same brown suit and red necktie as yesterday. Cuts from a bad shave dotted his face.

"Thanks." Martin sounded lifeless. "Why are you in such a good mood?"

"Why are you in such a bad one? It's Christmastime – we should all rejoice."

Something's going on, Martin thought. *Keller isn't religious.*

When they reached their desks, Keller leaned over and said, "Don't tell the captain, but his niece is great. She's a lot of fun and a different person outside of work. She's a good athlete too. She's a better skater than I'll ever be."

That's why he's so happy. I should have known. Can today start any worse? "I told you to stay away from her."

"But, Gil."

"We have work to do. First, we have to interrogate Schiller some more. I need your mind on your work." Martin tried to calm his angry stomach. "Let's go."

They walked to the interrogation room in silence. Schiller shivered in its damp cold. He hadn't touched his breakfast of lumpy mush. "I need a cigarette."

"Not more than me. You aren't getting one." Martin snapped back. "You've been giving information to Woehler. You're a traitor, and I'm going to make you pay." *Calm down*, he told himself.

"Gil, can I see you outside for a moment?" Keller pulled Martin into the corridor. "Look, I know you're mad at me. We can talk about that later, but remember this interview is important. This guy is terrified. If you attack him like that, he's not going to tell us anything. Relax for a minute. When you've calmed down, we'll go back in. Take a deep breath. I'll run this interview."

Martin closed his eyes and forced himself to concentrate on the case. "Fine. Let me get something to settle my stomach." A bicarbonate of soda helped. Several minutes later, they returned to the holding cell. In the time they were gone, Schiller had turned paler, and his teeth chattered nervously.

"Are you going to cooperate?" Keller placed his chair in front of Schiller. "If you don't, I'm going to make sure you're locked up in the coldest cell in New York State."

"Sure. Sure. Of course. How can I help you?"

"Tell us about your deal with Woehler."

Schiller gulped, bowed his head, and told them everything. At the start of the war, he, a German-American, went to the German Consulate in New York and volunteered to do special projects. He heard nothing for several months until Woehler called him in early April this year and asked Schiller to meet him at the Hotel Chelsea. Woehler was patriotic and bought Schiller an expensive steak dinner. He asked a lot of detailed questions. He knew everything about Schiller's job at Morgan Bank and offered Schiller a twenty-five dollar per week retainer, doubling his pay.

The first papers Schiller brought him were copies of express bills, which show when goods are delivered, where, and who carries them. Later, Schiller brought Woehler telegrams from the Allies that detailed payment terms, details of the shipping contents, processing details, and timing.

"Do you know what Woehler did with them?" Keller asked.

"I was helping Germany. That's all I cared about. Woehler told me he sometimes spent hours at night copying down all the info. He always made sure I had the documents back in time the next morning. He never missed once." Schiller rubbed his eyes. "Until now."

"I always wondered why Traub was late to work so often. Out of character. Now it makes sense," Martin said. "He set his organization in motion based on Schiller's information."

"You knew you were breaking the law. Were you ever concerned you'd be caught?"

"It was exciting. Herr Woehler kept telling me how important I was. The money was useful. I'm saving to buy a house." Schiller looked at them hopefully, but they left him shivering alone in the room.

Martin and Keller approached Morgan Bank from Nassau Street. The low-slung limestone bank building at 23 Wall Street reminded Martin of an ancient temple. They inquired at the front desk for John Wittig. The receptionist directed them to the southeastern corner of the building, where they found Mr. Wittig's door open. He was sitting at his desk reading documents. Martin knocked and entered.

"Mr. Wittig?" Martin flashed his badge. "I'm sorry to disturb you, but we need to talk with you."

Formal but respectful, Wittig stood up. He invited them to sit down and placed his papers on his desk in a neat stack. His well-pressed blue pinstripe suit hung evenly from his compact body. His striped tie was knotted in a perfect Windsor and his black shoes were freshly polished. "Can I offer you detectives something?" Wittig's voice betrayed his nervousness.

Once seated, Martin pulled out his notebook and briefed Wittig on the details.

"Yes, I'm aware of the situation. I was talking with our lawyers before you arrived." Wittig regained his composure. "Morgan Bank will cooperate with you to the fullest extent."

"Can you tell us how Mr. Schiller came to work for you?" Martin asked.

"I met Mr. Schiller through the German Red Cross. He impressed me. He had legal training and was smart and well-organized. When I needed a new assistant, I hired him."

"What kind of employee was he?"

"Up to now, the bank would have considered him a perfect employee."

"Why do you think he stole the documents?" Martin asked.

"Detectives, how could I know that? I assume he was bribed and gave the information to one of our rivals. The Fulton Street Bank is known for its dirty tricks. With that kind of information, they could undercut us or ruin our deals."

A competitor? Makes sense. A good lie or is that what you really think? "Any other reason you can think of?" Martin asked.

"No. Banking is a competitive business. Mr. Schiller's arrest has caused us many problems. Now, if you'll excuse me, I have an important telephone call to make." With a gesture, Wittig invited them to leave.

"Of course." Fishing for a reaction, Martin stood up, and said, "Do you know a man called Eugene Traub?"

"Never heard of him." Martin noticed Wittig swallowed hard. "If there's nothing else, ..."

Keller, who had remained quiet throughout the interview, left ahead of Martin.

Once on the street, Martin told Keller they hadn't seen the end of Wittig. "I don't know what to believe, but I don't trust him. He has too many connections to these Germans. Coincidence or not, I don't like them."

~

After the detectives left his office, Wittig's mouth turned dry and his shoulder muscles tightened into a knot. He was scared. Schiller's duplicity had inadvertently led the police to him. He tried to remain calm as he analyzed his conversation with them. Their questions exploded in his head like 18-pound shells. Why did they ask about Eugene Traub? How far would Beck go to achieve his aims? At least they hadn't asked about Dallmann's death last summer in Milton Point. He was trapped, and all he could do was hope Henry Ford's peace mission would succeed.

~

On the short walk west over to Traub's office at 45 Broadway, Martin decided to confront Keller, who had been testy all day and lacked his usual concentration and intensity. "I wanted to get through the day before we talked, but the way you're acting, I can't. What's gotten into you?"

"Now you're interrogating me?" Keller's cheeks turned red. "You're a pretty bad detective if you don't know why I'm mad."

"Shannon?"

"Of course. We've become friends. Our relationship doesn't affect my work. What we do on our time is none of your business, Sergeant."

"If it affects our relations with the captain, it does. She's like a daughter to him."

"What are you saying? I'm not good enough for her?"

"No, it's –"

"She's Catholic, and I'm Protestant. That's it, isn't it?"

"No." Martin hesitated for a minute. "Well, maybe." Martin's stomach knotted tight.

"Finally, the truth," Keller said. "You want to be Saint Gilbert, but you're still human. You have prejudices just like the rest of us. Admit it."

"It's not that." Martin didn't want to broach the topic, but had to. "I just don't like to know what you two do outside of work. If you love her, get engaged."

"I hope it comes to that. Our relationship is only in the fifth inning, if you must know. By the way, she's already told the captain she's seeing me. He said she's free to choose whoever she wants to see. If there's a conflict with work, he'll decide in favor of work every time. If that's good enough for him, it should be good enough for you."

Martin considered the situation. "I agree. Let's not talk about it again. You're a very good detective, but please keep your relationship with Shannon away from your work and me."

"Of course."

The pains in Martin's stomach eased somewhat.

~

Once inside 45 Broadway, they took the elevator to the top floor. There, Rudy Krebs, Traub's contemptuous secretary, patrolled the door to the offices of the Hamburg-American Shipping Lines like the guard dog he was. Martin handed him the warrant, which Krebs scrutinized until he could not find a reason to challenge it. He led them to Traub's office, which resembled his apartment: sparse and organized. Martin felt a twinge of satisfaction when he saw the phone they had tapped.

Krebs watched the detectives like a nervous German shepherd without its owner, which only made them search harder. After ten minutes, Martin peered behind a bookcase and said, "What's this?" He shoved the bookcase aside and found a floor safe hidden in an opening. The safe was high-quality dark-gray steel, about three feet tall and two feet wide. "We got any safe-crackers in the Bomb Squad?" Martin asked, already speculating about what he'll find.

"I think Griggs can crack a safe," Keller said. "I'll get him over here right away."

Krebs protested vociferously until Keller clamped his hand over his mouth, immobilizing his jaw, and said, "Shut up." Forcing his words out, Krebs said in German, "You, Herr Keller, are a traitor to the Fatherland."

Keller replied in English. "And you, Mr. Krebs, are a two-bit criminal."

~

An hour later, Griggs arrived with a peculiar looking tool kit. It didn't take him long to break into the safe. "Where did you learn to do that?" Martin asked.

"Let's say I had a different profession before I met Captain Tunney. He was the only man to give me a break. You want to take the first look, Sergeant?"

Martin kneeled down and reached into the safe. He found a German Luger with three extra clips of ammunition, several U.S. blank passports waiting to the filled out, good copies of police badges, and photo identifications of various people. Notes written in German were attached to each I.D. Keller read them and learned that Traub charged each operative for the expense. He also found train schedules and various maps of New York City, the Welland Canal, and some other areas he did not recognize. He was disappointed that he didn't find another black book.

He started to wonder if somehow the Germans were smuggling the bombs into New York from Mexico. Could a Boche boat have snuck into America? Long Island perhaps? Could Traub have been buying the bombs from anarchists or underworld gangs? Possible, probable, or wrong? Martin couldn't decide.

As Martin left Traub's office, his mind was filled with more questions than answers. He considered the possibilities. At the entrance to the Bowling Green subway station, they saw a crowd of people, three-deep, form around a magician working to earn some loose change. Keller began to watch.

The magician started doing tricks with connecting rings, pulling them apart and linking them together in intricate combinations. The magician challenged someone in the crowd to force the rings together. A volunteer clanged and twisted the rings, but he was unable to connect them. The magician ended his act by lighting the ends of four torches and juggling them faster and faster. At one point, he pretended to lose control, but he recovered in stage-worthy fashion. More laughter and applause. As a thank you, he blew an arc of fire across the crowd.

It was just after 7:00 p.m. when Martin and Keller arrived to brief Tunney. He kept them waiting for a bewildering twenty minutes. When he invited them into his office, Tunney seemed jumpy and impatient, something Martin had never seen before. "Get to the point, Sergeant. What did you find out today?"

Martin condensed the day as briefly as he could.

"What about Wittig? Is he connected to the Germans?" Tunney said.

"We don't know. He's hiding something. I'm sure of it." Martin sensed from Tunney's behavior that something was wrong, but he carried on. "I'll bet my badge on it."

"You might have to. One hooker on the street usually means a brothel's nearby. But that's not my biggest problem." Tunney's shoulders slumped.

"What's wrong, Captain?" Martin said, fearing the captain might fire him for lack of results.

Tunney put his index finger to his month. "I can trust you men. Sergeant, I know how much you want to get these Hun bastards. Detective Keller – you were my first candidate, but I cleared you. My niece defends you one hundred and ten percent, and she's the best judge of character I know."

"Captain?"

"Do you remember Traub's Special Operative 120 from his book?"

"Yes. Some curious references to him in the book. He seems to be another key informant," Martin said.

"While you were wearing out your shoe leather, I showed my niece Traub's book. That woman amazes me. She has an idea; it's bad." Tunney's face lost color. "I can't believe it."

"What?" Martin and Keller both said simultaneously.

"We have a traitor in our midst. She thinks he works in the Bomb Squad."

Chapter 40
Disappointment

Bronxville: December 1915

"Ford Heads Home. Peace Mission Continues"

Wittig read the Monday evening newspaper as he headed home on the train on his first day back at work after Christmas. The paper reported that Henry Ford, who had become sick when a wave drenched him on day three of the voyage, was abandoning the peace mission. He had started back to the United States. The peace mission would continue its work in Europe, but Wittig knew that without Ford, the mission was as dead as a sentry in a sniper's sights.

The two men sitting in front of Wittig on the train discussed the matter. "I've lost all respect for Ford."

"Arrogant fool. Now he's caught a cold and has to go home to mommy."

"Would have been more use if he'd walked naked through no-man's land."

"He's a Jew-hater too."

Wittig knew the men were right. The war would continue. He felt like a boxer on the losing end of a 15-round match. Gasping for air, bleeding from unseen wounds, Wittig tried to sleep, unconsciousness his only reprieve from reality.

"Next stop, Bronxville."

The conductor's words shook Wittig from his daze. He threw on his coat but didn't bother to button it. He reached down and picked up the newspaper still folded on his seat. He staggered to the exit and was the last commuter to reach the door.

Wittig slipped on the train's slippery steps. He fell and hit his skull. With a bruised head and his insides aching, he struggled to a bench. Ignoring the twenty-seven degree chill, he sat down in a frozen puddle of water and started to tear up the newspaper – first in long strips, then piece by small piece by smaller piece. When the pile next to him spilled to the ground, Wittig tossed the rest into the air. The wind scattered them. Several pieces landed back on Wittig. He looked at them dumbly when they clung to his coat. Then he buried his head in his hands and wept.

SECTION IV

EL TRAIN ON 6th AVENUE

New Years Eve 1915 - April 1916

Chapter 41
Operation *Gericht*

Jagdschloss Grunewald Hunting Lodge,
Berlin, Germany: New Year's Eve 1915

The Kaiser rested the barrel of his Gewehr 98 bolt-action Mauser rifle in the nook of a tree, took aim, and fired. The twelve-pointed buck scampered deeper into the snow-covered Grunewald forest. "*Verdammt*." He shook his fist at the retreating deer. He handed the rifle to his aide, who congratulated him on his excellent shot. "A near miss, Your Excellency. The deer ran just as you pulled the trigger."

Fog rolled in. Despite fur-insulated winter boots, his feet felt cold. "Enough of this sport. I need schnapps," the Kaiser said to his companions, Army Chief of Staff Erich von Falkenhayn and Colonel Walter Nicolai, head of Section III-B – German Military Intelligence. They headed to the nearby 16th-century hunting lodge. In the distance, the Kaiser saw its sandstone-framed bull's-eye windows in the porch and the polygonal staircase tower. He walked by a pile of carcasses from previous hunts. The bones had been picked bare by scavengers. He noticed wolf prints in the new-fallen snow.

The three men entered the main lounge where a fire sputtered in the fireplace. The Kaiser picked up a poker with his good hand and stirred the embers. He added two logs to the fire. It spit back to life with sounds like firecrackers. The men gathered in front of a large oak table. It was covered with maps and papers like so many bandages on the floor of a hospital ward. Apples and nuts sat on the table. A captain served hot spiced wine.

General von Falkenhayn opened a detailed map of France. “Your Excellency, you have asked me to outline my plan for our upcoming offensive on the Western Front. I call it Operation *Gericht*.”

“Place of execution; how appropriate.” Nicolai chomped into an apple.

“It is scheduled to begin in February. Let me show you. It is here, in Verdun.” He pointed to an area 150 miles east of Paris, along a bend in the Meuse River.

The Kaiser leaned over and listened as von Falkenhayn explained. He stated that the current stalemate on the Western Front demanded a change in strategy. He argued that France, already at the breaking point, could be knocked out of the war in a concentrated battle of attrition. He had selected Verdun, an old Roman fortress town, as the optimal killing ground for three reasons. The French military considered it sacred and strategic ground; they would fight to its last man to protect it. The German lines across from Verdun were near a major railroad junction; it would be easy to supply the army. If Germany broke through, the road to Paris would be open. Its capture would be imminent.

“With our artillery massed along the eight-mile front, we will chop the French into pâté.” Von Falkenhayn’s bristled hair seemed to stand at attention.

“A scale of carnage that Alexander would envy, isn’t that right, Herr von Falkenhayn,” Nicolai said.

“And how will our forces fare?” The Kaiser picked through the nuts.

“As long as we annihilate the French, it will not matter.” Von Falkenhayn rolled up his maps. “The war will be over.”

The Kaiser walked away from the table and sat back in a deep, cushioned lounge chair. He thought for several moments. "Yes, a knockout blow. I concur. Let us end this war." He picked up his glass of wine and tasted it. His eyes squeezed shut. "Sour." He put it down and stared at his chief spy. "Herr Nicolai, I am concerned about your setbacks in New York. We have spent tens of millions dollars, and I am afraid we have not seen adequate returns on our investment. What do you say?" His face sank into a scowl.

The head of Section III-B sat upright and appeared confident. "You are correct, Your Excellency. The death of our man Traub, and the loss of our dockyard operations are unfortunate. Merely a setback, I assure you; we have alternatives."

"In the event that Herr von Falkenhayn's predictions prove mistaken, we will have to improve our efforts to neutralize America's contributions to the Allied war effort."

Von Falkenhayn twisted his hands in his lap. "I would not worry about the Americans. However costly, my plan to draw France into a death struggle will succeed."

"I fear one point is correct. It will be costly," the Kaiser said. "But, we cannot depend on the Verdun offensive alone. What do you propose to do in America, Herr Nicolai?"

Nicolai picked up a file from the desk. "Have you read this, Your Excellency?"

"What is it?"

"My man in New York's plans for a new phase of operations."

"Yes. Beck. Devious man. Good mind. Ruthless." The Kaiser scanned the pages. "What does he suggest?"

"His plan is bold, but it may be risky. He wants to focus on a few objectives. I need your approval because, if successful, the Americans will be outraged."

"Summarize it."

After Nicolai finished, the lines across the Kaiser's face receded a bit. He asked von Falkenhayn his opinion.

"Dangerous, but necessary; it's what I would propose. War is different today – no constraints."

The Kaiser heard rifle shots outside. He looked at his pocket watch. "Gentlemen, it appears the New Year has arrived. He stared at Nicolai. "Tell Beck to wait. If the attack on Verdun stalls, tell him to proceed." He raised his glass. "*Prost*. To a successful new year."

Chapter 42
New Year's Eve

Police Headquarters: New Year's Eve 1915

At the end of their shift on New Year's Eve, Tunney stood on a chair in the Bomb Squad's main area and toasted his men. With the death of Traub and the arrests of eight Hamburg-America Shipping Line captains and many more German lighterboat men and dockworkers, everyone was confident they had dismantled the German bomb-planting operation. One spy in particular, Karl Brandt, had been convinced to help and was revealing details about their Mexican operations and German political developments that could prove useful.

Now, understanding his men needed to relax and enjoy their success after a demanding year, Tunney had authorized the party. The mood was festive and upbeat, except for Martin, who sat at his desk while the other men laughed and passed around glasses of cider. He was nervous about Corinne's health and not sure he was ready to be a father. He glanced at everyone in the room – *I can't believe one of these men is a traitor.*

He wanted to go to the top of the Woolworth building, the tallest building in the city, and yell. He considered Tunney's order not to speak about the traitor to anyone a burden. Never before had he withheld anything from Corinne. Each night he carried home his recent case notes, and when Corinne asked him what he was doing so late every night, he would lie.

Martin's attention shifted when Keller started to laugh. Griggs, who had just picked his pocket, explained how he did it.

Keller gave him a good-natured tap on the chest, but warned Griggs not to cross him again. Even though he also knew the existence of a traitor, Keller seemed unaffected, and Martin started to question his loyalty – the unspoken threat of the traitor made Martin question everything and everyone. The situation between them had worsened, since Martin could not disguise his disapproval of Keller's relationship with Shannon. For the last week, they had rarely talked about anything except their cases.

Tiny Mrs. Bauer mingled among the men and enforced proper decorum with gentle scolding and matronly finger-pointing. She passed around her home-baked oatmeal cookies. Martin took one and told her she looked more relaxed than she had in a long time.

"It's a new year, Sergeant. I always become hopeful at the start of a new year," she said.

"I wish I could feel the same," Martin said.

"I try to make the best of every situation. Listen, I'm just a Southern girl trying to earn some money, which I really need, and get by in a foreign land."

"Why do you say that? The Civil War ended fifty years ago."

"Did it? Back home they tell me I'm a turncoat for coming up north."

"Why did you come?"

"I was tired of reconstruction and carpetbaggers. I wanted adventure, a chance for a better life. When I was eighteen, I moved to New York. I met Mr. Bauer here. Living with you Yankees doesn't bother me none. If you'll excuse me, I'd like to give out the rest of these cookies."

The captain finished talking with his men and returned to his office looking tired. Since Traub's death, he had kept even longer hours and rarely visited crime scenes. Every morning, he emerged from his office with dark rings under his eyes and the same wrinkled clothing as the night before. On most mornings except today, Shannon came to his office, pulled down the shutter on his door window, and stayed there the rest of the day. No one was allowed to enter. They spoke in hushed tones, and the men began to make comments.

A few minutes after Tunney ducked into his office, Shannon arrived looking elegant and feminine with a classy, dark evening dress and a stylish coiffure that highlighted her thick red hair. Everyone's eyes turned toward her except for Keller, who looked away, trying to hide his obvious approval. She said hello to the men and headed to her uncle's office. Detective Everett Howell made an obscene gesture, and Keller charged him with a nightstick. Martin rushed to break it up. He never liked Howell.

After things quieted down, the party finished and everyone prepared to leave. Martin returned to his desk to finish some work but worried about the growing distance between Keller and him instead. He realized he had to change his attitude toward him. If they were going to solve the mystery of the internal spy and defeat the continuing, though lessened, German threat, Martin knew he needed Keller. He promised himself to try to sort out their problems on Monday when they returned to work. When Keller grabbed his coat to meet Shannon at the front desk, Martin asked, "What do you plan to do tonight, Paul?"

Keller didn't answer at first. He seemed taken aback by Martin's question. "Shannon and I are going to a dinner dance, and then we'll walk to Times Square. I want to see that seven-hundred pound ball drop down that flagpole at midnight."

Martin understood that Keller's statement was a declaration of his relationship with Shannon and decided to accept it. "You and two hundred thousand others. It's the party of the year." He tried to sound positive.

Keller wrapped a scarf around his neck and asked, "What are you going to do tonight?"

Martin tried to smile. "After Mass, I'll just go home and stay with Corinne."

"How is she?"

Martin wiped off his desk with his hand. "The war in Europe makes it hard to celebrate. We don't even know if some of our relatives in France are still alive. They live in German-occupied territory. We've had no word from them in sixteen months."

"I guess I'm lucky. All my relatives came over a long time ago." Keller started to leave, but he turned back and asked, "You got a New Year's resolution, Gil?"

"Peace on Earth; good will toward men."

~

"Peace on Earth and good will toward men. Amen." Caarsens looked at the crucifix above the altar in the small cathedral somewhere in Mexico. After the incident with Traub, he had retreated to Mexico to rest, recover, and stay away from New York. It was his first rest in years, and he didn't like it. At least his wounds were healing, and he was safe. He was anxious to return to his work, but before he could do that, Beck had ordered him to undergo special training with the Mexican military. After that, Beck promised, Caarsens would be more lethal than ever.

~

In Bronxville, Wittig went to bed before Nora early on New Year's Eve. He had little to celebrate and dreaded the coming New Year.

Chapter 43
Weil's Problem

New York Yacht Club, Manhattan: January 1916

Caarsens hesitated as he approached the six-story Beaux-Arts clubhouse of the New York Yacht Club at 37 West 44th Street. The British flag over the entrance made him tense. In front, a carriage driver covered his horse with a coarse blanket. Felix Beck had summoned him here for a meeting. With its nautical-themed limestone exterior, he had the impression the Yacht Club's building was designed for the Royal Navy. Greek columns, about three stories high, separated the three windows on the left side of the building. Large intricate stone carvings sat above the lintels. They resembled the stern of a ship of the line in Lord Nelson's time. Heads of sea monsters poked out of either side of the carvings. Caarsens hated ships, serpents, and confined spaces.

Caarsens had not seen Beck since he had killed Eugene Traub. Upon his return from Mexico a few days ago, he stayed in his secret neighborhood location and waited for his next assignment. He checked the Lutheran church daily for messages. Often, he met Jelly Brown near the Negro area of the Brooklyn dockyards. He wanted to return to the New Haven Projectile Company, but he knew Traub's death had changed his role. He hoped today's meeting would determine how.

Caarsens entered the Yacht Club and found Beck in the game room. "It looks like you've healed well." Beck studied Caarsens's face. "No visible scars. How is your arm?" Beck patted the area where Traub had gouged him.

Beck's touch hurt. "My arm is fine."

"Our other party has not arrived yet."

"Who's that?"

"Matthias Weil, a colleague."

While they waited, Caarsens studied a painting of *Victory*, Nelson's flagship at Trafalgar, which hung on the center wall of the game room. Why do the British keep winning?

A waiter with a white coat and black trousers, whose pleats were as sharp as those of a German housewife's linens, approached. He announced that Mr. Weil had arrived. Beck and Caarsens followed the waiter to the main room. It looked like the central hall of a trans-Atlantic liner. He had sailed in many such vessels on voyages in the Mediterranean and North Atlantic. Caarsens passed numerous ship models. Light beamed in from the ceiling-high windows. The room smelled of furniture polish and reeked of superiority. Men with chests-full of ribbons and spit-polished shoes talked in small groups.

Weil was sitting at a velvet-covered U-shaped bench that curved around the right bay window. His left arm was casually draped across the window sill. Looking like a Roman senator eating grapes, he fingered a chocolate taken from a plate on a small table in front of him.

As Beck and Caarsens approached, Weil stood up and bowed low enough to acknowledge their presence but high enough to indicate authority. Weil had short blond hair the color of bleached straw and looked to be in his forties. Beck introduced Caarsens to Weil as Herr Knopp, currently second-in-charge of the New Haven Projectile Company. Weil's firm handshake matched Caarsens's.

Caarsens suspected Weil knew the truth about him, or as much as Beck cared to reveal, and intended to say as little as possible.

"We can continue in German," Beck said. "Herr Weil has been based in the United States since 1897. He is familiar with our work."

"Longer than anyone else at the German embassy." Weil reached for another chocolate.

"Herr Weil runs our propaganda efforts in the Northeast, but he helps with other things."

"We help each other." Weil winked. "Let's get to the reason I needed to see you today, Herr Beck. I have a problem concerning some newspapers that have, how should I phrase it, taken an unfriendly position toward the Fatherland. It needs to be addressed immediately."

"Before we get into details, let us play some poker. Anyone watching will be less suspicious of our discussions," Beck said.

"May I suggest, Herr Beck, that we move to the card room? The club encourages gaming there. It should be empty this time of day." Weil licked his fingers.

"Fine, we have just come from there. It is a good place to talk." Beck bowed his head ever so slightly.

When they reconvened at a poker table, Weil handed Beck a deck of cards. "We can discuss things as we go along."

A waiter brought another plate of chocolates.

"Before we get started, I have a question, Herr Weil." Caarsens reached for a chocolate.

Weil's eyes narrowed, and he looked at Beck. When Beck nodded, Weil answered, "*Ja*?"

"If you are so involved with Germany's propaganda efforts, why weren't you at the peace rally last June? I'd have guessed such an event would be important for you." Caarsens tasted the chocolate. It was bittersweet and too small to satisfy his hunger.

"I was away in Panama," Weil said. He waved a chocolate in front of his face as if it were a trophy and placed it in his mouth.

"On vacation." Beck rushed to say. "Herr Weil performs several duties for us. Over the years, Herr Weil has acquired many portfolios." Beck held up the deck. "Five-card draw?" Beck shuffled the cards with a croupier's panache and slid the deck toward Weil. "Please cut them."

~

After four hands, Caarsens had won one hand with a full house – jacks high, and a pair of fives – and another with a good bluff. Weil had won one hand with a diamond flush – a lucky or suspicious win, especially since he had dealt the hand. Beck took the fourth with three eights.

Caarsens wanted to get to the reason for the meeting: what was next. "With Eugene Traub gone, is our main bomb-making operation secure?"

"We certainly can't move it, but I think it is secure. The police have no idea where it is. Even if they did, they cannot get near it. For once, the law is on our side." Beck smirked. "Another hand?"

Caarsens didn't understand his reference about the law. He wanted to learn more. Beck was rarely so talkative. "Of course."

"Last hand. I have to go in a few minutes. Your deal, Herr Beck." Weil passed him the deck.

Beck dealt the cards. "One-eyed Jacks wild."

"My man in New Jersey needs more TNT. The police have tightened controls. Raw materials are harder to get. I'm looking for a new source. I might have found one." Weil picked up his cards and arranged them. His face remained expressionless.

"Where?" Beck examined his cards.

"Never mind."

"Be careful, Herr Weil. I know that sometimes you move too fast."

"Don't worry. I've lasted a long time on my wits. Once I'm satisfied, my man can buy what he needs."

"You always use a middleman; do you not, Herr Weil?" Beck asked.

"Of course."

Weil puts others at risk. Caarsens looked at his cards. The hand was promising – three hearts: an eight, a nine, and the Jack; the nine of diamonds; and the four of spades.

"What are your plans, Herr Beck? You've just suffered a reversal." Weil rearranged his cards.

Beck kept his cards hidden in his lap. Caarsens couldn't read his face. "The best thing we can do is to stay low. Our dockside operations are in shambles right now. Let the police think they have won. They will become complacent. We will stop our bombings for a while – we have to anyway until we can reorganize. In the meantime, I will keep tabs on them." He rearranged his cards. "Just to keep the Bomb Squad occupied, I am sending them false manifests – anonymously, of course."

"And they have to check every one, I suppose," Caarsens said.

Weil looked up from his cards. "Very good, Herr Beck. That will keep them occupied."

"What do you want me to do?" Caarsens asked Beck. He discarded the four of spades. "One." Beck dealt him the ten of clubs.

"Wait. You will soon be very busy." Beck turned to Weil. "Cards?"

"Two. How is our friend, Herr Wittig? He seemed a bit on edge when I saw him at Ford's departure to Europe." Weil carelessly threw his discards on the pile.

Caarsens hoped to learn more about Wittig.

"Two." Beck flicked two discards onto the pile and dealt himself two more. "He has been most cooperative of late. He has stopped making propaganda suggestions and helps whenever I ask him for something. Final round – cards?"

"One." Caarsens gave up the nine of diamonds. He had a better chance for a straight. "I want to go back to the New Haven Projectile Company, Herr Beck."

"Herr Bier has things under control. Without Herr Traub, I need you here." Beck dealt Caarsens the seven of clubs.

"One card." Weil took the new card and folded it into the others. He rested them against his chest. "I'm glad. I have to admit that some of his ideas were excellent, but I don't trust his pacifist views. He might act unpredictably."

"I know, but he's on our side. He is not strong enough to do anything else. I must say, Herr Weil, that Wittig acts nervous whenever your name comes up."

"He doesn't like me. We had a quarrel once. Nothing important." Weil examined his cards, then looked up. "Has Herr Wittig's career progressed as we had hoped?"

"Yes. He recently received a promotion."

Caarsens turned his head to hear better.

"Just as you predicted." Weil's eyes seemed to dance. "Very good."

"Wittig is now in position to help us greatly. We have to wait for the right opportunity. Then we will ..., no need to conjecture." Beck dealt himself a card. "Final bets, gentlemen."

"I'll raise you ten dollars," Caarsens said.

Weil tossed in the money without a word.

"I call and raise you fifty dollars" Beck said.

Weil folded.

Caarsens was sure Beck was bluffing but didn't want to antagonize him. Knowing Beck became belligerent if he didn't win, Caarsens decided to take a tactical loss. It was Beck's money anyway. "I'm out." He scattered his cards face-down into the discards.

"Two pair. Kings and fours." Beck showed his cards and scooped up the pot.

"What about that matter with the *Providence Journal*, Herr Beck?" Weil took the last chocolate.

"Oh, yes, Charles Reynolds. His editorials against the Central Powers have been inflammatory and sensational. He's asking too many questions about our affairs." Beck counted his winnings.

"He must be stopped," Weil said.

"I agree." Beck placed his winnings into his coat. "Let Herr Knopp handle it. He will solve your problem."

Chapter 44
Speaker's Corner

Police Headquarters: January 1916

Martin returned to work on Monday, January 3rd anxious to sort out his problems with Keller. But his partner broke one of the captain's unwritten rules and was late. This was not how Martin wanted to start the new year. Twenty minutes later, Keller crept into the squad room and couldn't disguise his good mood.

"The captain wants to see us," Martin said abruptly. He wanted to change his tone as soon as he said it. They went down the hall in silence. As soon as they walked into Tunney's office, it was obvious he had been working all weekend. Stacks of open case reports and old files were scattered on the floor. Pages of notes and diagrams in Tunney's meticulous handwriting covered his desk. Tunney removed glasses that Martin had never seen before. He gestured for them to close the door. "I want to talk to you men about Traub's book."

"Everyone is pretty happy," Keller said breaking protocol again – the senior man, Martin, should have spoken first.

"Why? One victory does not win a war." Tunney moved his head in a slow circle to loosen the muscles in his neck. Martin heard a faint crack. "We've shut down the bomb-planting ring and protected the shipping for a while. But the Germans are still out there."

Martin knew Tunney was right, but the files on the floor meant something else. "Captain, have you made any progress on the –"

"Let Shannon and me worry about the traitor. I want to know where the hell Fritz makes his bombs. Find out how the bomb-makers get their materials. Who sells it to them? New York City has tight control on the necessary chemicals. The Germans are getting them from somewhere."

"Let's get started," Keller said, excited to do something new.

"Wait. We're going about this all wrong." Martin recalled Corinne's advice and said, "We need to think like the bomb-makers." Martin began to pace. "We know what they need, correct? Instead of us finding them, why not let them come to us?"

Tunney curled his face into a hunter's grin.

"Are you suggesting ..." Keller hesitated.

"Precisely. Let's sell it to them."

~

For the next two weeks, Keller set his trap every afternoon at the Speaker's Corner along Broadway near Macy's department store at 33rd Street. Standing on his soap box, he shouted over the voices of other men arguing about religion, politics, and temperance.

From his position near an inebriated man who preached about the sins of liquor, Martin listened to Keller fifteen feet away. Martin shivered as the wind cut through his overcoat. Martin's feet and hands were cold. Today was the last day he'd wear socks with a hole in the big toe. He'd ask Corinne to darn them tomorrow. He could wait for his next paycheck to buy new baby clothes. He gnawed on a salty pretzel and marveled at Keller's ability to talk on and on, and win every debate with hecklers. Keller knew when to be intimidating, when to be conciliatory, and when to be clever. Had he not known better, Martin would have thought the speech was scripted by German propaganda writers.

No one would have recognized Keller. His angry gray face was a marked contrast to the relaxed boyish one everyone in the Bomb Squad had come to know. He had the scratchy beginnings of a beard and greasy knotted hair. He wore a workman's cap, a threadbare coat, and gloves with no fingers, like one of those anti-czarists the newspapers were writing about. In a mix of English and German, Keller ranted about the government; he ranted about business; and he ranted about suffragettes. He attacked everything American. "Teddy Roosevelt is a war-crazed madman. William Jennings Bryan is an insufferable old bore and a has-been. Martha Washington was ugly and a bad wife."

"Boo," someone jeered. Another person tossed a smelly piece of cheese at him.

Keller dodged it. "Germans, on the other hand, are a great people. They have courage against great odds, a disciplined national character, and the best generals in the world."

"What about General Lee?"

"He lost, didn't he?"

Normally, the police would halt such a speech, but, because of the captain's arrangements, no policeman ever bothered Keller. The only policeman who ever approached the speaker's corner when Keller spoke was Sean Clancy, Martin's old colleague from the dockyards and newly assigned to the Bomb Squad. He and Martin acknowledged each other with an ear scratch and a nose pinch, gestures they had used before.

By now, Keller had captured the audience's attention. He shook his fist. "I don't care what you read in the papers, Germany has every right to fight this war. Once Russia and France mobilized,

Germany had no choice. Attack? Of course they had to attack." Spit flew out of Keller's mouth.

One man walked away.

"*Scheisskopf*. Go ahead, leave." Keller wiped his mouth with his crusted sleeve and continued. "America is interfering in Europe's war. They should either stop shipping munitions to the Allies, or they should break the damn English blockade."

Right on cue, Shannon Connolly appeared dressed as a seamstress wearing a tattered shawl. She started to heckle Keller with rehearsed vigor. "Who are you to talk like that? You're a traitor. You and all your drunken German friends should go back to Europe and let the British kill you."

"You have a problem with me, madam? If you don't like what I got to say, go."

"No. I like to see a man make a fool out of himself."

"Who's the bigger fool? The nagging female or the man who drinks to avoid her? Since I'm lacking a flask and you've said your piece, why don't you leave?"

Cheers and claps.

Shannon dropped her face and pushed her way through the crowd. She gestured to Martin as she walked by.

A man with short white-blond hair and a pronounced widow's peak laughed louder than anyone else. A German recruiter trolling for new volunteers? Could be, thought Martin. The man looked German enough. Martin had seen him here before, and he was paying more attention to Keller today.

Keller closed his talk with his standard bait. "I have valuable war-making materiel, and I'm willing to help anyone who supports my cause." After the speech, the German-looking man approached Keller and whispered something in a Saxon accent. They walked away together.

Martin followed them to Frankfurt House, already noisy and crowded with after-work drinkers. Martin waited outside, shuffled his feet, and batted his chest with his arms to fight the chilling wind. He wanted a cigarette. A half-hour later, Keller and the Saxon man exited the restaurant and parted company. Keller signaled Martin to shadow him.

~

They met back at the station house an hour later. Martin didn't see Shannon anywhere. Before he had a chance to speak, Keller asked, "What happened?"

"I lost him." Martin wiped sweat from his brow. "That man knows how to avoid a shadow. He walks down the street, stops, and buys a newspaper," Martin said. "Thirty degrees, and this man buys a newspaper. He just sits down on a bench and reads it like it's a summer day."

"Strange," Keller said.

"This man learned from Traub. I'll swear to it," Martin said. "Then the man stands up, folds up the paper, and starts to walk north. Mid-block he turns back and follows my movements. Do you know how?"

"No."

"Windows."

"Windows?"

"Yep. This man can lose someone better than Traub. Never thought of it before, but windows act like mirrors. Saw every step I made and never turned his head. He circled the block, headed toward Penn Station, and went into the subway at 32nd Street. I get on the car with him, he jumps off just as the doors close. Now, tell me what he said to you."

When Keller had finished, they were a team again and back in the hunt.

Chapter 45
Weehawken

Brooklyn: January 1916

After Keller's success at the Speaker's Corner, Martin returned home cheerful and excited. He skipped up the stairs to his apartment and unlocked his door. "Darling, I'm home." The yelling in the apartment above distracted him. He opened the bedroom door and found Corinne awake.

"What was that?" Rubbing her eyes, she looked up at Martin. "You're here? Sorry, I was napping. Let me get up and fix you dinner. I ..." Corinne tried to get up but fell back into bed. "Give me a minute," she said in a quiet voice.

Martin went to Corinne, fluffed her pillow and straightened the blankets. He kissed her softly on the cheek. She placed her hands over her expanded belly and winced.

"Something wrong?" Martin's concern and inability to help ate into his gut.

Corinne gritted her teeth. "He's just kicking something awful." This was the first time Corinne had mentioned a boy.

"Are you sick?" Martin sat on the bed.

"Don't worry. You have so much to worry about at work." Corinne's face brightened. "Hope springs eternal. I want a boy so much." Corinne reached up and pulled Martin to her. She kissed him tenderly.

"You sure it's a he?" Martin's heart jumped. "I want a boy, too. I never dared say it before."

Corinne smiled warmly. "Tell me about your ..." She shivered.

Martin placed another blanket on the bed. "Do you want some tea?" he said kindly. "What's wrong with me?"

"Tea would be wonderful. It will warm me up."

The couple upstairs stopped fighting. Martin went to the kitchen, burned his hand on the kettle, but stifled a grunt. He returned with two cups, steam swirling from them, and summarized the day's events.

Corinne sipped her tea. "Gil, did you consider that this might be a trick?"

"I don't think so. We have the name of the Saxon man's contact in New Jersey. Man named Frisch. He wants to buy TNT from us."

Corinne pulled the blanket up to her neck. "That's good. What about you and Paul?"

"What do you mean?"

"I know that you two haven't been getting along."

"That's true. I've been mad at him for acting like we were finished with the German sabotage ring."

"I think you've been upset because of his friendship with Shannon."

"Well, maybe. But we're good now. Tonight, Keller admitted that Tunney had told him to act cocky. The captain didn't want anyone to get suspicious. You see ..." Martin held his breath for a moment. "We have a traitor in the Bomb Squad."

"What?" Corinne sat up.

"The captain told me I couldn't tell anyone, not even you." Martin sat next to her and wrapped his arm around her shoulders.

“So that’s what you’ve been doing at night with all your notes. Thank God.” Corinne put her hand to her mouth.

Martin didn’t understand.

Corinne fought back tears. “I thought you had second thoughts about the baby or something. I don’t want to go back to our troubles before the war.”

“Me either. It was all about the traitor. I didn’t realize you were so upset.”

“Of course I was, but I didn’t want to upset *you*. I see more than you think I do. You get so involved in your police work.” She looked into his eyes and held him tight. “But why can you tell me now?”

“I couldn’t hide the secret from you any longer.”

“So what’s next?”

“We’re going to meet Frisch at his shop in Weehawken.” Martin put his ear on Corinne’s belly. “A boy, you say?”

~

Martin and Keller boarded the West 42nd Street Ferry to Weehawken five hours before their 3 p.m. meeting with Max Frisch. Traub’s book never mentioned his name or gave any hint of his existence. To Martin, the Palisades across the river looked like castle ramparts he had to scale. The temperature edged below freezing, and the wind along the Hudson turned it colder. Halfway across the river, the water became so choppy two passengers became sick.

Local police had provided them information on Frisch, whose record was clean. He lived in a boarding house at 41 Park Place, near his clock-making shop. The address matched information the Saxon man had provided. Frisch ran a legitimate and moderately successful business with a reputation for good work and honesty. He had been disfigured in the war, but people said he managed without complaint. According to his neighbors, Frisch did not go out at night and bothered no one – a model citizen. Frisch spoke perfect English, and the Weehawken police guessed that he might have lived a while in Canada.

Martin and Keller crossed the ferry's gangway and hiked the hillside road into town. At the top, they walked by the old rectangular water tower where an oversized American flag waved from its roof. The sight made Martin proud he was American. Arriving at Frisch's boarding house, they knocked on the door and waited. Before their agitation turned to aggression, the landlady answered, and they introduced themselves. Leaning heavily on a broom, she wore a dusty red-checkered bandanna tied at her forehead and no wedding ring. She told them Frisch was a quiet gentleman. "One of my best tenants. Opens a door for a lady. Always pays the rent on time. Lives alone. Rarely has a guest."

"Ever go into his room?" Martin asked.

"Once a day to clean. He pays me good for that."

"Ever notice anything unusual? Something you don't see anywhere else. Something that seems out of place."

"His big table is filled with diagrams and charts. 'New clock designs,' he says. Don't mean nothing to me. Why you asking?" She untied her bandana and shook it, scattering dust in all directions.

"We're conducting an investigation. He might be an important witness." Martin lied. "Do you know where we can find him?"

"Go to his shop, Black Forest Clockworks, 212 Main Street.

Couple of minutes down the road. He don't like uninvited company. He never puts an 'open' sign in his shop window. He's funny about that. Knock and he'll answer or he won't. Sometimes his hearing ain't so good. The war ..."

Martin patted her shoulder. "He's expecting us."

"Then I expect he'll see you."

~

Although it was mid-afternoon, the sign on the Black Forest Clockworks door said "Closed." Keller, still looking like a Russian anarchist, knocked. Martin, dressed in rough old clothes to look like a ruffian, saw a curtain near the window part, then close. "Just a minute," a guttural voice called from inside. After a time, a head stuck out the door. "What can I do for you?"

"*Herr Frisch*?" Keller started the conversation in German.

"*Ja*?" Frisch opened the door and stepped into the frame. Although Frisch's landlady had said he was maimed, Martin was not prepared for the sight. Frisch wore a patch over his left eye. The left side of his skull appeared somewhat flat. Strands of hair drooped over what remained of his left ear. The left side of his face had been burned and looked like half-cooked sausage. Martin smelled antiseptic. Frisch's little finger was gone and a one-inch stump was all that remained of his ring finger.

"*Guten Tag*. We were told to meet you here at this hour. We are friends of Eugene Traub," Keller said in German.

Martin waited to see how Frisch reacted when Keller mentioned Traub's name. Maybe, if Frisch thought they did business with Traub, he'd connect himself to the German saboteur network.

"Isn't Herr Traub dead?" Frisch spoke in German.

He knew – Frisch was a German agent. Traub's death had never been published in the papers. Sensing danger but feeling confident, Martin assessed their vulnerability.

"Why don't we come inside and talk about it?" Keller asked.

Frisch stepped back and nodded inside with his head. The detectives walked into the shop. It smelled of pine, metal, and lubricating oil. The floors were swept clean, and the shelves were organized and tidy. They held a collection of fine clocks that ticked away in complete precision. The face of every one showed the same time: 3:12. "Maybe you can tell me what this is all about." Frisch adjusted his eye patch.

"*Natürlich, aber –*"

Frisch pointed his right palm up and said in English, "Halt. What about your friend? Does he speak German?"

The detectives had anticipated the question. Keller replied, "No, but in our line of work, we have to use all kinds of men. That's how we fool these stupid Americans." Keller laughed.

Frisch did not react. "What kind of work might that be?"

"Helping Germany. That's why we're here."

"Humpf. Follow me," Frisch said in English as he led them to a small, dark office behind the counter. Frisch sat on a wooden folding chair and pointed to two other folding chairs leaning against the wall. "There." Looking straight at Martin, he asked, "What's in it for you?"

"Money."

"And love. He's friends with Traub's niece," Keller said.

"Renate Kleinmann. Do you know her?" Martin asked. Another test.

"Love. Ha. I hope she's worth it." Frisch snorted.

Martin pressed. "What work were you doing for Traub?"

Frisch tensed. "Why do you ask?"

Keller interrupted in German. "This *dumkopf* doesn't know the rules. He's an explosives smuggler. We know you need TNT. It's tough to get large amounts without some – how should I say it? – connections."

"How well do you know Herr Traub?" Frisch rubbed his burned cheek.

For fifteen minutes, Keller answered Frisch's questions in German and revealed convincing details from Traub's notebook. Finally, Frisch stood up. "Good. Schnapps is in order. I'll get some." After Frisch left the room, Keller smiled at Martin.

Frisch returned carrying a tray with three shot glasses and a quart milk bottle filled with clear liquid. "I made it myself. I call it kirsch." Frisch poured and handed a glass to each detective. "*Prost.*" The three men lifted their glasses and toasted each other.

The kirsch tasted like turpentine and cherries and burned Martin's throat. He almost gagged. As they started a second shot, Keller asked, "How did you end up in Jersey?"

Speaking in English, Frisch told them he was thirty-six years old. He was born in Freiberg and studied at the Karlsruhe Institute of Technology. After graduation, he completed German officer training and served two years as a lieutenant. He moved to Canada in 1903 to design farm equipment. In 1905, he relocated to Chicago and worked as a bookkeeper and a purchasing agent for a railroad company. Three years later, he moved back to Germany and opened a machine shop in Mannheim. At night, he designed mechanical devices.

When Germany mobilized at the start of the war, he was called up and promoted to captain. He led an elite demolitions company. He fought with the Sixth German Army pushing through France. He was wounded a month later near the Ourcq River, as the Sixth Army was trying to cut off the French around Verdun.

"The war has cost you," Martin said.

"I'm a soldier. Soldiers take casualties. Nothing I can do but press on and help Germany. I'd sacrifice more if I had to."

"Your injuries, how did they happen?" Keller asked.

"It was the end of the day. I was leading a counterattack. We were dynamiting French positions but had to return to our lines to get more explosives. We went to the old farmhouse where we stored ammunition. Just then, the French opened a barrage."

Silently, Martin cheered the French.

"A French round landed nearby. It ignited a box of flares my sergeant was carrying. Good man. Loved Italian opera. Had a wife and four children. Brave; never complained. Boom." Frisch's hands mimicked an explosion. "Gone. The flares ignited and shot toward me. My clothes caught fire. I rolled on the ground to put out the fire, but I fell into a drainage ditch when the next round hit. All I remember is the flash and the noise of the explosion. I woke in a hospital like this." Frisch waved his right hand across his face and body.

"How awful." Martin imagined the pain Frisch must have endured.

"I'm lucky. Men hurt worse than me. It actually looks worse than it is. I miss my eye and fingers. Nothing internal got damaged. I've got a steel plate in my head." Frisch reached up and touched the side of his skull with the rounded stub of his ring finger.

"How did you get to America?" Keller asked.

Frisch said he took several months to recover from his injuries. Just as he prepared to leave the hospital, German Military Intelligence – Section III-B he called it – contacted him. Despite his protests, they refused to send him back to the front lines. They were interested in a report he had filed before he was injured. After each battle, he had studied French shells whenever he could – live shells they had captured and unexploded ones that landed in their lines. He concluded that their high quality was due in part to superb American explosives. Because of his English, mechanical skills, and explosives training, Section III-B realized he could help Germany's newly forged sabotage efforts in America. He was excited to go. An intelligence officer gave him four thousand dollars. On April 23, 1915, he sailed to New York on the *S.S. Rotterdam* with many ideas.

"I can't imagine the war in France – the carnage," Keller said.

"No one can."

"I'm sure the pain is constant," Martin said.

"I manage." Frisch moved to his workshop. "Do you want to see what I've been working on?"

Martin controlled his enthusiasm. "Of course. I might have some suggestions."

All the benches were covered with clocks in various stages of completion. Frisch removed a tarp that covered the last bench. On it was a bomb, the design of which Martin had never seen. "I'm proud of this. I think it has real potential. Section III-B sent me here to make bombs that would do real damage. I believe I've succeeded."

"I'm impressed," Keller said. "How does it work?"

"I call it a rudder bomb. I've designed it to fit onto a ship's rudder. A rod is attached to the rudder. Each swing of the rudder blade winds a ratchet inside the device." Frisch mimicked the action with his hands. "The ratchet serves as the timing mechanism. After so many revolutions, the hammer will strike a percussion cap, which ignites the TNT packed in the container. I'll time it to explode when a ship reaches open sea. I've fitted the bomb chamber with rubber gaskets to protect the explosives. I'll pack enough explosives in the bomb to mangle the screw and split the shaft – the whole back of the ship, in fact. I guarantee I can incapacitate the most heavily armored dreadnought."

Keller whistled. "Can I look at it?"

"Of course. It's not armed."

Keller picked up the bomb and examined it from every angle. "The workmanship is excellent."

"Naturally."

"Ingenious," Martin said. "Have you used one of these yet?"

"I'm getting close."

"How will you plant them?" Keller asked.

"By boat. I have a motorboat in Weehawken near the ferry stop; it's one of the fastest on the river. At night, I plan to float up to a docked ship from the water side. No one will see me. I'll put on a diver's suit, and ..."

"Can you manage to do that alone?" Keller asked.

"I'm quite capable, I assure you." Frisch looked at them clinically. "I'll attach the bomb to the rudder."

"What about police patrol boats? Security along the docks is getting tighter," Martin said.

"I know their movements. I've already made tests. I'm so

confident this will work that I plan to shut down New York Harbor," Frisch boasted. "Maybe even Philadelphia and Baltimore."

"Did anyone help you design and build these?" Martin asked.

"No."

"What about your hand, you must have needed –"

"I am right-handed. Besides ...," Frisch held up his left hand and wiggled his three-and-a-half fingers. "These work fine. My rudder bomb is perfect. Seventy or eighty pounds of high explosives will blow a hole in the bottom of any ship."

"So you need a lot of TNT?" Martin looked right into Frisch's good eye.

"Yes. From what you say, you can get it."

"Let's just say I have access to government sources. Seventy to eighty pounds a bomb. How many bombs do you intend to make?" Martin took out a pencil.

Frisch became defensive. "Your friend asks too many questions. I think our business is completed. Will you please –"

"Did you ever see anything like this?" Martin showed him a picture of the *Kirk Oswald* bomb.

Frisch spoke German. "*Nein.* Where did you get this?"

"You didn't make that?" Keller's nostrils flared.

Frisch sneered and flipped the picture back to Martin. He reached into a desk drawer and pulled out a Luger.

Chapter 46
Silence Him

New York Public Library, Manhattan: January 1916

Three days after he had met Felix Beck and Matthias Weil at the New York Yacht Club, Caarsens leaned against the base of one of the two lion statues that guard the New York Public Library and fumed. Weil was late for their meeting. Was Weil trying to demonstrate superiority or display contempt? No matter. He'd leave in five minutes if Weil hadn't arrived by then.

Because of the weather, few people were in the vicinity. Dressed in a heavy woolen coat and a knitted cap, Caarsens peeled the roll of paper away from a pack of peppermint Life Savers and threw its covering on the ground. He resented the idea that Beck had ordered him to solve Weil's problem and despised Weil's presumed authority over him.

Caarsens tolerated Beck and his German organization because they were his enemy's enemy. He didn't care about the other warring powers. The fate of France, Austria-Hungary, Russia, or the Ottomans meant nothing to him. He wanted to be a farmer again, but he knew it would never happen.

Five minutes were up. Caarsens had better things to do than to wait for someone who treated him like a serf. Just as he started to leave, Caarsens saw Weil fight his way across Fifth Avenue and 42nd Street, one of the busiest intersections in Manhattan. Exhaust-spewing cars, confused horses, and frantic people charged the intersection from every direction. The noise was louder than a stampede. He hoped the mechanical herd would trample Weil.

Weil moved fast and managed to cross safely. He was alone, but he carried a dangerous-looking walking stick. German agents in Istanbul concealed long, narrow blades inside such things. As Weil neared, he said to Caarsens, “You like open spaces, don’t you?”

Caarsens didn’t move. “I like to be careful.”

Weil laughed. “For God, the Kaiser, and *Deutschland*, correct? Let’s conclude our business, shall we?”

“Of course.” Caarsens glowered and pulled out another Life Saver. “How do you want me to handle Mr. Reynolds?”

“Silence him. I don’t care how, just do it. Keep me out of it.” Weil, acting suspicious, walked up two steps so he could look down on Caarsens.

“What about a bribe?” Becoming distrustful, Caarsens spit out his Life Saver and watched Weil for any sudden moves.

“See what he’ll take. I’m willing to go to twenty thousand.” Weil grasped the handle of his walking stick.

“Is that all?” Caarsens reached inside his coat for the handle of his Demag.

“All right, thirty thousand. I want this matter taken care of immediately. Understand, *Kaffir* boy?” Weil stuck the tip of his walking stick into Caarsens’s ribs.

Caarsens knocked it away, grabbed Weil’s coat, and pulled him close. “Understand something. I don’t work for you, you *pisskop*. I don’t work for Beck. I’m not even German. I’m here because I want to be. I can leave just as easily. I’ve a mind to *steek* the blade in your walking stick up your arse.” Caarsens shoved Weil against the lion’s base and pointed his finger at him. “Don’t ever threaten me again.”

“If you don’t solve my *Providence Journal* problem, you’ll

regret it, Caarsens. I'm sure the police would want to know that you're a wanted man in Britain. Reynolds visits New York next week. Take care of it."

Caarsens let him go.

Chapter 47
Fifty Thousand

Weehawken, New Jersey: January 1916

Martin reacted immediately and knocked the Luger aside. Keller wrestled Frisch onto the ground and turned him face-down. He drove his knee into the back of Frisch's neck and pinned his head to the floor. Martin picked up the Luger. "You're under arrest."

Frisch stopped struggling. "Please loosen your hold."

Keller looked at Martin, who agreed. He released Frisch and stepped away warily.

"Thank you." His calm restored, Frisch stood up, brushed off his shirt, and straightened his collar. "May I see some identification, please?"

Martin pulled out his badge. Keller grumbled and thrust his badge into Frisch's face. "See. New York City Detective." Keller held it inches away from Frisch's good eye.

Frisch pushed it away. "With all due respect, you men cannot arrest me. This is New Jersey. You have no jurisdiction here." Frisch walked past them and headed to the door. "You are nothing but government scum. Go." He dismissed them as if they were servants.

"Nobody treats me like that." Keller charged. Martin let him. Keller lifted Frisch by his armpits and flung him into the wall. Some books stored on a shelf crashed to the floor. He placed his left arm against Frisch's neck and head-butted him. "You know what? I don't take kindly to insults."

"Are you going to get this monster away from me?" Frisch sounded groggy.

Martin shrugged his shoulders.

Keller punched the wall next to Frisch. Chunks of plaster broke away.

"Wait." Despair thickened Frisch's voice.

"Here's what I'm going to do." Keller thrust his index finger at Frisch's good eye. He stopped when it was inches from the cornea. "If you don't cooperate, I'm going to poke it out."

Martin looked away.

"Then, I'm going to call the Weehawken police, and they'll come and arrest you," Keller said. "I have a good friend there who's German-American like me. He hates rats like you as much as I do."

"Let me go. I'll cooperate." Frisch croaked out the words. "Let's proceed like gentlemen, shall we? Last year, I could have killed you both; not now."

"Sit. We need to talk." Martin picked up his chair and slammed it down.

Frisch said, matter-of-factly, "Since we're all reasonable men, I have an offer."

"I'm listening." Martin was curious. How important did Frisch consider his work?

"I'll give you any amount of money if you will let me go." Frisch reached into his pocket. Keller lurched. "Calm down, Detective. I'm just reaching for my cigarette case." He pulled it out. "See? Do you want one?"

Martin resisted the temptation to smoke. He decided to play along with Frisch. "How much will you give me?"

"All you want – I have resources."

"Fifty thousand?" Martin quoted an outrageous sum.

“Yes, fifty thousand, if you want it.”

“The price includes some information first,” Martin said. “Who is the contact between you and Traub?”

“Listen, you want the money? Let me get it, and then I’ll answer your questions.”

“Where is it?”

“Down the hall.” Frisch pointed. His hands were steady.

“Get it.” Martin wanted proof of the bribe. He motioned to Keller to follow him.

Frisch walked ahead. After several steps he stopped and grabbed his head as if he were in pain. In the next second, he kicked backward and hit Keller in the groin. Before Keller could recover, Frisch ran into a bathroom. Martin was too slow to help. A lock turned. Keller recovered and started to kick it down.

“Get away from there,” Martin shouted. He dived for cover.

Keller sprinted down the hall.

Seconds later, an explosion rattled the house. Clouds of dust and splinters sprayed Martin. When he opened his eyes, he looked up and saw the sky. Keller lay on the ground covered with debris. His ears still ringing, Martin hurried over. Keller was unconscious but breathing steadily and bleeding from numerous superficial wounds.

Keller woke up coughing. “Holy Christ. That was close. Thanks, Gil.”

“You owe me one.”

Martin inspected the area around the explosion. The walls were misted red. The only remains of Frisch were his shredded eye patch and fragments that Martin guessed were bone. The wooden floor started to burn. Martin beat out the fire with his coat and lifted Kelller up. “Let’s get out of here and call for help. This place isn’t safe.”

Martin helped Keller outside. No longer in danger, Martin patrolled the grounds and found Frisch’s right boot; his warm foot was still in it. Still groggy, Keller sat under a tree and held his head. A steam-powered horse-drawn fire engine pulled up. One of the firemen examined Keller while the others unreeled the hose and ran into what remained of the house.

When the fire captain declared the building safe and Keller fit for duty, the detectives searched the remains of Frisch’s shop. They found no clues related to German sabotage operations, but in his desk, Keller discovered a chart of New York Harbor that revealed all its piers and fortifications. In the supply room, they collected a number of half-finished bombs. In a packing case in the basement, Keller discovered four completed rudder bombs. In addition to the finished bombs, Martin and Keller uncovered 25 sticks of dynamite, 400 detonation caps, and 200 bomb cylinders in his garage.

“Amazing these didn’t ignite with the explosion.” Martin began to comprehend how close he had come to death.

“Different part of the house. Your luck held today, Gil.”

His hands still shaking, Martin sifted through rubbish. “Maybe Frisch was just someone on the fringe, but I’ll tell you this, his bombs are sophisticated.”

“What do we do now?” Keller picked up a piece of mangled wood and smashed it into toothpicks to vent his anger.

“We’ll tell the papers Frisch was an inventor. One of his experiments went bad. The Weehawken police will back us up. We’re not defeated, yet.” Just as Martin prepared to leave, every working clock in what was left of the shop chimed 5 p.m. in jeering unison.

Chapter 48
What's That?

Hudson River: January 1916

Caarsens laughed as he sped Frisch's motorboat away from Weehawken. Once again, Beck was ahead of the police. Following Beck's urgent order, Caarsens had just confiscated one of the fastest boats in New York Harbor and in the process had gained the same wide range and flexibility of movement that he had as a Boer horseman and commando. At first, the motorboat handled like a wild mustang, but he tamed it quickly and enjoyed the hum of the powerful engine as it glided over the choppy Hudson River, spraying his face with cold salty water. The speed, his control over the machine, and his feeling of invincibility gave him a deep satisfaction he had not experienced in a long time.

He headed back to Jelly Brown's dockyard area, the only place where he knew he could hide the motorboat. He waited for Jelly, who had become the closest thing to a friend he had had since he left South Africa, to arrive that evening. Despite their different backgrounds, Brown was a fellow warrior, a savvy operator, and an uncompromising outcast. Both men had courage, fortitude, and strong religious convictions.

When he saw the motorboat, Brown's eyes widened with admiration and respect. "My, my, my, that's one fine-looking boat. I'da mind to trade my woman for it. I'm smart enough not to ask where it come from, but I'm sure gonna ask what you gonna do with it."

"Let's share it," Caarsens said. "I trust you, and I need your help with it."

"I'll help, but that's it. If'n any white man sees me alone with this here fancy boat, he'll be asking more questions than a jealous woman. He'll sure be wondering what some colored man doin' with it. I'll hide it, and I'll teach you how to use it, but I'd be a fool to use it myself." Brown and his two most trusted men, Sam and Quincy, powered up the engine and streamlined the boat's contours. To disguise it, they painted it and added a collapsible canvas top. After the changes, Caarsens was confident that no one would recognize it at a distance. They hid the motorboat in a covered boathouse attached to a small run-down shack alongside the dock.

When the transformation was complete, Brown took Caarsens out on the water and taught him everything he knew about boating. Even though Caarsens had never lived near the ocean, he leaned quickly. Navigating on water and using the sun and stars to determine locations wasn't much different than riding on the veldt. Together they scouted New York Harbor, Long Island Sound, the Hudson and East Rivers, and even a few miles up and down the Atlantic coast. Caarsens's excellent visual memory enabled him to remember markers and shore points. With his sharp intellect, he learned everything else fast – tides, currents, depths, dangers.

Soon, Caarsens knew hiding places, the inner waterway escape routes, and shallow areas that most boats could not navigate. To give the motorboat additional range, Caarsens carried extra gasoline in cans. In case he was spotted by the police and could not escape, he set an explosive charge that he could detonate if he had to.

The first time Jelly took him past the Statue of Liberty to the Jersey side of the harbor, Caarsens spotted a mile-long causeway stuck into the water like the shaft of a Zulu spear. Seven piers jutted out from the shaft. Cargo ships, barges, and tugs crawled among the piers like crabs at low tide. “What’s that?”

“That there’s Black Tom Island,” Jelly said. “It mostly landfill. It got its name from some old fisherman who lived there a while back. It’s the biggest loading and shipping center I ever seen.”

Caarsens studied the depot with an artillery spotter’s eye and a saboteur’s deadly sense of opportunity. “*Ag, man*. That’s a mighty big target.”

~

That night, Caarsens returned to his quarters in Chinatown still thinking about Black Tom Island. Despite its close proximity to the Police Headquarters on Centre Street near Canal Street, he felt safe in Chinatown and tolerated the crowded and strange surroundings. For the most part, the police let the locals make their own rules and enforce them however they wanted. When Caarsens had first arrived in New York, he met Mock Duck, the head of the Hip Sing Tong, a Chinese organized crime band, through Turkish connections he knew before the war. After completing the necessary formalities and payoffs, Mock arranged for him to stay in a room above the Wing Sing restaurant on Doyers Street deep in Chinatown.

Mock made it clear to the Chinatown residents that he protected the Western stranger. His word was final, his temper fearsome, and his sentences harsh. His chain-mail vest, missing fingers, and conspicuously visible hatchet added to his authority. People walked across streets to avoid him or bowed and kept their eyes to the ground if they mistakenly got close to him.

In the months he lived there, the local people began to accept Caarsens. He paid well, never asked questions, and most important, he treated them as equals. They somehow understood that, despite his blue-eyed Anglo-Germanic looks, he wasn't accepted in America, either. The difference between his Chinese hosts and him was he chose not to belong.

They called him Mr. Barrymore after the famous moving picture star because he claimed to be an actor and dressed in various costumes. He didn't understand why, but the Chinese accepted each others' deceits. If they thought it was strange that Caarsens looked different every day and traveled at odd hours, they never said anything.

In exchange for Mock's protection, Caarsens provided a well-funded gratuity, but he knew the day would come when his bribes would not be enough to satisfy Mock's self-interest and greed.

Chapter 49
The Unexploded Bomb

Midtown Manhattan: February 1916

It was midday; Caarsens had three hours to get ready for the two missions he needed to accomplish today. The first was to complete the assignment Beck had finally given him a few days ago. It seemed curious, but he knew Beck was planning something spectacular later this year. He figured this task was part of a grand scheme. The second task, completing Weil's orders, would be tricky and distasteful.

Through his reconnaissance of Broadway and Sixth Avenue, Caarsens had decided that the best time to complete Beck's first assignment was 3 p.m., when activity was light. Carrying a knapsack, he headed to the Lutheran Church and found Beck's note. It directed him to a briefcase hidden near the organ. He checked its contents thoroughly. It was all there; Caarsens had to admit Beck was efficient.

In the men's latrine at the church, Caarsens changed into common businessman's clothes, made sure the device was set correctly, and walked to his target. He wore a dark pin-striped wool suit, a waistcoat over a stiff white shirt, and a fedora. Only his worn-out shoes looked out of place, despite their polish. To consume time and to survey his target, he ate some pancakes and coffee at Hartford's lunch counter on the corner that overlooked the entire block. When he was ready, he paid the bill and dropped just enough coins on the table so he'd be forgotten. When he left the restaurant, he looked up through thick glasses and saw a huge tire advertisement overhead. Strange city. A trolley car clanked past him.

He crossed the street and was almost hit by another trolley car coming from the opposite direction. Its clanging bell had warned him just in time. He found safety in a small pedestrian island in the street between the two trolley lines. A northbound elevated train rolled overhead. The afternoon's sun's rays reflected off its copper skin. Caarsens felt its vibrations and had to place his hands over his ears to muffle deafening screeches.

When the street was quiet, Caarsens headed toward the base supports for the El train. He looked around and pulled a paper bag from his satchel and lit a cigarette. With the cigarette in his hand, he reached into the bag. A fizzing sound, which did not concern him, began. He placed the package under one of the large train supports and walked toward the subway entrance across the street. After a few minutes, he doubled back to the bag to stare and poke at it. Suddenly, as if someone had lit his trousers on fire, he started to run around, his arms flailing, and yelled, "Bomb. There's a bomb!" He pointed and backed away in fake horror. "Help! Somebody help."

When a roundsman neared, Caarsens fled, knowing the bomb would not go off.

~

Martin stopped humming when he left the subway. Keller, who had been searching for Frisch's boat, was waiting for him at the entrance. They were the first demolition experts to arrive on the scene of the unexploded bomb. Despite having cordoned off the area around the base of the El train at Sixth Avenue and Broadway, the police were struggling to retain order. Passengers from the El trains that had been ordered to stop flooded angrily onto the street. Crowds blocked the trolley tracks. One disruption created another. Angry businessmen stood around and griped to anyone who would listen. Curious spectators wanted information. Anxious people wanted assurances.

Martin looked at the confusion in front of him. "I was having a good day until this," he told Keller.

~

Keller was nervous and tried to hide it. This was the first unexploded bomb he would have to defuse without supervision. To distract himself, he said, "I wonder what these Hun bastards are up to now. It's been a week since Frisch killed himself, and we still can't find his God-damn motorboat."

"We'll find it."

Pushing through the throng, Keller heard their chatter. "Why so many police?" one person asked. "It's a bomb," another said. "You're wrong. It's nothing. The police caused this mess." People behind the barricades craned their necks to get a better look. "The anarchists are back." Others tried to push forward. "Let me see."

In silence, the detectives moved into the restricted area and walked to the El train supports. A nervous cop stood near the unexploded bomb. He shuffled his feet and tapped his leg with his night stick. "I understand you're the roundsman who reported the bomb," Martin said.

"Yes, Sergeant. There." The roundsman pointed and kept looking back at the bomb as if he expected it to explode any second.

"We'll take care of it, but first tell me who found it," Keller said.

"Some businessman shouted 'bomb' and I came running." His tapping sped up. Keller told him they'd want more information after they disposed of the bomb and ordered him to safety across the street. He dashed away like a riderless horse fleeing a battlefield.

Keller approached the bomb with the utmost caution. Martin followed close behind until Keller stopped and pushed him back. "Let me do this. If something goes wrong, I want you to see your baby, Gil." Martin hesitated, but Keller remained firm. "I'm not touching that bomb until you move away."

When Martin was out of harm's way, Keller approached the bomb, which was contained in a paper bag, the kind used to carry groceries. He looked at the supports to the El train and the overhead tracks above to assess possible damage. *If this had gone off, it could have been a disaster*. The bomb would have blown a gap in the tracks. At least three Jewett train cars, each carrying up to 160 people, would have crashed to the ground. Injuries and deaths could have reached the hundreds.

Pushing all other thoughts aside, Keller focused on the bag. *The only way someone could have seen a bomb is if he had gotten really close to the bag. Why would someone do that?* Keller wondered. Careful not to touch anything, he stood over it and looked inside. All he could see was a cardboard container a little bigger than a shoe box and a fuse that looked as if it had failed. Utmost caution was still required; whatever was in the box remained dangerous. His mouth turned dry, and his armpits became wet. He breathed deeply a few times and looked under the bag – was it resting on a pressure plate or something else that could set it off?

Convinced it was not, he followed Bomb Squad protocol and sniffed the box. Every explosive component has its own smell. *Dynamite – thank God it's not nitroglycerine!* He crossed his fingers and looked to the sky, a step he added to the protocol in deference to his obstinate and superstitious great-grandmother who at ninety-one years old was inexplicably healthy. With a steady hand he reached for the knife strapped to his leg and cut the bag away to expose the bomb. When he finished, he stepped away to wipe the sweat from his brow. Water could create a fatal short circuit.

"Be careful, Paul," Martin shouted from a distance.

The words distracted Keller for a moment. He closed his eyes, collected his thoughts, and prayed he'd remember everything he'd been taught. Certain that Martin's life and his impending fatherhood were more important than his, Keller fought back his fears. He examined the outside of the bomb for moisture but saw none. To gauge its temperature, he felt the box – still cold, a good sign. He examined the exterior of the box and found the seam, which he cut away surgically.

He reached the most dangerous step. Shannon's image flashed through his mind. He held his breath and opened the lid. Four sticks of dynamite taped together were attached to a fuse of lightweight paper wrapped in gunpowder. A simple device, it was nothing like a cigar bomb or the sophisticated rudder bombs. He studied the fuse, which was coated with lacquer, and concluded it had fizzled out because it had gotten wet. *How had that happened?* He removed the fuse and declared the bomb safe.

Martin ran over and patted Keller on the back.

"Thanks, Gil. I have to say I've never been more scared in my life." His heart rate returned to normal.

"Sure didn't seem that way to me. Great job. Great job. Why did the bomb fail?" Martin asked.

Keller explained. “It doesn’t make sense. Nothing complicated about this bomb. That fuse shouldn’t have gone out. The bomb was either made by amateurs, which I don’t believe, or it was designed to fail.”

“With all the arrests and deaths, maybe we’ve reduced the Germans’ bomb-making skills to this. That bomb was the best they could do.”

“I don’t think so.” Keller scanned the neighborhood. “This whole scene, something about it is planned. The bomb, the businessman who found it – I can’t believe he found it by accident. It’s like the Germans deliberately wanted this bomb to fail. But why? A diversion?”

“Maybe they’re trying a new tactic – terror, like the Black Hand used,” Martin said.

Keller dreaded what might happen next. Just then, another policeman arrived and told them a bomb had just exploded at the City Hall subway station. The only person killed was a *Providence Journal* reporter.

Martin’s face showed his worry.

Keller said, “That’s no coincidence. It’s a new wave of bombings.”

Chapter 50
Where Does He Live?

The German Club, Manhattan: February 1916

At the same time Martin and Keller were examining the unexploded bomb, Wittig was finishing his regular lunch with Felix Beck at the German Club on 59th Street. Beck seemed anxious and bored. "Herr Wittig, you have not told me anything new."

Because Beck, through his friendship with Matthias Weil, knew about his complicity in the murder at Milton Point, Wittig was careful not to annoy him. In a delicate and dangerous balance, Wittig answered most of Beck's persistent questions but concealed details about the enormous profits his Morgan Bank unit was compiling. "What do you want to know?" he asked guardedly, feeling himself balancing on the edge of a cliff.

"Tell me about your boss, Swanson. Where does he live?"

Ever since Wittig received his promotion into Swanson's group at the bank, Beck had maintained a special interest in Swanson. Clever and subtle, Beck had initially asked general questions about Swanson but did not press for information. This was the first time he made such a direct inquiry. Taken aback by the question, Wittig said, "He's a very private man and lives on a houseboat in New York Harbor."

"Come, come. I read that in the papers. Give me something more. How many men guard him? Where does he eat? Does his wife ever visit Manhattan alone? Where do his children go to school?"

Why does he want to know all that? Wittig's stomach turned. He honestly didn't know.

Beck became belligerent and demanded more. "The Fatherland needs you. What big thing is about to happen? You are not telling me everything."

Nervous and intimidated, Wittig held nothing back except some Morgan Bank secrets, but Beck pushed further. After he had nothing else to say and under duress, Wittig revealed that Morgan Bank had started to organize a week-long conference in April with military, banking, and business officials from Britain, France, and the United States. Hearing this information, Beck's mood changed, and his antagonism morphed into curiosity and then excitement. He pressed for more information: time, place, names of attendees and security measures. Wittig promised to provide details as the plans finalized.

Wittig left the German Club certain he had disclosed too much.

Chapter 51
What's Wrong?

Broadway, Manhattan: February 1916

With the bomb defused, Martin announced that the area was safe. Soon, the El trains were running again, and the crowds thinned. "Something's not right." Martin rubbed his jaw with thumb and index finger and looked down Broadway. Ice was starting to form on the three lone poplar trees near the subway entrance. Two subway trains, heading in opposite directions, passed below him. Martin cupped his ears and felt the vibrations. He saw Keller's mouth move. "What did you say?"

"Shannon." Keller pointed to the subway entrance. "What's she doing here? She told me she had a doctor's appointment."

Shannon walked toward them. Her head was bent down and sideways to fight a strong wind. With one hand, she wiped her nose with a white handkerchief, with the other she held her coat tight against her body. A shawl was wrapped around her neck. Martin noticed that she walked hesitantly, as if she was afraid of stepping on something. Her eyes and nose were red, and she had trouble speaking.

"What's wrong?" Keller asked.

She shook her head and avoided Martin.

"Shannon. What's wrong?" Keller pulled her close.

She nudged him away and tried to straighten up, but the wind forced everyone to huddle down. When she managed to stand erect, she looked at Martin. "I'm so sorry." She broke down and started to sob. Her head fell onto Keller's shoulder.

Keller patted her back and whispered something to her.

Martin braced himself. “Tell me.”

Shannon sniffled and wiped her eyes. “You’d just left the stationhouse when we got the news. We –”

“What?”

“We tried to call you, but ...”

“Shannon, for God’s sake, what happened?” Panic crept into Martin’s voice.

“A nurse called from the hospital. Your wife was taken there three hours ago.”

“My God. Did she have the baby? Is she all right?”

“No.” She choked on her words. Shannon took a deep breath and finally said, “She died in childbirth an hour ago. She hemorrhaged. They couldn’t stop it. The doctors –”

“And the baby?”

“Struggling.”

Chapter 52
Beck's Grand Plan

Penn Station, Manhattan: March 1916

Caarsens sat next to Beck on a bench in the crowded waiting room at Penn Station during afternoon rush hour. "This is your most critical job to date. It represents a new phase in our operations," Beck said. "I am suspending all your other assignments." A uniformed man walked through the area, cupped his hands around his mouth, and shouted train arrivals and departures. People hurried in all directions depending on the information, and the commotion made it difficult to hear.

Beck folded his paper to the sports news. "Says the Giants are expected to have a better team this year. I hope so – another distraction away from us. The city is happier and more relaxed when they win." Beck leaned over. "Our investment in John Wittig has paid off. We can finally eliminate Swanson." Beck revealed what Wittig had told him about the upcoming Morgan Bank conference.

"But how will I get to him? He'll be inside a hotel, so I can't shoot him from across the street. I might be able to walk up to him and stab him, but I'd never get away."

"You'll get close enough to shave him, and no one will know a thing."

"How?"

"Through his connections, our friend Herr Weil has gotten you a job at the Biltmore Hotel. Go. Tomorrow. You will be a waiter disguised as a French-Canadian, Philippe Charbonneau, who was born in Maine."

"What about my other duties?"

"I have wanted to kill Swanson for a long time. This is our chance. The Bomb Squad is disorganized now. They are chasing their tails investigating the false manifests I have sent them; morale is low. They don't know if we have disappeared, become incompetent, or started new smuggling operations. They think anarchists, not us, are responsible for our subway attacks."

Caarsens was less optimistic. "Don't underestimate them. Those men are good."

"Come, let us walk. I don't want to stay in one place too long." They sauntered through Penn Station while Beck explained his new strategy. "I'm Germany's answer to John D. Rockefeller. Like his Standard Oil, I am going to vertically integrate my operations. We will attack every step related to the U.S. munitions supply."

"Explain."

The first thing Beck had tried to do when he arrived in New York was to stop the physical flow of materiel to the Allies. He wanted to prevent the supply ships from delivering their cargo. That seemed easy enough. Through Eugene Traub and the German bomb-makers, they organized an effective ship-bombing campaign. They damaged or sank tons of munitions, but there was a problem. Too many ships carried too many munitions. Germany had underestimated America's ability to expand its industrial capacity. America had become an economic colossus.

Caarsens had participated in Beck's next phase: interruption of the flow of goods by blowing up railroads and destroying bridges. German saboteurs, including Caarsens, attacked the plants that manufactured the goods. But there was another problem – limited manpower to attack all the targets. Worse, the security in places where sabotage could make the most impact, like the Welland Canal, was too tight. There was always another plant, a different route to take. They wouldn't stop trying, but Beck needed to do something more.

After that, Beck went after the people who produced the goods. The labor disruptions caused by union unrest were clever. The New Haven Projectile Company's ability to hire away key workers, corner important raw materials, divert or buy finished goods, or ruin companies that produced them was his best work yet. "You don't have to blow up an artillery piece to render it ineffective; you just need to destroy its firing mechanism," Beck had told Caarsens.

With Wittig's latest information on the upcoming conference at the Biltmore, Beck had the ability to hit America at an even more vital level. Hence, the next step in Beck's vertical integration. "I want to stop the key people who run the operations. That is where you are needed." Beck patted Caarsens on the back.

"What happens if none of your plans work?"

"Then we will move to the last phase. We will attack their economic nerve center itself, downtown Manhattan."

"I've wanted to do that since I arrived."

Beck looked around. The commuter crowd had started to thin. "Let's talk outside."

They walked out to Eighth Avenue and crossed west on 32nd Street. A cold March rain had made the streets slippery. People running late nudged them as they headed toward the refuge under the Corinthian columns of the two-city-block-wide Post Office building. Caarsens wiped his face and waited for some men to walk by them and enter the building. When they were alone, Caarsens asked, "Why can't I attack Wall Street now?"

"It will provoke America into declaring war. If they do, Germany will lose. If things go badly, we will strike it as a last resort."

"Tell me about your plan for Swanson."

Beck revealed his plan. "No one else can be hurt. You will murder Swanson without anyone realizing you did it."

Caarsens waited for more post office customers to walk by. Making sure no one could hear, he stressed his point. "With so many important people in one place, we should blow them all up."

"No. Let me repeat. We cannot risk pushing America into the war." Beck spoke too loud and a passerby glanced at him and moved on. In a quiet voice, he said, "But, if we make people think it was an accident, something that can't be traced to us ..."

"Why haven't we been able to assassinate Mr. Swanson by now? Surely –"

"We've tried, but Mr. Swanson is a careful man. He travels with armed guards, but with Herr Wittig's information, poisoning him will be easy."

Chapter 53
First Day Back

Saint Cecilia's Catholic Church, Brooklyn: April 1916

At the end of a two-month leave of absence imposed on him by Captain Tunney, Martin left his house and started to take his normal route to work. He was anxious to get back to the Bomb Squad and hoped his work would allay his restlessness and anxiety. In his daze, he somehow ended up at Saint Cecilia's, his regular church. He had not been inside since the funeral, and, once there, he had to enter. Leaving would betray his strict religious upbringing and Corinne's wish he go to mass at least once a week. Inside, Saint Cecilia's felt cold, dark, and comforting.

Battling a perplexing mix of reverence, anger, and remorse, Martin stood by his regular pew and glared at the crucifix. Martin moved to his seat and knelt but did not pray. What the hell difference did praying make, anyway? God didn't listen. He started to leave, but just as he picked up his coat, an inner force moved him to pray. Not used to praying, his knees ached from kneeling.

After he finished, Martin recalled all the services he and Corinne had attended. Vivid details about her came to mind – how she combed her hair, the way she said his name, her loving look when she told him she was pregnant. Already missing her good-natured common sense, he was reassured he'd see her again and comforted that she was never far away. He talked to her every night when he lit a candle before he went to bed.

The church lilies reminded him Easter was less than two weeks away. It would be the first Easter he and Corinne would be apart since they met at Saint Cecilia's ten Easters ago. He remembered her dressed in her favorite white and daffodil-yellow bonnet. This year it would remain in her closet collecting dust. He could not give it away. Maybe he'd burn it. Ashes to ashes; dust to dust. He tried not to think about the baby, who had survived a day. The cramp in his legs reminded him that he was still alive to share his loss with millions of others whose families had already been destroyed by the war.

Why should his family be excluded? Men choose to go to war. They die. Women and children mourn them – it's been that way forever. But his loss contradicted the natural way of things – he had lived and his wife and baby had died. Why, he wasn't sure. This was America. The war should not have invaded its shores, but Martin knew that it already had. No man should have to bury his baby. How did other men in his situation manage? He knew that, like him, such men would never be the same, and he would forever share an unspoken bond with them.

Martin looked up when Father Luke started to preach. His thoughts turned away from the service toward tangible things. Things he could understand. Things he could affect. Things he could defeat. First among those were the German saboteurs. When the Mass was over, Father Luke approached him. "It's good to see you back, Gilbert. I was beginning to wonder when you'd return. You look better. A bit thin, maybe."

"Thank you, Father." Martin's freshly cut hair and cleanly shaven face felt strange after so many weeks without attention.

"You have suffered a great loss. How is your faith?"

"My faith?" Martin didn't know how to answer. "Corinne would want me to ..." Martin looked away.

"When you are ready." Father Luke gently placed his hand on Martin's shoulder. "Healing takes time. Remember, God is always with you."

Is he? Before he left church, Martin lit two candles. As the candles melted, he asked God several questions. Would he be as good a cop at work as he was before? Would he ever be a father again? Did he want to be? Would he ever find someone else to love again? He imagined he saw Corinne. "You've let too much time pass, my love. Continue your work. You fight a good cause. You'll succeed; I know you will." She faded into the smoke from the candles. Enough self-pity. An assassin's still lurking about. After he was caught, there'd be time to work things out with God.

~

When Martin entered the main hall of Police Headquarters, most people smiled briefly, expressed their sorrow, and said they were glad to see him. A few, not knowing what to say, kept their distance. One detective nodded, speechless, blew his nose, and moved on. Keller bounded down the long curving stairs to meet him in the high-ceilinged front hallway. Before he reached Martin, Keller hesitated, to control his energy, and approached. "Gil, it's good to see you. No time to explain, hurry."

Confused, and after two months without much physical activity, Martin struggled more than usual to catch the fleet Keller. When Keller reached the back staircase that led to the basement where their motorcar was parked, he turned to Martin and said in a rat-a-tat cadence, "Last night I shadowed this German officer to a warehouse downtown. First break in a month. I just got my warrant." Keller waved a piece of paper like it was a winning bet at the track.

Keller jumped in the driver's seat and Martin cranked up the car, a reversal of their normal roles. Martin felt odd but said nothing. Like he approached everything else, Keller drove up the northern ramp onto Broome Street and accelerated fast to the point of recklessness, unconcerned the other two police vehicles assigned to his detail lagged farther and farther behind.

Eyes fixed to the street, scouting for any chance to gain ground, Keller explained. "Remember that brownstone on 15th Street we were watching?"

"123 West 15th. The one we thought was a brothel?" Always suspecting it was something more, Martin began to feel Keller's enthusiasm.

"Yeah. The one the captain said we couldn't touch. Orders from Washington. 'Don't upset any German officials.' Shit." Keller veered sharply to the left to avoid a daydreaming pedestrian. Back on course, Keller continued. "While you were away, I observed it in my off-hours. Even spotted the German ambassador, Count von Bernstorff himself, go in."

"Watch it!" Martin feared for a distracted delivery man about to cross the street.

Keller beeped his horn and accelerated by him. "Last night, a German officer left there; he was drunk and up to no good. He hailed a taxi, and I followed him to this warehouse. This officer gets out, acting real suspicious-like, and looks around to make sure he's alone. I stay hidden while he unlocks the gate and rolls it up. Before he gets it closed, I spot cases of weapons. I'm sure of it. We're going to investigate."

Since the start of German sabotage activity, the Bomb Squad

was concerned about the possibility of an uprising of German sympathizers and sailors. Together with German-Americans loyal to the Fatherland, there were enough men to form a regiment, but the question, like Irish revolutionaries in Dublin and Derry, was their access to weapons. If Germany could arm them, these men would become a threat.

Keller stopped the motorcar at 200 West Houston Street so hard Martin nearly hit the windshield. "There." Except for some scavenging dogs, the street was empty. Five minutes later, the rest of Keller's detail arrived. Keller told one team to watch the back as he went to the trunk of his motorcar. He handed Martin his favorite weapon, a Winchester Model 12 pump-action shotgun. The powerful gun felt good in his hands. Keller reached for a blacksmith's sledge hammer and led Martin and the other two roundsmen to the gate. "Step back." Swinging the sledge like a baseball bat, Keller smashed the lock with home-run power.

The lock yielded to the force with a metallic groan. Keller tossed the sledge away and rolled up the gate. Revolvers and shotguns at the ready, the policemen entered the warehouse in a military wedge – Keller at the front point, Martin to his right a few feet behind, and the other two men angled to his left. "Police!" Keller shouted.

The warehouse was dark and empty. Keller moved to the crates he had seen last night. "Here it is." After completing their inventory, Martin and Keller counted two thousand 45-caliber Colt revolvers, ten Colt machine guns, seven thousand Springfield rifles, three million revolver cartridges, and two and a half million rifle cartridges. Just before they were about to leave, a man claiming to be the owner appeared. Indignant, he demanded to know what they were doing. Keller slapped the warrant into his hands and arrested him.

"But I've done nothing wrong. These weapons are going to British India," he protested as a roundsman dragged him away in handcuffs.

Keller turned to Martin and said, "Not bad for your first day back."

"That's a lot of firepower." Martin shuddered to think of a street-to-street war in Manhattan.

"We've missed your luck. Glad to have you back, Gil."

~

Back at headquarters, Martin was surprised to find his desk was tidy. "Everyone wants to help – Shannon, the captain, Griggs, Regan at the front desk, the whole squad," Keller said. "You can talk to them later, but we need to see the captain first.

On their way to Tunney's office, they saw Mrs. Bauer laboring down the steps. "Oh, Sergeant. It's so good to see you," she said in her matronly way. "There are no words to express my sadness. I cried for days when I heard the news."

Martin thanked her and followed Keller. "By the way, Paul, I never thanked you for taking care of things at the hospital when Corinne ..." Martin couldn't finish.

Keller hesitated to find the words. "It was the least I could do. Now, let's get these German bastards. We owe her that."

Martin agreed and flicked away a tear. Still grieving, he wanted to change the conversation. "How are you and Shannon doing, Paul?"

"Fine. If anything, your tragedy has brought us closer."

"Good, I like her," Martin said, realizing how his perceptions had changed.

~

After lighting a cigar, Captain Tunney went through the key events since Martin went on leave. The bombing at City Hall had scared the mayor so badly he forced Tunney to redirect his efforts to finding the perpetrators. After he redeployed half his men to the increasingly futile investigation, two more subway bombs failed to detonate. For seven weeks, they had chased their backsides. Tunney postulated that someone, most likely a German, was either taunting or distracting him.

Tunney described his other problem: ship manifests. Someone had sent the Bomb Squad leads that falsely documented German smuggling efforts through Holland, Denmark, and Finland.

"Where are we getting the information?" Martin asked.

Tunney reached into his desk and pulled out a stack of letters and tossed them on his desk. "The mailman. These letters are full of information about falsified manifests."

"Very detailed." Keller gave a handful of the letters to Martin. "The problem is they don't lead anywhere."

"But we can't ignore them." Tunney chewed the end of his cigar.

Martin shuffled through the letters. "The handwriting looks the same on all the letters. What does it mean?"

Tunney pounded his cigar stub into the ash tray. "Another wild goose chase. That's what it means, and I don't like it." Tunney poked at the ashes with his cigar butt. "I fear the Germans are up to something big."

Chapter 54
The Faustian Bargain

Bronxville: April 1916

Daylight started to overtake night, and desperate thoughts forced Wittig awake. He wasn't sure what he feared more – his nightmares or his current situation. He imagined himself walking a tightrope over the East River. He considered bringing his revolver with him. It was hidden in the cold storage room in the cellar on a high shelf behind home-made pickles the girls never ate. He didn't like to have guns in the house, but after Milton Point, he sensed danger, and menace surrounded every aspect of tonight's Morgan Bank conference at the Biltmore Hotel. Would he need the revolver tonight or not? Would he use it? Wittig couldn't decide.

He had obtained the revolver from the only source he could think of – Beck. Beck had been delighted to provide it. He acted surprised by Wittig's request. Didn't every man have a gun in his house? The next time they met, Beck handed him a Colt – 1915 Army Special 6-shot double action 32-20 revolver and three boxes of ammunition. He asked Wittig if he knew how to use it. He did. Wittig's father had insisted that every young man should know how to handle weapons. When he was twelve, his father took him to an open field and taught Wittig to shoot birds and squirrels. Wittig hated the lessons but wouldn't disobey his father. Despite his disgust, Wittig became a good shot. He believed that understanding the lethal nature of guns and killing helpless animals had made him a pacifist.

Nora stirred next to him. He pretended to sleep. "I know you're awake, John Wittig. You've been jittery for the last hour. You got home so late, I didn't have a chance to speak to you. I've got something important to discuss."

Wittig's relationship with Nora had improved over the past months, and he didn't want to disturb the marital calm he had worked so hard to restore. "You're awake?" He tried to sound concerned.

"The uprising. It's about to happen."

"What?"

"The Irish Revolution, of course." Nora sat up and told him about the letter from her brother, Rory Fitzpatrick, a leader of the Irish Republican Brotherhood. Rory hinted that, while Britain wasted its energy on the war, this Easter was the time to strike. "At last, we're taking charge of our own destiny," she said full of Irish patriotism.

"Dangerous and foolhardy." Wittig rubbed his eyes. "The British will fight back, hard. If they win, they'll shoot the ringleaders."

"Rory is willing to die." Nora pushed the covers off. "Rory says their Volunteer and Citizen's Army has more than one thousand people. They're planning to attack Dublin's main buildings."

My God, thought Wittig. This is crazy. They'll never win.

"I want to go over and help."

Weary from lack of sleep and concerned about Beck's plans for the conference tonight, Wittig had neither the energy nor the patience to contend with new problems. "What about the girls?" he asked cautiously.

"Hannah can come. She's old enough. Mary can stay here. I want to be by my brother's side. I've waited all my life for this chance."

"You'd place Ireland above your family?" Wittig couldn't believe she was serious.

"Yes."

Wittig's head dropped to his pillow with shock. He said nothing the rest of the night, and at dawn he dressed quickly and rushed to catch the first train to the city. He knew it was going to be a dreadful day.

~

During the walk to the train station, Wittig tried to understand everything that was happening. He decided he couldn't do much about Ireland, and hoped Nora's judgment would improve. His financial situation was another matter. Because of his new job, he had not had the time to invest properly. He had taken too many risks and had suffered losses. Recovering them would take time. Time he didn't have.

When he reached the station, he felt impotent, isolated, and angry – at Nora, at himself, at life. In his rush to leave the house, he had forgotten to bring the revolver. A constriction in his neck muscles ran down his left shoulder. Other commuters waited silently around him. A person yawned; another scanned his *New York World*; the man next to him closed his eyes. Wittig envied them all. Given a chance, he would have traded places with any one of them.

A New York City-bound express train rounded the curve leading to the Bronxville station and powered into view. The train seemed to pick up speed. Its shrill whistle warned it wouldn't stop. Everyone but Wittig moved back a step.

The whistle blasted three more times. Wittig's mind jumped back to thoughts of the conference tonight. Suddenly, he understood what Beck had intended to do. How come he hadn't realized it before? He had ignored the obvious. He'd been manipulated like a naive boy and began to loathe himself. A burst of pain ran through his head. Fighting dizziness and disorientation, he confronted the possible consequences of his actions at tonight's conference with clarity and courage and made a fateful decision. He would not be part of Beck's plan. Looking skyward, he recited the Lord's Prayer.

The speeding train was seconds away. It was time to end his Faustian bargain with Beck. Death would be a relief. Wittig took a step and closed his eyes. One more step to go. He hesitated. The girls. What would be worse – continuing on, or jumping now?

Before he could decide, Wittig felt the vacuum as the train roared past him. Once again, events overtook him. As the next train slowed down, Wittig took a long look at Bronxville, the town he and his family loved. *How long before I see them again?*

~

Early that same evening, the telephone interrupted Martin and Keller's discussion with the captain, who ignored it. But after three more rings, the captain, increasingly distracted, picked up the receiver. "Tunney." He did not hide his annoyance. "Sergeant ... Slow down. What is it?" Tunney pressed the phone hard against his ear. "Yes, I see. What else?" Tunney's face tensed. "I'll get on this right away." Tunney returned the phone to its hook and tapped his finger against the side of his face. Martin detected a sly grin. After a few seconds, Tunney looked at the detectives. "Do you men remember John Wittig?"

"Of course," Keller said with alert interest.

"Captain, what's going on?" Several possibilities ran through Martin's mind.

"He's in police custody at Grand Central Station. He has

something big to tell us and says he needs protection. He'll only talk to you." Tunney lowered his voice. "Get to Grand Central as fast as you can."

Chapter 55
The Biltmore

Biltmore Hotel, Manhattan: April 1916

Caarsens had been working as a waiter at the Biltmore Hotel at 335 Fourth Avenue on 43rd Street for three weeks. He had worked hard and established trust while he planned the assassination. He expected no problems tonight. He carried a tray of glasses filled with vintage champagne through the "Cascades," the grand ballroom. Chilled droplets burned his wrist between his white glove and waiter's black jacket.

Caarsens evaluated the guests and searched for Swanson, who was expected to arrive at any moment. He offered the glasses to the dignitaries, businessmen, and guests. They were dressed either in tuxedoes or dress uniforms replete with rows of ribbons, broad vertical stripes up each pant leg, and competing sizes of epaulets and lengths of gold cord. In their stiff military postures and strutting walks, the French and British officers acted like roosters and seemed equally unthreatening.

Caarsens checked his watch: 7:32 p.m. John Wittig had not yet arrived with Swanson. Where were they? Caarsens went to a window and looked down the twenty-two floors. Through the storm, he couldn't see much. He didn't like to spend so much time among his enemies. He preferred to strike fast and evade. He was worried that, despite his language skills, one of the French officers would realize that his French-Canadian accent was wrong and his bald head and makeup a disguise. For once, he was unarmed. His waiter's outfit was too tight to hide his Demag. Tonight's weapon was safe in a small glass vial in his pocket.

Caarsens headed back to the kitchen. He passed through the crowd and saw a face he recognized from grainy newspaper photographs. He almost dropped his tray. Treasury Secretary William McAdoo lifted a glass of champagne from Caarsens's tray. Beck had not told him McAdoo would be here, but here he was, within touching distance.

Two burly men with bad haircuts stood behind McAdoo. They wore ill-fitting tuxedos. One man kept squirming and tightening his shoulders. The other man patted a bulge on his left side under his arm. They looked Caarsens up and down then moved their attention to anyone close to McAdoo. They were an inconvenience, not an obstacle.

Killing McAdoo would have been as easy as making change for a dollar bill. McAdoo was a target of army-sized value. Caarsens didn't care for his own life. Trading it for McAdoo's would be a bargain. Caarsens evaluated his options. He knew he had no escape. The ballroom was isolated at the top of the Biltmore and full of military men, any one of whom Caarsens could have eliminated with one strike. Collectively, they could overpower him. The thought of taking down a few more British officers was an attractive bonus. However, ...

Instinct and hate turned to adrenaline. An invaluable target was near. Attack. Prepare for counterattack. Escape. Caarsens looked for a weapon. One of the French officers carried a ceremonial sword. Impractical. Something smaller. A knife from the dinner setting? Too far away. Bare hands? Maybe, but no guarantee. Wait. He could use the vial of poison on McAdoo and not Swanson. No. He had enough for only one man. McAdoo might not stay for dinner. Caarsens would never get closer to McAdoo than he was right now. Caarsens glanced down to his tray. Yes. A broken stem from a champagne glass could become a stiletto. With a vicious thrust into McAdoo's carotid artery, Caarsens could kill McAdoo before he hit the ground.

Caarsens prepared to attack but held back. Beck had been adamant. "It is vital no one else gets hurts." Caarsens decided to wait and continue his assigned mission. His success or failure would be determined in the next minutes.

~

He would fail. A few minutes before eight, the maître d' walked through the crowd and asked everyone to sit. Dinner was now being served. Caarsens watched everyone go to their assigned places. Swanson's seat remained empty. Caarsens looked around for the Treasury Secretary. Gone. Decision point. A good soldier knows when to attack, when to fall back, and when to stay put. Caarsens walked through the kitchen and overheard the head chef complain to the maître d'. "Why the delay? What the blazes is going on?"

The maître d' scratched his head. "Don't know, but I'm telling you, something's happening."

"My soup is cold. The chateaubriand is overcooked. The wine was opened too soon. My reputation is ruined," the chef said.

"If I'm right, no one will remember your wine." The maître d' tightened his coat. "The boss told me to act normally, serve the meal, and finish the night without an incident. Military police and the cops are arriving as we speak."

The chef spotted Caarsens. "You, get moving. Do your job."

Caarsens felt trapped. One of McAdoo's goons watched the elevator; the other watched the fire escape. There were no other exits. Fighting his way through twenty-two stories would be suicide. He was not willing to surrender his life without having a victory first. He decided to keep to his post as the waiter and look for an opportunity to escape to the lobby. Then he could disappear. If he was right and the police thought there was an assassin on the premises, they would question the whole staff. His story would hold up only so long. Less if they suspected German saboteurs, a likely scenario, and especially if they called in the Bomb Squad detectives, who might recognize him from previous encounters.

If he did not report to work again, Caarsens was sure the police would make the connection between him and Weil, the man who got him the job. Weil would be questioned. He assumed that Weil would have a credible explanation about his involvement. If he did not and the police arrested him and ... well, worse things could happen. The only problem was that Weil knew Caarsens's real identity.

Assassin had turned to escapee. Caarsens had to dispose of the poison. He dropped the glass vial on the ground, crushed it underfoot, and then dropped a champagne glass. Before the broken pieces mixed with the poison, Caarsens picked up a shard and hid it. He cleaned up the mess with a rag while the chef scowled at him. When the chef turned away, Caarsens cut himself deeply in the soft fatty area below his left thumb. When the flow of blood was sufficient, he cursed and raised his hand. He looked at the chef who said, "Get out of here. You can't serve food like that." Caarsens wrapped a towel around his hand and marched to the elevator. Caarsens waved his bloody hand in front of the goon, who called for the elevator.

When Caarsens reached the ground floor, there was much commotion. Police had started to arrive. Caarsens walked up to the nearest cop, waved his hand in front of the man's face making sure blood dripped onto his uniform, and said, "Hospital."

"Go." The cop did not look up and tried to clean off the blood with spit and a handkerchief.

Just as he walked out of the Biltmore and onto Fourth Avenue, the cops arrived. *They're getting closer each time.* He wondered what had gone wrong.

Chapter 56
What Went Wrong

Police Headquarters: April 1916

It was over. Relieved, Wittig blessed the isolation of the undersized holding cell in the basement jail of Police Department Headquarters. Its clammy dampness soothed him, and the stale mildewed air smelled refreshing to him. He plopped down on a rickety three-legged stool, closed his eyes and relived the day's events.

It had been a horrible day. From the time he had boarded the morning train until the end of the working day, he had struggled with fear and remorse. Twice, he approached Swanson, but retreated at the last minute, fearing reprisals from the Germans. Together with Swanson and his two bodyguards, Wittig left the Morgan Bank building just before 6 p.m. Because of the rain, no taxis were available, so they took a subway train to Grand Central Station instead. When they reached the underground corridor that connected to the Biltmore Hotel, Swanson stopped and said, "You have done outstanding work for me, Mr. Wittig. I know it has placed a burden on your family. I can't thank you enough."

Wittig gagged with appreciation, embarrassment, and fear. Confused and crushed by the day's strain, Wittig confessed. Struggling to get the words out, he turned to his boss. "I have reason to believe there will be an attempt on your life, sir. Tonight."

Swanson's bodyguards sprung into action. One pulled Wittig aside and fired questions at him, and the other pulled a revolver and stood to defend them. Wittig pleaded with the guard. "Mr.

Swanson is in danger. We need to go to the police. I have information the Bomb Squad needs to know – immediately." In order to convince them of the danger, Wittig revealed the Biltmore plot and urged them to get Swanson to safety.

Swanson intervened. "Mr. Wittig, do you know what you are saying?"

"You're in danger. I'm not lying." One of Swanson's men applied a hammerlock to Wittig, and they hurried to a police holding area somewhere in the bowels of Grand Central. After Swanson explained to the police who he was and what was happening, they jumped to life and called police headquarters.

~

Within an hour, Martin and Keller arrived. Wittig recognized them from their meeting in his office last December. Martin's Gallic features and calm demeanor were unmistakable although the lines on his face had hardened. Keller's unkempt brown hair, threatening intensity, and soft eyes had not changed. They asked some questions and clarified the situation. Wittig felt safe from the Germans for the first time in nearly a year.

~

Martin told one of the uniformed policemen to take Wittig to 240 Centre Street and hide him in a detention cell. The detectives ran to the lobby of the Biltmore Hotel and took charge. Martin instructed every policeman to guard the exits and interview everyone in the vicinity. He learned that one of the waiters had just left to go to the hospital. He and Keller ran outside where a taxi driver told them the waiter headed toward Grand Central. *Not the hospital?*

~

Blood dripped from his hand as Caarsens dashed away from the Biltmore Hotel. He looked back and saw scores of police gather around the Biltmore. Without a weapon, his safety depended on his ability to disappear through Grand Central Station, a block away. Once inside, Caarsens removed his bowtie and tied it tight across his wound and around his wrist. It made an effective bandage, and the blood trail stopped.

He walked into the station's Grand Concourse. Coatless on a cold night and dressed in his waiter's white shirt and black trousers, Caarsens was conspicuous. Acting like any other commuter, he blended into a group of people waiting around some benches in the waiting area. How to escape? He guessed the police would rush to the subway, believing he'd grab a train, but the subway presented an unacceptable risk. At this time of night, Caarsens might have to wait five minutes for a train. Such a delay would be fatal. To confuse the police, Caarsens headed toward the IRT station, planning to double back when he had a chance.

The police flooded into the Grand Concourse. If he had had more time, he could have gone to his locker for a change of clothes, a disguise, and his Colt, but his natural instinct to fight would have left him dead. He considered hiding somewhere in Grand Central Station, but he knew the cops would search until they found him. It was a coward's gambit anyway, something abhorrent to his aggressive nature. Besides, he might have to hide all night. Too long. His wound needed attention.

He walked toward one of the underground connections to the street along the train lines, but he stopped at the last moment. No good. The cops might also know these connections and be waiting for him when he emerged. An idea struck him when he saw a wino beg for handouts. Caarsens enticed the drunk with a dollar. "Follow me." The wino kept pace. When they were alone, Caarsens gave him five dollars for his stained overcoat and greasy cap. They reeked. All the better. Caarsens put them on and told the man to sit down with him. The wino was too busy fondling the bills to listen. Caarsens yanked him to the ground and grabbed his bottle. He took a big swig, splashed some wine on his face, and said, "Here's twenty if you walk out with me."

The wino grabbed the money. "Mister, I don't want no trouble, but for that kind of dough, I'll do whatever you want."

"If you say anything, I'll snap your neck. If someone stops us, let me do the talking." Caarsens put his right arm around the wino's shoulder and tucked his bandaged left hand inside the coat pocket. As they started to walk, Caarsens whispered in his ear. "Another twenty if we get outside. Do you know any chanties?"

They began to sing. "*What'll we do with a drunken sailor, what'll we do with a drunken sailor, earl-aye in the morning?*" A cop approached them, but Caarsens steered the drunk into him. They all collided, and Caarsens staggered up and belched. "Sorry." He pulled his companion to his feet. "Evening officer." He made sure the cop smelled his breath.

The cop stepped back. "Have you seen ..."

Caarsens pretended to fall again. "What? I don't know ..." Making sure to hide his bloody hand, Caarsens pretended he was about to be sick.

"Get out of here." The cop nudged them along with his nightstick. No one else stopped them. At 39th Street, Caarsens gave the wino his money and headed south. He knew tonight's failure would have serious consequences.

~

Voices in the corridor jolted Wittig awake. He opened his eyes and adjusted his position on the stool. His mouth was as dry as stored gunpowder, and his leg jiggled nervously. He stood up and paced. What was taking the detectives so long? He walked toward the small opening in the locked door covered with wire mesh. The clock in the hallway said 8:49, and after a while, he realized its hands hadn't moved. He saw a policeman escort a man, handcuffed and in leg irons, down the gloomy corridor. *My fate, too.*

Wittig returned to his stool and decided it was good he hadn't jumped in front of the train. He berated himself for even contemplating it. If he had killed himself, Swanson would be dead by now. He also realized his daughters were all that mattered. He wondered if his destiny had been decided when Germany went to war. Before he could answer the question, he heard footsteps, the same sound Edith Cavell had heard in her last few minutes on Earth.

~

Still angry that Swanson's assassin had escaped, Martin was anxious to talk to Wittig. The frantic events of the last few hours had energized him and made him feel more useful than he had felt in months. For the first time since she had died, Corinne's memory faded into a quiet place in his mind.

He kept pace with the taller Keller who sped down the corridor toward Wittig's cell. Martin jumped ahead when they neared the door. He raised his hand to block the determined Keller from opening it. "I know you're angry, Paul, but no rough stuff."

"What do you mean?" Keller snarled.

Martin held Keller back. "I want to make sure we do this right, Paul. The stakes are high, and –"

"I know what the stakes are. That bastard in there needs –"

"Quiet."

"Gil, he's one of them." Keller looked like a hungry dog ready to attack a juicy bone.

Martin gently put his hands on Keller's shoulders. "We've got better ways than to pound him into dog food."

"You've been away too long. Have you forgotten what these Huns have done?"

"No," Martin said, although he knew that Keller was partially correct. "Wittig came to us, remember? He's a decent man, not a thug. He just got caught up in something he couldn't handle."

Keller's eyes narrowed. "He's got a lot to answer for."

"He's been pushed and bullied. Tonight, he got desperate and cried for help. He doesn't want to be in there." Martin pointed to the door.

Keller retreated. "But if he doesn't give us something good in ten minutes, I'm going to take a swing. We can debate my approach with the captain." Keller's look confirmed his aggression.

"Agreed." Martin unlocked the door and felt Keller's breath on his neck.

~

Wittig heard two men quarreling outside his cell. Although he couldn't hear the words, their angry tone made him nervous. He moved to the far corner of the room and waited. When the argument stopped, Wittig smoothed his hair, brushed his pants, and mopped his face with his sleeve.

He heard the lock turn open and went to the door. He would meet his confessors with as much dignity as he still had. His knees almost buckled, but he managed to stay upright. Sergeant Martin led the way, followed by Detective Keller, his face flushed. Keller set up two folding chairs.

"Hello again, Mr. Wittig. Please sit." Martin pointed to the wooden platform that served as a cot. "Who's your main German contact?"

This was the question Wittig had most dreaded. He had trouble saying the words. "Felix Be ... Beck."

~

"The German consul?" *Of course, it had to be*, Martin thought.

"Sweet Jesus. What about that weasel?" Keller's voice betrayed his urgency.

"I advised him. Economic policy, ideas. I wanted to help Germany."

"Which you did willingly," Martin said.

"America has no right to side with the Allies."

When Wittig challenged America's right to support the Allies, Martin became angry. "I don't give a Chinaman's pigtail what you think about America's rights." He turned to Keller. "Paul, I think my ten minutes are about up."

"I think you're right." Keller pulled up his sleeve, and swatted Wittig across his head just low enough to graze his hair.

Martin got close to Wittig and shouted into his ear, "Now, tell me something useful!" His voice echoed in the cell.

Wittig looked petrified. He fumbled for his next words. "Did you know that Matthias Weil is a German spy?"

The head of the German-American League in New York? Martin couldn't believe it. Weil's name had never appeared in any of their investigations.

"And he's a murderer." Wittig recounted last summer's events at Milton Point, unable to hide his obvious fear. He concluded by saying, "I helped hide the body in Long Island Sound. Forty feet down."

"Nothing we can use, is there, Gil?" Keller said in clear frustration.

"No, but we'll make things uncomfortable for Mr. Weil when we find him. Thank you, Mr. Wittig." Martin wrote something in his notebook.

"What will happen to me?" Wittig sounded like an old man.

Keller exploded. "What do you think is going to happen to you? You've hurt every good German-American in this country. You're a traitor."

Wittig stood up. "I'm a decent man. I've got a wife and two daughters. They need me."

"Sit down." Keller pushed him back on the cot. You're lucky you live in this great country. In Germany, they would have shot you by now." Keller turned his ring inward and prepared to strike. Wittig raised his arms to protect his face.

"Calm down, Paul. I'm sure he has more to tell us." Martin motioned to Keller to back away. "Can I get you anything else, Mr. Wittig? A cigarette maybe?" Martin craved one for himself.

Wittig shook his head and started to shiver.

"Who killed Traub?" Keller glared at Wittig.

"That man terrified me. I don't know who killed him. I wasn't part of their operations. Look, I did what they told me. What else could I do?" Wittig swallowed hard.

Martin thought, *I'll push this man as far as I have to.*

~

Wittig's despair grew. *Why are these detectives attacking me like this? I've told them the truth. What more can I say*? "But I'm trying to help you. Didn't I help Mr. Swanson today?" Wittig, desperately wanting a friend, told them about all his German connections and mentioned a man named Knopp, who visited his house with Beck. Martin pressed him for details.

After Wittig finished, Martin said, "Except for the hair and some other details, he sounds like the waiter." He scratched his head with his pencil. "I've seen this man before. I'm sure of it."

"Where does he live?" Who is he? What's he to Beck?" Keller rattled off questions without giving Wittig time to answer.

Questions, questions. Why don't they lock me up? At least I'll be safe. "I don't know. I've already told you everything I know."

"I doubt it." Martin stood and approached Wittig so that they stood nose-to-nose. "Think, Mr. Wittig. Are the Germans running some operation or conspiracy right now?"

Wittig remained silent for several seconds. He ran his hand through his hair and said, "Have you ever heard of the New Haven Projectile Company?"

Chapter 57
The Police Sketch

Fifth Avenue, Manhattan: April 1916

The day after the debacle at the Biltmore, Caarsens pretended to hobble up Fifth Avenue. Dressed as an old man, he noticed a policeman studying a sketch. In big letters at the top of the drawing, the word “Wanted” flashed at him. He adjusted his fake glasses and glanced at it as he walked by. Not a bad likeness, but not so good he’d be recognized on sight – his disguise was too good.

Men in uniform had been his personal enemy since he was captured by Major Westerly toward the end of the South African War. After he had escaped, he continued to fight with aggression and vengeance. He led a small commando unit that became notorious for it cunning, its recklessness, and its use of deadly force. Just before the war ended, the British accused him of trapping and burning to death seven Welsh soldiers in a blockhouse. A Boer traitor lied when he confirmed the accusation. He also swore that Caarsens had shot a captured British lieutenant whose body had been dismembered and sodomized with a knife.

The British tried Caarsens in absentia, found him guilty, and sentenced him to hang. Caarsens had been a fugitive ever since and had always avoided men in uniform like the policeman who continued to ignore him.

At 59th Street, Caarsens turned and headed toward the Plaza Hotel. The doorman bowed and opened the door. The old man raised his gloved left hand and said, “*Merci.*” He entered the hotel lobby and headed to the dining room.

Beck sat facing the entrance. When Caarsens sat down, Beck touched his lips with his napkin. "I was not sure if you would make it, old friend." He spoke in French. "They are looking for you. I have never seen so many cops around here."

"The police are circulating a sketch of me." Caarsens adjusted his false glasses.

"Is it accurate?"

"No." The waiter brought Beck coffee. Caarsens ordered scrambled eggs and bacon. He eyed the waiter until he disappeared into the kitchen.

"I am sure an old French Canadian won't bother them."

"It was for nothing." Caarsens's stomach growled. "We failed."

Beck ripped his roll in two. "We had Swanson. It was a good plan." Beck looked at the glove on Caarsens's hand. "Are you hurt?"

Caarsens told Beck the details of last night's failure. "It's your fault, *Monsieur* Beck. I knew I could never trust your organization. You tried to do too much and made some mistakes. Now we'll pay. I'll be the first casualty." Caarsens contemplated his next move.

The waiter approached Beck carrying a silver tray. On it was a small envelope with Beck's name written on it in a light, delicate hand. "This just arrived for you, Mr. Beck."

Beck picked up the message, but hesitated until the waiter left. Beck opened the letter with his table knife. He glanced at it briefly. "Code." Rows of precisely aligned letters filled the page. Beck took out a notebook and scratched down the translation without hesitation. When he was done, Beck lit a match and burned the original note and the decoded message in the ashtray. Beck stirred the ashes into powder. "Our worst fears are true. It seems that John Wittig has told the police everything. This morning, Captain Tunney started barking orders. His people are scurrying around the police station like cockroaches."

"What do you want me to do?" Caarsens poked at the powder in the ashtray with his finger. Despite everything, Caarsens could not abandon Beck and his sabotage work.

"You must leave for Connecticut immediately. New Haven Projectile is our first problem. You have to attend to it."

"I don't like that waiter."

"He's not my regular one. I already asked about him," Beck said.

Caarsens relaxed. "Before I go, I'll lose anyone shadowing me in the elevators." As he prepared to leave, Caarsens noticed an attractive blonde woman talking to an older man two tables away. Something about them wasn't right. Who were they? Lovers? No – they weren't gazing at each other. Niece and uncle? No – they were not related. Their clothes indicated they came from different backgrounds. Friends? Body language wrong. They were looking around too much. Why hadn't he noticed them before?

Chapter 58
A Lot to Do

Police Headquarters: April 1916

Leaving Wittig's all-night interrogation, Martin was almost speechless. The scale of German activities was larger than anything he could have imagined. He turned to Keller and said, "We have a lot to do."

"I've never seen Shannon speechless, but this will shock her." Keller shook his head. "Unbelievable. The Germans hit a grand slam with that New Haven company. What do we do about the Biltmore waiter, Gil?"

"If we don't have him yet, he's escaped," Martin said. We'll get an artist to draw a picture of him. It's something new the captain's trying out. We'll give copies to every policeman in the city. He can't hide forever. We'll watch every move Felix Beck makes, too." Martin looked at the clock on the hallway wall. It said 8:49. "I hate that thing." Martin reached up and moved its hands to the right time.

"Why bother? That clock never works."

"It's more right than it was." Martin banged it. Its hands moved a tick then stopped. "I'll get it fixed sometime. Come on, Paul, we need to see the captain." As he locked the door to the cell, Martin looked through the window and saw Wittig on his knees, praying. *Good idea.*

Although it was 5 a.m., Martin sent Keller home and returned to his desk to complete his report. Then, he walked to Tunney's office and placed it on his desk. On his way back, he told the desk sergeant to let no one talk to Wittig without Captain Tunney's written approval. He returned to his desk, rested his head, and slept.

Early the next morning, Keller, the first man to appear in the squad room, looking fresh and energetic, woke up Martin.

Tunney ordered Martin and Keller to his office mid-morning. The captain acted like a bloodhound who had just picked up a lost scent. He had just finished talking to William Flynn, head of the U.S. Secret Service, who was going to see Secretary of the Treasury McAdoo later that day. Tunney had sent out an order across every New York police precinct and neighboring state to detain Matthias Weil on suspicion of murder. "I've started to move on our friend, Beck. Shannon?" he called out.

A blonde woman walked into Tunney's office. Shannon? She looked so different that Martin hardly recognized her. Keller seemed as surprised as Martin to see her. "Hello, Detectives, Uncle. A good hairpiece can sure change things, can't it?" She looked at Keller longer than the others.

"I asked my niece and Detective Griggs to see what our friend, Felix Beck, was up to today," Tunney said.

Tunney's a sly fox, Martin thought, *always a step ahead.*

"Beck was there, just as he always is – late breakfast at the Plaza." Shannon described what happened. An old French-speaking man she had never seen before joined Beck. Nothing seemed unusual except the old man wore gloves and hardly used his left hand. Martin and Keller exchanged looks. *Couldn't be.*

"A waiter delivered a message to Beck, but he burned it. The old man left right afterward," Shannon continued.

"Do you think Beck noticed you?" Keller asked, more worried about Shannon than the old man.

"No."

"Did you shadow the men when they left?" Martin asked.

"It was just Griggs and me. When the men parted, I stayed with Beck. He walked up Fifth Avenue to Yorkville. Nothing happened along the way."

"What about the old man?"

"He lost Griggs on the elevators in the hotel. Impossible for one man to shadow someone in a place like that. Griggs checked, and the old man was not registered at the hotel."

"What's Beck up to?" Martin asked.

Chapter 59
Best Job I Ever Had

New Haven: April 1916

Thirteen hours after he left Beck at the Plaza, Caarsens tied his borrowed livery stable horse to the main office gate of the New Haven Projectile Company. He crept into the office building and became a burglar in his own company. His lantern provided the only light. Its shadows deceived him and slowed him down. Worried the police might arrive at any moment, Caarsens worked fast. He checked around to make sure he would be alone. Luck was with him – an overcast sky blocked the moon and the place was closed for Easter weekend. The plant was empty.

Anxious to finish, Caarsens went to the four hundred-pound steel safe in Karl Bier's office and worked the combination. He emptied its contents into his rucksack. It overflowed with thick bundles of cash and bonds, the secret ledgers, and their confidential contact lists. He closed the safe and opened Bier's cabinets. He spread the papers on the floor and soaked them with kerosene he took from the plant. He checked his old office next. On his desk were some papers and a triangular wooden block with the name "Pieter Knopp" engraved in gold. He flipped it upside-down. He gathered the papers and added them to the pile in Bier's office. As he left, he felt a pang of regret. *Best job I ever had.* The pang did not last long.

Caarsens picked up the rucksack and rushed to the plant. He spread kerosene throughout the factory. The last thing he did before he left was to light a cigarette and insert it into the box of matches. He carefully placed the matchbox just on the outside edge of a puddle of kerosene and ran from the plant.

Caarsens figured it would take the cigarette about three minutes to burn down to the matchbox. When it did, the matches would light in a short burst and ignite the kerosene. The fire would spread and become a conflagration when it reached the nearby explosives, lubricants, rags, and powder scattered around the work area. Once the wood floor and roof went up in flames, nothing could stop the blaze. It would spread to the offices. He hoped someone would think the fire started out of carelessness. He laughed at the irony when it struck him that New Haven Projectile would claim damages and demand compensation from its insurers.

Caarsens climbed on his horse and galloped a safe distance away. A cutting wind whipped across his face. When he saw the flames start, he covered his face. Minutes later, shells exploded with a deafening roar. The burning plant turned the sky red, yellow, purple, and then black. The crackling explosions sounded like a nearby gun battle between two heavily armed platoons. Clouds of smoke circled overhead like German Albatross biplanes.

Caarsens waited for the plant to consume itself. At daybreak, the police and firefighters had not yet arrived. By then, the fire had reduced the facility to ashes and smoldering equipment. The frame was a glowing skeleton. As he led his horse away, he tripped over the charred remains of a company sign that had been blown from the plant. He kicked it away.

BLACK TOM ISLAND AFTER EXPLOSION

April 1916 - August 1916

Chapter 60
There May Be Another Way

Treasury Building, Washington, D.C.: April 1916

Secretary McAdoo, responsible for America's internal security matters, had hoped to be with his family on Easter. Instead, the events in New York City and the mysterious destruction of the New Haven Projectile Company in Connecticut forced him to convene a meeting with Colonel Edward House, President Wilson's personal advisor, who, because the president was detained, took his place.

House entered and dispensed with the usual protocol. "This has been a bad day. Please get on with your briefing, Mr. Secretary."

"I would have preferred to speak to the president directly on this matter." McAdoo resented House's unofficial Cabinet-level status. *Why should I have to tell that man what I should tell the president directly? I'm a Cabinet minister, and House isn't even a colonel.* McAdoo was always surprised such an unimposing man could wield such power.

"The fact that I'm even here shows the importance we place on this week's events." House revealed that the president was considering severing diplomatic relations with Germany if it resumed unrestricted submarine warfare, as it had threatened. After McAdoo summarized the startling developments following the attempt on Robert Swanson's life, House asked, "Was Wittig a German agent or not?"

"Wittig denies it. He advised the Germans and got caught in something he couldn't handle. When he realized the Huns intended to assassinate Swanson, Wittig ran to us at the last minute. Brave man, considering."

"How does all this relate to the New Haven Projectile Company?"

"The attempt on Mr. Swanson is somehow linked to it." McAdoo connected Wittig to Beck and New Haven Projectile's lawyers to Wittig, concluding that Beck was associated with the New Haven Projectile Company. "If so, it supports Wittig's belief that New Haven Projectile is a front for nefarious German activities. That's Tunney's theory."

"THEORY? You're making a big leap." House's face narrowed into skeptical coldness.

"Wittig told Tunney that New Haven Projectile started with three million dollars, but Wittig suspects it's at least five times that much by now. No question of German involvement." McAdoo leaned forward, trying to intimidate House.

House didn't flinch. "You might be right, but so what?"

"The German Consulate in New York is a nest of snakes. No question about that now." McAdoo's face tightened with resolve. "By the way, Wittig claims Matthias Weil is a German spy."

"Matthias Weil – the head of the German-American League in New York?" House shook his head. "I can't believe it."

"It makes sense," McAdoo said, happy to gain an advantage over his adversary. "What do you propose?"

"We've discussed this many times." House took a deep breath. "Under no circumstances does the president want to compromise our neutrality. We need to prevent any incident that might incite Germany to declare war against us. We can't kick out Germany's entire diplomatic delegation in New York."

"At least let's recall Ambassador von Bernstorff in Washington."

"The president knows von Bernstorff is not dealing with us frankly." House tightened his jaw. "If true, Captain Tunney's information casts a veil of suspicion over the whole bunch."

"It does more than that," McAdoo said. "The president needs to –"

"Don't you dare tell me what the president should do. Let me remind you, sir, that the president is trying to keep America out of a war." House slammed the arm of his chair. "We must handle all German diplomats legally with all the correct protocol that their positions demand. No exceptions."

Silence. McAdoo and House dueled with their eyes.

"If the president will not reconsider expelling the diplomats, there may be another way." A wry smile crept into McAdoo's face. "It's a bit unorthodox, but I don't think my suggestion violates any diplomatic protocol. It might stretch it some."

"Go on."

"Give the information to the newspapers. They can find their own proof. We'll stand back and watch the fray as the newspapers try the Germans in public."

~

On his way to work the next morning, Martin stopped at the corner near the stationhouse when he heard the words. He couldn't believe them. To his usual call of "Extra, extra, only two cents," the paper boy added, "German company in Connecticut a fake. Germans try to stop goods to Allies." The boy was selling the *New York World* as fast as he could hand them out. His pockets filled with pennies, nickels, dimes, and a few quarters. He didn't have time to pick up change that dropped on the ground. With his shoe, the boy raked in his fallen profits. Several men milled around the boy, making comments: "Devious bastards," and "We should have declared war after they sunk the *Lusitania*."

Martin tossed the boy a nickel. "Keep the change, son." At Police Headquarters, Keller was already at his desk reading a copy of the *World*. He looked up when he saw Martin. "Can you believe the Washington politicians gave this story to the press?"

Martin read the article quickly. "Brilliant. I wondered how they were going to handle this. Someone earned his salary with this idea."

"Listen to this." Keller paraphrased the article. "The Huns bought and stored five million pounds of gunpowder and two million shell casings that they never intended to use. They must have more money to spend than Rockefeller."

"The *World* says representatives for New Haven Projectile claim saboteurs blew it up," Martin said. "They want their insurance company to pay."

"You've got to give those Germans credit – they'd try to lie themselves out of Hell itself," Keller said. "Their plant is gone, and we know the whole story."

Martin looked up from the paper. "Do we? I wouldn't bet on it."

Chapter 61
Getting Tough

Police Headquarters: May 1916

The next day, despite the public outcry following the newspaper disclosures about German activity, or maybe because of it, Tunney fired off questions at Martin and Keller while he paced his office. He looked more intimidating when he stood. Martin tried to answer, but Tunney gave him no time. "Where is Matthias Weil? What about that waiter? How can two men disappear? It's been three weeks since the attempt on Swanson, and you're telling me you have no leads?"

"Captain, we're doing everything we can," Martin said.

"For that matter, where are Traub's killer and the subway bomber?"

"Frankly, Captain, we don't know. We're as frustrated as you."

"What good was Wittig's confession if we have no arrests?" Tunney sat. The chair seemed to buckle under his weight. "The German Consulate is claiming they were set up. They say they invested some money in the New Haven Projectile Company, but the Austrians ran it."

"But that contradicts everything we learned from Wittig."

"Look at this." Tunney handed a file to Martin. "Dates, financial records, letters – all incriminating evidence against the Austro-Hungarian ambassador, Franz-Henrik Esterhazy."

"How did you get these?" Martin thumbed through the file.

"From New Haven Projectile's law firm, Webster, Locklie, and Weinz. When the news hit the papers, their managing partner walked right into my office and gave them to me."

"We know that firm is dirty, but are you saying the Austrians are in cahoots with the Germans?" Keller tightened his fists. "What will we do?"

"We'll claim victory and declare Esterhazy persona nongrata. Then we'll kick him out."

Martin, his anger and frustration growing, tensed. "Any chance the president will agree to kick Beck out of the country?"

"No. We have nothing on him," Tunney said. "If we did, I'd grab him by the seat of his pants and shove him on the next liner to Europe myself."

"So we can't touch Beck?" Keller asked.

"Not officially."

"Does that mean we can scare him a bit?" Martin asked.

"I don't know what you're talking about." Tunney walked to his window and looked out. "No harm in talking to him. Just keep your interview private. I can't protect you if something goes wrong."

"I know what to do." Keller flashed his ring.

~

Martin and Keller waited for the train coming into Manhattan's Pennsylvania Railroad Station from Baltimore. It had taken them several days to learn that Beck would be on it. When the train pulled into Penn Station, the underground platform turned steamy. Martin tensed when he saw the diminutive and well-dressed Beck get off the train. He was one of the last passengers to descend. They approached him. "You're a hard man to find, but we persuaded your lawyers to tell us where you'd be, Mister Beck." Martin showed him his badge.

"I have diplomatic immunity; I am in a hurry." Beck nudged Martin and started to walk away.

"Stop. I just want to talk to you as a friend." Martin grabbed his shoulder while Keller moved to block him. "We need to chat. Nothing official. It won't take long."

"We can be nice or –" Keller dug his heel into Beck's foot.

Beck raised his hands in surrender. "We can do this like gentlemen, but let me warn you, my consulate knows where I am."

The detectives escorted Beck to a secluded loading area outside of Penn Station. Keller pushed him against the brick wall.

Beck straightened himself up and asked, "What do you want?"

"We're looking for someone," Martin said in a stern tone.

"So what?"

"We have information he works for you."

"Who does?"

"Matthias Weil."

"An acquaintance. We have met a few times. He supports German-American causes. In your terms, I think you call such men patriots."

"He's a criminal."

"Doesn't a court of law determine that?"

"Where have you been?" Martin asked.

"Consulate business. If you do not let me go, I will complain to your State Department."

"Who cares?" Keller frisked him.

"What's your connection to the New Haven Projectile Company?" Martin asked.

Beck shrugged his shoulders. "I invested some money in it. From what I understand, that is not illegal. The Austro-Hungarian ambassador is also an investor. He knows more about it than I do. The newspapers –"

"John Wittig told us –"

"Wittig? Hah. He is a liar and a coward. I believe he is under arrest, yes?"

"That's another matter," Martin said.

"I have answered your questions. Now, may I go?"

"Not yet," Keller said. "You're going to lose."

"What? I have no idea what you are talking about. My patience is –"

"Germany. It's going to lose. It has lost its gamble." Martin couldn't resist taunting Beck about the improving French military situation at Verdun.

"What do you mean?" Beck tried to look bored.

"Verdun. *Ils ne passeront pas*! They shall not pass." Martin recited the current French battle cry. "Your great offensive has stalled."

"Brave words, but meaningless." Beck dusted off his coat. "Germans are superior in quality, character and leadership. French soldiers are outclassed and outgunned. Their casualties are unsustainable."

"So are yours." Keller sprayed out the words.

"You make me laugh, Detective. We will be the next great power. I insist you detain me no longer."

"You're not going anywhere." Keller turned Beck around and put him in a hammerlock. He looked over at Martin. "Make sure we're alone."

Martin checked the area and nodded. Keller released Beck

and pulled out his revolver. Beck's eyes narrowed. Keller rubbed the edge of the barrel across Beck's cheek. Martin watched, his arms crossed.

"Are we in Russia now? Will you dump me in the river or bury me in New Jersey? I thought you Americans prided yourselves on your moral superiority." Beck calmly looked down the barrel. "I am an innocent man and a German consul. You –"

Keller pushed the barrel of the revolver into Beck's mouth. "I don't know what you're talking about. We're just having a friendly conversation. I just want you to understand my point of view." Keller forced the gun deeper into Beck's throat.

Beck gagged. Keller pulled the revolver from Beck's mouth and wrapped a handkerchief around the barrel. Martin looked away.

"You will not get away with this."

"Away with what? I don't understand." Keller waved the revolver in front of Beck's face. "Worried?"

"You do not scare me. You are nothing but a low-level policeman." Beck stared at Keller.

"You should be scared." Keller eased the hammer back and placed the side of the gun against Beck's head and pointed it upward. Beck gulped just before Keller pulled the trigger. The bullet sped past Beck's head. His arm snapped toward his ear.

"Your hearing will return by tomorrow, Herr Consul." Keller holstered his gun.

His ears ringing, Beck roared, "That was a mistake, Detective."

"Are you going to have me arrested?" Keller looked at Martin. "Did you see anything, Sergeant?"

"You men had an argument. That's all. Let's go, Detective. I think you made your point." Martin started to walk away.

Keller turned to Beck and said, "You won't get away from me. I'm going to stay on you like stink on a corpse."

"I can always wash off the smell."

"It will never go away."

Beck's face turned red. "Let me tell you this." Beck jabbed his finger into Keller's chest. "Now, it is personal between us. I will make you pay for this outrage. I know your weakness, and I will exploit it."

Chapter 62
Grant's Tomb

Grant's Tomb, Manhattan: June 1916

At dusk, Caarsens steered Frisch's motorboat up the Hudson along Manhattan's west side. He slowed down when he neared Grant's Tomb and looked for a safe place to land. Caarsens chose the most inconspicuous spot. He pulled the motorboat onto land, secured it, lowered the canvas top and concealed it with fallen branches. He placed his fully loaded Colt in the pocket of his coat. His hidden Demag pressed reassuringly against his side.

He started to hike up the hill to meet Beck. After walking one hundred yards, Caarsens looked back to make sure the boat was safe. Its low profile and dark color made it hard to see from a distance. After checking from a number of angles, he was satisfied the boat blended into the brownish-green surroundings. Thinking of it as dependable, fast, and responsive as a good horse, he couldn't afford to lose it.

Because of the police sketch, the hunt for Swanson's assassin, and the notoriety surrounding the New Haven Projectile Company and its destruction, Caarsens had stayed hidden until now. This meeting with Beck was his first since their breakfast at the Plaza. When he reached the crest of the hill, Caarsens circled the area. Grant's Tomb was an excellent meeting place – out of the way, quiet, and open. The tourists had gone. Caarsens glanced at the square marble mausoleum. It was topped with a rounded dome that looked like a huge artillery shell encased with Greek columns. The words

"Let us have peace" stared down at him. "Get out of Europe's affairs and you will," he muttered.

Beck sat alone on the steps at the southern entrance. He clutched an unlit cigarette in his left hand, the signal that it was safe to approach. Caarsens walked past Beck and tipped his cap, the countersignal. Beck joined him, and they strolled together on the walkway in front of the tomb. A few cars and carriages drove by them on either side. Beck spoke first. "I see you have managed to stay safe."

"I stay hidden and change my look often. I keep it simple. Some wigs, spirit gum to apply the mustaches, and different hairstyles help." Caarsens, proud of his disguises, was dressed today as a common delivery man. He looked as different from the police drawing of him as a toothless hound does to a wolf.

"You should be in Vaudeville. I hardly recognize you myself." Beck looked toward the river and sighed. "John Wittig ruined everything."

"What happened to Herr Bier?"

"Gone." Beck lit a cigarette with his fancy lighter.

"Is he safe?"

"He is sitting in the sun south of here; someplace the Americans cannot touch him. I am sure he has got his arm around some young whore and is enjoying himself."

"What do the cops know about me?" Caarsens didn't care about the growing danger, just how to confront it.

"The police have not pieced your story together." Beck pulled in a deep lung-full of smoke. "They are still looking for the French-Canadian waiter named Philippe Charbonneau. The police are looking for Pieter Knopp, too. It will not be long before they learn that he and the waiter are the same person."

"What's happened to Weil? Wittig must have given him up, too."

"Weil's career in America is over. He is in hiding right now. I am working on getting him back to Germany."

"What about me? I want to get back to work."

"You are still useful." Beck flicked his cigarette onto the walkway and rubbed it out with his foot. "Have you picked out your next target?"

"Yes – the one in New Jersey you suggested. I've wanted to attack it for a long time."

"Nothing to stop you now. We must return to sabotage. That is an ideal target. Your attack will make the police forget about Swanson. When will it happen?"

"I still need time and more explosives. I've run out." Caarsens looked over his shoulder to make sure they were still alone.

"There is a shipment of goods due to arrive in Baltimore in about five weeks," Beck said. "It will have two trunks containing what you need as well as some specially designed items for you. Inspect them. When you are satisfied they are what you need, the people onboard will arrange to deliver it to this address." He whispered the address into Caarsens's ear.

"But that's in the center of Manhattan."

"I know. Very convenient, don't you think?"

Chapter 63
Black Tom Island

Black Tom Island, New Jersey: June 1916

Caarsens approached Black Tom Island on his motorboat for a close look. It was about one mile long and, connected to mainland Jersey by landfill, no longer an island. Seven hundred yards away, the back of the Statue of Liberty rose up, so big it seemed closer than it was.

Caarsens had motored around the New Jersey shoreline for several days to assess possible approaches and weaknesses. Hobo camps lined the southern shore area below the depot. Hard-to-navigate marshes drowned the area north of it, and above those, the Communipaw ferry was located near the point where the Hudson River flowed into the upper bay of New York Harbor. He estimated the walk from the ferry to the center of Black Tom Island would take about twenty-five minutes. Gazing at the high-rise buildings of lower Manhattan across the river and the overflowing warehouses on Black Tom Island, he felt the power of America's enormous economic might.

Impersonating a French-Canadian businessman, Caarsens landed near the piers and started to reconnoiter the grounds. In disguise, he was certain no one would recognize him on the small chance that the police sketch of him circulated in New Jersey. If anyone asked what he was doing here, he would say he had acquired a large shipment of explosives destined for Calais and wanted to see to the security himself.

Caarsens was amazed by the size of Black Tom's munitions

center, which resembled a small city. Goods flowed into the facility by train and water in staggering volumes. Trains arrived and departed one after the other at the northern end of the terminal, delivering long rows of freight cars that could be stored in the complex or transferred immediately by barge to one of the piers, which seemed to buckle under the weight of all the material they bore. Inside the complex, groups of men labored their way across a network of roads and tracks seemingly more numerous and interconnected than a spider's web.

At the center of the depot, twenty-four warehouses, some longer than a New York City block, and many five stories high, contained hundreds of tons of salt, sugar, grain, clothing, cleaning powder, military goods, weapons, and explosives. *If the Boers had had this many munitions, we would have won our war*, he thought. Telephone poles and wires stretched everywhere.

Even with his extraordinary sense of direction, Caarsens became disoriented in the maze until he sketched a map that he later used to memorize every building, railroad track, and street corner. After four more visits, he knew every inch of Black Tom Island.

~

Tonight, his sixth visit, Caarsens needed to evaluate security on a Saturday evening, the ideal time to attack. He landed above the marshes and walked unchallenged through the complex, as if he were going into Central Park. Everything seemed quiet under the poor lighting. There were no security gates, barriers to cross, or patrols, either on land or in the water.

He headed down a narrow passage between two warehouses to a small maintenance shack he knew was always occupied, knocked on the door, and entered. A man with his feet on the desk read a newspaper. He stumbled up, but relaxed when he saw Caarsens, who looked like an unthreatening businessman. "What do you want?"

Caarsens recited his cover story.

"I guess it makes sense. Don't really care myself." The man offered his hand. "Aloysius Murphy." He had dreamy eyes, an intelligent face, and sticky hands.

After they talked for several minutes, someone in a bowler, a handlebar mustache, and a holstered revolver barged in. "Murphy, do you know ..." He stopped when he saw Caarsens. "Who's this?"

"A friend."

Caarsens introduced himself and repeated his story. The man called Murphy a dumb Mick, grunted something and left.

"Rude bastard." Murphy's neck veins bulged. "Always insulting me like that."

"Who was that?"

"That's Mr. Albert. Don't know his first name. He's one of the private detectives the railroad hired to look after things. A blind nun could do a better job. He and his partner act like they own the whole damn railroad."

"You don't say." Caarsens sat down, intrigued to learn more about another weakness. "May I offer you some whiskey?" He pulled out a flask.

"Never turn down a taste."

After a long conversation, Caarsens had a detailed description of Black Tom Island's schedules, the rules and which ones the owners didn't enforce, and who did what. He asked about Albert last. By that time, his flask was dry. Murphy explained that Albert and his partner worked for a private agency and supervised six detectives employed by the railroad company. The railroad men didn't like Albert either, so they pretended to follow his instructions. It was common for Albert to make the rounds on Black Tom Island late Saturday afternoon before he sashayed over to nearby Jersey City to visit his favorite whore for the night. Murphy had never seen him after 8:00 p.m.

Caarsens also learned that Murphy needed money to move to Boston. Before he left, they arranged to meet again.

Black Tom Island was more vulnerable than he could have imagined.

Chapter 64
For Sale

Bronxville: June 1916

The Harlem Division train of the New York Central Railroad neared Bronxville. It began to emerge through the woods that flanked the tracks. The detectives disembarked, and Martin saw a sign, "Village of Bronxville, Population 2,240." Opposite the tracks, he recognized the rounded Village Hall with two-story columns that Wittig had admiringly described. On the bluff near the tracks, the popular Gramatan Hotel, built in Spanish Mission style, stood over the town like a castle.

"I think we need to head that way." Keller pointed west.

"Let's ask," Martin said. Along the station tracks, workers were digging an underpass. Horses pulled wagons, and men hammered wooden planks into a temporary bridge that supported the tracks. A policeman observed the work. Martin walked up to him and asked directions. The policeman spoke over the noise that seemed more appropriate for a city. "That train crossing is dangerous. This should have been done a long time ago."

"You misunderstood me." Martin showed him a piece of paper and pointed to an address: "2 Dellwood Road – where is it?"

The policeman nodded and turned away from the construction. He had to yell. "See those nice apartment buildings over yonder? That's Alger Court. Go past them and stay on the road leading away from town. It's called Swain Street. Lawrence Hospital will be on your left. When you pass the Ward Leonard Electric Company, you'll cross over the Bronx River; it's more like a stream.

Stay on Swain Street till it drops a bit, then forks up a small hill. The other fork is Dellwood Road."

"How long will it take?"

"No more than ten minutes. Good day to you." The policeman tipped his hat.

The detectives walked along the scimitar-curved Swain Street. New York City seemed a long distance away instead of fifteen miles. They rounded a corner, an outcropping of rocks on either side, and looked down the little hill. Martin saw the fork and another sign, "Welcome to Cedar Knolls."

"That must be Wittig's house – the big one on the corner, just like he described it – same style as that hotel," Keller said.

"My God, John Wittig lives there?" The sight of the grand house with white stucco walls and a brick-red tiled roof startled Martin. "I live in a box compared to that." When they got closer, Martin said, "What a great place for kids to play. Look at that front yard."

"I don't like it. It's too big. Imagine the work to keep it up."

"I guess if you have enough money like Wittig did ..."

"Not for me." Keller pulled his derby tight on his brow. "It's too quiet. Where's the excitement?"

As he approached Wittig's yard, Martin was surprised to see a "For Sale" sign. Martin hesitated when he spotted a swing hanging from the crabapple tree by the side of the house. "That swing brings back memories." Martin wiped his nose. "I loved to swing when I was a kid. My father pushed me so high I was almost parallel to the ground. I'd swing for hours. I always wanted to do that with my kids. Now, ..." Martin's voice cracked.

"You will, Gil. Give it time. I forgot Wittig had kids."

"He's a family man, not so different from us, really. It's our families who are our treasures, aren't they?"

"Come on. The sooner we're done here, the better." Keller picked up his pace.

"Corinne and I dreamed of a place like this. Wittig had everything and tossed it away. For what? Germany? The man was a pacifist. I can't figure it out."

"People value different things. I'm sure Wittig regrets this whole business," Keller said.

"He's a bigger fool than I thought. Corinne and I would have given –"

"Corinne was happy just to share her life with you. Fancy things and big houses didn't mean much to her," Keller said. A crow cawed from the tree. They followed the brick pathway leading to the front porch.

Wittig had already given them much information, but Martin needed to talk to Nora Wittig. He particularly wanted to know about Beck's visit to their house last summer and the man who had accompanied him. Wittig had talked little about him.

Wittig mystified him. How did a decent man go so far wrong? But, when the critical moment arrived, Wittig chose to save Swanson. Martin had hoped he could understand Wittig better by visiting his house. Now, he was more confused.

They knocked on the door. No response. Martin looked through the side window next to the door. He saw a stack of suitcases. Finally, a small woman walked down the steps and answered the door. She looked older than Martin had imagined. She had the same distant look that soldiers have after a costly retreat. The detectives introduced themselves.

"So you are the men who arrested my husband." Nora spit out the words.

"Don't you care how he's doing?" Martin had visited Wittig in prison several times since his arrest.

"I know how he's doing."

"Mrs. Wittig, I am sorry for any problems our visit causes you, but we would like to ask you some questions," Martin said in his firm but polite police voice.

"Come in if you have to." Nora showed them to the living room. "Please sit, but I am busy as you can see." Hannah ran into the room. Nora sent her outside to play.

"Are you taking a trip?" Keller asked.

Nora scowled. "If you must know, I am planning to go to Ireland."

"Now? Is that wise?" Martin asked.

"I have relatives there. They are in trouble."

"Does this have anything to do with the Easter rebellion?"

"The English have captured my brother. He's about to face a firing squad. I need to help him."

"You have my sympathy, but let me get to the point," Martin said. "Your husband has provided many details about his dealings with the Germans. I was hoping you could help clarify a few things."

"Doubt it, but ask." For fifteen minutes, Nora answered their questions but provided nothing useful. Martin finally asked about Beck's visit.

"My husband and Mr. Beck are acquaintances."

"What did they discuss?"

"A business deal, that's all I know. I'm just a woman."

"There was another man with Beck, a Mr. Pieter Knopp, wasn't there?"

"If you know so much, why ask me?"

"Can you describe him?"

Nora gave an unhelpful description.

"Except for the age and general physique, he doesn't sound like our man," Keller said.

Or maybe he was; who could know from that description? "Did he have an accent?" Martin asked.

"We all have accents." Nora affected a thick brogue. "Beck and me husband spoke in German."

"Where was he from?"

"Timbuktu. How should I know?"

Martin pressed his questioning. "Canada?"

"Could have been."

"Germany?"

"Couldn't say."

"Holland, maybe?" Nora's shifting eyes told Martin that he was on the right track. He pretended not to notice. "But he looked European?"

"As opposed to what? Colored? No, he wasn't colored."

"Mrs. Wittig, I want to show you something." Martin unfolded the police drawing of the waiter. "Can you identify this person?"

"Let me guess, Charlie Chaplin?"

Martin returned the drawing to his coat pocket. "What can you tell us about Mr. Knopp?"

"He was a gentleman. More than I can say about you." Nora stood up and tightened her apron strings with a determined pull. "Please, hurry up. I have work to do."

Keller pulled away from the conversation and drifted to the library at the back corner of the house. "Detective, where are you going?" Nora followed him.

"Mrs. Wittig, wait a minute. I have some more –"

The telephone interrupted Martin. Nora ignored it. "Momma." A child cried from upstairs. The telephone kept ringing. Nora picked up the receiver and smashed it back down on the hook. "Momma. I need you." Nora ran upstairs.

Martin waited for Nora in the front hall while Keller scouted around. Ten minutes later, Nora used the handrail as she came downstairs. Strands of hair fell over her face. "How is your daughter?" Martin asked.

"Wish I knew." Nora guided them back to the living room. She slumped on the couch.

"What's wrong?" Martin hated to hear innocent children suffer.

Nora explained that, for the past week, Mary had complained of headaches and a sore throat. When she developed a fever, Nora summoned a doctor who prescribed rest. Last night, Mary complained of pain in her neck and back muscles. "I'm really worried. I've heard there's some kind of epidemic hitting the city. Who knows where she's been playing or what she might have picked up?"

"I'm sure she misses her father, too." Martin's voice was calm and soothing.

Nora looked away. "They were close."

"Mrs. Wittig, I am sorry your daughter is sick, but you need to tell us everything about Mr. Knopp," Martin said.

"What do you want to know? He helped Mary when she fell."

"How?"

"She broke her leg. Mr. Knopp rushed to her and took charge. He said he'd set legs before. He knew what he was doing."

"Was he a doctor?" Keller asked.

"No." Nora thought a moment. "A soldier, I think."

Martin and Keller exchanged glances. Wittig had said he was the one who had treated Mary. Martin began to realize that Wittig had misled them about Knopp. Wittig must have been jealous of Knopp and had tried to make himself the hero that day. Nora's account began to make more sense. Knopp was not just a director at the New Haven Projectile Company.

"But he's a businessman," Keller said. "How could he –"

Before Martin could silence him, Nora's defiance returned. "I've talked enough. I've answered your questions. Now please go."

"One more question ..."

"I'm sorry. I have to attend to my daughter. Good day." She guided them to the front door. It slammed behind them.

They walked away from the house. Keller said, "I didn't think she would be too cooperative, but I wasn't prepared for a Salem witch."

"I think I understand Wittig better now." Martin's mind shifted back to the case. *Knopp was a soldier?* Martin's mind assessed the possibilities.

"What are you thinking, Gil?"

"It's far-fetched."

"What is?"

"Could it be that Mr. Knopp and the Biltmore assassin are the same man?"

"Why do you say that?"

"Change the hair and add some theater makeup and maybe they look the same. Age and body type are the same. Both have military and weapons training. Both are connected to Beck. Why couldn't they be the same man?"

"Maybe. If you're right, could Knopp be our subway bomber, too?" Keller suggested.

"If you gave me some good odds, I'd take that bet." Martin had his thousand-mile-away gaze.

"And Traub's killer?" Keller asked.

"Don't know." Martin said. A squirrel scampered across the road.

"And where is he?"

"That's what we need to find out."

"We need to rethink our investigation."

Martin closed his eyes and concentrated. "I know where to start – remember that case we were asked to review last winter about a drunken man who died in Grand Central last winter?"

"The one they found in the toilet with his head bashed in?"

"That one. I never agreed with the police findings," Martin said. "Seemed like his death was more than a random robbery or a bar fight. I asked the investigators to do some more follow-up, but they were busy. That man was in Grand Central for a reason. What?"

"The detective in charge never got back to you, did he?" Keller said.

"That doesn't mean anything. We were busy, too, but we've learned a lot since and realize things are more connected than they seemed to be a few months ago. Maybe we should do a little more digging into that case."

"That murder was too violent. But what's the connection to Knopp and the waiter?"

"I just have this feeling," Martin said. "The location may be Grand Central Station. The victim. He didn't look like someone who gets drunk in bars. His clothes were too expensive. They were ... foreign. The way he died. I saw the police photographs. I remember thinking he was killed by someone who had killed before. That case always bothered me."

Chapter 65
The *Deutschland*

Baltimore: July 1916

When Caarsens arrived in Baltimore harbor, it was full of curious and excited spectators. He saw several tugboats escorting the German U-boat *Deutschland* into the harbor. The massive U-boat dwarfed the sturdy tugs. Although it was a submarine, the *Deutschland* was classified as a cargo ship, not a warship. Therefore, it was allowed into neutral U.S. waters. It had just completed a dangerous and unprecedented crossing of the Atlantic.

Caarsens stood amidst the throng and pretended to cheer. The *Deutschland* impressed him, but he had more important considerations. As well as a cargo full of dyestuffs to sell in America, the *Deutschland* carried two steamer trunks full of weapons and explosives just for him. Explosives he needed for his next operation, his first since the Biltmore debacle. Caarsens left the harbor and presented himself to Curt Bruckner, head of Baltimore operations for the North-German Lloyd Shipping Company. "So you're the man from the consulate," Bruckner said.

"*Ja.*"

"We've been expecting you." Bruckner reviewed Caarsens's papers. "Of course you want to inspect your goods. Once you're satisfied, we will deliver them to New York City. What's the address?"

"123 West 15th Street, New York City. Please keep it confidential."

Bruckner reached for a pen. Caarsens stopped him. "Memorize it."

Irritation filled Bruckner's face. "I'm aware of the sensitive and – how shall I say – irregular nature of this request. I am a German patriot, and I know how to follow orders. Don't insult me by implying I don't know my job."

Caarsens, too, was irritated. He wanted to finish this assignment quietly and get back to New York. Visiting Baltimore was risky. The *Deutschland's* arrival was too public. He would be too exposed. Too many newspapermen were covering the story. Police and government officials were certainly watching the *Deutschland*'s every move and studying people who came in contact with its crew. There was a strong chance that, despite his disguise, someone in the crowd might have seen the police sketch of him as the Biltmore waiter or the newspaper photograph of him as a labor organizer.

But Beck insisted he meet the *Deutschland*. "You will be the one to use these items. I do not want anyone else involved." Caarsens's attention shifted back to the North-German Lloyd man.

"Perhaps you could use one of our uniforms." Bruckner pointed to a closet.

"I was just going to request one." With his hair dyed dark brown, a bowl haircut, and a trim beard, Caarsens already looked like many of the Lloyd men.

When the *Deutschland* docked, Caarsens joined the other North-German Lloyd employees working their way to the pier to meet it. When he reached the U-boat, its skipper, Captain Paul Koenig, was already talking to newspapermen. The skipper was dressed in a smartly pressed blue uniform jacket and white pants. His blue navy cap was tilted at a dashing angle. His confident military bearing made the small athletic captain seem taller than he was. Koenig seemed to be enjoying himself. Caarsens overheard the newspapermen's questions.

"Captain, you're a hero," one reporter said. "How large is your ship?"

"I understand President Wilson has extended an invitation for you to visit the White House. When will you go?"

"How long did it take you to complete the crossing?"

"This is the largest submarine in the German fleet. As you can guess, it is about 300 feet long, 30 feet wide and over 9 feet high. It carries a cargo of approximately 800 tons. I have not heard about President Wilson's invitation, but it would be an honor to meet him."

A North-German Lloyd employee introduced Caarsens to the *Deutschland's* lieutenant, who escorted him onto the ship. They lowered themselves to the main deck. "It took us three weeks," the lieutenant said. "It was a rough trip. Even I got seasick. Most of the time, we had to keep the hatches closed. We dodged several Royal Navy warships. Nighttime saved us at least twice."

The newspapermen, captivated by the glamour of the historic journey, would have written a different story if they could have seen *Deutschland*'s interior. Condensation ran from the bulkheads. Water leaked around loose rivets. The temperature inside matched the hottest African summer Caarsens could remember. "How big is your crew?"

"Twenty-nine men."

As they walked through the ship, Caarsens saw several grimy sailors in their undershorts. "Can I have some water? I hate confined spaces."

The lieutenant handed him a canteen. “You get used to it.”

The water tasted like diesel oil. Caarsens almost spit it out. “Can you show me my trunks?”

“Follow me.” The lieutenant escorted Caarsens to the cargo hold where two steamer trunks sat in the far corner behind some large crates. A strong padlock secured each one.

Caarsens didn’t understand what was so important about them.

“We loaded the second trunk at the last minute – special request from on high. We had to delay launch until it arrived. Don’t know what’s in them, and don’t want to know. All I know is that you are the only person authorized to see them.” The lieutenant looked at Caarsens, hesitated, and volunteered more information. “An intelligence major with lots of ribbons – he acted like he was the fleet admiral – supervised the loading into our hold. Two civilians were with him. The type you avoid. I have never seen the captain so deferential to anyone who didn’t outrank him. We had to off-load some cargo just to make room. The captain ordered me to guard them. I’ll be glad to be rid of these trunks.”

The lieutenant pressed the keys into Caarsens’s hand. He snapped his heels together, saluted, turned 180 degrees, and marched a discreet distance away.

Caarsens opened the first trunk and mentally inventoried the goods. “Excellent.” It contained a large supply of dynamite, detonation devices, and grenades. When Caarsens began to open the second trunk, the lieutenant said, “Be careful with that one. I was told to tell you that.” He backed farther away.

Caarsens opened the lid with both care and curiosity.

Carefully packed was a captured British Stokes mortar. Recent events began to make sense. When he was in Mexico after he had killed Traub, Beck had arranged for him to visit Mexican military intelligence. They trained him to use mortars. Now, he knew why and once again applauded Beck's foresightedness.

The mortar would be ideal for his next sabotage operation following his attack on Black Tom Island. He and Beck had talked briefly about the target, and from what Caarsens saw in the trunk, he knew the sabotage operation would be more lethal than anything he had ever previously attempted.

Caarsens wanted to examine the mortar to see what changes had been made. It was a simple weapon. When operational, the mortar weighed one hundred pounds. A smooth-bore tube rested on a support plate to absorb recoil. A bipod mount supported the top of the tube and was used to adjust elevation and range. Caarsens knew from the four-inch diameter of its cast iron bomb cylinder that it had been modified from the standard model he had used in Mexico. The mortar had an effective range of seven hundred yards. Normally, it needed a two-man crew to assemble it, but once set up, one man could operate it.

Caarsens also found twenty regular mortar shells carefully packed in boxes. He'd have to use several of them to practice. In a separate box marked with a skull and crossbones, he found seven more shells. The last items in the trunk were several gas masks. He repacked everything and locked the trunks. "Let's go," he told the lieutenant. "I hate this steel can." He knocked his head on a pipe. "There's more room in a prison."

"These steel cans will win the war." The lieutenant wiped sweat off his face.

On his way out, Caarsens met a man in a German officer's uniform who had just boarded. He removed his cap, revealing whitish blond hair and a pronounced widow's peak. He looked too old for active U-boat service. The man said nothing, but turned away when he saw Caarsens.

Caarsens recognized Matthias Weil from the Yacht Club. Beck had engineered his escape.

On the pier, Caarsens saw some of the German crew mingling with the spectators who were cheering the sailors, patting them on the back, and begging for souvenirs. One sailor pulled off a button and gave it to a pretty girl. She handed him something in return. Caarsens saw another man yank the stripes off his tunic and exchange them for money.

Caarsens longed to return to New York. The trip had set in motion Beck's ultimate plan to strike America hard.

~

After the trunks from the *Deutschland* were delivered to 123 West 15th Street, Caarsens collected them and transported them in a wagon Jelly Brown had borrowed to the shed where he hid the motorboat and his operational funds. He was ready for the next step.

Chapter 66
Shannon's Breakthrough

Police Headquarters: July 1916

Martin looked at Shannon and noticed a change in her demeanor. "Look at this timeline I built," Shannon said excitedly at the end of another hot, fruitless day. It matched all the sabotage operations around New York with suspected sabotage operations along the East Coast.

"Do you see a pattern?" Martin asked. Despite himself, he had begun to like and respect Shannon, so different than most women.

"No, but I'm sure there's one." She studied the timeline one more time.

"I couldn't find one, but Shannon is smarter than I am," Keller said. "Not as good with a gun, though."

"I'm still practicing, Detective," she joked.

Martin liked her approach but suggested she expand the timeline to include non-violent work. "After all, Pieter Knopp was a businessman, and we know from Mrs. Wittig that Swanson's assassin and Knopp are the same person. Maybe he was up to something outside of the New York area. Figure out how New Haven Projectile fits into the puzzle, too."

A few days later, she returned and described an incident in Maryland she had read about. It concerned some black workers who tried to unionize. "I only mention it because there were reports of violence against the KKK, something our friend Knopp is capable of. This is a lead; I know it."

They all looked at each other, but Keller dismissed the incident, saying it was a coincidence. Having come to trust her judgment, Martin asked her to do some more research.

A week later, at the end of their Friday shift, Martin wanted to finish the day and go to church. Today, July 28, was his anniversary – and he was anxious to light a candle for Corinne. Keller was talking about the latest Brooklyn Robins victory and asked Martin to join him at the game tomorrow. With his mind on other things, Martin agreed without realizing what he was agreeing to.

Just then, Shannon burst in with a copy of the *Baltimore Sun* newspaper. "I found it," she said elatedly. She opened the paper, spread it out on Keller's desk, and pointed to a picture. "Who's that? A coincidence, Detective Keller?"

"What is it? I don't see anything," Keller said.

"Look harder." Shannon had also brought the police sketch of the missing Biltmore Hotel waiter and placed it next to the newspaper photo. "See a resemblance?"

"My God." Martin took out a magnifying glass and studied the photograph. "Could it be?"

"Let me look." Keller nudged next to Martin. "It's possible."

"That's Knopp, sure as I'm Irish. I'd bet my bloomers on it," Shannon said.

Martin scrutinized the pictures. "You might be right."

"Do you know what I think?" Shannon said. "Someone should go to Baltimore and talk to that Negro leader Madison and those Klansmen who got beat up. Bring that police drawing – they'll confirm it's him."

"You might be right, but the captain's away. We'd need his

authorization." Martin continued to examine the picture. "Let me study this over the weekend. Nothing will happen until Monday, when Tunney gets back." Martin had a gut feeling he should act, but uncharacteristically ignored it.

Chapter 67
It's Hell Over There

Battery Park Ferry Terminal, Manhattan: July 29, 1916

On the morning of Saturday, July 29, Caarsens met Murphy, now a committed and capable collaborator, at the Battery Park Ferry. He confirmed the bribes had been paid and was excited to say the ammunition storage facility at Black Tom Island overflowed with new supplies. Several fully loaded fuel tanks had just arrived and would not be unloaded for another day.

"I've done everything you wanted, but something else has come up," Murphy informed him. "You'll never believe our luck." An eighty-by-thirty-foot barge, the *Johnson 17,* fat with 417 cases of detonating fuses and 100,000 pounds of TNT, was tied up at a Black Tom Island pier. "It's crazy, but it's there because the owner didn't want to pay a special $25 towing charge. Serves those cheapskates right. If the *Johnson 17* goes up, everything else on Black Tom Island will blow up, too." Caarsens paid him two thousand dollars and told him to disappear.

~

That afternoon at Ebbets Field in Brooklyn, Martin cheered halfheartedly as Casey Stengel of the league-leading Brooklyn Robins drove in the go-ahead run in the bottom of the eighth with a triple. He hadn't wanted to go to Ebbets Field today, but Keller convinced him they needed a change from work. Martin planned to relax the rest of the weekend at home.

~

Caarsens landed in the marshes north of Black Tom Island that evening just after nightfall. He anchored his motorboat in the shallow water and waded onto shore. It was a perfect spot for an ambush. He pulled out his Colt, took a deep breath, and scoured the area for bushwhackers, but Black Tom Island was unguarded; the bribes had worked. Prepared for a fight but relieved not to have one, Caarsens holstered his automatic and, keeping to the tree line, snuck past some workers huddled around lighted smudge pots trying to avoid mosquitoes.

Hugging the shadows, he stopped – this was too easy. He looked in every direction, at all possible ambush points, at every movement. The boats headed out of New York Harbor in a normal stream, hungry fish patrolled the shallows for food as usual, and except for the men distracted by mosquitoes, there was no human activity. The only noises were the water splashing onto the shore and the gentle wind rustling through the trees. Moonlight reflected off the Statue of Liberty, so near, so big and so peaceful, just like Black Tom Island.

Convinced he was safe, Caarsens boarded the *Johnson 17* unseen and flicked on his torch, treading lightly on the creaking floorboards. He walked by the captain's quarters and heard snoring. When he reached the main cargo hold, he pointed his torch at the cases of detonating fuses. The stacks towered over him. Cases of dynamite filled the rest of the hold. Murphy's information was right. Sensing victory, he felt exhilarated.

From his rucksack, he removed a stick of dynamite with a four-hour fuse and lit it. He would be back in Chinatown when it went off, creating a series of explosions up and down Black Tom

Island. In the next forty-five minutes, he placed more long-fused dynamite sticks for maximum effect in the warehouses, railroad cars, and other barges, imagining the devastation soon to come. Feeling confident his work was complete, he headed back. To his surprise, he saw a vagrant searching for clams in the shallow water fifteen yards from his anchored motorboat. Caarsens guessed he lived in one of the derelict camps nearby. He was thirty-five going on sixty and stank of liquor, body odor, and the sea.

Pretending to be a guard, Caarsens called, "Hey you! What are you doing here?" Mumbling something, the vagrant stumbled and fell into the ankle-deep water. Caarsens reached him while he was still on his knees. Caarsens sliced into the man's soft wrinkled neck with his Demag, causing blood to spurt out and turn the water black. The vagrant grabbed his throat, splashed face-first into the water, flailing for a few pathetic seconds. *I pray God will treat you better in the next life than he'll treat me.* Still unchallenged, Caarsens sped away in his motorboat, its low silhouette disappearing into the night.

~

At 2:00 a.m., Caarsens, naked and burning with anticipation and sweat, lay awake. Peping rolled over next to him. "One more time?" she giggled. In the thirteen months since he had stayed with Mr. Li, Caarsens had found refuge and solace with his daughter, a tiny woman just over twenty years of age with bound feet and a jet-black pigtail that reached to her waist. They shared secrets they never discussed, dashed hopes for a good life they'd never have, and joyless intimacy. For them, a present with no future was enough to keep them distantly close and comfortably distant.

"Go to sleep, Peping." Caarsens stood up and went to the window to escape the heavy air and his sticky sheets. Heat released from the ovens cooling in the kitchen one floor below and the day's lingering humidity made his bedroom feel like the Chinese laundry down the block. Garbage in the alley mixed with dung and waste. Gray swirls of opium from the den across the street circled up like formless ghosts. Caarsens imagined they were men he had killed.

He checked his watch – 2:05 a.m. – and retreated to bed. Three more minutes. He lay on Peping to shield her with his body. "Stay down." He held her, and she, used to obeying male authority, said nothing and remained still.

The first blast detonated as planned at 2:08. Caarsens felt the thrill of adrenaline shoot through his body with such power he thought he would explode himself. The force from the distant explosion shook the alleyway and shattered the windows in the room. Dishes crashed in the kitchen below. Knowing more explosions were imminent, he rolled Peping off the bed and covered her small body with his own. She cried out with fear, but Caarsens's firm hands and steady grip calmed her down. When the primary explosions had finished, he lifted her back onto the bed, but she continued to shiver and clutch him tightly.

Caarsens lay silent, on his back, bathed in a feeling of pride and satisfaction. Peping poked his ribs with her elbow. "Mister Barrymore, what you think about?" He shook his head and sat up straight. Peping reached toward him and tried to kiss him, but he pulled away and started to dress.

"Where you go?" she said anxiously.

"See what's going on."

"You gwai-lo all same. Why can't mind own business?"

Caarsens reached under the bed and took his Demag and Colt.

"Why you always take?"

He avoided her eyes.

~

Walking south from Chinatown, Caarsens joined more and more people emerging from their apartments. Some were fully dressed; several were missing shoes or shirts; others wore night-clothes. One man was tying a tie as if preparing to go to a wake. Caarsens reached Battery Park just as the night sky began to turn into the pasty yellow of smeared mustard, and the stars melted into the expanding glop overhead. Bombs and ammunition burst over the harbor, some as high as one hundred feet. The smell of gunpowder and burning wreckage fouled the air around him. Across the harbor, secondary explosions rumbled and fire engines shrieked. The water turned into a devil's brew of dead fish, floating debris, and chemicals. In front of the erupting volcano that was once Black Tom Island, the Statue of Liberty glowed orange.

A ferry boat loaded with people from Ellis Island had raced to the relative safety of Manhattan. A few people had jumped off before it docked. A man in a white coat was supervising a group of panicked immigrants scurrying down the gangplank like rats. Once on land, they scattered, one man begging forgiveness from the Lord, another spinning around like a dervish before he took off and was chased by the man in the white coat. "They're from the insane wing over there!" he exclaimed, gesturing toward Ellis Island as he ran past Caarsens.

The blaze continued during the night. Brooklyn and Manhattan Coast Guard cutters sailed into the volcano. A fireman, his face blistered and his arms covered in soot and ash, returned from Communipaw. "It's hell over there."

"You don't know what hell is," Caarsens said.

Black Tom Island continued to die.

~

The 2:08 explosion had jolted Martin out of his sleep in his Brooklyn apartment. At first, he thought someone was shooting at him, but then realized the continuing explosions were far away. "What the hell?" he exclaimed, peering out the window. Something was grievously wrong. Smoke was rising from lower Manhattan.

When he arrived at Police Headquarters the next morning, Black Tom Island was in its final convulsions. Chaos, confusion, rumors, loud voices filled the station. As calls for help flooded in from around the city, the only thing anyone agreed on was that there had been a massive explosion in the harbor. All over town, police responded to false reports of burglaries and calls from night watchmen fearing break-ins and the end of the world. Roundsmen were dispatched all over the city. After what seemed like hours, Martin, learning less each minute, decided to investigate himself. As he walked toward Battery Park, church bells pealing reminded him it was Sunday. Unshaved and still dressed in civilian clothes, he fought lack of sleep.

All routes to lower Manhattan were jammed with taxis, motorcars, horse-drawn wagons, and pedestrians. Streetcars were packed; kids rode on their sideboards with amusement park bravado. On Broadway, an enterprising young man sold Cracker Jacks.

As he approached Battery Park, Martin saw the direct effects of the blast, which had caused unprecedented destruction. A combination of ash from Black Tom Island fires and fine particles of glass from countless shattered windows covered the streets like a freakish summer snowstorm. Hearing shouts, he walked into the Battery Park Aquarium to investigate. Its entire roof had collapsed. Employees dove into the tanks that had survived, desperately trying to prevent the fish from ingesting glass shards and debris.

Unable to help, Martin continued on and soon reached the Whitehall building at the end of West Street. It appeared to have taken a direct hit. No front or west-facing window had survived. Piles of jagged, silver-dollar-sized pieces of glass blocked its entrance. He nearly tripped over a door that had been blown off its hinges.

Finally reaching the southern tip of Manhattan, he pushed through throngs of curiosity-seekers all staring at the remnants of Black Tom Island, still smoldering and coughing up live munitions. He called headquarters and described the situation to the desk sergeant, who told him Captain Tunney was finally restoring order and Keller was heading downtown.

Tense, angry and tired, Martin met Keller at the ferry. He ordered the ferry captain to head over to New Jersey and joined some firemen, the only other passengers. As they neared Communipaw, the caustic, smoke-filled air intensified and thickened. Dreading what they would find, they disembarked and followed the New Jersey Central Railroad tracks toward what was left of Black Tom Island. For half an hour, they walked across the salt marshes littered with the carcasses of bufflehead and ruddy ducks. Those that had survived flopped around grotesquely as if insane.

War had come to America. Black Tom Island was as much a battleground as Verdun. Scattered along the railroad bed were signs marked "Hazardous!" and "Flammable!" Twisted and melted railroad tracks and splintered ties lay everywhere. Charred freight cars were thrown around like children's toys. Power lines tilted at steep angles, and the warehouses burned at temperatures so intense Martin had to back away. Scattered wildly all around them were broken wooden cases, metal fragments, and artillery casings. Firemen and other workers removed debris by hand. One out-of-breath man wearily remarked, "We'll never finish."

A fireman shouted at them, "Hey. Be careful! This is a minefield. We haven't cleared your section. Go the other way." The man pointed toward a dirt path thirty yards to his left. Martin quickly understood that the workers could not use shovels or picks. An unlucky strike could detonate a live shell or trigger an explosion. A moment later, someone yelled, "Watch out!" Several bullets exploded and men dove for cover, including the detectives. One round zinged by Martin's head, missing him by inches. In all his years on the force, no bullet had ever come closer. He fell on something warm. It took him a while to realize that it was a melted bottle.

Unfazed by the danger, Keller appeared in his element. When other men tensed, he remained calm. When they ducked, he often stood firm, somehow sensing which bullets posed no threat. When they hesitated to act, he moved forward. "Follow me, I'll show you the way," he yelled, as Martin rushed to keep up.

They stopped at the crater, the most startling sight of all – a hole as wide and long as a football field and so deep that groundwater percolated up from below into it. A man came up to him. "We think this is where a train full of railroad cars was resting when it went up," he said. "Eighty cars filled with dynamite, right here." The man kicked some dirt into the hole and turned again to the detectives. "My name is Aaron Carmichael, captain of the Jersey City Fire Department. I'm in charge of the clean-up here. Massive operation. No one from the railroad company has shown up. Who are you?"

They introduced themselves and showed their badges.

"Glad to meet you." The fire captain extended his hand. "Just be careful."

Martin ordered Keller to check the shore. "Have you ever seen anything similar to this?" he asked the fire chief.

"Not in all my twenty-two years on the job, and I was in San Francisco during the aught-six quake. Want to hear something curious? One of the secondary blasts blew the shoes off one of my men. He still can't believe he's alive."

"Can you assess the damage here? I've already seen what it did to Manhattan," Martin said.

"Come with me." Carmichael escorted Martin to the shore. "Let's start from the water. There were seven piers; only the one to the south is useable. Four are destroyed and two will have to be rebuilt. Hundreds of barges and railroad cars disintegrated. Thirteen warehouses disappeared. There's so much debris we're having trouble figuring out where they stood. One of the men working here estimates that each warehouse held about a hundred tons of dried goods – grain and salt."

"Is that what I smell? It seems sweet," Martin said.

"Oh, and sugar. The warehouses were full of it," Carmichael said. "When it burns, it smells like that. Sickening, isn't it? I don't think I can ever eat Cracker Jack again."

"What do you think happened last night, Captain?" Martin was still trying to comprehend the devastation. "At the police station, the feeling was that it was an accident."

"I heard some reporter say the same thing. The Jersey coppers agreed."

"Down!" came a yell as more bullets exploded. Martin was on the ground faster than Carmichael. Something nicked him.

"You hurt?" Carmichael indicated it was safe to stand.

"Just a scratch." Martin wiped away some blood on his left arm but it continued to flow. "What were you saying about the Jersey police?"

"They got here right after my men. They arrested the five guards who were on duty last night and yanked them away for questioning. One man accused a guard of lighting a smudge pot last night. It might have started there. He denied it, of course."

"Even if he did, do you think that could have caused such destruction?"

"Possible. Apparently, the fire started near the *Johnson 17*. That blast could have spread sparks all across Black Tom Island."

"You think this was an accident?" Martin asked.

"From what I've seen, it didn't happen that way. The explosions weren't random – one detonation creating another and then another with no pattern. No, this seemed more like a series of explosions from multiple sources. We may never know for sure."

~

As Keller continued to investigate, Martin returned to headquarters. It was filled with as much confusion as when he left. "The churches are full," Mrs. Bauer reported. An old-timer mentioned that President McKinley's assassination hadn't attracted as many parishioners.

Griggs didn't seem to care. He said the attack was across the Hudson, and New Jersey should handle it.

Howell complained that he'd been called into work on a Sunday.

Martin ignored him and went to see Tunney in his office. The captain shouted orders into the phone and finally hung up. He looked at Martin. "What did you find?"

"I don't care what anyone else says, this was sabotage," Martin said in his most compelling tone.

"You're jumping too fast," Tunney said. "Tell me what you saw."

"The captain of the Jersey City Fire Department is smart. He thinks it was likely deliberate," Martin said.

"We must be careful," Tunney said. "The repercussions of making a mistake are huge."

"I'm aware of the repercussions. The Germans did this. I know it."

"I agree. Push the German émigré community. Get someone over to those German boats stinking up New York Harbor. We might not have jurisdiction over them, but keep asking the sailors coming ashore. Someone must know something. Rough them up a bit. Scare them. I'll get extra men from the mayor. Now these Huns have gone too far."

"Yes, Captain."

"Also, double the reward for information on that waiter. Eight thousand dollars should shake the trees. Our saboteur's out there, and I think he's involved in this mess. We have to find him."

"Captain, I'm sure you've considered it, but don't you think it's time we raided 123 West 15th?"

Chapter 68
God Is Doing Good Business Today

Saint Luke's Lutheran Church, Manhattan: July 1916
The morning after the attack, Caarsens sat calm and satisfied in his regular bench near the back of Saint Luke's church. The stink from debris still burning on Black Tom Island and the lingering odor of gunpowder from across the harbor filled the church like some hellish incense. Last night's sudden and powerful explosions had driven large numbers of frightened parishioners into the church, as well. *God is doing good business today*, Caarsens thought.

Like the rest of the congregation, Caarsens sought union with God, but for different reasons. Since he was a boy in South Africa, Caarsens had attended church regularly. Instead of rejecting the church's Calvinist teachings, as his best childhood friend told him he would do, the humorless and brooding Danie Caarsens embraced its Old Testament belief in an eye for an eye, its Boer reliance on individual responsibility, and its devotion to an unforgiving God.

He was glad the church was full. Numbers meant anonymity, and anonymity meant safety, but vigilance provided protection. His steel blue eyes studied the faces of the other parishioners and shifted from row to row as he looked for anyone who might be too interested in him. Did anyone deliberately avoid eye contact? Did anyone look out of place? Not today. He relaxed and prayed. He thanked God for his success last night and asked for the strength, wisdom, and courage to continue his task. Revenge is a heady burden.

At the end of the service, Reverend Hoogstrum raised his

hands to the sky and said, “The path for the lambs of God is peace. Have mercy on the souls of those who lost their lives at Black Tom Island. I ask forgiveness for any man responsible.”

Caarsens cringed. Under his breath, he said, “You’re wrong, Pieter. I don’t want forgiveness. I’m prepared for the consequences I face, but once subjected to the British yoke, a man has three options: betray his cause and join the oppressors, become enslaved, or fight. I fight.”

He left the church and headed into Chinatown, where he again felt engulfed by its clashing blend of cultures. The smell of raw fish and fried rice filled his nostrils. The old tenement buildings on either side of the narrow alleys seemed closer together than normal. The buildings looked like many others around New York, but characters, not words, formed most of the signs. Those in English seemed out of place: “Wang Tong Hook & Co – Chinese and Japanese Novelties.” Women in long pigtails and Oriental silk robes decorated with embroidered dragons walked next to tattooed men wearing Western suits and hats. A strange mix, but so was he.

He walked through Mott Street and then to Chatham Square before he headed to the Wing Sing restaurant. He heard Peping singing in the kitchen and climbed two flights of stairs to his room. When he opened the door, a fat cockroach tried to run under his bed, but Caarsens stomped on it first. Others appeared, and he killed several, but more kept coming.

Chapter 69
The Eastman Girl

123 West 15th Street, Manhattan: August 1916

Night was setting in. For fifteen minutes, Martin observed 123 West 15th Street with his team, including Keller, Griggs, and three roundsmen. He clutched his search warrant tight remembering that Black Tom Island had blown up three days ago. From a distance, the brownstone looked like the others on the tree-lined block. It had three stories, bars across its ground-level windows, and an eight-step stoop, about the height of an average woman, leading up to the front door. But, from his concealed position across the street, it seemed to him the brownstone stood apart from the other buildings like a pair of muddy boots at a dress parade.

In the squelching August humidity, all the windows on the block, except those of 123, were open. The other brownstones were unusually quiet. By contrast, 123's draped and shuttered windows only partially muffled the boisterous merriment inside. "That's the way it's been since Sunday, Detective," the roundsman mopped his brow.

"New York is staggering around like a groggy boxer at an eight count, and those Huns are having a party," Keller said. "Can't tell me someone in there wasn't involved in Black Tom Island."

When he heard a woman belt out *Die Wacht am Rhein*, Martin's fist clenched. The owner of the building, Marta Held, was a former opera star in Germany. That must be her.

"Let's go now." Keller fidgeted. "I hate these people."

Martin pulled him back. "Wait, not yet."

"You're always too careful."

Martin frowned. "We have only one chance at this. Remember, look for the waiter."

Over the next twenty minutes, a number of well-dressed guests arrived and left. A long string of taxis waited for them. "Word is they're good tippers, Sergeant. The goings-on would shock the Lord," one roundsman said. 123 West 15th Street had a notorious reputation. Everything added up to one thing: Marta Held managed a brothel and maybe much more. Everyone in the local precinct knew the rumors that Madam Held called French letters "Fritzes."

But, what struck Martin as odd was that some of the men entered and left not by the front door over the stoop, but by the street-level door leading to the basement. Every man looked from side to side as he exited. Another oddity: no women accompanied them. As a taxi accelerated away, a horse-drawn open carriage pulled up to the building. In the back of the carriage, Martin recognized Felix Beck. He fawned over an attractive young woman with stylish bobbed hair and an alluring dress. Martin thought he recognized her – but he couldn't remember where. Beck grabbed her hand and tried to kiss her cheek, but she pulled away. He chased her inside.

A few minutes later, people inside began to sing, *Deutschland, Deutschland Über Alles.* Martin turned to his men. "Now." He ordered one man each to guard the front door and basement entrance while he charged ahead. They sprinted across the street. A Negro servant opened the door. Keller and two policemen followed Martin inside. Pictures of a woman who must have been Mrs. Held covered the hallway walls. In each one, she was dressed in elaborate costumes at exotic locations – the Pyramids, the Taj Mahal, Victoria Falls, always with a different glamorous man in each picture. Copies of the latest edition of *The Fatherland* rested on a table. Well-dressed men in suits, ties, and waistcoats that seemed to constrain their girth cheered with schoolboy enthusiasm. Men in uniform congregated among them. Everyone held either a glass of champagne or a stein of frothy beer. Someone toasted the Kaiser – more cheers. A few attractive women stood in the background.

Just as Martin announced himself, a stout middle-aged woman with dark-blue eyes and shiny black hair barged forward. Her tent-like dress seemed to expand with each step. "Can I help you?"

"Mrs. Held?" Martin suspected that men's eyes no longer floated in her direction. His police instincts told him that her power resided in her wit, connections, and ability to provide introductions to women whose figures and allure she now exploited.

"No other." Mrs. Held rested her hands on her hips, thumbs forward.

"Detective Sergeant Gilbert Martin. I have a warrant to search this building."

"Give it to me, Sergeant." Mrs. Held examined the document like a trained lawyer and read every word.

Martin guessed that she was delaying either for dramatic effect or to let someone dispose of evidence. *Hurry up*.

"It seems in order." Mrs. Held handed back the warrant. "Please proceed. I ask you to be careful. We have many expensive items in this house." She played with her earring as she glanced at a woman in the dining room.

Detective Martin followed Mrs. Held's eyes to the brown-haired beauty who had arrived with Beck. Her arms were folded. In the well-lit room, Martin recognized her – Mena Reiss, the Eastman Girl. His wife admired her photographs and loved the gossip surrounding her. She approached him. "Excuse me, officer." Her pale gray eyes added to her mystery.

"Can I help you, madam?"

"Don't look at me like that, you swine." She slapped Martin across the face.

The Germans clapped.

He felt two things: a stinging numbness across his face and a small piece of paper move into his hand. He tucked it into his pocket and turned to go to the library at the far corner of the dining room. He froze when he entered. Over the fireplace was a French tricolor.

"A souvenir from the Franco-Prussian war," Mrs. Held gloated. "We'll get another one once our soldiers take Paris."

Martin forced himself to stay calm.

Sweeping through the top floors, his men reported they found nothing interesting except a few scandalous French postcards and ladies' undergarments. Martin and his men moved to the basement. "Check it." Detective Martin pointed to the open door where he saw a toilet. "I'll check the wine cellar." Behind a large wooden cask, Martin found a thick stash of money – U.S. dollars, British pounds, and French francs. From the front room of the basement, someone called. "Sergeant, come here. Look at this." In an old briefcase next to a side table were maps and drawings of New York Harbor. The outlines of Black Tom Island were clear.

They found a man in a German naval uniform looking behind the icebox, where a steamer trunk was hidden.

"What's in the trunk?" Martin asked.

"How would I know? I'm trying to find a ring I dropped," the sailor said in bad English.

"Please open it for me."

"How can I? It's not mine. I don't have the key."

Keller stepped forward and shot off the lock. The trunk was empty. He leaned in. "I smell dynamite."

Martin swallowed, "It's time we spoke with Mrs. Held."

"I don't know what you're talking about." She growled like a cat whose territory was being threatened. "I've never seen that trunk before. One of my guests must have put it there. You have no grounds to arrest me."

"No, but if I trace any explosives back to this trunk, or if I prove you've harbored a saboteur, I'm coming back, and I'll tear your house apart."

~

Martin checked his watch: 10:16 a.m. and Mena Reiss had still not appeared. He took out the note she had given him at Mrs. Held's. "Meet me at Grand Central Station ticket office tomorrow, 10:00 a.m. Can help." From the landing inside the Vanderbilt Avenue entrance, he could see the entire length of three-year-old Grand Central Station. He saw no woman at the ticket window below him. The cavernous building, almost one and a half football fields in length, made him wonder if he'd see her at all or if she'd recognize him. Where was she?

"Don't worry, Gil, she'll show up. That slap proved she wanted to get your attention."

"Sure did." Martin's face still showed the mark.

Keller pointed to the ceiling one hundred fifty feet above them. "Which one are you?"

"What are you talking about?"

"The zodiac. I'm Leo. Up there."

"I don't know. I was born June 17. Who cares?"

"Gemini, of course." Keller showed him each of the constellations painted on the ceiling. They're backwards."

"What?"

"They're not from the Earth's perspective. The artist painted them as if he was in the heavens looking down on Earth."

"How would you know?"

"Shannon."

"Everything is backwards these days."

"Look." Keller tapped Martin. "There." Mena Reiss emerged from the tunnel below them that connected to the lower level. She looked over her shoulder. She was taller than many of the commuters. She wore an ankle-length beige cotton dress and a circular hat with a wide brim. She walked past the ticket window and quickened her pace.

They followed her across the concourse toward the IRT subway. Martin tracked her through the crowd by following the squeak made by the low wedge heels of her laced shoes. He caught her just before she reached the ramp leading into the subway station. "Excuse me, madam, you dropped something."

Mena Reiss turned around. "I think not, sir. Thank you anyway, I'm in a hurry." She avoided eye contact as she dug into her purse to find a token.

"You wanted to see me," Martin said.

"No longer. Good-bye."

"Wait." Detective Martin's large hand wrapped around her slender left arm. "Maybe I can help you."

"Let go. You're hurting me."

Detective Martin pulled his arm away. Mena Reiss rolled up her sleeve. He saw bruises up and down her arm. "What happened to you?"

"I'm being followed, see. Where can we talk?" She rubbed her arm.

"Follow me." Martin took her to the basement room in Grand Central where he had arrested Wittig. He told Keller to stay behind to make sure no one followed them.

Once in the room, Mena calmed down. "You're safe. Let's start with those bruises. How did you get them?" Martin thought she was no longer the defiant woman at Mrs. Held's. She had become an abused young girl.

She removed her hat. A few angry red marks blemished her face. "Mr. Felix Beck."

"That the same gentleman I saw you with last night?" Martin became excited.

"He lost his temper."

"What happened?"

"We were fighting before we arrived at Mrs. Held's last night. He was becoming inappropriate in the carriage ride. He got angrier when I asked him questions about Mrs. Held. He told me never to talk about her, see." She sat down and crossed her legs demurely.

Martin sat far enough away to avoid threatening her. "Go on."

“We get back to the hotel – don’t know why he never takes me to his place. He takes off his dinner jacket. I know what you’re going to say. I need money so I put up with him. That’s why I do modeling, too.”

“Modeling?”

“A while back, I took this picture at Niagara Falls with this fat German, and I became the Eastman Girl. Then, I met Mrs. Held. Money came and went – I don’t manage it so good. Soon every prominent German-American in New York wants to meet me, see.”

“That’s how you met Mr. Beck?”

“Yes.”

“Can you tell me what happened at the hotel?” Detective Martin started to write down his notes.

“He got real angry. Seems like he saw me give you the note. I tried to calm him down, real nice-like.” Mena smoothed her dress.

“I understand.”

“Wrong move!” she screeched. “He got excited and became rough, see. He says to me, ‘I’ve always wanted to play THIS game.’ He licked his lips and looked down at his ... uh ...,” She gestured to Martin’s waist. “That was when he took off his suspenders and wrapped them around his fist. I panicked. I tried to run, but he hit me and threw me on the bed.”

“Did you try scream?”

“For a small man, Mr. Beck is very strong. Tough, too. I bite him. He hits me and stuffs something in my mouth – his sock, maybe. Then he tells me to be quiet and threatens me.”

“How?”

“My mother – he knows where she lives. Then he tells me he’ll throw acid in my face if I don’t do what he says.”

"What did you do next?"

"What he wanted. He rips my dress down to my waist. It was a beautiful dress, too. It was mostly off, anyway. 'I have to punish you for giving that note to that policeman,' he says. Then he starts to ..." Mena Reiss pointed to her arm. "See?"

"Did you ever admit to giving me the note, Mena?"

"'There is no note,' I tell him again and again. Each time I denied it, he swung harder. I don't know how many times. One, two, ..." She pointed to each mark. She stopped counting at six.

"When did he stop?"

"I don't know. He punched me in the face and I blacked out. I woke up in my undergarments. What was left of them, anyway. That's when I decided I had to get away."

"Did this ever happen before?"

"No."

"Did he ever take you anywhere?"

"He liked me. We went all over – once even to Washington."

"Can you verify that?" Martin assessed the legal implications of Beck taking Marta out of state for carnal purposes.

"Because of my modeling, I have to keep a good record of meetings. I have the details in my book. That man is sick."

"Why did you give me the note last night?" Martin asked.

"I was angry. Mr. Beck was ... I can't explain. All that singing after such a horrible event. I wanted to do some good. I didn't think it through too good, see."

"I understand. I can help you." He patted her hand. "I have a few more questions. Were you at 123 West 15th when Black Tom Island exploded?"

“I got there the next day.”

“Do you know anything more about the explosion?” Martin loosened his collar. The room was getting midday hot.

“No, I’m sorry. It was all they talked about. You would have thought the Germans won the war by the way they celebrated.”

“Anything else you can tell me?”

“Yes, I overheard this German navy captain brag about bomb-making materials in his ship.”

“Really? Do you know which one?” Martin’s eyes narrowed.

“It might be the *Frederick*-something. Mr. Beck and I were waiting for a taxi. The captain was in front of us. That’s the name he told the driver. I have no idea if it’s true, but I thought it was important.”

“Of course. We’ll look into it. Do you ...”

“Excuse me for interrupting, but I want to say something.”

“Of course.”

“Please don’t take offense, Detective, but I don’t think you understand these people.”

“What do you mean?”

“Except for Mr. Beck, these are not bad people, see. Mrs. Held is looking to regain her success. We all want that, don’t we?”

“I suppose so.”

“For the Germans, this is a terrible war. They feel America hasn’t been neutral. America is keeping the Allied war effort going, while the British navy is starving the German people. The Germans are just fighting back however they can. From their perspective, the explosion at Black Tom Island just evened things out a bit. These Germans believe in their cause.”

"They have no cause. They're criminals."

"They're patriots, trying to help their country, see. We would do the same thing in their place."

"Any final thoughts, Miss Reiss?"

"Only one thing." Mena Reiss hesitated. "They could win."

MORGAN BANK BUILDING

August 1916 - September 1916

Chapter 70
Mounting Debts

Treasury Building, Washington, D.C.: August 1916

Four days after Black Tom Island exploded, Secretary McAdoo sat long-faced and sullen. He was too busy to wait for tardy people, even Colonel House. House arrived fifteen minutes late and made no apologies. He walked in careful deliberate steps. “I appreciate you taking the time to see me, Mr. Secretary.”

“The president insisted on it. Please sit.” McAdoo gestured toward the stiff leather chair in front of his desk.

“Let’s get down to business.” House wrestled off his coat and gasped when he sat down.

“How is your back, Colonel?”

House struggled to get comfortable in the chair. “What can you tell me about Black Tom Island?”

“Here are the facts.” McAdoo spoke like a stock broker quoting prices. “Two million pounds of explosives detonated. The attack created $20 million in damage. It may be more.” McAdoo waited for a reaction.

House folded his long spindly hands on his lap. “Proceed.”

McAdoo resented House’s condescending attitude. “The East Coast has seen nothing like it. It jolted the Brooklyn Bridge. People in Philadelphia felt the blast. Folks in Maryland thought there was an earthquake. Windows in Manhattan were shattered as far north as Times Square. Telephone lines in New York and New Jersey went dead.”

“What about the harbor?” House frowned.

“The explosion created some craters, but navigation is still manageable.”

“And the river?”

“The blast shook the tunnels connecting New Jersey and Manhattan, but they’re still intact.”

“Any deaths?” House toyed with his pen.

“At least five people. A railroad guard, two policemen, and a baby who was blown out of his crib. The captain of the *Johnson 17* is missing. We assume he’s dead. Hundreds were injured, mostly due to shrapnel and shattered glass.”

“Unfortunate. We were lucky the casualties were so low.” House jotted down some notes. “*The New York Times* has suggested it was an accident. What do you think?”

McAdoo’s ears twitched backward like those of a cat. “It was sabotage.”

“I was afraid of that.” House’s face tightened. He reached behind and massaged his back. “We have to dispel any notion of sabotage. Keep the newspapers thinking it was an accident.”

“Doing that already. The police will be careful what they tell the press.”

“Don’t forget the election’s coming up,” House said. “Don’t want this country howling for war the way they did in 1898. Despite everything, the Germans haven’t provoked us too far. The president wants to keep it that way. His re-election depends on it.”

“Of course. There is another small matter.” McAdoo picked up a report on his desk marked *Confidential*. “Our navy has informed me that we’ve lost another ship.”

"Which one?"

"The animal transport ship *Henry Morgan* was sunk in the Mediterranean. All hands were lost."

"What happened?"

"It hit a mine planted by a German raider."

"Pity. Thank you, Mr. Secretary." House started to collect his papers. "Anything else?"

"Yes, but you may want a whiskey."

"Is it that grave?" House sat back down. His eyes narrowed.

McAdoo leaned forward. "Our economic situation is precarious."

"What?" House straightened up. "The U.S. economy is booming."

"Correct. We are providing steel, food, equipment, everything to the Allies. Business is good, but ..." McAdoo took a deep breath. "It's artificial, a balloon about to burst."

"I don't understand," House said. "All our estimates indicate business has never been better."

"Short-term results. It's paid for with massive debt. Our economic growth may not be sustainable. Since the war began, the U.S. economy has grown over fifty percent. Our rail transportation system can't keep up with the demand. Our estimates indicate the U.S. will need 140,000 new freight cars by mid-year."

"Why is that a problem?"

"Since mid-1915, the English have underwritten all the loans for Italy, France, and Russia. Everything has been repaid so far, but we're reluctant to float more loans on today's terms."

House scratched his head.

"Britain has no more collateral, Colonel. They will be bankrupt next year."

"My God. What can we do, Mr. Secretary?"

"I've talked with the British foreign secretary. We've agreed that England will send us twenty tons of gold. Secretly, of course. That will be the first shipment of collateral. We want the British to give us a show of good faith."

"That's a lot of faith. For safekeeping, I assume."

"Naturally. With the gold, the United States will extend them more loans. The first shipment will arrive in New York in three weeks on the *U.S.S. Tucker*."

"A destroyer?"

"Yes. It should be safe from U-boats. If the British lost this gold, it would be a catastrophe. The United States could not issue any more loans. If our loans stop, the war stops and Germany wins. It's that simple."

Chapter 71

The *Friedrich der Grosse*

Pier along the Hudson River: August 1916

From his hiding place behind a ten-foot stack of crates in the warehouse section of the covered pier, Martin watched his trap unfold. Rays of sunlight peeked through the wooden roof. Keller drove the horse-drawn wagon alongside the long pier beside the *Friedrich der Grosse*, the largest liner in the North-German Lloyd fleet. It was one of eighty German liners, freighters, and other ships the British navy had chased into neutral New York Harbor at the start of the war. As a neutral country, America could not refuse sanctuary. So it tied up the ships and detained the sailors, who were free to roam around the city. Under international law, the ships were considered German territory and not subject to U.S. jurisdiction.

Keller stopped the horse at the first gangplank and waited for the Germans to disembark and collect his delivery of sheet-lead. In order to make cigar bombs, the Germans rolled sheet-lead into cylinders to form the outer shells. For months, the Bomb Squad had investigated sheet-lead supplies, but finding the ultimate delivery points had proved impossible until Mena Reiss talked.

Once Martin learned that the *Friedrich der Grosse* was the bomb-making source, he and Keller started to watch all deliveries there. They followed one sheet-lead delivery wagon back to its original manufacturer in New Jersey and checked its records. They learned that it had sold bomb-making material to several companies that existed only on paper.

Three German sailors came down the gangplank of the *Friedrich der Grosse*. The chief engineer, Karl Schmidt, led the way. Keller sat in the buckboard of the wagon and flipped a baseball into the air while he waited.

"Once they touch that dock, they're on U.S. soil. When they take Keller's sheet-lead, they're ours," Martin said to the two roundsmen assigned to his detail.

Chatting in German, the sailors approached Keller. "*Wo ist Korbach*?" Schmidt asked.

"Sick. *Ich bin Folkmann*." Keller handed them the delivery papers.

From his concealed position, Martin was close enough to hear their conversation and forced himself to hide his excitement. He charged forward when the sailors started to unload the sheet-lead. "You're under arrest."

The three Germans just gaped. After a few seconds, Schmidt started to laugh. "Good joke, Folkmann. For what?"

Keller laughed back. He reached for a baseball bat he had placed under his seat in case of trouble. When Martin reached the Germans, he said, "Conspiracy to destroy ships with fire-bombs."

"You can't arrest us," Schmidt said in a superior tone.

"Why?"

"*Ich bin Deutsch*. You not have authority over me. We leave." Schmidt waved his men back to their ship. "*Rasch*."

Martin blocked them. Keller raised his bat. The other two roundsmen drew their weapons. "When you're there," Martin pointed to the *Friedrich der Grosse*, "you're correct. But now you're here." He stamped his foot down. "In America."

"*Dummkopf.*" Keller grinned at Schmidt as he clamped handcuffs on each sailor.

Martin searched Schmidt and discovered a small leather notebook. "My God, what have we here?" The notebook contained dates, facts, and figures. "It's in German, Paul. What does it say?" Martin's heart beat fast as he handed it to Keller.

"Mother of God." Keller dropped his bat and flipped page after page. "The detail! This documents their purchases, suppliers and amounts, delivery dates – the whole ballgame."

"That good?" Martin said.

"Better than that. It lists their bomb production. Says that at its peak, they made fifty cigar bombs a day."

Schmidt held his head high. "We are the best."

"Gil, look. This book identifies every ship they attacked. By name." He stopped counting at thirty-five.

"We would have blown up more ships except the Irishmen we used cheated us. They threw the bombs overboard instead of planting them," Schmidt said.

"I thought you used German lighterboat men?" Martin asked.

"We used what was available."

"Your thoroughness will get you a lot of time in Sing Sing. Take them away," Martin said. The two roundsmen shoved them toward a paddy wagon waiting in front of the pier.

"I serve my country proudly. Arrest me. I'll be back on my ship by tomorrow," Schmidt said.

"Keep talking and you'll never set foot on the *Friedrich der Grosse* again," Keller said.

"Traitor." Schmidt struggled with the handcuffs.

"What did you call me?" Keller picked up the bat and tightened his hands around the handle.

"*Verrater*. You're German, aren't you? Why aren't you fighting for the Fatherland?"

"I'm American – born and raised here."

"Your parents are German, *ja*? That makes you German."

"No."

The conversation between Keller and Schmidt started Martin thinking. He hadn't considered the complexity of conflicting nationality, birthright, and cultural inheritance. Born in New York, he always considered himself American. But, he was French, too, wasn't he? He spoke French, understood its culture, and had studied its history. For him, it was an easy balance, not like Keller, whose two nationalities were on the verge of war. Keller had always called himself a German-American – but with a a small "g." and a capital "A." What did that mean? Would Keller's children call themselves that? What if he married Shannon? Could someone be German-Irish-American? At some point, doesn't someone just become American?

Chapter 72
An Emergency Message

Saint Luke's Lutheran Church: August 1916

Three weeks after Black Tom Island and five days after the arrest of German sailors from the *Friedrich der Grosse*, Caarsens sat in his usual pew in Saint Luke's and contemplated violence while Reverend Hoogstrum preached peace. Caarsens closed his eyes and prayed for the souls of his wife and daughters. When he opened them, he stared at the Bible in front of him. When he had arrived for services, the Bible was turned upside-down and sideways – Beck's signal that he had left a hidden emergency message.

Although they had exchanged numerous messages at Saint Luke's, this was the first time Beck had ever used this secret communication. Caarsens considered the possibilities; every one was bad. When the service ended, he slipped the Bible under his coat and left.

Needing to go somewhere quiet and isolated, he took a subway to Brooklyn. He walked the rest of the way to Jelly Brown's shed near the motorboat, where he had hidden Beck's money and the contents from the *Deutschland* chests. When he arrived, the shed was dank and dark except for some afternoon light that crept through the cracks in the wallboards. He lit a candle stub, which started to drown in its own wax.

He found Beck's earmarked page at *Revelations 8, Verse 7*: "The first angel sounded his trumpet, and there came hail and fire mixed with blood … ." Those lines were underlined in pencil, Beck's confirmation marker that this page contained his message. Except for that, the page seemed normal, but Caarsens detected a whiff of lemon juice and knew better.

He held the candle close behind the open page and Beck's note appeared:

> *Careful. Reward doubled. Police have connected Rasmussen to Knopp. Time short. Meet Milton Point.*

How had the police made the connection between his union alias and his New Haven Projectile Company name? The newspaper photograph? It didn't matter. They still didn't know where he was. With a higher reward, it was only a matter of time before they would. He burned the Bible. While he considered his next move, he heard the unmistakable click of a revolver's hammer.

Caarsens pointed his Colt at the sound.

Chapter 73
What's He Want?

Police Headquarters: August 1916

In the five days since Martin had arrested the *Friedrich der Grosse* sailors, he and Keller had concentrated on Felix Beck. With the captain's approval to use Mena Reiss's testimony against Beck, Martin planned to prosecute Beck through the Mann Act, the 1910 law that made it a felony to take a woman across state lines for immoral purposes. The arrest would ruin his reputation.

"Just make sure you can document everything that Reiss woman told you. Diplomatic immunity or not, after Black Tom Island, the public won't allow Germany to keep a consul here who's a pimp." The corner of Tunney's mouth curled up. "Even if they don't recall him, we'll have grounds to kick him out. We get rid of him either way, and Germany can't claim it has anything to do with our war policy." Tunney's face turned serious. "But if this doesn't work out, I'll have your heads."

Working round the clock, Martin and Keller verified Mena's statements and had documentation to prove it. Martin had just finished summarizing his findings when the desk sergeant called. "Get down here."

"What is it?" Anxious to finish his report, Martin tapped his pencil on his desk to hide his annoyance.

"Some Chinaman's down here insisting he talk to you."

"What's his name?" Martin's tapping quickened.

"Ree or Lee, something like that. Says he's the owner of the

Wing Sing restaurant in Chinatown."

Martin repeated it to Keller. "Doesn't mean anything to me. What about you, Paul?"

"Me either. I don't go into that God-forsaken place unless I have to."

"What's he want, Sarge? I don't have time to –"

"He'll only speak to you. Says it's important."

"You sure this isn't a waste of time?"

"At first. Then he asked about the eight thousand dollar reward."

Chapter 74

We Can Help Each Other

Brooklyn Dockyards: August 1916

Caarsens recognized Jelly Brown's outline in the shadows. "*Jo*. Is that you, Jelly?" He lowered his Colt.

"Mr. Carpenter?" Brown flashed a light at Caarsens.

"Yes. Put your gun away. We're alone."

"What you doing? I nearly shot you." Brown secured his revolver.

"Just checking some things."

"Where you been? I ain't seen you in a long time." Jelly's broad smile relaxed Caarsens.

"I've been busy."

"Busy hiding, I reckon. You something, you is."

"What do you mean?" Caarsens scattered the ashes from the charred Bible with his foot.

"I'm impressed. I know you was more than a union organizer when I first met you. I figured you was all sorts of things, but I never figured you was a bomber."

"I don't know what you're talking about." Caarsens became concerned – Jelly knew too much.

"Don't tell me you don't know nothing about that little fire over yonder a few weeks ago." Brown pointed in the direction of Black Tom Island.

"I didn't –"

"Don't lie. I know you used your motorboat that night. When the fireworks started, I came here to make sure things was all right

– the engine in your boat was still hot."

"But you haven't Judased me." Caarsens circled toward the door to make sure they were alone. "Have you?"

"If I'd a wanted to, I could have sold you down the river before this, Mr. Carpenter. We friends. You been better to me than any other white man in this harbor. I'm glad you here. I've been looking for you."

"Why?"

"I know something big is coming down. If you is what I think you is, we can help each other."

"How?"

"Do you want to steal some gold?"

Chapter 75
Chinatown

Police Headquarters: August 1916

When the desk sergeant mentioned the reward, Martin hung up and ran across the hall to the main desk. Keller and he took Mr. Li to a consultation room where Li told them everything about Mr. Barrymore. He identified him as the man in the police sketch of the Biltmore waiter. “He wear many disguises.”

Martin had guessed that was the case; he was glad to get confirmation. “Where is he now?”

“How I know? He there this morning. Be careful my daughter. She like him.”

“Is he armed?”

Li turned his head at a funny angle like a confused dog. Martin guessed Li didn’t understand and asked if he had seen any guns or explosives. “Not know. Me stay out of his room.” After several more unhelpful answers, Martin ended the conversation.

“How do you want to play this, Gil?” Keller asked after they left Mr. Li standing with his hand out.

“We’ve only got one chance.” Martin stopped to think. He hated his options. Chinatown was unfamiliar territory to him. “Get the men.”

~

Early that evening, Caarsens returned to his room in Chinatown. Peping was crying; her cheek was bruised, and one eye was closed. She looked up. “You go.”

"But, you're hurt." Caarsens looked at her wounds.

She pushed him away. "Disobey Papa. Deserve hit." She fought back tears. "You good man. Kind to Peping. No time. Papa go to police."

He noticed that she had packed his things in a small carry-sack. A small suitcase with Chinese symbols sat beside it. For a moment, he feared that she'd want to go with him. "Peping, you can't –"

"No worry, Mr. Barrymore. I go back China with Papa. He say he now have money. He buy business. 'Good life,' he tell me. He remarry. Find good husband for Peping."

Caarsens checked his bag.

"Hurry. Papa tell police everything. Must leave," Peping said.

"Will you be all right?" He gathered a few things from under the bed Peping had forgotten.

"Yes."

"What about the Tongs?"

"Papa say he talk to Mock Duck. Split money. We fine. Police come, five minutes. Go."

On his way out, he grabbed Peping's coolie hat and gave her a thousand dollars. The last words he heard were, "Good-bye. Love you. Stay alive."

Caarsens ran from the Wing Sing restaurant, crossed the narrow street, and crouched down. He placed his bag behind him and pretended to be a beggar. He was putting on the coolie hat when he saw two police motorcars turn south onto narrow, winding Doyers Street. The first car swiped a man pulling a cart. He fell. The second car's brakes screamed to avoid the fallen man. Six uniformed policemen emerged from the car. Armed with shotguns, Springfield rifles, and high-caliber revolvers, they came ready for a fight.

From the other end of the street, a third car arrived. A man in civilian clothes jumped out and ordered the men to surround the building. Caarsens recognized Sergeant Martin and suspected there were more than the ten men he had seen. For a moment, Caarsens considered fighting. He could have killed at least four policemen, but he forced himself to stay inconspicuous for two reasons: Peping might be hurt, and Brown's information about the gold. With Brown's help, Caarsens had a chance for a final, spectacular attack, the one he had hoped to do since he had arrived in New York.

Under his breath, he said, "Thank you, Peping. I hope your father made a good deal. Both our fates are now sealed." Bowed low and watching the policemen from the corner of his eye, Caarsens shuffled away like an old man.

~

Martin led the charge up the stairs of the Wing Sing restaurant and found a Chinese girl cowering in the corner of a small bedroom. "Where's Barrymore?" he demanded.

"No English." Peping shivered with fright. "No help."

"Is this him?" Martin shoved the police drawing of Caarsens in her face. She pushed it away.

A moment later, Mr. Li accompanied by Keller entered the room. "You disobey your papa?" He approached and slapped her across the face viciously. She confessed that Mr. Barrymore left five minutes ago.

"Shit," Martin howled and punched the wall so hard he left an indentation.

Chapter 76
Where's Shannon?

Brooklyn Dockyards: August 1916

Early the next morning, the noise of dockworkers woke Caarsens. For a moment, he was disoriented, but he remembered he was in Brown's shed, having escaped last night's trap in Chinatown. In the morning light, the shed seemed smaller and more decrepit. Feeling older, he rubbed his cramping leg and aching back. Famished, he ate some bread from his haversack and considered his dwindling options.

The situation reminded him of the end of the Boer War. Caarsens had seen tough fighters, men accustomed to the hardships of guerilla war, men who had lost everything give up as the odds against them mounted. Unlike them, Caarsens had not given up then; he would not give up now.

He decided to follow Beck's instructions and go to Milton Point. Knowing it would be a long trip, Caarsens checked his motorboat and found that, once again, Jelly had filled the spare gasoline cans.

~

About the time Caarsens headed up the East River, Martin and Keller walked silently to the captain's office. Embarrassed by last night's failure in Chinatown, Martin's ego hurt worse than his hand. Keller told Martin that he could accept a demotion if Tunney would allow him to continue to see Shannon. Feeling like a man heading to a sentencing by a notoriously strict judge, Martin entered Tunney's office with Keller close behind. No sooner had they sat down than

Tunney started to give Martin the toughest rebuke he had received since his rookie roundsman days. He was even tougher on Keller and threatened to kick him out of the police department. Tunney gave them three more weeks to capture the saboteur.

When they were alone, Martin commented that it could have been worse. "How?" Keller asked. "I'm about to get fired. Only one thing to do."

Martin agreed. "It's time we had another private session with Mr. Beck. If he won't talk, we'll arrest him."

For the rest of the day, Martin and Keller hunted Beck unsuccessfully. On the way back to their headquarters, their motorcar hit several holes in the road, and at Fulton Street, a tire ruptured. In the heat and traffic, changing it took longer than Martin had expected. To restart the motorcar, Martin worked the crank. Each time, the engine sputtered and died. He gritted his teeth, took a deep breath, and cranked as hard as he could. The motorcar came to life.

Grimy and frustrated, they walked up from the basement garage of Police Headquarters and went to the desk sergeant. "Where's the captain?" Martin asked and wished he could start the day all over again.

"His office. He's in a terrible mood."

"Why?" Martin asked, sure Tunney was going to give them another rebuke.

"Not my business. I'll know when I need to know."

Martin knocked on Tunney's door while Keller stood back and thought of Shannon. A weak "Enter" followed. Tunney gestured for them to sit. The butts and ashes of three cigars filled his ashtray.

The vein on his right temple pulsated. "Did you get Beck?"

"No," Martin said vigorously, deciding he would stand up to the captain.

Tunney looked dejected. "Then it's worse than I thought."

"What do you mean?" Keller looked puzzled.

"Griggs didn't report in this afternoon. Shannon's disappeared."

~

To reach Milton Point, Caarsens headed up the East River, passed through Hells Gate and crossed through Flushing Bay, slowing down to go through the Throgg's Neck. He sped through Eastchester Bay, going between Hart and City Islands and into Long Island Sound. Along the way, Caarsens had time to reflect on Brown's information.

At first, Caarsens remembered he had been skeptical when Brown told him about the gold shipment a few days ago. How did he know? "I know everything that goes on 'round the docks," Jelly had said. "I got my sources. White folks tend to forget we around. Shoe-shine boys, office cleaners, messengers – they smarter than you think. Hear lots of things, too."

"Relax. So what are they hearing?" Respecting Jelly and knowing he had reliable contacts, Caarsens was excited.

Brown acted jumpy. "We partners, right?"

"Of course."

"I wouldn't be telling you this if I didn't needs your help."

"Jelly, what the *bladdy hell* is it? If you want my help, you've got to tell me everything."

"I know someone who sweeps the Treasury building. He found some papers throwed away."

"And ..."

Brown moved close. "Those papers say that England is shipping twenty tons of gold to New York on the *U.S.S. Tucker*. Arrives September 14 at the U.S. Navy Yard, Brooklyn. Then they drive it over the Brooklyn Bridge in ten Sanford trucks to the Treasury building on Wall Street."

Caarsens calculated in his head. Gold bars weighed about twenty-seven and a half pounds. That's about nine thousand dollars per bar. Twenty tons amounted to around thirteen million dollars. "You sure?"

"You want to see the paper my man fetched out the trash?"

"You want to steal it?"

"Much as I can." Brown's smile broadened across his face.

"How do you plan to do this?"

"They could take several routes to Wall Street. I figures we'll attack them when they stop at the Treasury building."

"Which side?"

"The front. That be where they going – right in the front door."

"We'll block off all the other roads just to make sure." An expert saboteur, Caarsens was already planning the operation. "What then? They'll be heavily guarded."

"That's where I need your help. I got about eight men. We got weapons."

"I have an idea. I may be able to make all the guards run away." Caarsens began to believe their attack could succeed. "I'll help you." They shook hands and agreed to proceed with the operation. What Caarsens didn't say was that he would use the robbery to blow Wall Street into kingdom come.

~

"Shannon's gone?" Martin was shocked. "How?"

Keller was speechless.

"Ever since Miss Reiss confessed, things have moved fast," Tunney said. "While you were investigating her story and arresting the German sailors, I had Griggs and Shannon shadow Beck."

"Why them?" Keller asked.

"Who else? They're the best shadows we have." Tunney's expression showed he didn't like to be challenged. Or maybe he was angry with himself.

"She never said anything to me," Keller said.

"When was the last time you saw her, Detective?"

Keller slumped. "Last week."

"You sure she's gone?" Martin asked.

"Griggs called the desk sergeant on Saturday afternoon. Nothing to report. Beck was walking uptown. They were following him." Tunney finished his cigar and lit another.

"Maybe Beck spotted them," Martin said.

"Let's hope not." Tunney opened his desk and pulled out a bottle of whiskey and three glasses.

"And no one has seen them since?" Keller asked.

"Calm down, Detective." Tunney poured the liquor. "I only got worried two hours ago when they were supposed to report back to me."

"Captain, are you sure we can trust Griggs?" Martin swirled his glass but didn't drink.

"That bastard Griggs has been involved in our investigations from the start. You've cleared everyone else of wrongdoing, haven't you, Captain? He must be the traitor," Keller said.

"You're jumping to conclusions, Paul," Martin said. "Griggs is a good cop. Must be an explanation. He's helped us enormously during our investigation. He's saved Shannon more than once."

"All the better to gain our trust." Keller tightened his neck to stop it from shaking with rage.

Tunney's telephone rang. He picked it up. The desk sergeant. They talked for less than a minute. "You sure?" Tunney's face showed no reaction. "Yes, thank you. I'll send a team over immediately." He put down the phone and looked at the detectives. "They just found Griggs's body in an alley near Saint Luke's Church. His head is caved in."

"I can't believe it." Martin looked blankly at the telephone, not sure he had heard correctly.

"We have to assume the worst about Shannon." Tunney drained his glass.

"My God. Beck's got Shannon. I know it." Keller looked like he'd been hit by a haymaker from John L. Sullivan.

"And we have no idea where Beck is," Martin said, trying to concentrate on the facts and forget the implications to Shannon. "Griggs was killed near a church. Why?"

"Shannon told me she thought that Beck might have met the assassin there. She and Griggs must have followed them."

"Wherever he is, I bet he's using a motorcar. It's the only way he could take her hostage," Martin said.

"She'd claw and fight. Somehow, Beck subdued her," Keller said, fighting his fear for her.

They discussed possible locations to look for her, but nothing made sense. At last, Martin suggested, "Only one person who can help. It's a long shot."

Tunney and Keller looked at him.

"He's in the Tombs awaiting trial – John Wittig."

~

Pushing the conversation with Brown out of his mind, Caarsens skipped his motorboat across Long Island Sound as he headed to Beck's house at Milton Point. The well-oiled engine roared. A spray of salt water stung his face and invigorated him. He felt good, free and glad to be away from the choking confines of Manhattan. He was a soldier again, with an upcoming mission.

Beck's directions to the consul's house on Milton Point were good. By early evening, Caarsens reached the hidden cove. He shifted the engine to neutral and studied the shore. Calm. From the water, Caarsens could see a light in Beck's house. The shore appeared deserted, but Caarsens proceeded with caution. He loaded his Colt and checked the Springfield. The Demag rested comfortably in its usual place. He headed in.

Caarsens heard high-pitched screams after he moored the motorboat. He recognized the anguished sound. They stopped. Where had they come from? He waited for more screams and looked at the circular scars across his arms. A victim never forgets. The woman's screams started again from the house. Each new scream was more piercing, more desperate, more prolonged. The perpetrator appeared to apply his work like a piano-tuner. More screams. The victim had not cracked. Only one thing causes such regulated agony. Caarsens understood torture's excruciating pain. The relief from passing out. The breaking points. The hatred that allows someone to endure. The desire for revenge.

Caarsens readied the Springfield and ran to the screams. *No one tortures a woman.* The cycle of screams stopped. Caarsens crouched low and rushed to the house as if he were attacking a British position. He reached the front door and listened for the next round of screams. They started again from the cellar. Caarsens checked the back door – not locked. He pointed his Springfield and moved inside. By the time he found the door to the basement, the screams had stopped again.

He reached the bottom of the stairs and saw Beck slip his arms out of his suspenders. The small man turned. "Herr Caarsens, you are just in time. Do you want to join the fun?"

The sight of the red-haired woman tied spread-eagled on the billiard table infuriated and mortified him. The torn remains of her silk slip clung to her body. Any semblance of modesty was in tatters, but she somehow seemed defiant. He understood her pain when he saw the marks across her legs and upper body. He could feel the burns on her arms and smelled scorched flesh. He saw a fireplace poker with a glowing red tip next to the table. When she lifted her head, Caarsens could see purple marks across her face, and blood dripped from her nose. Her lips moved. "Help me."

Beck appeared intoxicated by his dominance and seemed to enjoy an audience. He put his hand on her temple and leaned over her. She turned her head away, but Beck grabbed her chin and forced her to look at him. "Please continue to fight. I will enjoy breaking you even more."

Caarsens interrupted him. "What are you doing, Beck?"

"My dear Caarsens, I would have thought a man with your violent nature would understand."

Caarsens noticed the woman's head tilt up. "This woman is not our enemy," he said.

She fainted.

"That's where you are wrong. She has been spying on us. She is Captain Tunney's niece," Beck said.

"She's a woman for Christ's sake. You can't kill women just because they get in the way. I've seen too much –"

"She is a pretty one, but not for long." Beck grasped something that looked like pliers. "She needs to learn a lesson. I'm sure she will be more cooperative after I take a fingernail or two."

"Don't touch her." He pointed his rifle at Beck.

"Since when did you get any morals?"

"You never understood me. Move away."

"Don't tell me what to do. You're just hired help. Why don't you wait upstairs? We can talk once I am finished." Beck took the woman's hand and exposed her little finger. When she didn't respond, he slapped her.

She revived. "Water."

"Don't hit her again." Caarsens poked Beck with the barrel of his rifle.

Beck looked at him with beastly black eyes. "Nobody interferes with my pleasures."

Caarsens forced Beck away from her with several prods of his rifle barrel. "Drop those pliers."

~

Martin and Keller arrived at the Tombs about the time Caarsens headed into Milton Point. Walking to the visitation room, Martin feared Wittig would be uncooperative. At first, he was right. Wittig, his face a mask of uncaring defeat, ignored him.

Before Wittig could say anything, Keller jumped on him demanding to know where Shannon was. Martin pulled him away and asked the guards to escort Keller out of the room while he talked to Wittig alone. "I'm sorry about that, John. How are you?"

Wittig scowled. "One daughter dead from polio. Another in Ireland with my wife doing God knows what. My house is gone. So is my money. My life is ruined. I feel terrible. How do you think I am?"

"I know you've had a bad time, but we need your help." Once Martin explained what he wanted, Wittig cooperated. His mind was sharp and his recollection of detail impressive. After some thought, Wittig guessed that Beck had fled to the German consul's summer house on Milton Point, the same place where he had witnessed the murder.

Martin called the Rye police and demanded they meet at the house, but the officer complained they were understaffed. The Bomb Squad was much better equipped for such situations. It would take time for the Rye police to get there, even if it was really an emergency.

"If the captain's niece is harmed, ..."

"We'll do the best we can," the Rye policeman said.

Martin concluded that Keller and he would have to handle the situation themselves. They borrowed a police motorcar and headed north. Martin drove, and Keller kept checking his revolver. "How soon?" Keller asked every few minutes.

Martin wasn't sure. Wittig had drawn them a map and explained how to get to the house on Milton Point. He made a point to say the private road to the consul's place was hard to find. Worse, night was setting in.

Keller urged Martin to drive faster. He complied, skidded around blind corners, broke hard only when he had to, and attacked bumps. He hoped the car would survive and prayed Wittig had been right.

~

With his rifle, Caarsens directed Beck away from the woman. The small man shook the pliers at Caarsens. "You are nothing but a poor farmer from a pathetic country that no longer exists."

"We fought better than your great German army is doing now." Caarsens noticed the woman slip in and out of consciousness. "You're an animal and a lunatic."

"Why do you say that? She's nothing but chattel. Besides, I am not done. I suggest you have a drink? The liquor cabinet is –"

"I don't want a drink, you *fokking* bastard. I don't want anything to do with you. Give me those pliers or –"

"Put the gun down, Herr Caarsens." Beck made a calming gesture, but his eyes turned rabid. He moved closer. "You had such potential. I never expected you to have any scruples."

He watched Beck's every gesture. "Too many innocent women have already died. Someone needs to protect them."

"Who cares about them? Only the strong deserve to live. Pity, but you and I are ..." Beck charged.

Caarsens anticipated Beck's attack and moved aside. As Beck went by, Caarsens jabbed him in the back with the butt of his Springfield. Beck gasped and fell, but he forced himself to his hands and knees and scampered toward the poker. Caarsens cursed himself for leaving it there. "Stop."

Faster than Caarsens had expected, Beck grabbed the poker and swung. He knocked the rifle out of his hands. Beck stood up, took a fencer's stance, and pointed the poker at Caarsens. "I might have more fun tonight than I expected. First, the woman; now you."

Caarsens dodged Beck's first lunge. He reached for his Demag in time to parry Beck's second thrust. He forced his bayonet down to the poker's hand guard with his right hand. The scraping sound of the Demag's steel blade against the iron poker seemed to last forever. He moved into Beck and punched him in the face with his left. Caarsens felt Beck's nose crack.

Beck reeled back, blood flowing from his nose, and used the poker to right himself. Caarsens didn't need Beck's frightened expression to see his vulnerability. He attacked and buried the Demag deep between Beck's ribs. Caarsens needed all his strength to withdraw it. He then drove it into his heart. As he wiped the blade across his trouser leg, something shiny on the floor caught his eye. He picked it up – Beck's two-headed silver dollar. He flipped it – "Heads you die" – and let it fall to the ground.

He approached the cringing woman. Without saying a word, he cut her loose and covered her with Beck's coat. He collected his weapons and ran to the motorboat.

~

When Martin couldn't find the turn-off to Beck's house, Keller turned frantic. Wittig had surely misled them. Keller quieted down when Martin spotted the dirt road Wittig had described. He parked the motorcar a hundred yards from the house. They drew their police revolvers and approached on foot. He heard no noise and saw no activity in the house. He was at the front porch when he heard a powerful motor engine coming from the water.

Martin told Keller to check the house while he ran around back. By the time Martin reached the dock, the motorboat was eighty feet out to sea. He yelled a warning and emptied his gun, but the motorboat sped out of range. Martin got a good look at it and, except for some obvious differences, was certain it was Frisch's motorboat, the one he had been looking for since the rudder-bomber had died.

~

Caarsens heard the shots fall short and pushed the engine to full throttle. He turned back and squinted in the darkness. Sergeant Martin again. *The next time we meet, one of us is going to die.* He disappeared into the Sound determined to reach Brown's shed in Brooklyn, his last refuge. At night, the journey would be dangerous, but he needed to get to his hideout before the police could form searches and water patrols. He was confident he could navigate the trip using the stars, the full moon, and his knowledge of the water. With Beck dead, Caarsens was alone except for Brown, but he liked the idea of being independent again.

~

Outraged the motorboat had escaped, Martin turned toward the house and heard Keller. "In here, Gil." Martin found them in the basement. "We won't have to arrest him anymore." Keller pointed to Beck's inert body; its last expression was one of disbelief and agony. "He got what he deserved," Keller said.

Covering herself with the coat, Shannon stumbled over to the body and kicked it with pent-up rage. She didn't stop until Keller came over to comfort her. "Who saved me?" she asked, before she collapsed.

Chapter 77
The Traitor

Brooklyn Dockyards: August 1916

Caarsens arrived at Brown's shed in Brooklyn just as the sun was rising. His fuel gauge showed empty. The gasoline he stole from a small marina in the Bronx had been just enough to allow him to get back. Now that Sergeant Martin had seen the motorboat, Caarsens considered scuttling it, but he decided he still needed it, one more time. He tied it up and checked the shed to make sure the contents of the chests from the *Deutschland* and the buried tin box with Beck's remaining money were safe. Finding they were, he secured his weapons and counted the money – it was enough. This would be his last operation in New York. He didn't bother to plan beyond that.

~

Three days after the incident at Milton Point, Martin visited Shannon in Mount Sinai Hospital on Fifth Avenue and 100th Street. Keller was already there. Keller had stayed with her since they had rescued her. Her condition had improved and yesterday her doctors moved her from New Rochelle Hospital to Mount Sinai.

Martin talked to Keller outside Shannon's room. He was grateful to learn that she had not been raped and was making a fast recovery. The scars from her burns would fade. The doctors were less certain about the scars to her mind, but Keller insisted she was resilient and anxious to help.

"She ready to talk to us?" Martin asked.

"Yes." Keller looked tired and mentioned she recalled events unevenly. Uncertain what to say, Martin walked into her room. Shannon looked thin and pale.

She clutched Keller's hand tightly, but right away and in a strong voice, she said, "I know who the traitor is."

~

Martin dashed back to Police Headquarters. The information he had learned from Shannon startled him. He was angry at himself for not identifying the traitor before now without Shannon's help. He and the traitor had worked together, helped trap Traub together, and shared grief together. They had been friends. Martin couldn't decide if this would be the hardest or easiest arrest he would ever make.

Detective Regan was manning the front desk. Martin would have preferred someone more discreet. Fighting a dry month, Martin took a deep breath before he spoke to him. He asked Regan if Officer Clancy was working his rounds today. "Just came in. Over there, Sergeant." Regan pointed to a bench near the entranceway. "What's going on, Sergeant? Shouldn't you be ..."

"Never mind."

Clancy was talking to an angry Italian woman. Martin waited for him to calm her and used the time to collect his thoughts. He owed Clancy for saving his career and hated to approach him like this. He felt a tap on his shoulder.

"You let another one get away, didn't you, Sergeant?"

Martin turned and saw Detective Howell. Through clenched teeth, he said, "Doesn't matter that the captain's niece was kidnapped and nearly killed, does it, Howell?" Martin pushed him aside. He was sorry Howell wasn't the traitor. "You've been as much use on this case as a blind man in a boxing ring."

Howell pulled his arm back to take a swing, but Clancy, having finished with the angry woman, stopped him from landing a punch. "Detective, why don't you go back to doing whatever useless thing you were doing? You don't have too many friends around here. Don't make it worse." Clancy released his grip.

Howell held his ground.

"Leave." Clancy shoved him away.

"Thanks, Sean," Martin said. "Can I see you in private?"

They walked to a consultation room in silence. Martin would rather have faced Traub's assassin unarmed than to have this conversation. When they were alone, Martin put his hand on Clancy's shoulder. "Sean, I can't believe it, but I must. I'm sorry."

"What's wrong, Gil?"

"I know she's like an aunt to you, but I have to tell you that Eloise Bauer has been helping the Germans. She's a traitor."

Clancy's face showed incomprehension and shock. "How?"

"I wanted to tell you before I arrest her."

"Not possible."

"Where is she?"

"Kitchen. Can I come?" Clancy looked sick.

They found Mrs. Bauer washing glasses. "Oh, my goodness. I'm glad to see you, Sergeant. I've been so worried since I heard the news. I've been praying. How is Shan ..." Martin's icy stare silenced her. She looked at Clancy. "Sean, what's wrong?"

Clancy looked away.

"We're here to arrest you." Martin studied her wrinkled face.

She dropped a glass. "My God, no."

Martin recalled Keller's words before he left the hospital. "I hope she hangs." For a moment, Martin hated her, but he still couldn't accept hanging a frail old woman.

Clancy kept his distance from her. "Why did you do it, Eloise?"

Mrs. Bauer turned defiant and years of venom spit out. "You're the cops; you should know. I hate the North. I was born in Georgia. I was nine years old when Sherman's men marched through. They killed our pigs and stole our grain. We nearly starved that winter."

"That's no reason to betray us," Clancy said.

"I haven't finished, Sean. Some Yankee shot my daddy dead at Petersburg, Virginia. Carpetbaggers feasted on us for years after the war. I'm still a Confederate."

"That's why you helped Germany? So they could help the South secede again?" Martin asked.

"Nonsense. I don't care about Germany. What could Germany do to help the South? I look after myself and my kin. That's all."

"How did you meet Mr. Beck?" This was not the conversation Martin had expected.

"The German Red Cross."

"What were you doing?" Martin asked.

"Volunteering. Mr. Bauer, God rest his soul, loved Germany. I wanted to help as a gesture to him. Besides, I know how terrible a war can be and feel sorry for the innocent victims."

"Did Mr. Beck recruit you?"

"No."

"When did you start talking to Beck?"

"After a Red Cross meeting. That was about the time I was

helping you intercept Eugene Traub's telephone calls. Mr. Beck seemed to appear wherever I was. He knew a lot about me and was a true gentleman."

"When did he ask you to spy on us?"

"He didn't. We became friends."

"I thought we were your friends," Martin said.

"You were my supervisor. Mr. Beck was different. He knew my daughter's medical history. How did he know all that? You never ask about my family, Sergeant. You never cared that I was a Southerner."

"I didn't want to intrude."

"Exactly. Mr. Beck offered to help her. He knew a German doctor who specialized in her condition."

"Why didn't you come to me for help?" Clancy asked.

"You were always so kind after my husband died, Sean. But her treatment was too expensive – you never could have afforded it."

"But ..., I could have found a way. It would have been better than ..."

"Mr. Beck cared. We talked often. It just seemed natural to tell him what was going on."

He had manipulated Wittig in the same way, Martin thought.

"I told Mr. Beck whatever he wanted to know. Sometimes I called him late at night."

So that's how he got to Kleinmann so fast. And how she warned Charbonneau to get out of Chinatown.

"My daughter started to improve before Christmas."

Martin remembered her good mood on New Year's Eve.

"I always wondered why she got better. It seemed like a miracle; I guess I never thought about it." Clancy slumped.

"You couldn't have known, Sean," Martin said.

"I'm sorry I almost got Shannon killed. I like her." Mrs. Bauer started to faint, but she righted herself. "What will happen to me?"

"That's for the courts, Mrs. Bauer. You won't get any sympathy from me. We have to go." Martin reached for his handcuffs and wondered if they'd be too big for her bony wrists.

She looked at Clancy with panic. He gestured for her to go.

Another one of Beck's victims. Martin hoped Corinne would be proud that he felt compassion and pity for the old lady despite her betrayal. He decided this *was* the hardest arrest he had ever made.

~

On the western part of New York City in Staten Island, Caarsens and Brown carried the mortar across the deserted Staten Island marshes to the beach and his motorboat. They were done. Caarsens's practice tests confirmed his skill with the mortar.

Chapter 78
We're After One Man

Police Headquarters: September 1916

"Of course. It has to be." Martin leaned back on his chair and called Keller to his desk. "We're after one man. Look here." Martin explained the diagram he had just completed. Fingerprints at Milton Point matched those taken in the bedroom above the Wing Sing restaurant and were identical to those of the Biltmore Hotel waiter. They proved that Mr. Barrymore and Philip Charbonneau were all the same man. Shannon had already identified Pieter Knopp of the New Haven Projectile Company as the union organizer, Jens Rasmussen. With the help of the police sketch of the waiter, Nora Wittig confirmed that Philip Charbonneau was Pieter Knopp.

Who is he? Martin asked himself. "Paul, what have you learned about the murder of that drunk in Grand Central last January?"

"That damn detective in charge won't call me back," Keller said.

"I'll talk to Captain Tunney. You'll get your call."

~

Later that afternoon, Martin received a call from the detective. When he hung up the phone, Martin cursed so loud everyone in the squad room looked at him.

"What's wrong?" Keller asked.

"I can't believe it." Martin told Keller what he'd learned. After the Bomb Squad was consulted in the case, British Military Intelligence contacted the New York police department and inquired about a missing British officer, Colonel Westerly, who was in New York on war-related business. One of their agents came to New York to investigate. He identified Westerly as the drunk from a post-mortem picture. He mentioned that Westerly had planned to visit the New Haven Projectile Company the day of the murder.

"Shit. If we had known that ..." Keller kicked the waste can.

"It's worse," Martin said. "The British agent and the detective in charge visited the New Haven Projectile Company."

"And they didn't talk to us?"

"No. The detective said they had no cause. Back then, we didn't know about New Haven Projectile's connections to the Germans or Knopp's association with Beck."

"It's Black Tom Island all over again. One group of cops doesn't talk to another."

"Turns out they interviewed Karl Bier."

"The same Karl Bier we can't find now?" Keller said.

"He told them that nothing unusual had happened during Westerly's visit. Bier said he resolved all of Westerly's concerns and thought nothing more of the matter."

"And they believed him?" Keller's face turned red.

"The British confirmed it. Based on what they knew at the time, I might have thought the same thing," Martin said.

"What did they do?"

"Dropped the New Haven Projectile line of inquiry. Seems that Westerly had a history of drunkenness and disorderly behavior. They concluded he died from a bar fight or an attempted robbery and kept the incident out of the papers."

"Let me guess the rest," Keller said. "By the time the police learned that New Haven Projectile was a German-run operation, Westerly's death was a closed case and the detective in charge was too busy to follow up or mention it to us. So, we're the first ones to connect the murder of the drunk to the New Haven Projectile Company."

"Exactly, which brings us to our saboteur. We need to talk to the British Military Intelligence agent who came here, Paul. Tell them our theory of the case. Send them Rasmussen's newspaper picture and the drawing of Charbonneau. Maybe they can help."

A week later, Keller received a dossier from the British. It identified Knopp as Danie Caarsens. They had been looking for him since the end of the Boer War. Attached to the dossier was a note: "If you find him, we want him."

Martin slammed the dossier down. "So do I."

~

When Martin arrived at headquarters the next morning, Keller was waiting for him. "Glad you're here."

"Anything new with Caarsens?" Martin was focused on finding him.

"I've just come from Mount Sinai," Keller said.

Martin shifted his attention. "How's Shannon?"

"Better, thanks. She remembered more of Beck's discussion with the assassin." Keller hesitated and swallowed hard. "Not good."

"Lower your voice." Martin put his hand on Keller's shoulder and moved close. "What?"

Keller cupped his hand around his mouth and whispered into Martin's ear. "Something big's about to happen."

Martin froze. "What do you mean?"

"Shannon swears she heard Caarsens say, 'I'm going to destroy America's economic heart.'"

Chapter 79
You'll Have Ten Minutes

Broad Street, Manhattan: September 1916

The blind Spanish-American War veteran swept his cane back and forth like a metronome. His loose-fitting clothes and contorted body hid his strong physique. Caarsens rattled a tin cup and was surprised how quickly it filled up. For the second time today, he walked north on Broad Street. Behind tinted glasses, he noticed every roundsman and identified every change from yesterday. Stopping to mop his brow, he looked for ambush points and escape routes.

Caarsens passed the New York Stock Exchange and turned left onto narrowing Wall Street, counting each step along the way. A Good Samaritan helped him cross Broadway in front of Trinity Church. When he had a chance, he removed his glasses and discarded his cane. He reversed his coat, switched hats, and took out a small notebook and pencil. Looking like a foreman assessing a job, he walked around the church's graveyard and decided this was a perfect spot to position the mortar for the attack. It was well within the mortar's effective range and close to the corner of Broad and Wall Street, by the Treasury and Morgan Bank buildings, his targets.

Caarsens crossed back over Broadway and paced off the distance to a lamppost on Wall Street that he could use as an aiming stick. He walked up the Treasury building steps and sat next to George Washington's statue. Three minutes later, Jelly Brown, dressed in a work shirt that pinched his biceps, joined him. His jaw swollen with chewing tobacco, Brown spit out a thick brown wad. He tipped his cap and acted subservient. He whispered, "Here the underground maps you asked for. Had to call in lots of favors. Lucky my brother-in-law works in City Hall."

"Good work." Caarsens took the papers and scanned them. "Just what I need. You got the gas masks for your men?"

"Weren't easy, but yah. I got this, too." Brown removed a British infantry captain's brass whistle from his pocket. It fit into the palm of his hand and was a little thicker than his index finger. "Sounds different from a cop's whistle."

"Let's give it a try. Give me three minutes and blow it." Caarsens walked across Broadway and waited. The shrill high-pitched bark from Brown's whistle was unmistakable. Brown joined him in the tree-lined Trinity Church graveyard, and together they studied the underground maps. They walked over to the place on Pine Street that interested Caarsens, who was pleased the manhole cover was right where the map indicated it would be. "I'll look down there tomorrow."

They returned to Wall Street and stood near the Morgan Bank building. Caarsens paced off the distance indicated on the map's scale and stood on the spot where he wanted to detonate the explosives. He turned to Brown and said, "We need the truck right here." Caarsens stomped his foot down on the spot to emphasize his point. Without questioning why, Brown agreed but suspected Caarsens wasn't telling him everything.

Separately, they walked to Fraunces Tavern at the corner of Broad Street and Pearl. Outside the restaurant and amid the chatter of the pedestrians, Caarsens took out his notebook and detailed his plan. When he had finished, he asked Brown if he had any questions.

"How much time we got?" Brown asked.

"Depends on the chlorine gas. It's unpredictable."

Brown frowned. "You sure that mask gonna protect me good?"

"Ever faced poison gas?" Caarsens asked.

"No." Brown's eyes widened.

"No one else has, either." Caarsens pointed up Broad Street. "You and your men will have masks. Everyone else will panic. They'll scatter faster than cattle at branding time."

"What's it like? A poison gas attack, I mean." Brown shivered.

Caarsens explained that a yellowish green cloud forms when the gas is released. For a few minutes, visibility shrinks to a few feet. Since the chlorine gas is heavier than air, it concentrates on the ground. It has a strong odor. People will be confused and their eyes will begin to sting and water. Their breathing will become labored. They'll start to cough. In the worst case, a person will get a terrible headache.

"How does folks die?"

Caarsens opened a pack of Life Savers and crunched one. "Chlorine gas asphyxiates you."

"What the shit does that mean?"

"You suffocate. Drowning may be a better description." Caarsens told him gas becomes fatal when it reaches a certain level – about the same as a drop of oil in a quart of water. It destroys the tissue in the lungs and causes fluid to build up. The fluid prevents oxygen from reaching the blood. "Just before he dies, a man coughs up greenish froth, and his skin turns dark green and yellow."

"Lots of folks going to die."

"Does that bother you?"

"No. Won't be many colored folks around. I just want my gold and my lungs whole."

"Listen, Jelly, the number of deaths will depend on how much gas we use. I've only got seven gas shells. That's enough to panic everyone in the area. Won't be much time before the air becomes tolerable and the police and the Treasury people start to fight back. You'll only have ten minutes."

"That enough. My boys and me will drive off with them gold trucks before then."

"After ten minutes, I light the explosives – if your men are around or not."

"I know. That our deal. What you do after that is your bus'ness."

Caarsens fixed his eyes on Brown. "Good."

~

They shook hands, and Caarsens, his spirits high, walked away. He opened his wallet, looked at the well-creased picture, and his thoughts moved to his wife and their home on the veldt. He became Danie Caarsens again – farmer and mining engineer, husband and father, happy and God-fearing. Two memories of the farm his grandfather had built near Bloemfontein flashed through his mind. The first was when he rode to war in October 1899. The second was the last time he saw it in July 1902, several months after the British had ravaged it. By then, the Boers had just signed a peace treaty with Britain, but Danie was a hunted man. Despite the risk, he returned home. The scene sickened him. The house was a charred frame, only the stout chimney remained. Varmints occupied the old living quarters. The sun-bleached skeleton of his milk cow baked in the place that was once a corral. The farm's once rich fields were barren and deserted.

He placed three makeshift wooden crosses on the small hill above the farm overlooking the stream where the girls loved to play. There'd be no remains underneath the crosses. He carved their names on the wood: Johanna, his wife; Annette, his older daughter; and Ruth, his younger daughter and favorite. Next to their names, Danie added their birthdates and the year they died. He didn't know the days.

Ruth had died first. That much he knew from Johanna's letters. She had sent them to a sympathetic pastor who kept them until Danie could claim them. According to the letters, his family became victims of British tactics designed to end the Boer War. The Boers had fought an effective and stubborn guerilla campaign. Although Britain had sent the largest overseas military force in its history, 250,000 men, they could not defeat the Boers. When British casualties and frustration mounted, they retaliated ruthlessly. In an attempt to break the resistance of the Boer people, the British attacked their farms in a policy British General Kitchener called "scorched earth." His troops spared nothing. Women, children, livestock, food, and the land itself became British targets.

From his wife's letters, Danie learned British cavalry had attacked their farm in late 1901. At that time, Danie was fighting with General Christiaan de Wet. For a good part of the day, Johanna kept the British at bay with her Mauser. She killed their officer and two soldiers. She wounded three more. But she watched helplessly as more soldiers, out of range, salted the fields and poisoned the well. Next, they rounded up the cattle and shot the milking cow.

The end came when Johanna ran out of bullets. The British approached the house on foot, carrying torches. They kicked down the door and grabbed the two girls. Johanna wrote in her letters that she'd never forget the sound of their heavy boots and hateful faces. "My mates died; now you'll pay. One of you for every one of us. I don't care if it's a man, woman, or child," the red-faced sergeant had said in bad local Dutch. When she slapped him, he pistol-whipped her. Johanna lost two teeth and the hearing in her left ear. They dragged Johanna and the children from the house, and set it ablaze. When the fire reached the sleeping quarters, she heard barking from the house. Ruth cried, "Nugget, he's trapped." Held by the soldiers, Johanna fought, clawed and kicked, but she couldn't break free. Ruth ran into the house. A minute later, the roof collapsed.

Johanna and Annette suffered a worse fate. From a neighbor who had survived, Danie learned that the British had forced them to walk six miles to a railroad depot. With the tips of their bayonets, the soldiers pushed them inside a railroad car reeking of animal feces and urine. They transported Johanna and Annette to the Bloemfontein concentration camp. Six thousand women and children lived in rows of bell-shaped tents.

The tents were overcrowded; theft was common; fights were frequent. The guards kicked and beat any woman who disobeyed them. The sun baked their skins dark. During bone-chilling nights, the incarcerated women and children slept on bare ground with no blankets or pillows. Shoes wore out and clothes became rags. Despite the ceaseless rain, water was scarce. Women lined up for hours to fill their undersized buckets.

Increasing numbers of flies tormented them. Lice forced them to crop their hair. Toilets were holes in the ground with splintered plank seats, and anything that could be used for toilet paper became valuable. Food was scarce and medicine so rare women scavenged the fields for herbs and relied on traditional remedies such as cow dung poultices to heal skin disease. They crushed insects to treat convulsions. Women prostituted themselves for medicine and extra rations to save their children. Measles, dysentery, pneumonia, and typhoid reached epidemic levels. Every day, carts collected the dead. Women tried to conceal deaths in order to receive the rations of the deceased.

Because the British knew her husband was a commando, they labeled Johanna an "undesirable." As such, she received fewer rations. Defiant and proud, she encouraged people to sing. Her sprit was stronger than her body. Within months, her muscles withered and she became a hollow-eyed skeleton. Annette struggled, too. She contracted measles and died. Down to ninety-five pounds, Johanna was too sick to bury her. The next day, carts collected Annette's body like discarded trash.

After Annette died, Johanna contracted dysentery. Someone found her remains face-down in the latrine. No record where they buried her.

After the war, Danie read that Johanna and Annette were among 28,000 Boers to die in fifty British concentration camps. Of these, 24,000 were children under age sixteen, one-half of the entire child population. The rest were women. An entire generation of Boers was murdered. Almost 120,000 people, a quarter of the population, had been interned. Thirty thousand Boer farms had been destroyed.

Caarsens recalled the Lord's curse on the Egyptians.

Chapter 80

The Fire Truck

Little Italy, Manhattan: September 14, 1916

Caarsens drove the shiny 1916 LaFrance Combination fire truck through the dark streets in one of Little Italy's poorest sections. It was after 1 a.m. Caarsens, Brown, and Brown's two best men had just stolen it from the one volunteer firehouse in lower Manhattan that was not manned all night. The dirty streets were deserted except for those who had more to fear than four strange men in a fire truck – a downtrodden few, and thieves and assassins looking for prey.

Brown jumped off the running board and opened the garage door of a dilapidated warehouse a short drive away from the site of the next day's attack. Caarsens had rented it from a gambling acquaintance who spoke poor English, liked his liquor too much, and had even less use for the police than Caarsens. He paid double the going rate and gave the owner two months rent in advance on one condition – no questions. The man took the cash, counted it carefully with greasy hands, and agreed. "Who I going to tell? This money save my hide." He gave Caarsens the key to the lock and skulked away.

Caarsens backed the fire truck into the warehouse, and Brown closed the garage door. He parked the fire truck next to a stack of wooden boxes, all marked "explosives," each about half the size of a milk crate. Together the load was about eight feet long, two feet wide and two feet high and totaled seven hundred and fifty pounds of TNT. Caarsens had obtained them the night before from the downtown armory, where he had bribed the guard with such an agreeable sum that he had even helped Caarsens load the heist.

Caarsens called Brown and his two men over and thanked them for their calm, vigilant work. He gave Sam, a former boxer who was blind in one eye, had lumberjack arms and a twenty-two inch neck, a five hundred dollar bonus. He had just finished a prison sentence for aggravated assault and armed robbery. He thanked Caarsens and folded the money into his pocket. "This a tip compared to what we gonna have after tomorrow. I'll leave it for my lady just in case. She never seen this kind of money." Caarsens studied Sam's angry and steady eye. "I'm ready. I know the plan."

Caarsens turned and gave Quincy, the stocky man with an accusatory glance and jumpy nerves, the same amount. He took it without comment.

"Tell me again where you'll stop the fire truck." Caarsens always repeated critical points just before an attack.

Quincy knelt down and sketched a picture of Wall and Broad Streets on the dust-covered floor as the other men looked on. "I stops and points the fire truck at an angle facing southeast and blocks the gold trucks here. I leave the engine running, and when we ready to scoot with the gold, I move the fire truck a few yards toward Broad Street and put it just so." He jabbed his finger into the floor into the exact spot Caarsens had wanted it. He looked up at Caarsens. "Why so exact-like?"

"That's where I want to detonate the TNT." Caarsens purposely left out his other reason – the secondary gas explosion below the manhole cover on the spot under Quincy's finger. He expected the first explosion to crater the street and crack the Consolidated Gas Company's line underneath, causing a massive gas leak. He would ignite the escaping gas with a burning flare and cause an underground explosion all along the gas line.

Quincy stood up and moved close to Caarsens. Tapping his fingers against his leg, he said, "Me and Jelly gone over this so many times, I dream about it. You just make sure we far away when you light that match." He gestured to the wooden boxes.

"I'll give you all as much time as I can, but I can only wait so long. When the TNT goes up, none of us want to be near the blast. I need time to get safe, too." Caarsens saw himself standing on the flatbed of the fire truck. In his mind's eye, he took out a stick of dynamite with a four-minute fuse and a flare from his rucksack, placed the dynamite into a crate of TNT, and jumped off the truck. He then activated the flare, dropped it near the manhole, and before the TNT detonated, ran to the safety of the Trinity Church graveyard, where there were no underground gas lines.

"You sure that stuff ain't goin' to explode before you want it to?" Sam asked.

Caarsens looked at each man. "TNT is very stable. A 30-caliber bullet won't detonate it. Not even one from this 45-automatic would do it." He half-removed the Colt from his trouser pocket. "The plan is good. Everyone, cops too, will be so confused you'll have those gold trucks over the Brooklyn Bridge before anyone cares they're gone. You'll have time to get to Brown's dockyard area and get rid of the trucks. What you do after that is up to you."

"I got that all covered." Brown told his men to be back at the warehouse by seven the next morning and dismissed them.

"Sam is good," said Caarsens, who admired his controlled aggression and intimidating demeanor.

"He's my best man." Brown added, "I like him. No one mess with him. He'll do what he say. That's why he got the hardest job."

"Agreed. What about the jumpy one, Quincy?"

"He fine. The time to worry is when he ain't fidgety. His daddy beat the crap out of him, but he's smart and a good mechanic. He's the best driver I got and don't scare for nothin'."

"They know to keep their gas masks on? I don't want anybody asking what the hell four Negroes are doing on Broadway in a fire truck that obviously doesn't belong to them."

Brown seemed relaxed and confident. "That fire truck be heading down Broadway mighty fast. My boys be cranking the siren and driving like crazy. With them gas masks, they'll look like monsters. Nobody gonna dare get in their way. If'n they do, my boys ain't gonna stop."

"Let's get to work." Caarsens walked over and opened one of the crates. He ran his finger over the wrapper covering the toxic whitish-yellow trinitrotoluene. A solid compound, it felt like hard, dried clay, and upon detonation its energy would travel at 22,000 feet per second. With that force and the position of the fire truck, the TNT would functionally destroy the Morgan Bank building, or at least render it unusable for months, blasting a hole in America's economic heart.

The last and probably the most destructive aspect of the explosion concerned the underground gas lines, plotted according to the underground maps Brown's informant had provided. The devastation would be incalculable, several times greater than that of Black Tom Island. The physical destruction of the two blasts and its terror factor would paralyze Wall Street and divert much of

America's resources toward a massive inquiry into what had happened and how to stop future attacks. America's diminished support for the Allied war effort would give the Central Powers enough time to win.

By the time Brown and he were done that night, the fire hose and reel from the back of the truck sat on the cold warehouse floor. In their place was the stack of wooden crates that covered more than a third of the flatbed space. They put two layers of sandbags over the crates to tamp the explosion, driving it downward and sideways, thus maximizing its destructive force against the adjacent buildings and into the street. They tied everything down with rope and a burlap covering.

When they finished, Caarsens looked at Brown and said, deadly serious, "Jelly, this will be a hard fight tomorrow. Some people may die."

"We be fighting all our lives. After tomorrow, we gonna live like the King of Siam or not. Either way, our current mis'ry be over. We know the risks."

"That's it, then." Caarsens collected his things and headed back to Brown's dockyard area in Brooklyn to get some sleep.

When Caarsens left, Brown pulled up a chair next to the fire engine and placed a loaded pistol on his lap. "That's it, then," he said.

Chapter 81
The Attack

Police Headquarters: September 14, 1916, 10:50 a.m.
"The downtown armory just reported seven hundred and fifty pounds of TNT stolen. I don't have to tell you what damage it can do," Tunney said to the hushed Bomb Squad. "My guess is that Caarsens has it, and you can bet he intends to use it."

Martin shivered at the prospect. Could the hospitals handle all the casualties if the TNT exploded in the city?

"It gets worse," Tunney added. "The Treasury Department is escorting a shipment of British gold from the Naval Shipyard to the Treasury building this morning. I just learned about it."

"When does it arrive?" Martin asked, fearing the worst.

"They're unloading it now. The Treasury people don't want us around because we had a traitor. But they don't know Caarsens like we do, or that he's got a truck full of TNT. I'm betting Caarsens is going to use it to intercept the gold. I don't give a crap what they think. This is my city, and we're going to stop him!"

On their way out of the squad room, Martin said to Keller, "No wonder we haven't heard from Caarsens in weeks – he's been busy planning this attack." The detectives bounded down the stairs of 240 Centre Street two at a time and ran to their parked auto in the basement of the building. Martin jumped into the driver's seat, and Keller furiously cranked it to life. Martin mashed the gas pedal to the floor as Keller jumped in, and they sped away with tires spinning to Battery Park, guessing Caarsens would arrive by motorboat and start his attack from there.

Martin accelerated down Nassau Street, crossed over to Fulton heading east, and south again on Water. He weaved around slower vehicles and swerved to avoid panicked horses and angry pedestrians. Keller, riding shotgun, cursed at anything that blocked them, once shooting his revolver in the air to get a horse-drawn cart out of their way.

~

At 11:02 a.m., a few minutes after Martin sped away from Police Headquarters, Caarsens eased his boat into Battery Park at one-quarter throttle. His long silver wig chafed his neck, and his false glasses rubbed the bridge of his nose. The cloudy skies worried him – rain would minimize the impact of the gas. The plan was risky, with only a ten-minute operational time frame, but he was sure Brown's men could steal a large portion of the gold. If they didn't, no matter. His main purpose was destruction, panic, and intimidation.

The trucks carrying the gold were scheduled to arrive within the hour. Caarsens felt a familiar and satisfying pre-battle tension. He became a finely tuned machine propelled by adrenaline, highly acute reflexes, and unflappable nerves. The mortar sight, his Colt, twelve extra clips of ammunition, and two boxes of matches were in his pockets. His Demag hugged his ribs, and his knapsack was heavy with pistols, dynamite, grenades, and a flare. It also contained a change of clothes and a gas mask.

One of Brown's men waited for him onshore. Caarsens tossed him a line. "Take care of her. I won't be long." He walked up Broad Street amidst normal traffic and pedestrian activity. At Wall Street, he looked at Morgan Bank on his right and saw a bicycle leaning against the wall twenty yards east of the main entrance. Brown's men had followed his orders. He turned west and crossed over Broadway to Trinity Church on the other side of the street.

Two of Brown's men, shovels in hand and sweat on their backs, waited for him in front of the church graveyard. The older man with owl eyes and a scar across his face tapped his forehead and said, "Everything like you wanted, boss." A smile spread across the pockmarked face of the other man, revealing a gap between his teeth. "We'se dug the pit about four foot down, wide as two graves. Right?" Caarsens nodded. The men had surrounded the pit with wooden sawhorses and yellow warning flags. A foot-high embankment of newly dug dirt circled the hole. Passersby ignored them – they were another nameless work crew on another street in Manhattan.

Caarsens jumped into the pit, pulled off his disguise, and put on a workman's jacket. "You know the plan. I'll be back in fifteen minutes. Keep working." He took two sticks of dynamite from his rucksack, stuck them inside his shirt, and headed one block up.

He turned right onto Pine and walked another block, where he met Sam standing near a manhole cover right behind the Treasury building. He signaled when he saw Caarsens. "I glad you here," he snarled. "I'd a stopped them Treasury trucks myself if'n I had to." He patted the sawed-off shotgun he carried under his coat.

Caarsens lifted the cover and disappeared underground. He placed the dynamite where Brown's source had indicated the sewer ran next to the water line. He lit the fuse and returned to the street. "We've got forty seconds. Go to your next post," he said to Sam. Caarsens heard the explosion when he reached the corner of Pine and Nassau. Water spouted up to flood the street. *There's only one way those gold trucks can approach the Treasury building now.*

Caarsens returned to the mortar pit where Brown's men waited for instructions. He removed a trench coat from his knapsack and put it over his work clothes. He glanced under the mildewed tarp that covered the mortar. Satisfied, he reached into his knapsack, handed pistols to the two men, and ordered them to go to their assigned posts near the Treasury building. The pockmarked man, his pants rattling with bullets, brushed down his clothes and said, "I gonna be a rich man."

Or dead. Caarsens waited for some pedestrians to walk by, then lifted the tarp and knelt down to sight the mortar. He fit the sight into a groove in the tube. Using a lamppost that he had identified and paced off for an aiming stick, he recalibrated his distances, fixed the mortar's position, and sighted it again making minor adjustments with the tube crank. He was on target.

A minute later, Brown's runner, a skinny young man wearing a moth-eaten Brooklyn Robins baseball cap, scampered up to the sawhorses. "They comin'," he declared, out of breath.

Caarsens stood up from the ditch. "How much time, *hey*?"

"Ten minutes. Maybe fifteen. I'm gonna kill me somebody." He flashed a switchblade in his hand, and a smoke bomb poked out of his rucksack.

"Put that blade away, and cover up that rucksack, you *domkop*. Use this." Caarsens tossed the runner his Spanish-American War jacket. *I hope Brown's other men are better than this one.* "Get in position."

"Whatever you say, boss." The runner loped away.

~

Martin reached Battery Park and stomped on the brakes in front of the aquarium. Keller jumped out, opened the trunk, and loaded a Remington Slide-Action 38 Caliber Rifle. Martin joined him and fed six 12-gauge shells into the magazine of a Winchester Model-12 pump-action shotgun. With sweating hands, he filled his pockets with extra shells and checked his revolver, knowing this was going to be the fight of his life.

At the shore, Martin recognized the boat Caarsens had used to escape from Milton Point. "Hey, you! I want to talk to you!" he called to the guard. Keller followed with his Remington at the ready, his finger on the trigger. The guard cowered behind a rock and raised his hands high. "What you want? I ain't making no trouble."

~

At Trinity Church, Caarsens stood up in the pit and scanned for potential threats. Minutes to go. His worst fear materialized when a man in a long black robe exited the church, turned, and headed directly toward him. *No. Get out of here!* He scrambled to cover the mortar and shells with the tarp, as the vicar leaned over and peered into the pit. "Good morning, my son. I've been watching your men work. I was wondering what's going on."

Caarsens jerked the rest of the tarp over the mortar and tried to block his view. He cleared his throat to give himself more time to think. "Good morning, Reverend. I thought my men told you. We're trying to fix a water pipe, but we're being respectful to the ..." Caarsens gestured toward the graveyard.

"That was a strange-looking piece of equipment." The vicar's eyes narrowed and his face turned cold with suspicion.

Caarsens tried to bluff. "I'm a surveyor, I'm –"

"No, you're not. That's a mortar under there!" The vicar nervously backed away two steps, then turned and dashed toward the church.

Caarsens jumped out, ran after the vicar, and reached him just as he was closing the church door. Caarsens barreled through the opening with a force that knocked them both down. He stood up, grabbed the vicar by his robe, and closed and bolted the door. "Where can we go in private?"

The vicar's eyes widened. "You're safe. I'm alone."

Caarsens covered the vicar's mouth with his hand. "I've never killed a man of God before, but I will if I have to. Understand?" The vicar nodded. "Good. Listen, I'm a man of God too, and I'm in a hurry. Now move." He marched the vicar up to the altar, ripped his robe into strips with his Demag, and tied him up. He stuffed a wad of material into the vicar's mouth, and secured it by wrapping a long piece of fabric around his lower face. He pushed the vicar onto the floor and shoved him under the altar.

Caarsens exited the church and raced back to the mortar. It was fine. He checked the street again, no imminent threats. He closed his eyes and felt a drop of rain. *No! Not now*. He prayed Brown's attack would start soon.

Across the street and a block away, Brown's man inside the Treasury building yelled "Fire!" Caarsens heard the clamor pour into the street, signaling the start of the attack.

The two ditch-diggers began throwing smoke bombs in front of Morgan Bank and the Treasury building at ten second intervals. Caarsens bent down and readied the first shell as the smoke drifted west toward him.

Quincy raced the stolen fire truck, bell clanging, down Broadway. "Outta the way!" He gestured wildly from the open driver's seat, sending screaming pedestrians every which way. Three more monsters in gas masks, high on adrenaline and the thought of gold to come, gesticulated wildly in the back of the truck. Racing so fast it almost took the turn at a tilt, the fire truck skidded onto Wall Street and careened into a crowd of panicked, desperate people, scattering them like bowling pins. They shrieked in fear and bellowed in pain.

Caarsens dropped the first shell into the mortar tube, moved his hands away fast, and ducked low. *The strong shall inherit the Earth*. The shell blasted out with a distinct *thump*, lobbed over Broadway, and exploded with a boom a block away. Brown's signal followed, two shrill blares from the British captain's whistle, telling him he was on target. Excited and confident, he launched the first poison gas shell. It detonated a few seconds later, followed by two more whistles. He turned the side crank of the mortar ever so slightly to launch the next shell eight yards farther, and continued the same procedure until he had fired all the poison gas shells.

Strapping on his gas mask, he grabbed his rucksack and rushed across Broadway, forcing his way through the pandemonium of frightened animals and stampeding people. He shoved and braced, pushing his way through every opening, only to fight past the next obstacle. Smoke clouded the air and mixed with the yellow chlorine gas, but he breathed easily through the mask.

As he broke through the crowd, the chaos on Wall Street unfolded before him. Angled across Wall and Broad, the fire truck, pointed toward Morgan Bank, formed a barrier blocking ten gold-filled Sanford trucks facing it. Two dead pedestrians lay sprawled in the street, and trampled bodies writhed on the ground, screaming, weeping and crying in agony. A few bewildered civilians staggered along the sidewalk, gasping for breath and begging for help. Three of the truck drivers floundered on the street, coughing and rubbing their eyes – the rest of the drivers and their companions were either dead or had disappeared. It remained for Caarsens to overcome two Morgan Bank guards and an unknown number of Treasury men.

Hearing shots, he glanced to his left. Brown's man dashed from the Treasury building with two guards wearing gas masks in hot pursuit, shooting as they ran. Brown's man fell to the sidewalk, immobile. One Treasury man took cover on the steps behind Washington's statue, and exchanged fire with Quincy and two of Brown's other men, who were crouched behind the first truck on the opposite side of Wall Street. Another Treasury man bled out on the ground in front of them.

The tall buildings and narrow streets turned the block into a canyon and intensified the sounds. The gunfire was deafening and the numerous muzzle flashes blinded Caarsens through the smoke. Shielding his eyes, he spied the two bank guards, wet cloths to their faces, sneaking up behind Brown's men. Dodging bullets and ricochets off the street, he ran to intercept the guards. He shot one in the back, but the other dropped one of Brown's men with a bullet before Caarsens blew part of his head away in a splatter of blood and brains.

From his lookout by the bank, Brown zigzagged over to Caarsens and his men, who had taken cover behind the first truck. More well-armed Treasury men exited the building and opened fire.

To Caarsens's shock, they all wore gas masks.

Now to get the gold. Brown barked orders to one of the men to move the idling fire truck. The man took two steps and was cut down by heavy fire. Quincy followed, but quickly retreated. Brown turned to Caarsens. "Got to move that truck!" he cried. "Gimme a grenade!" He pulled the pin, stood up, and threw it in the midst of intense fire. It exploded near Washington's statue and silenced the Treasury men. The shrapnel and concussive force expanded toward Caarsens and Brown, but they were safe behind the first gold truck. Caarsens noticed gasoline leaking onto the street from the truck, but he could do nothing about it and refocused on the fight.

Quincy ran to the fire truck but returned. "What's wrong?" Caarsens shouted.

"The tires is all shot to hell." Quincy, Brown, and Caarsens looked at each other with dismay.

Twenty yards east, the mortar pit crew exchanged fire across a gold truck with another Treasury man on the right side of the building. Smoke and poison gas had reduced visibility to near zero, forcing the men to fire blind. With accuracy impossible, volume of shots mattered, and the Treasury man worked the bolt of his Springfield with skill and determination. One of Brown's men took a hit in the heart, and the other abandoned his position and ran eastward down the line of trucks. Caarsens moved into the open and shot the Treasury man in the lung; he died spitting up blood.

More Treasury men appeared on the roof and main entrance, all surprisingly in gas masks. They unleashed a heavy fusillade toward Caarsens, but their angle of fire and the thick, cloudy air hindered their aim. Bullets bounced off the street and zipped through the air, but Caarsens bent low, dodged and scrambled back to the safety of the first gold truck.

Out of breath, he peered over the truck to determine his next move. Sweat accumulated inside his mask, distracting him for a moment. The defense was stubborn. A rifle shot cracked from the front of the Treasury building and hit a pit digger by the fifth truck in mid-stride. He fell on his face as blood spurted upward into the toxic air.

Caarsens had to eliminate the man at the entrance thirty yards away. Ignoring the danger, he steadied his Colt with both hands on the hood of the truck, took careful aim, and pulled off two shots. His target was dead before he hit the ground. He counted the men remaining: himself; Brown; Quincy; the runner, wherever he was; and Sam guarding their rear. Caarsens had expected losses, but not this many, not this quickly.

To Caarsens's horror, a guard emerged from the front of the Treasury building and opened fire with a hand-held Lewis machine gun. A powerful burst ripped into the engine of the first truck, releasing a cloud of steam and burst of oil. The bullets made a sharp piercing metallic sound as they struck the truck again and again. "Jelly, use this." Caarsens gave Brown another grenade, but the torrent of bullets spitting from the Lewis gun was too heavy for Brown to stand and throw it.

He crouched back down for cover. "What now?"

The Lewis gunner moved forward and continued to pour fire on them.

"Flank him." Quincy stayed behind the truck and sprayed covering fire as Caarsens and Brown split up and approached the

Lewis gunner from opposite directions. Caarsens, his ammunition low, snuck west. Brown ran east, protected by the line of trucks. Dropping his rucksack, he crossed over to the north side of Wall Street.

Concentrating his fire on the fire truck, the gunner riddled Quincy with bullets. Brown moved out into the open, hoping to toss the grenade when the gunner stopped to change magazines, but before he could pull the pin, the gunner finished reloading and shot the grenade out of his hand. Bleeding from the wrist, Brown dove behind another truck just in time to save himself from a murderous burst.

The gunner had left himself exposed. Caarsens circled behind him, moved closer, and aimed his Colt. His gas mask hindered his vision, but did not ruin his accuracy. The gunner grabbed his gut and cork-screwed onto the street.

At the tenth truck, Sam discharged both barrels of his sawed-off shotgun at a cop charging from the eastern end of Wall Street. The cop returned fire and hit the fuel tank, causing a fiery explosion. The cop was dead, but Sam, badly burned, crawled to safety. With the lead truck blocked by the fire engine and the last truck in ruins, the chance to escape with any of the gold trucks had vanished.

Caarsens looked at Brown and gestured he was free to go. Brown tied a rag around his wrist, found his rucksack, and filled it with bars of gold from the nearest truck. Straining to lift it, he nodded curtly to Caarsens and lumbered to the subway.

Caarsens was alone but unfazed and determined. The poison gas had driven away the truck drivers and civilians, but the Treasury men, supplied with gas masks, were more numerous, had showed more courage, and possessed more firepower than he had expected. Rather than making off with half the gold trucks, Brown had merely carried away the few bars he could seize. The chlorine gas began to dissipate, pushed south by a breeze, but Caarsens was not beaten – the TNT gave him the advantage.

Chapter 82
One of Us is Going to Die

Wall and Broad Streets, Manhattan: September 14, 1916

As Caarsens assessed his losses, Martin ran north on Broad Street, ignoring the warnings of fleeing people. "You're going the wrong way!" "You're crazy." "You're gonna die!" By the time he reached the Stock Exchange, about forty yards below Wall Street, Broad Street was empty except for a widening yellow cloud. The acrid air constricted his lungs. Suffocating and disoriented, he fought back nausea and pushed forward until he gagged and fell to his knees.

Martin looked north and was surprised to see the gunfire had stopped. He refused to think Caarsens had won. He crossed himself and, using his shotgun as support, stood up and pressed forward.

The pungent air began to clear, but the chlorine gas still clung to the ground at a man's height. Martin tore off a section of his shirt and placed it over his mouth. It hardly made a difference – every breath became an ordeal; his lungs burned and his head felt heavy. He stopped, placed his hands on his knees, and gulped in the foul air, but he had to rest against the Broad Street side of Morgan Bank fifteen yards away from the front of the fire engine. *Lord, give me strength.*

A skinny man in a gas mask and Brooklyn Robins cap emerged from his hiding place and ran toward Martin with a switchblade in his hands. "Maybe late, but I in the fight now." Propped up by the wall, Martin raised his shotgun and waited for his assailant to move in. When he closed to four feet, Martin pumped two rounds of buckshot into him. The force knocked the man back and turned his torso into hamburger. Dizzy and fighting for every breath, Martin collapsed. A dark emptiness began to fill him, but he forced himself to crawl to the dead man and remove his mask. To his great relief, it still functioned. He slipped it over his head. His breathing steadied.

He raised his shotgun and pressed forward. Through the smoke and gas, he saw a man with a gas mask – *Caarsens?* – lean over a stack of crates on the bed of the fire truck. *The TNT!* Martin advanced, positioned himself, and fired the shotgun.

~

The blast missed Caarsens by inches. He ducked for cover, and a second blast went high. Crouching behind the crates of TNT, Caarsens realized the threat came from the front of the truck and Morgan Bank. He raised his Colt over the crates and fired blindly in the direction of the shotgun blasts.

~

Exposed, Martin dropped to the ground when he saw the Colt and rolled away from the gunshots toward the nearest cover, the front of the fire truck. He crouched low and pressed his back hard against the front axle, his head flanked by the headlights. Breathing hard, he reloaded his shotgun as fury and frustration stoked his last reserves.

~

Caarsens was anxious to complete his main task – set off the TNT. Enraged by the arrival of another attacker, he fed another clip into his Colt – only one more left – and tried to target the man crouched in front of the fire truck, but he had no clear shot.

~

A tense stillness settled over Wall Street. So close they could smell each other, Martin and Caarsens had reached a stalemate. The angle of fire and the barrier provided by the front of the fire truck and its engine block prevented either man from hitting the other.

Caarsens's heavy boots moved on the flatbed. Queasy, his energy draining fast, Martin made a risky gambit. He held his breath, discarded his gas mask to improve his vision, and rose up, pumping round after round in wild, deadly volleys.

~

Surprised by the aggressive attack, Caarsens dove onto the flatbed just in time, but he recognized his attacker. Sergeant Martin. *You bastard. One of us is going to die.* Short of ammunition, he briefly considered killing Martin and himself both with a grenade, but he did not intend to die. He fired two rounds to force Martin down and moved into a low crouch, hoping for a clean shot. Anticipating where Martin would appear next, Caarsens readied his Colt.

~

Martin circled to the Treasury Bank side of the fire truck, stood up again and aimed at Caarsens's last location. A 45-caliber bullet grazed his neck, and he fell to the ground where the heavy chlorine gas was still dangerous. Bleeding and angry that Caarsens had hit him, Martin struggled to breathe and desperately tried to retrieve his gas mask.

~

"Got you, Sergeant!" Caarsens exclaimed. Pressed for time and unwilling to expend another precious bullet, he pulled out his Demag and cut through the burlap to get to the TNT. From his rucksack, he pulled out a stick of dynamite, lit the fuse, and jammed it inside a crate of TNT. Four minutes to reach safety. He jumped off the Morgan Bank side of the fire truck, removed the flare from his rucksack, activated it, and dropped it near the manhole cover. It spit out noxious flames.

~

Martin reached the gas mask and put it on. Lying on his side, he heard Caarsens light the dynamite and saw him land on the street and drop a flare near a manhole cover. Terror and panic surged through his body as he suddenly realized that Caarsens had orchestrated double explosions – the TNT and a gas line.

~

Caarsens, down to his last clip, started toward Trinity Church confident he had done his job. A squad of policemen ran at him from the Treasury building shooting wildly. They blocked his escape, trapping him in front of the TNT about to explode. He reversed directions and dashed around the fire truck toward the bicycle. He had to get to William Street if he was to survive the blast.

~

Using the little energy he had left, Martin dizzily climbed onto the fire truck and found a stick of dynamite jammed inside a wooden box. Its glowing fuse was so short he couldn't pull it free. With only seconds left, he pried the stick free and with all his might tossed it as high and as far as he could. He ducked and covered his head. The dynamite exploded in mid-air with an enormous but ineffective bang.

~

Caarsens turned when he heard the explosion. Something had gone wrong. Frantic, he started to go back to detonate the TNT with a grenade, but a line of police was moving forward, spitting withering volleys that drove him back. Bullets struck the bank and ricocheted off the street. He'd be dead in seconds if he moved any closer to the TNT. Wall Street would survive.

Determined not to be captured, Caarsens reached the bicycle, tossed the gas mask away, and pedaled hard. A bullet narrowly missed his head while others cracked by him. Past the line of trucks, he reached the corner at William Street and leaned hard to his right. Crouched low, he looked back after forty yards and saw his pursuers far behind. He continued on William and then sped south on Water. *One more fight to fight.*

~

Minutes later, wind and a slight drizzle began to clear the air. Martin woke up when someone slapped his face. "Are you a priest?" he asked.

~

"No, Martin. It's Keller." Keller pulled Martin off the fire truck and kneeled down to bandage his neck. As Martin, white-faced and groggy, struggled to collect his thoughts, a new fear struck him when he saw a pool of gasoline from the first gold truck slither toward the still-spitting flare at a quickening pace. He gasped and tried to crawl to the other side of the fire truck for protection.

Seeing Martin's desperation, Keller recognized their peril. He shot to his feet and grabbed Martin around the waist. Ducking, they ran to relative safety behind the fire truck, where they covered their heads with their hands and bent low.

The line of gasoline along the street reached the flare and ignited into a fiery snake. It sprang at the gold truck. The fireball seared through the detectives' trousers as the blast sent metal fragments flying in all directions. Martin and Keller staggered away with blistered legs and shrapnel wounds, but the explosion failed to detonate the TNT – it had occurred too far away.

Through the ruins of the gold truck, Sam, near death, staggered toward them. Keller thought he was an injured civilian until he saw the pistol aimed right at them. He reached for his Remington, but Sam shot it out of his hands. The next bullet grazed his side. As Sam lurched toward them, Keller grabbed the knife from his leg strap and flung the blade straight into the man's chest. Sam spit out blood and collapsed on top of them.

~

At the end of Water Street, Caarsens dropped the bicycle and disappeared into a mob of confused and curious onlookers. Mounted police galloped to the scene of the fight, followed by other cops. No one noticed Caarsens, another anonymous civilian heading to Battery Park, where he discovered three policemen guarding his boat. "What's going on?" he asked casually as he walked toward them.

One of the policemen watched Caarsens approach, took a card from his pocket and pulled out his revolver. "That's him!" Before the officer could aim, a 45-caliber bullet went through his liver. The second policeman hesitated. A bullet drilled him through the eye. The third cop ducked for cover. Caarsens drove him into the water with two more rounds and shot him as he swam away.

Caarsens untied the boat and started the motor. As a crowd approached the shore, he raised his Colt and fired off his last round. The crowd dispersed, but a group of cops formed at the water's edge. *I can't kill them fast enough. Even the fokking British didn't have this many men.* He lifted a plank near the steering wheel, seized the

Springfield rifle he'd hidden there, and fired off a full clip. The cops froze, and Caarsens gunned the engine.

~

His body aching, his lungs constricted, Martin leaned on Keller as they hobbled down to Battery Park, determined to apprehend Caarsens. Martin stopped every few minutes to catch his breath and drink from a roundsman's borrowed canteen. The water provided little relief for his burning throat, but he gained a bit of strength each time he stopped. Hundreds of stunned and fearful Wall Street workers emerged to share rumors, exchange horrors, and chatter nervously in the streets amidst growing numbers of policemen.

Hearing gunfire, the detectives hurried as best they could to the site where they had arrested Brown's man. Police were shooting at Caarsens's boat, already fifty yards into the harbor. Martin tried to speak but could only wheeze. "That's our man!" Keller shouted. He borrowed a rifle from one of the cops and squeezed off round after round.

Caarsens shifted the engine to neutral, loaded a new clip into the Springfield, and returned fire. He hit one cop in the chest and another in the shoulder. Caarsens's next bullet struck Keller in the thigh. "Jesus, I'm hit," he cried as he fell.

"My God, not you." Martin ripped open the remnants of Keller's trouser leg and examined his wound.

"Christ in heaven." Keller said through clenched teeth. "How bad is it, Gil?"

"It didn't hit bone. You're bleeding bad, Paul, but you'll walk again." Using a shoelace from one of the downed cops and the barrel of his revolver, Martin applied a tourniquet. The other men shouted words of encouragement and stepped up their fire.

Keller leaned forward, grimaced, and said something Martin didn't hear in the gunfire. "What, Paul? What is it?"

"Get that son-of-a-bitch." Keller fainted.

~

Well away from Battery Park, Caarsens shifted his engine into gear as two police boats patrolling the outer harbor headed toward him, sirens splitting the air. Ferries and transport ships in the harbor moved away. Working as a team, the faster police boat headed right at him, forcing him toward Governor's Island, where the slower one, armed with a mounted machine gun, moved to cut him off. It opened fire. Bullets struck the side of Caarsens's boat with a crackling force that splintered the wood and sent deadly fragments toward him.

A few shards cut his face and arms. Was this his last fight? Part of him hoped so. As the police boats drove him toward Brooklyn, away from open water, he muttered a short prayer, sped up, and maneuvered away. As if in answer to his prayers, the machine gunner stopped shooting to change barrels. Caarsens slowed his boat and shot back, hitting the machine gunner and wounding the pilot.

Speed and daring his only hope, Caarsens pointed his boat toward the outer harbor and pushed his engine to full throttle. With his bow skimming over the water, he skipped over the waves, churning a wake of salty mist, and dashed straight at the startled police in a powerful burst. Passing through the gap between their boats with a few yards to spare, he cheered with excitement as he started to break free. He pulled a grenade from a drawer near the steering wheel, pulled the pin, and tossed it onto the deck of the first boat. He veered left to avoid the explosion, which rocked his boat and sent shrapnel flying in all directions.

The second boat renewed its pursuit with a new pilot, but Caarsens was faster and started to pull away. His luck changed. The machine gunner completed the barrel change, loaded new rounds and fired a sustained burst into Caarsens's boat, hitting the engine. The pungent industrial smell of leaking oil and gasoline made him gag as his boat lost speed and the police boat closed in for the kill. Bullets drilled into the side of his boat with improving accuracy and shattering effect.

The police were twenty yards away and closing. Crouching low, steering his slowing boat from side to side, Caarsens struck a match to light the explosives he had stowed away for such an emergency when a bullet grazed his shoulder and spun him around. He fought to reach the charges, but he lost his balance and gashed his head on the side of the boat as he fell into the rough, chilly water.

Knocked almost unconscious, bleeding from his head and arm, Caarsens bobbed up to see his boat disappear in the blast. Governor's Island was hundreds of yards away. His strength waned and his adrenaline evaporated. Still believing in his cause, he realized he never had a chance against the odds he had confronted all his life. Now he was at the end of his long struggle – a soldier knows such things. He accepted the pain, closed his eyes, and sunk into the water's cold embrace.

Johanna's voice called out to him. "Keep going. You can still fight, Danie. Avenge us. An eye for an eye. We'll meet in a better place." Her words jolted him awake. He fought to the surface, gagged on seawater, and spit it out. He ducked under the water and began to swim.

Chapter 83
Where's the Body?

New York Harbor: 5:47 p.m.

Martin leaned over the rail and looked into the murky water. Ripples from the police boat rolled across it. Fading sunlight reflected off the spreading oil slick. Debris from Caarsens's boat bobbed to the surface. "Where are you?" Martin tried with agitated concern to see through the oily shroud. He labored to breathe.

One of the crewmen approached Martin. "You're a hero."

Martin barely heard him. He squinted at the man. "What? No. How can you –" He wasn't sure what to say. "I just did my job."

"Whatever you say, Sergeant." The crewman extended his hand. "I just want to shake the hand of the man who saved Wall Street."

Martin smiled blankly and grasped his hand. "Thank you." He returned to his search.

Men with long poles poked into the black broth. No body appeared, but they churned up a billfold. In it, Martin discovered a picture of Caarsens as a younger man. With him were a woman and two girls behind a farmhouse and green fields. "You had a good life once, didn't you, Danie?" Martin also found a folded piece of paper, its creases so worn they began to tear when Martin opened it. It was a copy of Paul's letter to the Corinthians, 1:13: "Love is patient, love is kind. It does not envy; it does not boast; it is not proud ..." Written in a heavy but easy-to-read script, it had been one of Corinne's favorite scriptures. Shocked to find it in Caarsens's billfold, Martin read it twice.

The police boat circled for hours, but Martin refused to believe they couldn't find the body. The ship's pilot explained that the currents in the harbor were fast and tricky – the body could be anywhere. Martin insisted they continue. "Get closer to Governor's Island. If he's alive, that's where he'll be." They found nothing.

The pilot turned to Martin. "He's dead. No man could have survived that swim."

"I have to make sure. Keep searching."

After darkness bled into the water like black dye, Martin agreed it was futile to continue. Caarsens had vanished as mysteriously as he had arrived.

~

To Martin, everything seemed different as he entered Police Headquarters through the front hall. Opposite the entrance, he walked past the bronze plaque of heroes modeled after a similar one at West Point. Frank Larsen, the newest Bomb Squad member, greeted him and mentioned his name would be there soon. Martin objected, "No, you have to be dead to get your name on that."

"Not in your case," Larsen said.

Martin cringed, and his thoughts moved to Corinne. He felt her presence and hoped that somehow she knew what he had done. The main entranceway's new coat of paint made the building look brighter. People he hardly knew and Bomb Squad members he had never worked with congratulated him. Officer Clancy gave him a bear hug, something out of character for the reserved Irishman. Even Howell shook his hand. His breathing had improved. The doctor had told him he had not inhaled enough gas to threaten his health permanently.

Clancy told him the damage to Keller's leg wasn't life-threatening, but it would hamper his ball-playing. Keller was furious when he heard the news and vowed he'd return better than ever.

Although he hadn't found Caarsens's body, Martin was confident they had stopped the German sabotage ring at last. Manhattan was safe for now, but Martin knew it would always remain a target.

~

When Martin approached the captain's office, three newspaper reporters were there. Through the open door, Tunney waved him in and introduced him. "You did good today, Sergeant, please sit." He pointed to a straight-backed chair in the corner. "Gentlemen, let's continue your interview."

The newspapermen fired off questions. The captain answered each one in turn.

"Yes, it's true one of the robbers had a mortar. No idea how he obtained it. He used a special type of tear gas that had a toxic smell and yellow color. A south-easterly wind dissipated the gas quickly. The attackers also used smoke bombs and grenades. They commandeered a fire truck, and one of the perpetrators ran through the Treasury building yelling 'Fire!' This was a well-planned and executed robbery."

Martin wondered what robbery the captain was talking about.

"Civilian casualties? Unfortunately, there were several. A few civilians succumbed to the gas. Their condition is unknown at this point. Another man had a heart attack when the explosions started. Two people were trampled in the panic. One civilian was shot in the crossfire. Several more were in the hospital with minor wounds or shock – nothing life-threatening. I'll know more soon."

More casualties than that.

"Yes, there were explosions, but the biggest blast came from the Treasury building. A fire started there and spread to a weapons cache. I believe it was a coincidence and unrelated to the robbery."

Impossible.

"Yes, a shoot-out occurred. It only lasted a few minutes. Rumors that it lasted longer are exaggerated. The combined efforts of the Treasury men and the New York police stopped the robbery quickly. I believe they planned to rob Morgan Bank."

Martin covered his face.

"A water main broke on Pine Street. This occurred before the robbery."

A half-truth at best.

"Fireball explosions? Yes, two occurred near Morgan Bank. We believe they were caused by leaking gas."

If they only knew what could have happened.

"No, the trucks were delivering special equipment to the Treasury building. It came from England. I'm not at liberty to say what it was."

Some truth.

"Witnesses? Many people observed the robbery from their buildings. However, the smoke prevented anyone from seeing clearly. In cases like this, such witnesses prove unreliable."

That much is true.

"Perpetrators? Seven robbers were killed at the scene. Their bodies are at the morgue. The coroner is examining them. I'll tell you more when I see his report."

Good dodge.

"Anyone arrested? We have one man, a Negro, in custody for questioning. He was guarding an escape boat. One man is still at large. We'll find him."

Yes, we will.

"The ringleader? He presumably died in New York Harbor trying to escape."

Did he?

"We will continue to look for the body."

We'll never find it. I bet Caarsens survived somehow. He was a strong swimmer.

"A racial aspect to the robbery? Definitely not. Some of the robbers were Negroes. Their apparent ringleader was a white man. We are trying to identify him."

We already have.

"Our casualties? Several Treasury men were wounded. They're at the hospital. No deaths. Two Morgan Bank guards are unaccounted for; we believe they fled the scene. We lost some policemen in the harbor when their engine caught on fire. That's all I know right now."

I counted at least six dead Treasury men, and I walked over the corpses of the Morgan Bank guards.

"German involvement? Let me repeat, and I cannot emphasize this enough. There was none. This was nothing but a well-planned robbery. We quickly stopped it. NO German agent was involved."

He was South African.

"Thank you, gentlemen. I have a lot to do, if you will excuse me." Tunney stood to show the interview was over. When the newspapermen left, the phone rang. The captain picked it up. "Tunney." He buttoned the top of his tunic. "Yes, Mayor. He is with me right now. Thank you. I've already told him. I will extend your congratulations."

Martin fidgeted in his chair.

"I agree, we were lucky," Tunney said. "We'll never admit to the public we suffered a poison gas attack or almost lost lower Manhattan. We don't want to cause a panic. Did the newspapermen believe me?" Tunney laughed. "Of course they did. I'm a good storyteller ... We need to make sure everyone keeps to the script."

I hope they don't ask me about this incident.

Tunney picked up the telephone and ordered dredges for tomorrow's search. He asked for volunteers to walk along the harbor's shores. He even requested an aeroplane to swoop around the area. Tunney hung up. "Keep looking, Sergeant. I won't relax until we can identify Caarsens's corpse."

"Me either," said Martin.

AFTERMATH

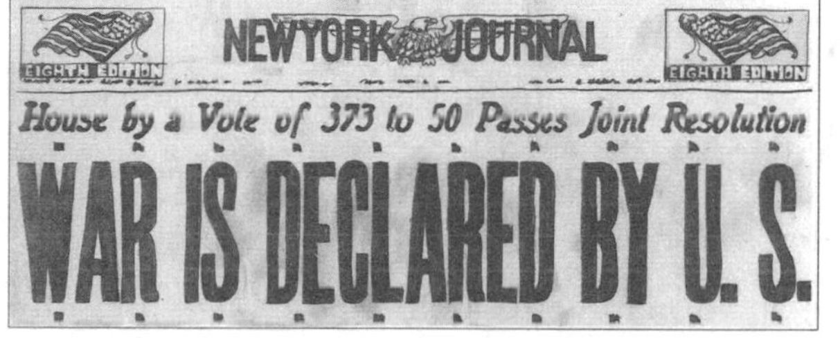

NEW YORK JOURNAL

EIGHTH EDITION — EIGHTH EDITION

House by a Vote of 373 to 50 Passes Joint Resolution

WAR IS DECLARED BY U. S.

Aftermath

Treasury Building, Washington D.C.: February 1917

Colonel House barged into the office with his usual abruptness. Today, Treasury Secretary McAdoo accepted House's rudeness without comment. Nation-changing issues were at hand. He knew from secret Cabinet meetings that Germany was about to restart unrestricted U-boat warfare. In meetings McAdoo had attended, the president's course of action had wavered. House was here to convey the president's decision.

The small man with the ten-gallon ego unbuttoned his coat and sat down. "It's hot in here," he said with a hint of Texas twang.

"What did the president decide?"

"Tomorrow, he will announce that the United States is severing diplomatic relations with Germany," House said. "Ambassador von Bernstorff and the rest of the German delegation will leave immediately."

"That's something, at least. That embassy was the center of their spy ring and its paymaster." McAdoo relaxed. "I gather there will be no declaration of war."

"That will come."

~

Captain Tunney's Office: April 1917

Martin folded the newspaper under his arm and walked into the captain's office. Keller followed and closed the door.

"Thank you for coming, men. You can all smoke today."

Tunney opened a box of Cuban cigars, took one himself, and offered it to them. "It's finally happened. The United States is at war with Germany."

"It's about time." Keller took a cigar.

Martin declined. After being exposed to poison gas, he had no interest in smoking. Besides, now wasn't the time for a victory cigar. "What does that mean for us, Captain?"

"We can finally tighten security around important buildings, as we've wanted to do for a long time. The government will issue passes and identification cards. No more chance for another Black Tom Island."

"Is that all?" Keller's annoyance was apparent.

"No, Detective. Anyone convicted of sabotage will face the death penalty. Whatever's left of the German spy network will run to Mexico."

"What's next, Captain?" Martin asked.

"We have a war to win."

~

Police Headquarters: June 1917

Martin and Keller waited with the other Bomb Squad members for Captain Tunney to address them. Martin felt his shoulder muscles tighten.

"Men of the Bomb Squad, our work has not ended," Tunney said. "I called you together to tell you about the latest developments. Yesterday, Congress passed the Espionage Act."

"Finally," Keller said.

"We have the full legal authority we need."

A few men applauded. Tunney motioned for silence and read

a statement. "The law now prohibits anyone from interfering with the operations or success of the armed forces of the United States. It is a crime to promote the success of our enemies. Conviction brings up to thirty years in jail and possible execution. In addition, in times of war, the law also forbids anyone from making a false report or statement with the intent of aiding our enemies. Punishment is a ten thousand dollar fine or up to twenty years' imprisonment, or both. I have posted a full copy of the law by the day's work orders. Any questions?"

Martin raised his hand.

"Yes, Sergeant."

"I've heard rumors that the Federals are going to get involved with our sabotage cases. Is that right?"

Tunney hesitated for a moment. "That's correct. One lesson we've learned over the last two years is that these cases need to be coordinated. One team must be responsible for monitoring all leads across all jurisdictions. New York police handling one incident and New Jersey police another possible related incident can no longer happen. The attorney general has called me. From now on, he will use the Bureau of Investigation for espionage cases. Next week, he's sending one of his officers, a man named Hoover, to talk to us about our ongoing cases."

The room was silent. "What will happen to us, Captain?" Martin asked.

Tunney cleared his throat. "This is still unofficial, but I've been authorized to tell you that the Bomb Squad will be transferred to a new group in the Military Intelligence Division. The nation is calling for our help. Men, we're joining the Army."

~

Sing Sing Prison, New York: January 1918

John Wittig was hunched in a hard metal chair when Martin entered the visitor's room. An armed guard stood over him. Martin waved him away. Wittig had aged since his trial. Thin unkempt gray hair had replaced his thick brown hair. The lines on his face had turned to unshaven crags. "How are you, Mr. Wittig?"

Wittig continued to stare at the ground. "It's a prison; I manage." He twisted his hands together and looked up and seemed surprised by Martin's U.S. Army uniform. "I'm sorry, Lieutenant Martin; I have too much time to think. How is Miss Connolly?"

"Fully recovered. She's engaged to my partner. They both send their regards."

"Congratulations to them both," Wittig said softly.

"They owe you a lot."

"Glad I did some good." Wittig slumped in his chair. "I appreciated the things you said about me at the trial. Can I help you with anything?"

"I'm sorry about the verdict. It was harsher than I expected."

"Deserved it, I guess. How's the war going? I don't hear much."

"Russia's surrendered. Germany's going to move a huge army west. The war will be won or lost this spring. We'll be going over with the troops soon."

"Good luck."

Martin noticed Wittig still wore his wedding ring. "She's dead, you know."

"I know. Shot in the streets of Dublin – so I'm told. A mistake

– so I'm told. She died quickly – so I'm told. Not that it matters much."

"I'm sorry."

"Don't be. She died fighting for Ireland. That's what she wanted. She loved Ireland more than me." Wittig became quiet.

Martin folded his hands and kept still.

"We had a good life. She did love me."

Wittig's honesty forced Martin to confront something he'd tried to forget but couldn't. Martin realized he shared something with Wittig. "Corinne almost left me ... once."

"It's not my place to –"

"About three years ago." Martin's eyes started to close. He needed to tell somebody.

"What happened?" Wittig asked.

"Small things became big things. Big things became arguments. She had trouble conceiving. She said we never talked."

"Happens."

"She was right. That's what hurt the most. It still hurts. She was the most sensible woman on Earth, but I didn't listen. I was too busy," Martin said.

"What changed?"

"The war started. I lost my parents. I got sick."

"You don't have to tell me –"

"Influenza. I almost died, but Corinne never left my side."

"You're lucky."

"Sorry. Didn't mean to burden you. I've never told anyone this before." Martin felt relieved to talk about it. "Please, don't tell -"

"I have enough secrets, Lieutenant Martin. I won't tell anyone else's."

"After that, we became closer than ever. She always knew what to say. Now that she's gone, I realize how much I miss her."

"All things end. Even this horrible war will end."

"Do you still believe peace is the only solution?"

"More than ever."

You may be right. Martin wanted to forget the war, the losses, his heartbreak. "Mr. Wittig, let me get to the reason for my visit."

"What is it?"

"I have good news for you."

Wittig didn't react.

"You're being released."

Wittig stared blankly.

"Did you hear me? You're going free."

Wittig remained granite-still. After a few moments, he started to blink. He turned to Martin. "I don't deserve to be free." He held out his arms. "I don't understand."

"You helped save Miss Connelly. Without your help, she'd be dead. She's everything to Captain Tunney. He's taken an interest in you. He knows you're a decent man. You were placed in a horrible situation. The captain spoke to Robert Swanson about your case. You saved him, too. They both spoke to Secretary McAdoo on your behalf. The secretary convinced the governor to let you go."

Wittig muttered something.

"Everyone agreed the Germans manipulated you. When the crucial time came, you did the right thing. The governor had to let the trial go forward. After that, things had to settle down. Yesterday, he commuted your sentence to time served. I've got your release right here." Martin patted his vest. "I'm here to escort you out."

"Don't know what to say." Wittig had trouble getting the words out.

"Keller's outside to drive you away."

"But, I have no place to go. No money. Nothing."

"Mr. Morgan has helped get you a job. He forgives you. It's in a small bank in Pennsylvania. It's run by some enterprising Quakers who share your pacifist views. Not much, but it's a start."

As they left the prison, Wittig stumbled but righted himself and threw his shoulders back. As he walked outside the prison gate, Wittig turned and said, "That's a beautiful sight."

At first, Martin didn't know what Wittig was talking about. Then Wittig placed his hand on his heart and looked at the American flag waving against the sky above the prison entrance. He moved his lips. Martin guessed he was reciting the Pledge of Allegiance.

Keller was waiting for them. He stood next to an unmarked motorcar. He was dressed in a U.S. Army sergeant's uniform. Shannon sat in the back seat. Her face was turned away. Wittig didn't seem to notice. Martin turned to Wittig and said, "We have another surprise for you, Mr. Wittig."

"Wh ... what?"

Keller opened the rear door. Shannon stepped out. "Mr. Wittig, I want to –"

"Papa." Hannah jumped from the motorcar and ran to her father. She almost knocked him down. Wittig clutched her. Hannah wrapped her arms around her father so tightly it seemed she would never let go.

Martin, Keller and Shannon moved away. None of them could speak.

"How?" Wittig wiped his eyes.

Martin explained that after Nora had died, British authorities found Hannah on the street outside her house. She told them she was American. They contacted the American ambassador, who sent her back to New York when Shannon volunteered to take her in.

"Thank you. Thank you from the bottom of my heart." Wittig buried his face into Hannah's shoulder.

Martin turned away to hide his eyes.

~

Later that night, Martin returned to his apartment in Brooklyn. He shivered when he entered. He'd forgotten to close the window. His wedding photograph rested on the front table in its polished silver frame. Above it hung a painting of lilies in full bloom he had bought after Corinne died. He paused to look at it. How much luckier he had been in marriage than John Wittig. But, Wittig still had a daughter.

What did he have? Memories were fading. He went to the phonograph and played his favorite song, Irving Berlin's *When I Lost You.* He closed his eyes and imagined himself dancing with Corinne. She had been right that night after they saw *Birth of a Nation.* He was like Caarsens. Like him, Caarsens had lost his wife and children. Martin understood that no man could suffer such losses without changing. Like him, Caarsens had fought for his country with skill, steadfastness, and courage. Martin wondered if he would have been as determined and brave had he confronted the same obstacles. Like him, Caarsens loved his God, his country, and his family. Martin wanted no less for himself.

Had he been in Caarsens's place, would he have behaved

differently? He wasn't sure. He wasn't sure of a lot of things. He knew that, like millions of others, he had paid a high price over the last three years. Two witnesses under his protection had been murdered. A friend had betrayed him. An enemy had nearly killed him. He'd almost lost his faith. His wife and baby had died.

The needle on the phonograph skipped and repeated the last words to the song: *I lost the gladness that turned into sadness, when I lost you.*

Author's Note

It is time to set the record straight and separate fact from fiction. German sabotage in America was real and far more extensive than the incidents described in this book. While two major events in the book – the poison gas attack in lower Manhattan and the attempt to assassinate a major U.S. figure – are fictional, as are many of the major characters, the novel incorporates numerous actual figures and events.

The most prominent internationally known historical figures are Kaiser Wilhelm II; Treasury Secretary William McAdoo; Edward House, who served as President Wilson's chief foreign policy advisor; Grand Admiral Alfred von Tirpitz; Field Marshall Erich von Falkenhayn; Foreign Minister Gottlieb von Jagow; and Colonel Walter Nicolai, head of Section III-B, the German military intelligence unit during World War One. Count Johann von Bernstorff was Germany's ambassador to America. For all of them, I have tried to be true to their physical characteristics but any personality traits, words and depictions of these people are creations of my imagination. In the process, I apologize for any inconsistencies or exaggerations that I may have made.

Captain Thomas Tunney, well known in New York, led the city's Bomb Squad during World War One. I am indebted to him for his book, *Throttled! The Detection of German and Anarchist Bomb Plotters* (1919). It has provided me a deeper understanding of the events. Specific references to my character Eugene Traub's journal came from Captain Tunney's description of a book kept by the real

German dockyard boss, Paul Koenig. Shannon Connolly, Captain Tunney's niece, is a fictional character and any similarity to any real person is unintended.

The character of Robert Swanson is very roughly based on a real person, Edward Stettinius, who was responsible for coordinating all Allied purchases of American goods and materiel during the war. Swanson's personality, words, and description are mine. The economic figures I use in the book are taken from factual sources.

There was an actual *rudder-bomber*, Robert Fay. The bombs he designed and his intent to use them as revealed in *Over Here* are generally accurate. My fictitious rudder-bomber, Max Frisch, in no way represents him. My portrayal of how the Bomb Squad investigated and arrested the real rudder-bomber purposely deviates from actual events.

Mock Duck, a noted New York criminal, led the Hip Sing Tong, the dominant Chinese organized crime ring in Chinatown in the early 1900s. Lesser-known characters are Marta Held, the alleged German madam who ran the meeting house at 123 West 15th Street in Manhattan; Mena Reiss, "the Eastman Girl," a model for Eastman-Kodak Company advertisements and a known consort for German dignitaries; and the key informer, whose real name was Friedrich Scheindl (named Klaus Schiller, a completely fictional character in the book), who supplied shipping and dockyard information to the Germans. For all of these people, their actions, personalities, and descriptions in this book serve the fictional narrative and are not meant to be true likenesses.

The attack on Black Tom Island is genuine, live New York history. A marker exists on the actual site to memorialize the incident. My description of the explosion and its after-effect are as accurate as possible. An international commission in the 1930s concluded that German saboteurs were responsible. They awarded America a judgment of $50 million, including $29 million in interest. Adolph Hitler refused to pay. The debt was finally settled in the 1950s.

In addition to the attack on Black Tom Island, historical events in *Over Here* include the following, listed in chronological order: the sinking of the *Lusitania* (May 7, 1915); the peace rally at Madison Square Garden (June 24, 1915, although I moved its starting time to the morning); the execution of the humanitarian nurse Edith Cavell by the Germans (October 12, 1915); the Henry Ford Peace Mission (December 4, 1915); the arrival of the German U-boat *Deutschland* in Baltimore (July 9, 1916); the labor march up Fifth Avenue by 10,000 African-American workers (July 2, 1917; moved up to August 1915 in *Over Here* for purposes of the plot).

Unexploded cigar bombs actually found on the steamship *Kirk Oswald* led to the investigation of the bombers in much the way I describe.

The 1915 Denver economic conference really occurred. It established U.S. lending policy to the Allies. Britain did pledge gold to America as collateral for loans. In *Over Here*, the gold shipment to the New York Treasury Building, and the attempt to steal it, are fiction.

German agents used anthrax to poison pack animals sent to the Allies. The description of the *Henry Morgan* came from details of an actual animal transport ship of the era.

Other German activities in the U.S. between 1915 and 1917 include: planting bombs on numerous ships (the names used in the book are real), blowing up American factories, and attempts to destroy the Welland Canal in Canada. German agents did try to organize unions and rally the African-American community to support its side. The Germans established a company similar to the New Haven Projectile Company that had the same aims. The German company did not achieve the same successes as those in the book largely because American officials detected it early. As in *Over Here*, the U.S. government used newspapers to disclose it to the public. Germany did have an informer inside Police Headquarters, but similarities between this book and reality end there.

I have tried to make 1915-1916 New York City come alive, taking demographic and economic information from historically accurate sources and pictures and postcards from that time.

I made my German saboteur a Boer guerilla fighter because I wanted to capture the global dimensions of the Great War. At the same time, including Danie Caarsens's background gave me a chance to tell the neglected story about British concentration camps during the Second Boer War (October 1899 to May 1902). My description of the conditions of the camps and the deaths that occurred within them are sadly true.

German agents in World War One never attempted to assassinate any major American official. Pointedly, an anarchist of German heritage did try to blow up the Capitol Building on July 2, 1915 and then assassinate Jack Morgan, head of Morgan Bank, in his New York home. There is no definitive proof that these incidents were directly related to German activity against the U.S., although some speculation about German involvement remains. They were perilous times.

The book makes clear economic conclusions, which are my own, but are based on historical facts regarding the importance of American goods and money to the Allies.

Writing this book has allowed me to explore two deeply personal interests. The first concerns terrorism. Like everyone else, I was horrified by the 9/11 attacks. I grew up in the New York suburbs, attended graduate school in New York City, and lived in Manhattan's Upper East Side for years. Today, I live in nearby Central New Jersey. As I read more about 9/11, I was surprised to learn that it was not the first terrorist attack in New York Harbor. The attack on Black Tom Island was. The more I studied Black Tom Island, the more I learned about German sabotage. I became intrigued with the story and its potential for a novel.

Secondly, I am a German-American. My familial German roots predate the Revolutionary War. My maternal grandfather, a first generation German-American, was a significant part of my young life. I have always been interested in the contributions German-Americans made to this country and the challenges they faced along the way. No challenges were greater than those they confronted during World War One.

Like John Wittig, my grandfather was a successful executive in New York City during World War One. He moved his family to Bronxville, New York, after he built a house on Dellwood Road – both my mother and I grew up there. The house exists today, but I have let John Wittig borrow it. When I was a child, my family frequently visited nearby Milton Point, in Rye.

One final note. I have made every effort to make this book as historically accurate as possible. Any mistakes I have made are mine.

In addition to the deviations mentioned above, I have deliberately changed some facts, the most important of which concerns Caarsens's use of the Stokes mortar. In truth, the British introduced it on the Western Front months after Caarsens takes possession of one. The mortar was essential for his attack on Wall Street, so I ask the reader to please forgive me for using it earlier than history would allow. Likewise, my apologies to Brooks Brothers for opening their store a few months ahead of time. Finally, to tighten the narrative flow, I moved the Bomb Squad's offices to the Police Headquarters at 240 Centre Street from a space nearby.

Writing this book has been a labor of love and has given me the challenging opportunity to merge the complexities and realities of history with the intricacies and demands of fiction.

- James Hockenberry